When the Sons of Heaven Meet the Daughters of the Earth

When the Sons
of Heaven Meet
the Daughters
of the Earth

a novel by

FERNANDA EBERSTADT

Alfred A. Knopf New York 1997

THIS IS A BORZOI BOOK
PUBLISHED BY ALFRED A. KNOPF, INC.

http://www.randomhouse.com/

Library of Congress Cataloging-in-Publication Data
Eberstadt, Fernanda, [date]
When the sons of heaven meet the daughters of the earth /
by Fernanda Eberstadt.
p.   cm.
ISBN 0-679-44514-5
I. Title.
PS3555.B484W48   1997
813´.54—dc20   96-38579
CIP

Manufactured in the United States of America

First Edition

for Alastair

When the Sons
of Heaven Meet
the Daughters
of the Earth

Part One

One

WAKING . . . WAKING . . . WAKING. Sleep was seeping out of the slits of his eyelids like blood, sunlight was being injected in its place, the last dream–rankly coital, no doubt; his morning dreams, fathered by the chafing of an udderful bladder, slobbering, degenerate as the late Caesars, usually were–had already fled beyond his recall. Awake now, Mr. Gebler cocked an irritable eye at his own long plump godlike limbs saried in a winding cloth of bedclothes, splayed across the territory of mattress hours before vacated by his wife, at the breeze-billow of curtains. Now the brass band of last night's mixed drinks–margaritas, straight tequila, cheap Burgundy, brandy–was beginning to percuss upon his tympanum. Last night. Last night indeed. Last night had run well into this morning. Mr. Gebler had a sudden remembrance of prancing through the door just before his children were getting up for school. Oh shit, what else did I do that I shouldn't have? *Timor servilis*, the sinner's enslaving fear. No, none of that; he was far too old to dread the day. What duties and pleasures lay ahead–oh, the, oh no, the . . . fucking flowers for tomorrow night, oh no, he'd blown it but good, already hours too late to call the flower market. Remembering how he'd insisted on taking care of the flowers himself (this after all was what made the Geblers' parties so wonderful, that they chose every last lily or lamb chop themselves), I'll do it, he'd said, Dolly reminding, You know you have to be there by seven, yes, yes, he who adored markets above all things would take care of it, would call Morris and ask him to reserve what they needed, go down there himself to pick the flowers up. And where had he been at seven–well, till almost seven? Waking up, again he heard the siren that had cracked him out of sleep. The intercom. Deliveries, maybe . . . or . . . The buzz again, shriller. Was nobody else home?

Johnny . . . Carlotta—will someone for Christ's sake please get the intercom?

"I am warning you we are one messy family," confided Mr. Gebler. At the word "one," his voice, which was rich and carrying, sounded the long-drawn wail of a trumpet over a burial at sea. The prospective cleaning lady, alarmed, wiped her hands on her pink rayon dress, then fixed her eyes stubbornly on the inlaid border of the living room's parquet. This wasn't the effect he'd intended to produce.

"We're a family of incurable slobs," Mr. Gebler clarified, fishing harder for the proper response. His two daughters, who were sitting next door in the kitchen, giggled as they eavesdropped.

This time the self-satisfied smile on his lips assured Carmen that she wasn't being told the job was already taken or accused of having no green card, but was being asked to join in a joke. Carmen, baring an aisle of dental gold, smiled back at the red-bearded man in the silk dressing gown. All the gold of the Mexicos, it seemed to Mr. Gebler, enough minable metals in that crocodile grin to set a new Cortés sailing. Probably under twenty-five, he thought, and the teeth already poxed—a child of Coca-Cola and cuchifritas.

Carmen had come on the recommendation of their next-door neighbors, the Blums, who were going to Ann Arbor for a year and were anxious to find a home for their treasure. She was short, five foot at most. No neck, no waist. Torso like a tank.

Mr. Gebler stared, perplexed by that obduracy of form, all endurance, no superfluity. No joints, nothing that looked as if it might entwine or break. It was the jointed parts in people that made one's heart quaver: knees, throats, elbows, wrists. Eighteen months ago he'd fallen in love with a girl for the sake of her knobby knees and elbows: well, that was another story.

"And you don't mind staying late Monday nights to give the children their supper? We have a regular lady, Ernestine, who looks after them the rest of the week."

"No problem."

"The laundry room is right off the kitchen. Shall I show you the—?"

"Laaaaawn-ree?" She looked doubtful.

"You do laundry, don't you? The Blums said you did laundry for them. Washed and ironed. Sheets. Shirts." Mr. Gebler's hands scrubbed and ironed the air in encouraging dumbshow.

"Oh, noooooooo . . ." said Carmen, deprecatory but ready to smile in case the man in the dressing gown was joking again.

"Uh-oh," said Carlotta next door, splattering her lips in the noise of a razzberry.

"You *don't* wash clothes? You *don't* iron?" Mr. Gebler performed his mime again. "*Lavare?*"

Carmen was mystified. He strode to the bookshelf in the hall, pulled down a pocket dictionary, and strummed through its newspaper-print pages.

"*Planchar las ropas?*" he inquired, half triumphant, half sarcastic, already planning the dim-witted cleaning lady's dismissal. Well, if you don't iron, señora, you're no use to us at all. In the old days Ernestine had been a laundress nonpareil, but now she just looked after Leopold. Let's not waste any more of each other's time, Miss Carmencita.

The busybody Blums. They were so proud of what was theirs–their Carmen, their Martha's Vineyard, their Zabar's—so eager to help that one had to fend off their providings and matchmakings like Egyptian plagues.

But now Carmen, enlightened, met him with an equally condescending smile. "Sheets? Cloes? No problem."

"And you'll wax the floors and clean the windows? See, I'll show you how the windows pull out, like deck chairs," continued Mr. Gebler. Carmen appraised the acrobatic ease with which the windows swung in and out on their sashes, like a husband-and-wife trapeze team.

"Waxing's no problem? No ammonia base on these oak floors. You got to polish by hand, with the buffer." Wasn't it ridiculous the way one talked to foreigners always loudly, and a little bit in their own accent? So Mr. Gebler, hand rotating in polishing motions, found himself speaking broken English with the Puerto Rican janitor's accent.

"No problem," Carmen affirmed, pushing her lower lip out like a thumb.

She had been in the U.S. eight years, she told him, making the migrant's commute between work in the north and family in the south–an aged (probably forty-year-old!) mother and five siblings on the outskirts of Tegucigalpa, and until now her idea of luxury was doubtless the hokey-pokey ethnicity of the Blums' three-bedroom, which was all beanbag chairs and pottery by Mrs. Blum.

She was checking out the apartment with a frank curiosity Gebler enjoyed—didn't miss a thing, this one. Was she trying to crack its inhabitants from their appurtenances, was she counting the dust balls, or merely deciding what to charge? Their last cleaning lady had been efficient but inhuman as a zombie. Mr. Gebler caught himself hoping that Carmen would stay, or at least that his wife would fire her if need be. It wasn't every day that a visitor gave their joint so thorough a casing.

Mr. Gebler regarded the apartment as a test of character for guests. Well, for certain qualities. Such as: curiosity. Some people were so self-absorbed or so nervous that they barreled in blindfolded and sat all evening drinking, eating, chattering, with no more consciousness of their surroundings than if they'd been in an airplane. Others pried, inquired, took in, admired. And Mr. Gebler judged them by how they judged.

Each painting or piece of furniture the visitor hit upon, like a pin-ball machine's jackpots, gave off points. It was easy to gape over the Frank Stella or the Beuyses or the Agnes Martins, especially now that contemporary-art prices had gone through the roof; there was a desk inlaid in whalebone and mother-of-pearl, inherited from Dolly's father, that as far as Gebler was concerned set one below zero; it was acceptable, if banal, to admire the view. But there were hidden, quieter jewels—his own favorites—to whose admirers Gebler felt almost grateful, as if someone had been kind to an ugly daughter.

It seemed to him that so many people, his wife and three children among them, were devoid of curiosity, moving through their own lives like freight on a conveyor belt, inert, self-preoccupied, seeing nothing and hence understanding themselves least of all. You could plant Dolly in a strange city with five hours to kill between flights, and she would sit in the Clipper Club lounge unbudgeable. Unless there was a museum, there was nothing to see.

And then there was this brotherhood of nosiness which tinctured the world with wit and import, which cropped up in funny places—a canny flame in a Honduran cleaning woman's eyes that devoured the furniture and paintings in a room, and now were feeding off his daughters, sprawled on high stools at the kitchen counter, eating jam from the jar, scarcely able to stop giggling to say hello.

Mysterious the way women eyed each other. Here Johnny had taken in Carmen from head to toe with her oblique, flirtatious gaze that only moved at angles from beneath lowered eyelashes, while the Honduran woman stared with a more confident and forthright curiosity. What did women look for in each other? Men had no interest in other men's looks. Was it only in rivalry they gazed, comparing figures and weight, pricing shoes, or was it also from a more disinterested pleasure, an appetite for beauty, flesh, and eyes? Were women, despite their killer reputation, more generous and alert in fellow interest than men?

Johnny was surveying the social pages of the *Times*. A party at the Armory, and there was a photograph of her father wedged, inanely grinning, between two raddled blondes: Nancy Ayala and . . . "Who's Agostinha De Souza, Daddy?"

Gebler leaned over her shoulder. "A rich Brazilian hooker. God, we all look plastered."

"So what else is new?"

Mr. Gebler, giggling despite himself, squeezed Johnny tight. "Why aren't you bad children in school? This is no way to start off the year. Leopold goes to school every morning—what's with you girls?"

Johnny had just entered eleventh grade; Carlotta tenth.

"It's Environment Day," Carlotta explained, drawing her long legs up to her chin.

"It's—what?"

"You know, like, everybody's supposed to go to the park in the morning and pick up the trash, and then listen to lectures from recycling people and—"

"I'm paying forty thousand dollars a year for you kids to collect the city garbage? And why aren't you there?"

The girls rolled their eyes at each other. "We thought maybe we'd go a little later," said Carlotta. "There's this guy from the Amazon rain forest talking . . ."

"Well, I don't think you should be lolling around reading the society pages. I mean, talk about garbage . . . I've got two naughty daughters and a good son," he explained to Carmen, "and I don't know which of 'em gives me more trouble. Isn't that right, Lo? Have you got children, too, Carmen?"

Carmen clicked her tongue in mock despair. Her turn to boast. "One son. Two year. And oh—he *terrible*, terrible."

. . .

The Geblers lived at Seventy-ninth Street and Broadway in an apartment building raised before the First World War, a fortress-cathedral, blackened and corroded by age—as if fifty years in Manhattan equalled five hundred in Chartres or Rouen. From the Broadway entrance, tall iron gates and a sentry box admitted you to an inner courtyard, with a fountain at its navel, from which you then proceeded to one of the four staircases radiating from it. To Gebler's eye, the building had the look— gloomy, punitive, dwarfing—of one of those Moscow apartment blocks inhabited by top party apparatchiks and prima ballerinas, as well as by a police file of sooty lives collected in communal kitchens with only areaways and inner courts for sky. He had never completely got over his first associations of his new home with show trials, neighbor-informers, men being led through the courtyard at dawn into a waiting black car.

Back in the days when he had slept with anyone who would feed him, it was the kind of building he would sneak out of before the maid woke up.

For almost two decades now the Geblers had lived on the twelfth floor. It had been Dolly's bachelor pad—Gebler had moved in, protesting, and as their fortunes improved, instead of relocating to more humane surroundings, they had spread sideways, gobbling up the larger apartment next door after Mrs. Vishniac finally croaked.

The resulting conglomeration, admittedly, was all right: a fourteen-room stronghold—inlaid oak floors, stout walls, high ceilings—suspended over the Hudson and flooded by a silvery river-light that gave it the soaring gaiety, the uplift of a ship sailing above the geodesic crags of Manhattan. The apartment felt as if it were moving! Lying in bed, you could gaze out at the barges and tugboats chugging up the molten bronze river, and see, on its far banks, the docks and warehouses and wooded bluffs of New Jersey. Magical to be able to spy a different state from your own bed.

Once you descended to street level, however, you were assailed by the port-town slop that swirled and congealed about the building's underbelly. Recently, the old constituency of junkies, prostitutes, elderly Hungarian piano teachers, and middle-aged leftists with sandals and dancer girlfriends was getting spiked by a growing influx of young Orthodox (the women fat from too many children, their baby-faced black-hatted husbands harried, pale, superior), devotees of the inspirational synagogue ten blocks down, which had had the brainstorm of giving Jewish yuppies what they didn't know they wanted: GOD. Now head shops were reopening as kosher pita stalls, emitting a rancorous smell of fried chickpeas. His wife accused him of not liking Jews. And rising banally to the bait—I categorically deny that not liking falafel is synonymous with not liking Jews, replied Gebler, who was Jewish.

Every so often, in a fit of exasperation, optimism, Gebler threatened to move his family to the West Village, the Upper East Side, buy a house with a garden, a roof deck, escape this dingy bedlam. Since they were obliged to go to work every day right in the middle of the slummy Lower East Side, the least they could do is come home at night to somewhere more salubrious. What was the point of being rich as Croesus if you lived like a goddamn bum? Silence from Mrs. Gebler, who had very different ideas from her husband as to the point of being rich. His wife, who didn't notice their neighborhood was depressing because she went everywhere by car—in fact, who made a perfect fetish of buying up bad neighborhoods—would exert her aura of unbudgeability, and soon he'd resubside into inertia.

"Morning, Luis. We're expecting a lot of deliveries today."

"No problem, Mr. Gebble." "No problem" . . . the magic words. How come that soothing Latino mantra never failed to make his hair stand on end?

It was almost twelve by the time Alfred Gebler got out on Second Street. He and the taxi driver, a lanky Rastafarian, had sung reggae songs all the way down the West Side Highway, concluding with "Johnny you're too bad." The driver thought it was a riot he'd named his daughter after Johnny Too Bad. Or was it Surabaya Johnny? Johnny Guitar? Frankie and Johnny were lovers? None of the above. They'd named her after Dolly's friend Johnny Maine, a merry broomstick of a lady who lived by herself on the beach and made sculptures of driftwood and rusting metal. Johnny luckily had turned out a more worldly girl than her namesake. Although none of the children seemed to have inherited their maternal forebears' moneymaking genes.

Balmy September day, the sky a crazy blue. You could feel the leftover summer, still, in everyone's street manners—drivers mooing and catcalling as a busty girl in high heels tripped across First Avenue just as the lights changed. First cold snap and people's libidos moved indoors.

In the vacant lot turned greenspace opposite the office—owned by the Geblers, who intended to build an annex there for their permanent collection—Mr. Martinez was weeding his flower beds, attended by a phalanx of old ladies. Dominican houris. God knows what kind of neighborhood riots—a new Commune with gardening spades instead of pitchforks—the foundation was going to face whenever they got around to construction on the annex. The sight of the roses made Mr. Gebler feel a fresh twinge of guilt at not having risen in time to call Morris that morning. The flowers. Two choices. Either he could set the alarm for six tomorrow and pray to the patron saint of dinner parties that one of the stores in the market would just happen to have in stock a hundred perfect anenomes. Or he could stop by Renny's this afternoon and pay a king's ransom. Worse than the bill would be confessing to his wife his failure, his chronic, vicious, abject unreliability.

Mr. Gebler said good morning to Pete, the security guard, who replied insolently, "Good afternoon." Almost lunchtime. What was on his plate? He had a one o'clock lunch date with Jerry Mehl, the president of Cal Arts—Mehl was on their board of trustees—which was mostly an excuse to eat sweetbreads at Dominick's; a four o'clock meeting with a graphic designer who had offered a good price for doing a catalog for the group show in December (Arc, their old designer, had gotten too sloppy); and then tonight. . . . Thinking about tonight, Mr. Gebler emitted an anticipatory groan of pleasure, then cleared his throat to cover it up. Elevator door slid open silently, and Mr. Alfred Gebler, director, walked out into the gleaming white offices of the Aurora Foundation for the Arts.

It was a fact commonly known around New York that Mr. Gebler's money was Mrs. Gebler's.

Mrs. Gebler, born Dorothea Diehl, was an heiress from Chicago. The aspirin queen, her husband called her. Mrs. Gebler's grandfather Leopold Diehl had been an Alsatian chemist who immigrated to the Midwest after the Franco-Prussian War. It was his son Charles who'd built up his father's corner drugstore into one of the world's largest pharmaceutical companies. A foxy bastard, the right combination of greedy and patient.

Of course, to hear Dolly's version—she was her daddy's favorite—all

Charles Diehl lived for was art. They had a house full of Flemish Masters and abstract expressionists and a box at the opera and season tickets to the Chicago Symphony, and Diehl was on the board of the Art Institute. Best of all, he liked buying modern art: it was a gamble. For unlike most rich collectors, Charles Diehl was not content to hire a Berenson or a Duveen. He wanted to investigate for himself, to see how his paintings were made; he enjoyed the suspense of not knowing how the story would turn out. The same nosiness that when he travelled to Europe led Diehl to tour not just churches and museums but also prisons, factories, waxworks, agricultural fairs, made him visit the sculptor's foundry, listen to the orchestra rehearse, have Maria Tallchief explain to him how Balanchine's *Orpheus* differed from his later Stravinsky collaborations.

His wife, who lived out in the country in the house Diehl had built for her, was somewhat alarmed by his enthusiasm for culture. As a young girl, Dolly—watching her mother await all week in a fever of nervous love her father's Saturday-morning arrival—had already understood the price of not joining in his tastes. It was Dolly, the eldest of the three daughters, who went to concerts with her father, and visited painters' studios and studied at the Art Institute so she could be a help to him. In addition to her father's eye and appetite, she had somewhere acquired the belief that money must redeem itself from its gross origins and be converted into the immortal tender of lasting works.

In the 1950s, having already bought the bulk of his own private collection, Charles Diehl set up a foundation which gave money to museums, universities, orchestras, concentrating in particular on Chicago artists and institutions.

Diehl, who thought he would live forever, died in 1973, leaving most of his fortune to the foundation, with his wife and oldest daughter on the board of trustees.

Dolly, who had worked for the foundation during her father's lifetime, spent a year after his death trying to persuade the other trustees to get it transferred to New York, where she now lived, and put under her and her husband's control. The family and two other trustees were behind her, but the Chicago cronies blocked the move. In the end, she lost.

Diehl left his widow and three daughters a twenty-five-percent share in the company. With the income from her share, plus an annual grant from the Diehl Foundation, Dolly and Alfred opened up their own shop.

Still had to get the flowers for tomorrow night's party. Not so long ago Alfred might almost have trusted his secretary to take a taxi up to Renny's and follow his strict instructions, but Cecile after thirty-five years on the shelf had taken it upon herself to go courting and had now come quite unhinged. Mr. Gebler marvelled at that pulpy flesh at long last having been stirred by lust. Or merely loneliness?

Get a weekend package to the Caribbean, her office mates had urged when Cecile first expressed an interest in getting laid; go for Club Med. *Don't* answer the ads, *don't* go to bars. Cecile booked a flight to Kingston. For one week, work was suspended while all hands debated whether she should buy a bikini with a gold ring between the boobs or a classic tank suit, and whether to take the fuchsia or the turquoise separates or both. In Montego Bay, Cecile went for a moonlight swim with a car salesman from Bayside—a strutting little Guido with permed hair, whose subsequent wrigglings and evasions the entire staff was made to study. How soon after their return should Cecile call Mark if he didn't call her? Should she bring protection on their first New York date? Should she offer to split the bill? If he dropped her home after dinner, might she ask him up for a drink? But she shared an apartment with an ancient aunt; should she send Aunt Florence to Atlantic City for the night? What was the proper etiquette for asking a man if he was HIV-negative? Could you believe him if he said yes? Mr. Gebler, sometimes eavesdropping, sometimes chiming in, thanked his maker he had married before disease and sexual equality threw everything into anxiety and suspicion.

Mark didn't return Cecile's call. For one week Cecile stayed by the telephone every night till seven. Then Mark called. Cecile put him on hold while she shrieked like a fire engine in nervous triumph. They made a dinner date for Friday; he would phone in the morning to tell her where and when. Cecile came to the office Friday morning loaded in gold and high heels. At six p.m., when everyone else went home, she was still sitting there. Forget the little shit, let him rot in hell, advised the women. Startling to be reminded how much honest hatred the sexes bore each other, how lame, contrived, unspontaneous at best, how rife with blackmail, tears, guilt, hard bargaining, the game of courtship was. One side sitting by the phone near nervous breakdown, the other going happily about his business until a name appears on his message sheet—Who's she? Oh, her, Miss Ugly-but-willing—and then a week later when the latest squeeze is busy Friday night, Why not give what's-her-name a call?

Men and women. Must be a better way to perpetuate the species.

That was six months ago, and since they'd begun stepping out in earnest, Mr. Gebler's secretary in her war for marriage had forgotten how to type and treated a ringing telephone like a live present from the Hezbollah. Mr. Gebler suspected Mark would yet redisappear, be exposed as a bigamist, and then he would have his secretary back. Which was as it should be. She bored him, he trusted her: it was love, good as it got. What did a conceited young kid want from Mr. Gebler's long-in-the-tooth, thick-ankled innocent? If Cecile succeeded, he would be giving the bride away—Cecile called him "Dad" when she was feeling pretty—and nine months later, Mr. Gebler'd be looking for a new secretary. What would he get them for a wedding present, besides the wedding?

"Good morning, darlings."

A blur of flurried faces busy at telephones and Xerox machines and computers. He tripped through, hoping to sneak unobserved past his director's office, from which a plaintive voice twanged.

Cecile waved at him. "Al, there's a person—"

"Sssshhhh . . ." he forbade his secretary, one finger on lips, the other pointing at Andy's half-open door. She giggled in complicity. Clown. What a clown he was. A riot. Everybody's favorite boss.

"Oh, there you are." Caught. Andy had trailed to the door, looking so abstracted Mr. Gebler felt even guiltier.

"Good morning, Andrew."

"It's . . . uh . . . it's um . . . almost afternoon."

A fair, sheep-faced young man with a stubborn disapproving mouth, graduate of a women's college with a major in art theory. Uninflected, midwestern, trendy—the Geblers' smartest move in years, supposedly. Trained by the Walker Art Center in Minneapolis. So why did this lanky straw-colored boring *kid* make Mr. Gebler feel like an unfunny incompetent, a drunken layabout? Andy didn't see the point of

him, that was why. Without such sympathy, even from an employee—
employee, shit, even from the *wall*—you simply shrivelled up.

"How's the baby?"

The baby was a group show. It was called "Home: The Unsheltering
City," and Andy had talked them into it. The show was scheduled to
open in December. The notion was, in addition to their permanent
or longer-term installations, to invite in every now and then a guest curator to organize an exhibition that would address some issue of topical
concern.

This first concession to postmodernism was being curated by a
young artist called Casey Hanrahan, who made photomontages and
mixed-media installations about the city. Interviews with real-estate developers spliced with images of the homeless. Basically, what they had
done was give Casey $100,000 to ask his friends over for a party. Gebler
wasn't sure about the art, but he was amused by the idea of this cute
twenty-six-year-old inviting all his miniskirted-and-combat-booted girlfriends in to strut their stuff.

"The . . . um . . . baby is . . . well . . . still missing a few vital organs."

"No kidding. Every time I ask Casey how it's going, he says Beautiful, beautiful, no problem. So what's the story?"

Andy counted off his nail-bitten fingers. "Wieslowski has pulled
out. Corbett appears to be abroad."

"Where's that?"

"Well, his wife doesn't know where he is, and . . . um . . . didn't re-
ceive the impression she greatly . . . mmm . . . cares."

"Corbett's married? The kid isn't old enough to buy a drink in the
state of New York. Did you take a look at the Polaroid I left you of *Night
Fishing in the Harlem River?*"

"Huh? Oh—McGuinness's painting." Andy said "painting" like a
dirty word. He thought painting was pretentious and dead, preferred
video, neon, sand, dirt, photomontage, concrete, the bathroom sink.
"Yes, I did take a look at it."

"Well?" Mr. Gebler cracked his knuckles, challenging. This painting was his particular contribution to the exhibition. Amusing to mix
things up a bit, throw in an old master to confuse the critics and
make the younger artists mad. He had taken a car out to McGuinness's
hovel in Port Washington and told him he'd pay him thirty thousand
dollars (That's a hell of a lot of Smirnoff, Bill—shit, you can even switch

to Stoli) to produce a work about the city, and held his breath. It was McGuinness's first piece anybody had seen in several years, and it certainly didn't look like anything anybody else was painting these days—not that anybody these days was painting, anyway. The canvas was twelve feet by sixteen, blue-black, splattered-over, abstract, with an old man's spareness to it, something ropey, engorged, titanic.

Young people make bad artists, contrary to popular wisdom. Those concertos Mozart or Mendelssohn churned out aged four—mere bubbles and froth. Takes old folks to paint, write, compose. Just look at dying Titian's flayed martyrdoms; deaf Goya's hag-ridden peasants, conscripts; Beethoven's last quartets; the arctic oddness of Shakespeare's late plays.

"McGuinness—well, it is what it is," said Andy. "I mean, for three-quarters of the people who see it the only news is going to be that he's still *alive*."

"Too romantic for you, eh?" Yes, that meatiness would stick in his young director's narrow gorge. "*Night Fishing* is nothing short of a modern masterpiece. What else?"

"Jim and Barbara are ready to come do their installation whenever. Casey showed me the plans. I thought it looked, like, really outstanding. It's a homeless shelter."

"Oh yeah?"

"Actually, it's neat—just a row of cots with army-issue blankets. The bizarre thing is, it looks kind of inviting. Homey, almost."

"You don't say. Have you had any more thoughts about the catalogue?"

"I was wondering—what about Susan Grunwald doing the introduction that will go along with Betty's preface? . . . She writes for *Konsept*."

"Hmmm . . . rings a bell. Any good?"

"She has a piece on Duchamp in the current issue that is absolutely seminal."

"Seminal, eh?" God help us.

Three phones ringing at once. A lady from Philadelphia was downstairs wanting to talk to the director.

"Al," sang Cecile, "your lunch date called to say his plane's been delayed and he won't be in till two." Mr. Gebler's face fell. No sweetbreads, no Sancerre. No cakes and ale.

"I changed the reservation to 2:45."

"Angel."

Made it a little tight with the graphic designer, who was coming to the office at four. "Cecile, will you take all telephone messages for the next half hour? Tell people I'm in a meeting. I've got to get George on the phone before he leaves for–"

"Oh, and Al, there's a young–"

Mr. Gebler grabbed the cradle of messages Cecile was handing him, a pile of mail, magazines, and sailed into his own office. Home free, he closed the door behind him with a sigh–then stopped. There was a man in his chair. The man was as big as an ogre. In fact, he *was* an ogre. He had his feet up on Mr. Gebler's desk. He was humming. He was reading a book and he was humming. He was swivelling around in Mr. Gebler's chrome chair, rocking and swinging, his legs extended in the air, singing a little tune to himself. He was a kid, sort of. A sort of retarded kid, maybe. Oversized. Shaggy, and not very clean. A homeless person. Mr. Gebler backed up against the door, hand fumbling for the knob.

"Who–in Holy Jesus–are *you*?"

The tramp looked up at him from behind taped-together spectacles, and lumbered to his feet. "I wanted to know . . ." The sentence got muffled deep in his throat.

Mr. Gebler waited, fingers drumming.

"I wanted to know if I could . . . if . . . I'm looking for a job."

"Oh, you are, are you?" No, his head ached too much, and if Cecile really had let this creep into his office, well, it was just too much. "You want a job, huh? Well, I want you to get out of here. Now. I mean, what's the big idea? Barging into strangers' offices, plumping yourself down on their chairs! What do you think the telephone is for? Why do you think we pay a billion dollars a year for the U.S. Postal Service? Will you please leave *now*? And next time you want a job from somebody, I don't recommend bulldozing your way in like a . . ." By now Mr. Gebler had the door open and was ushering the intruder out of his office and to the elevator. ". . . bull of Bashan," he finished, just as the elevator door closed on a surprised young face.

"Cecile, why did you let that stranger into my office?"

Cecile, as was her wont when in the wrong, looked unconcerned bordering on huffy. "What stranger?"

"What do you mean, What stranger? That . . . *person* whom none of us has ever seen before, who wandered in without an appointment. Don't you know that the last time they let someone in off the street in this part of the world Andy Warhol ended up with sixty-four stitches in his stomach?"

Mr. Gebler returned to the violated sanctuary of his office. He hoisted open the window, shaken. Bird-brained Cecile. Sooner she got married, the . . . Then, seeing an unfamiliar heap on his desk, he swore aloud. The kid had forgotten a package. Wouldn't you know. He took a peek inside—a box of crayons—and put it in his out box for Cecile to deal with.

The encroaching lunacy of this city, swarming with walking talking pushy *maniacs*. Especially in this maniacal crackhead neighborhood. No refuge. Mr. Gebler, pushing out his lower lip in a shrug of amazed dismissal, opened *Konsept* and buckled down to the tranquillizing subject of Marcel Duchamp as prophet of postmodernism.

Two

WHILE MR. GEBLER WAS inhaling the fennel-scented steam arising from his monkfish—Dominick's had run out of sweetbreads by two—Mrs. Gebler was sitting in the ashy darkness of an empty theater. Beside her, a woman with a crew cut. Mrs. Gebler, stout, matronly, in a beige linen dress, was sitting exaggeratedly erect, handbag at her feet; her companion, a bone-thin girl in black, slouched, skull resting on the rim of her chair and wiry legs hooked around the seat in front of her. When they leaned together to talk, their heads almost touched.

They were watching the stage, which floated like an aquarium of light, a Milky Way suspended in the larger darkness. On stage, a fleet of women carrying rakes. Mrs. Gebler and her friend watched the women move across the floorboards in a kind of shivery antic Mother-may-I? dance without words or music, only a metronome: one in scissor leaps, one in giant steps, another in scuttling mousy mini-patter. In between steps the dancers manipulated the rakes with a frenzied waggling of the hips. The effect was gawky, awry. It made you laugh without your know-ing why. But Mrs. Gebler and her companion were stone serious. Every few steps, the woman beside Mrs. Gebler clapped her hands and inter-rupted the dance. "No, no, no, no, no! Joyce, I've told you a million times, Joyce . . . Joyce, go with the flow. Flow, Joyce, don't hunch your shoulders."

Then the dance resumed and the director clapped her hands again, this time climbing up on stage to grab Joyce and forcibly to rearrange the recalcitrant yoke of anatomy.

A minute later she was yelling, "Angeline, have you forgotten how to move your hips all over again?"

Angeline was a fat black woman from Trinidad. The director waved Angeline through the rotating motions. "Drop the rake—forget about the rake for now, let's just get the hips on line."

Angeline, rakeless, waggled. The director watched, then interrupted. "Too big, too big—little wheels of motion, and faster." Angeline waggled faster.

"Angeline, you don't get it, do you? Think of the pelvis—the pelvis is shaped like a spoon. A spoon. So stir that spoon. Come on, Angeline, let me see you stir." The director watched Angeline stir, then, exasper-ated, demonstrated with her own bony Protestant fishlike little butt what she wanted Miss Size 46 Girdle to do.

"Again."

"Again."

"Better, but keep it fast and small. Little wiggles, real fast."

Angeline wiggled, the director nodded. "Better. Now the rake."

After a dozen more rounds of waggling, the director resettled herself beside Mrs. Gebler for a full run-through of the rake dance, skinny legs flopped over the seat ahead, crew-cut head flopped back. "Cows," she muttered. "Light's still too . . . uh . . . too . . . kinda vanilla."

Both women pondered the light.

"I want something more . . . well, a kinda bathed, newborn kind of whiteness, maybe even a little clinical, like you don't know whether you're just born or died."

Mrs. Gebler grunted.

After the rake dance, after the cow dance, after the funeral dance, after the comet dance—and this was not including orchestra and chorus and the star from the Peking Opera—would come the lighting rehearsal. This penultimate lighting rehearsal would take five, six, seven hours, running into pretty swift Golden Time. Golden Time was what came after overtime ran out. Golden Time was right. It was the lighting that would make the piece a half-a-million-dollar spectacle. Dancers you could work like galley slaves; technicians were like burning money.

Mrs. Gebler sat in the folding velveteen chair motionless. On her face was an expression of concentration so all-excluding it looked like frowning bad temper, simmering fury. She waited. She was waiting to crack the genetic code of each dance. When over the course of the afternoon that moment came of breakthrough when the inner structure was revealed, then the director, satisfied, wandered back to Mrs. Gebler and said, "It's getting there." And Mrs. Gebler, looking up, said in her growly voice, "It's glorious."

The Aurora Foundation had turned out to be a very different kettle of fish from its Chicago progenitor. In 1975, the Geblers renovated an abandoned parochial school on the Lower East Side. Sts. Cyril and Methodius was on First Avenue and Second Street, in a burnt-out flatland of tenements, bodegas, drug dealers, market-gardens. Big city projects between it and the river. The Geblers converted the gym and cafeteria to exhibition space, the classrooms to studios and projection rooms. On the top floor were their offices. Back then, it was a simple operation. Alfred's best friend, Bobby Wasserman, was their lawyer, they had a bookkeeper and a secretary, and a young filmmaker named Costa Constantinakis whom they paid three-fifty an hour to install their shows.

Even in this earliest incarnation, Aurora was exquisite. Each light switch and door handle told you the Geblers meant business, that unbegrudged millions were going to be poured into exhibiting all that was most advanced in a setting pure as an ice palace. And Dolly picked the art.

Her own taste was for minimalism, whose practitioners used cubes, grids, the straight angle to create infinitely reproducible, mechanically repetitive works. Aurora became a showcase, too, for Arte Povera, a school of mixed-media installations, which showed an almost monastic reverence for raw or cast-off materials.

Aurora was where you went to see the wax and gray-felt mountains of Joseph Beuys, the rusting steel monoliths of Richard Serra, the quizzical smudged blackboard quantum physics of the expatriate Virginian Cy Twombly, the neon sculptures of Dan Flavin and Bruce Nauman.

In addition to these works displayed in Aurora's exhibition space on Second Street, Dolly invested heavily in artists who were creating works—land art, happenings—that deliberately could not be bought, sold, displayed. Anticollector pieces. It was Dolly Gebler's peculiar fortune to have become a patroness in an age when artists were hellbent on sacking the very idea of acquisition, ownership, or even permanence. In 1979, Mrs. Gebler proudly forked out fifty thousand dollars for a piece that spontaneously combusted.

The premise of Aurora was simple: to choose a few men and women of genius and bank them for life. Give them enough rope to hang the world. Dolly Gebler handed her artists scads of unfettered money; she bought them space and time.

In Nebraska Mrs. Gebler purchased four hundred acres of prime farmland for the sculptor Dean Johnson to make an installation so spread out it could only be seen aerially; in New Hampshire she bought an old summer camp where an artist named Orin Jubal created a series of waterworks, to be visited by application only; a Victorian Moorish castle in Easton, Pennsylvania, was converted to a permanent living museum for a forty-year-old light artist from Tulsa; she turned a former shirt factory in Long Island City into archives and projection rooms for a school of filmmakers who were exploring a new kind of documentary making; she gave an endowment for life to a young Slovene who had embarked on a cinematic autobiography, with world-historical backdrops, intended to unfold over the course of his natural life.

All during the real-estate slump in the seventies, the Geblers bought warehouses and storefronts, mostly in unsavory neighborhoods—the meat market, Williamsburg, Hunts Point, Long Island City. Some were rehearsal studios for dancers and musicians; some were converted into arenas for the permanent exhibition of one artist's work; one they turned—briefly—into an all-night café which held poetry readings and served as a lending library.

Ten years after purchasing Sts. Cyril and Methodius, eight years after buying two tenement buildings next door, the Aurora Foundation razed the whole lot and commissioned Frank Gehry to build a palace of metal and glass tile which would be all light, with one perfect glass staircase running up it, offices upstairs, and a garage next door. Forty thousand square feet of crystalline purity.

This is where the Geblers went to work every day. It was a poor neighborhood which they had changed by being there. Mrs. Gebler tried to make their presence less harsh by inviting the neighbors in. She ran an after-school program in which local kids could take workshops in painting and sculpture, she hired neighborhood boys to help set up Aurora's shows. Mr. Gebler, too, in the last several years had taken a particular interest in an arts program for juvenile prisoners on Rikers Island.

Mrs. Gebler didn't believe in nickle-and-diming; she thought art could change the world, and that anything that aimed for less wasn't interesting. She was unperturbed by the incongruity of her situation: a capitalist queen, a woman of conservative instincts and worldview, using her riches to subvert capitalism.

It was part of Mrs. Gebler's nerve that she did not rely on some uppity adenoidal curator, but trusted her own eye to greet patent greatness. She believed in a bedrock of genius, unmistakable, uncapricious, unparticular to era, class, culture. For the borderline cases, sometimes it was just whether or not you liked someone's face.

In recent years, Aurora had come increasingly under attack by younger artists and critics who maintained that its concentration upon white male artists creating works of mammoth ego, its notion of the transcendency of individual talent—or of talent altogether—was a validation of an oppressive power structure, designed to exclude women, persons of color, the Third World. "Quality" was a country-club code word invoked to keep out minorities, the underprivileged. Quality was in the eye of the beholder.

The Geblers didn't budge—or so it seemed. But then one day they budged perceptibly. They hired Andy Peebles as assistant director and

gave him one show a year. With that show, they hoped to pacify the
barbarians.

Three

THE YOUNG MAN who had been booted from Mr. Gebler's office was
walking across town. He moved in a loopy stride paced to cover long
distances at high speed. Eyes fastened on the ground, he marched
through red lights, human bodies, cars. He was heading west along
Houston, tracing the border of Little Italy and Chinatown, past the
gilded imps of the Puck Building, past the gas-station-cum-car-wash,
past the gleaming pink-and-black prow of the Angelika, and south on
West Broadway into the land of art galleries and boutiques. He walked
like a blind man in a hurry. Cars honked at him, drivers shouted. He
didn't notice.

He had grown up in the country, without a driver's license: he was
used, like some more aimless, roustabout Abraham Lincoln, to walking
eight miles across fields to get to the nearest town—"town" having been
to him a symbolic agglomeration of movie theater, video games, library,
human beings. Since he came to New York, he must have covered many
hundred miles on foot. He had hiked across the Brooklyn Bridge and
out as far as Coney Island and Canarsie; he walked north up to Van
Cortlandt Park and the Italian enclaves of Arthur Avenue. He rode the
Staten Island ferry and traversed that strange hilly hinterland where
Garibaldi, then working in a candle factory, had plotted the unification
of Italy with a fellow exile who invented the telephone; he visited the
rest home for sailors; the Tibetan Center; the white clapboard house
with its rose garden, nestled in the crook of the elbow of the Verrazano
Bridge, where was born and lived a lady photographer, Alice Austen—
lived there till she was evicted from it destitute in her old age and carted

off to the poorhouse. He crossed, recrossed the greater metropolitan area on his roamings, following his nose, travelling as the crow flies and walking along train tracks when his sense of direction failed, returning home with blistered soles and a still-popping brain. He walked to explore, he walked because his room was too small to stay cooped up in without going mad, he walked because he was too poor to ride the subway or go to the movies or make friends (disappointing, he had discovered, how dependent pleasure is upon hard currency), he walked to chastise and tame his boiling brain, to rock his unused body to sleep, to glean new subjects or to ventilate the old.

Now he was racing, almost, to rid himself of the smart of failure. Not just failure, but humiliation. Why must those in power be rude? How could a man so rich, so lucky, so all-possessing behave like the doorman of a nightclub? How could you have so much and not want to share it? How could you choose to act so small, so peevish? But maybe, he told himself, the man's child was sick; maybe his wife didn't love him anymore; maybe he'd heard bad news. You never knew what justifying anxieties sat behind that monotonous front of urban rudeness, rank-pulling. Yes, he had screwed up in five idiot minutes something it had taken him a month to get up the nerve to do, and it was going to take a whole new effort of will to adjust to the suddenness of this latest setback, the totalness of his rout.

He reached Prince Street just as Frank and Adam were opening up the store.

"Hiya, Ike."

"Dude, what's happening?"

"Humph," said Ike.

"Hey, guy, do you mind looking after upstairs today? We got some shit to do in the workroom."

"Mmmmph," said Isaac. He sat down behind the counter, buried his face in his computer chessboard—bought on Canal Street with his first paycheck—and waited for the customers to arrive. The other boys filed downstairs.

It was the previous spring that Isaac had found this first humanizing job. Acme was a storefront on Prince Street in SoHo. It was run by a man named Macklowe who twenty-five years ago had come to New

York from Indiana to paint: a long clean-limbed farmboy with wide-set translucent eyes that stared right through you and out the other side. Macklowe was good with customers. He was chatty in a slow meditative way; he had a great Protestant seriousness. Artists liked him because he gave them steep discounts, contemplated, discussed the works they brought in; buyers liked him because he conveyed a tacit admiration for their acquisitions and had an easy way of steering them into the correct mat and frame as if they'd chosen it themselves.

Isaac had taken one look at him and saw yards of blue sky the shade of worn overalls, smelled mown fields of rolled hay, and breathed deep. Isaac for the first time, almost, since his arrival in the city could relax, feel halfway accepted. He had learned carpentry as a boy—it bored him then, but now the shipshape perfectionism, the smells of glue and seasoned wood brought memories of childhood and of Isaac's father, now dead, who had sought sanctuary from a bruising home life in his basement workroom.

Among the familial country scents Macklowe and his store gave off, there was also something new. It was the first time Isaac, born and raised in a region in which people valued property, God, children, hard work and its rewards, had encountered the religion of art. There was sanctity to the frame store's air of work-proud awe: you might have been working in Joseph's shop in Nazareth, but the messiahs were made of paint and paper. Best yet, so democratic was Macklowe's habit of deference that it even extended to his employees. Each had his real vocation: Frank was an actor, Adam sculpted, Isaac too was trying to learn to make something with his hands—and framing, though it must be cleanly executed, understandably ran second to one's proper calling. It was this sympathetic latitude that had induced Macklowe to hire Isaac, who was unpresentable, tactless with customers, and audibly annoyed by most contemporary pictures. Plus, Macklowe was kind, and the boy, who at that time was looking to quit his job as a short-order cook at a diner on the West Side Highway, had come in like a stray cat, lonesome and hopeful.

Three days a week Isaac worked at Acme: Macklowe could only afford to hire him part-time, and was always apologizing about not being able to pay him better. Nobody could live in this city on part-time wages, but Macklowe didn't have any business hiring a third person, even three days a week. The lease was up for renegotiation this month; who knew if there would even be a store?

On the days Macklowe stayed home to paint, Isaac and Adam and Frank were in charge. Downstairs was the workshop, Ike's domain; upstairs a square white ark caged in jagged gold jaws of frame, where Frank and Adam took turns sweet-talking customers and doing the paperwork.

At lunchtime, one of the boys would go off to the Italian grocer and bring back a bag of overstuffed sandwiches, a big green bottle of volcanic water, and espresso in tiny white plastic cups. Isaac, scattering hailstorms of crumb, felt his frozen heart quicken and thaw, the pinprickle of blood return to his limbs. It was somewhere between rest cure and bliss-flavored freedom to spend his lunch break, feet up on the counter, eating, and surveying the commerce of Prince Street. Haughty girls in wasp-waisted riding jackets, carrying shopping bags with boutiques' names across them, painters with shaved heads and convict coats emerging from long limousines. And beyond, a backdrop of gray and olive-green cast-iron warehouses with fluted pillars and frilly colonnades, ornate yet massy souvenirs from an age in which factories, engines, skyscrapers thrilled with the romance of the Future.

After lunch, Isaac would descend to his lair, wield long blade through paper and glass, like a mower. Mount slivers of paper on cardboard like a lepidopterist pinning butterflies. Learn to stipple frames to make new wood look daintily mildewed. Play with hammers and glue. Sometimes when Macklowe wasn't there and business was slow, they closed early and went off to shoot pool. Isaac couldn't play, but he was pleased to sit in a corner and watch the stealthy way the good players fretted their cues, the darting pounce with which the cueball chased the shiny herd into their corral. Watch how sore Adam got when Frankie once in a blue moon beat him. "Look at the way he jabs that joystick, man. This isn't pool, this is rape," groused Adam. Soaking up the smell of liquor and warm company.

He had been as poor as a person can be without getting very sick, and now this intermission seemed to him blessed breathing space, nourishment against whatever new difficulties might follow. Three years ago, Isaac had left the small town in New Hampshire where he had grown up a local wonder boy, winner of National Geographic spelling bees and a scholarship to Harvard. He had kissed his girlfriend goodbye, promising to send for her when he struck gold, and boarded the bus for this city which everyone came to, on the supposition that here he would be better equipped to execute his life's work, whatever it might be, would gain from the inspiration—if God willed it—of comrades who had arrived at the same ideas as he. Soul mates. If not, not. He was used to rough conditions; he was strong as a mule, didn't need much sleep. Was willing to work to become great and win fame.

At first the equation had held good. He'd found a job in a furniture warehouse, and a basement studio in Inwood from a woman who was moving to L.A. The margins were slim—fifty dollars a week left for food, gas, electricity, pleasure. On fifty dollars a week you couldn't exactly go to town, but Isaac took this straitness as an injunction to gravity. All day he'd hauled sofas and chests of drawers, and at night, working in half-light to the tramp of feet above his head, he had written hopeful letters home to Agnes and crammed notebooks full of marching armies of words. A history of solitude, his book was to be. Even then, though, words and Isaac were falling out, and he hadn't much heart for the job.

Then one December evening, leaving work, he'd been jumped by two teenagers. A taxi driver found Isaac head in a puddle, wet clothes frozen stiff, and just coming to enough to realize his arm wouldn't move. The driver dropped him off in the emergency room at St. Vincent's, where, having learned he had no money and no insurance, after a fourteen-hour wait they'd plastered his arm and discharged him.

Back home, Isaac discovered that Toni had returned—L.A. hadn't worked out. She'd packed Isaac's stuff in a black plastic garbage bag. For the first night, Toni let him sleep on the floor, on the condition that in the morning he'd find somewhere else to live. You have friends you can stay with? Sure, lied Isaac. (How could a person *not* have friends?) Tacit was their realization that with a freshly broken arm Isaac couldn't go back to a job loading furniture and that with no job and no savings, he was unlikely to pass muster with even the slummiest landlord. The next night, Isaac curled up in the outside hallway, with the garbage bag as lumpy ground cover, but it was too cold and his arm hurt too much to sleep.

In the morning Isaac went back to Toni, who very kindly said she'd keep his bag until he'd found a new apartment. Of course, he never came back for it. The history of solitude was the history of loss.

For several nights, he had slept in the lobby of a building on Forty-ninth Street until he was persuaded to leave, and then he slept in a doorway or on grates. He hunkered down on park benches and in a tunnel under the West Side Highway, he got caught shoplifting a bag of Famous Amos cookies from the A&P, and all along he had stalwartly resisted the conclusion that this city was a harlot with paint over her pockmarks and a smile only for people with cellular telephones in their Mercedeses. Sometimes he dreamed of hitching a lift back to New Hampshire, but that was unpardonable. Having been seen off in anticipatory triumph, he could not now slink home a broken man. Home was where you returned famous or not at all.

After little more than a week, he'd been scared sufficiently prideless to call up his ex-best friend from college and beg for a bed. Come on over, said Casey, who was living on Vandam Street, working for a video production company. Where have you been all my life? said Casey, as if they hadn't fallen out in junior year. For eight sweet weeks he had slept in Casey's living room, waiting every day for Casey to come home and take him out to dinner. Casey picked up the tab for a proper doctor, a session with a physiotherapist. Casey wanted to know what Isaac had done that day; had he called so-and-so who was looking for a new assistant whatever? Let it last, Isaac had prayed; but just when he was getting almost healed enough to start thinking about a job, Casey explained that he was giving up the apartment and moving in with his girlfriend. Isaac didn't blame him—much: two bachelors together was joyless. Anyway, it had got him through the coldest bite of winter, and Casey had sent Isaac off with two hundred dollars, making him promise to stay in touch.

The next four months were a sad smear of strangers' sofas and floors. By the boat pond in Prospect Park, he'd met the disciple of an Indian guru—thirty years old, rich and harmless—who let Isaac crash in his living room for a couple of weeks. That was a gorgeous piece of luck—from then on, Isaac's lodgings became scragglier, more grudging. If he could rustle up enough change to buy a round of beers, he could usually end up with a place for the night from someone too drunk to do him any harm. For ten days he'd stayed with another friend from college he'd bumped into at Papaya King. After Gary, there was a lady Isaac met in a chess club, a locale not usually loaded with females—sex as well as food and sleep. Isaac felt bad about betraying Agnes, but his chess girl-friend kicked him out when she made up with her ex-husband.

In the summer, when it no longer mattered so much, Isaac had got a job working in the kitchen of a residence for homeless men on Henry Street, and a room nearby which he shared with a middle-aged Cantonese man. From seven in the morning till three in the afternoon Isaac worked in the Henry Street kitchen. After that he was free, but too tired to go anywhere. In the long summer afternoons, Isaac lay on his bed, playing computer chess or reading books from the public library. Thrillers, manuals—whatever. Waiting for it to get dark enough to sleep. In that sweaty nerveless lull, he began to realize, finally, just how scarring the last year had been, how seriously he had believed he was going to die in the streets, how unlikely it now was that he would ever accomplish anything. No fame, no delight, no grapple at immortality: just subsistence jobs and rented rooms. Nighttimes, his roommate would wake him, asking why he was crying. I wasn't crying, said Isaac, I was sleeping.

In September came salvation. Isaac got befriended by Melissa, who taught an art class at Henry Street. When he was done with his kitchen work, he would stop by Melissa's class and watch. Finger paints, charcoal, crayons, collages, papier-mâché. Sheets of wallpaper that you unrolled as you went along. Men standing at their easels, intent and goofy as babies—until the quarrels broke out—in a basement room so steamy it brought out everyone's stench like old food on a hotplate. Melissa asked him if he wanted to join them. No, said Isaac, sullen; he wasn't allowed to, he was staff, it wouldn't be right to hog expensive materials that were supposed to be for the residents. But then suddenly he wanted to—was hungry as a thief for orange and scarlet and green and purple crayons, for dry whispery charcoals, thick sheets of empty paper. Melissa got permission for Isaac to take part, on condition that he help her set up the easels before class and clean up afterwards. At first Isaac, having wanted to so badly, went blank. Caked-dry brain, hands too swollen-cracked from dishwater to hold a crayon. Looking at the colors laid in rows like the men in their beds at Henry Street, thinking of things he didn't want to remember.

And then she—Melissa—would come around, looking at the men's work, young boobs panting against her flimsy T-shirt, and all Isaac could do was feel silently murderous against this person who could flounce her tits at penned-up men, because at the end of the day she was going home to her own apartment, her own husband, love.

For Isaac, it seemed that every subject in the world was a brightly colored cluster bomb, every memory had a fizzing fuse on it waiting to blow up in your face. Then, after a few days of wanting to stab the teacher with a stapler, he started drawing what he saw in his head. In his dreams. In charcoal, then in ink, then in crayons and pastels. Small, medium, large, over and over.

What Isaac drew was his parents' house in Gilboa, New Hampshire. First he drew it in crayon: a yellow clapboard house, sitting on a wooded hill. He filled a whole page with drawings of the house from far away, up close, day and night. Then, in his mind's eye, he entered it. Now he drew the house room by room. Painstakingly, with as much precision as his ignorance of art allowed. The earliest drawings were of his attic bedroom. A tiny room, in which the pine floor, cockeyed from the damp, met the ceiling at a crazy angle. His cot against the wall, sheets crumpled, quilt awry, the pillow in its naked ticking, a crooked column of library books piled on the floor, and his desk beneath the open window. And through the window, trees, valley, church spires. At night, a starry sky outside.

The kitchen: long tin-topped table with curly red legs, porcelain stove, crude straw-bottomed chairs painted baby blue—oh, that interplay of heavenly blue and straw gold seemed to Isaac worthy of Beato Angelico. The quality of light he wanted was musty, granular, moted, like the light in a stable, but he didn't know yet how to acquire it.

The yellow house at night. Lit windows. Television set flickery blue like cold fire.

Now drawing pictures was all Isaac wanted to do. The energy he'd once unleashed upon politics, history, science, poetry—even friendship—now was funnelled solitarily into this one silent thing. Pictures seemed safer than words. With words you lied and cheated, ground people down, corrupted. Even commas were ways of wriggling away, colons two little holes leading nowhere. Spoken words, too: hadn't he sworn unchanging love to his girlfriend, Agnes, promised he'd come get her soon as he was settled, and didn't he now know that he would never be with her again, because he wasn't the same man who'd issued that false currency? Images were like starting from scratch, clumsy but free. For Christmas Melissa gave him a box of crayons and a block of paper. He was too pleased to say thank you, just took them away to his lair. Drew every evening now, propped up in bed, until his roommate gently turned out the light.

When Isaac had completed a series of pictures, he would bring them to art class and paste them together in panels onto one big sheet. A counterpane containing the kitchen, his bedroom, the den with a base-ball game on television, the vegetable garden, a fox running across a field—some in crayon, some in pastel, some in charcoal—in panels of five feet by five, six by six.

Melissa came around to appraise his latest arrangement. "That's wonderful, Isaac. You can really feel the emotion in them, the home-sickness."

His fellow students looked his work over. "Sick is right," said Scout. "Look to me like a house where someone been murdered. I think it real scary, man. *Nightmare on Elm Street Part Four.* No offense, man. Maybe that just me, bein' a city kid."

Del was more kindly. "This you house, man? Where you grew up an' all? Nice-lookin' spread, no shit. No wonder you lookin' sad and lonesome all the time."

"The legs of them chairs look kinda funny to me," said Luther, a burly southerner who considered himself an artist.

"How come there no people in it? All these empty rooms? Where they all gone?"

The empty rooms, so lovingly reconstructed, were haunted, irradi-ated by longing. It was guilt and regret that reconstituted every stick of furniture, as if he'd carved them himself from the living tree.

As a child, Isaac had been a collector. He wasn't happy unless he had amulets in his pocket or under his pillow. Bark, pebbles, ends of rib-bon, tape measures, even cigarette butts, shards of glass. His late father, who taught high school, had given him the box from the cigars he'd bought to celebrate Isaac's birth, and the boy had lined the Romeo y Julieta box in tin foil, made nests of cotton for his hidden belongings.

Now that he felt so unanchored in this moving city, Isaac once again clung to charms: the streets were strewn, Hansel and Gretel style, with messages for the initiate. Isaac scavenged a donut box—flimsy, but sided in cellophane—and made a snug home. A matchbox for the bed, the picture on the wall a cancelled postage stamp, the kitchen table a rectangle of tinfoil. Scraps of purple velveteen for the windows, a drawing of a red bear on the wall, and hanging above the bed like a sampler a fortune-cookie message.

Hesitantly, he tried his hand at human occupants. The first race was of dead people: an ink drawing of his father's coffin in a room full of faceless mourners. His father's soul flying out the window in his navy blue suit.

Something big had changed. Isaac, although he didn't want to admit it, thought it more honorable to stay crushed, was beginning to regain his appetite, grow almost perky. Simply, he had discovered he liked concocting pictures better than anything else in the world.

The painstaking, mechanical chores of it soothed and concentrated him—the washing of brushes, the tacking of paper to easel, the fixing of pastels. Like being the gardener in a monastery cloister. And then the reconnoitering: having to look at the world more big-eyed, wondering if he could maneuver his cataclysmic shortsightedness into some kind of advantage in the struggle to compile a color encyclopedia of things visible and invisible, of fugitive gestures, transitory light, smiles, shoes, shadows, women's behinds, men's unshaven chins, coffee shop counters. Lower New York. Upper Hell. Following Melissa around like an unsure but hopeful dog, begging for scraps.

The more he liked drawing, the less he liked working at the shelter, day after day with men angry enough to kill you just for breathing too loud. Worn out by that fending-off-menace watchfulness. Worn out, maybe, by trying not to catch their collective furies. Sick of coming home with institutional stink on him to a room that wasn't his own. Sad. Enough sadness for a lifetime. Wondering about what else there was in the city besides poverty, violence, disease.

His days of art classes and kitchen duty, his nights reading manuals and playing chess with his Chinese roommate, ended when one of the Henry Street cooks mentioned that he had a cousin named Sancho who worked at a diner on the West Side Highway. They were looking for kitchen help; at Sancho's good word, Isaac was hired for almost twice his Henry Street wages. As a present, Isaac painted Sancho in his soccer uniform, the black-and-orange nylon shirt with white highlights like pomaded hair. He wasn't pleased with the picture, but Sancho loved it. Sancho wanted him to stick in the family too, who lived back in Santo Domingo, but Isaac explained he couldn't draw from photographs.

In the spring, Isaac landed himself an easier berth than the Blue Sky Diner. He had wandered into the frame store almost by accident; Macklowe happened to be there that day, and the two men started talking. Fortuitous. Isaac, who must have looked as if he needed saving, got into the habit of passing by Acme every week or so, just to see if Macklowe was there.

Nowadays life was more lenient. His arm had mended, a little crooked; he had a pleasant job, and an apartment of his own in Hell's Kitchen, above a Turkish nightclub, for which he paid the exorbitant rent of $325 a month–$325 meant you could come home at night and lock the door and not see another human face till morning.

The room was dark, pokey. Only the bathroom, a communal bathroom one flight down, had a high window, sunny as a skylight, Mediterranean, blinding. You lay in the rusty bathtub and gazed out the high window, which tilted up into cerulean blueness, chiselled clouds, sometimes a tiny silver airplane, its arms splayed, carving up the blue.

Isaac, never much of a bather, took to spending hours in the bathroom, ignoring the hammering knocks of neighbors. Lay in the tub long after the water had gone tepid, gazing up at that square of blinding blue or charcoal gray, like the flag of a free republic. To the child's question of Why is the sky blue? he now had an answer. Because if it were brown or green or orange, planes would fall out of it, it would beat us flat in terror, leave us nothing to soar up into—indubitable it is that blue is the color of levitation, ascent. At night you could see stars out the window. One week the lightbulb blew and nobody could be bothered to change it. Isaac took baths by candlelight. The steam rising from the water hovered mothlike around the candle's flame.

These were his pleasures, but something in him was still raspy, fragile. The two years after breaking his arm had been too frightening not to leave a kind of rot. He was afraid of winter coming, and of getting sick, of not being able to keep up with the rent, and his own physical fear of the cold filled him with an anger he didn't yet understand. It seemed to him that the world was divided between the people who knew how easy it was to fall between the cracks and those who didn't. If he ever climbed far enough out of the hole, he would try to bring news to the lit world of where he'd been, but for now he was too singlemindedly bent on not falling back again.

After he got the job at Acme, Isaac had finally mustered the guts to write home. He had sent his mother and brother his first month's salary, and he had written Agnes to say he wasn't coming back. The weeks after sending his letter—of being left face-to-face with his own treachery—were a slower kind of scarring, punctuated by paroxysms of self-violence, by nights spent walking the streets, trying to gag himself from howling.

Her eventual answer—stilted, prim, but aboundingly gallant—only made it worse. The realization that he was ditching her now that life was looking up was what made him want to hang himself from disgust.

Then the news broke. Yes, Acme had lost its lease—so precipitously had SoHo chic-ened in the late decade that the owner of the building was now asking $4,500 a month. They would have to be out by October 1. Macklowe was trying to find a property somewhere less expensive, but didn't hold out high hopes.

The doorbell rang, a rosy man in a Shetland sweater with a square parcel under his arm. Isaac trotted downstairs to relay the man's request.

"Rich suck wants his prints unfoxed."

"What kinda prints?"

"Some rather clitoral depictions of water lilies. Nineteenth century. What's 'fox' mean?"

"A woman. If she isn't a dog, she's a fox." This from Adam, who felt he had to make up for his married state.

"It's a kind of speckling—fancy mold," said Frank. "Tell him we send it to a specialist who does work for the Metropolitan Museum if he insists, but that we prefer leaving it be. It's more authentically atmospheric, you understand. Unfoxing is molto unhip," he camped.

Isaac climbed back upstairs to reimmerse himself in the coralline innards of the water lilies, progeny of a Boschian imagination so rankly genital you would have thought nineteenth-century Bostonians would have shrunk from their display. "Nice change from all the electric chairs we usually get. Have you thought about what color mat you want?"

Doorbell rang. Isaac buzzed.

A reedy-looking fellow in a raw silk Nehru jacket. Raw silk looked like vegetables put through the blender. "Are my pictures ready?"

"What's your name?"

"It's the Lunar Gallery. The de Kooning drawings. You promised them for yesterday."

"Just a minute," said Isaac. "After this customer, I'll be with you."

"You said this morning the pictures would be ready after three."

"Hold your horses. I'm helping this fellow here." And to the other, "What kind of mat were you thinking of?"

"I have a car double-parked outside," persisted Raw Silk, voice rising.

Isaac, ignoring. "I could show you a gray-green to pick up the shade of lily pad. . . ." Who ever got the stupid idea that pictures and mats should match?

"What do you suggest?" asked the older man, made uncomfortable by the tantrum going on behind him. Isaac could feel he was about to say, Look, if you want to go get his pictures I don't mind.

"Listen, twerp, will you just get me my fucking de Koonings so I can get out of here?" Raw Silk's voice was pushing upwards almost to a scream. Intemperate city—what was it about too many miles of sidewalk and roofs too high off the ground that made people want to grind each other's noses in the dirt?

Isaac showed the older man a notched army-issue rainbow of grays and greens. "How about this dark gray?"

Raw Silk, ready to start breaking things: "I'd like to speak to Macklowe. Immediately."

Isaac, finally irritated, looked him in the eye. "Macklowe's at home."

"What's his number?"

"He's not to be bothered by customers' fits." And to Adam, who had appeared at the head of the stairs to see what the shouting was about: "Adam, you mind coming to butter up this abject little whelp?"

Where Isaac came from, you hammerlocked anyone who looked at you cross-eyed. If you didn't fight, it only got worse. Fighting back was known as honor. It was funny that honor—as in life, liberty, and sacred honor—was in modern times a concept confined exclusively to the working classes. As for Isaac, he could no longer take the whole thing seriously. When you went head-to-head with somebody, one of you was going to have to back down. Nowadays, it seemed to him that the more intelligent one was the one who stepped aside. That's what Confucius said: Small people concern themselves with territory, exemplary people with virtue. The less you had to lose, the more bitterly you defended it. Luther at Henry Street told Isaac he'd once seen a man bite a hunk out of another man's throat for trying to steal his blanket. What would Confucius have said about that?

Even so, customer relations weren't really his forte. Most pictures didn't need frames, anyway. He had seen those de Koonings earlier on—they'd all come to look at them, he and Frank and Adam, like stable boys when the Kentucky Derby winner is paraded. Macklowe himself had undertaken their framing. Gorgeous blowsy squiggles of pink-and-gold-and-turquoise femininity with gashes below. Senile Olympian, as if Rubens were still alive but incontinent, drooling. Apparently, you could still paint even after your mind went. Which told you something—depending on how you looked at the human race—either deeply disturbing or deeply reassuring about the nature of artistic talent.

"Where are you going to go when the store goes out of business?"

Isaac hiked up his shoulders. "Can a person go out of business, too?"

"Adam's going to work for his father-in-law." Adam's father-in-law was Piero Ancona, who owned one of the most prestigious galleries on West Broadway. "Some people really have to struggle, right? I'm, like, Oh, you poor thing."

"How about you, Frankie? You deserve a good time."

"I've been thinking about applying to NYU film school, starting January, if I can get a loan. It's so expensive it's a joke—like, twenty thousand dollars a year. So I'll still need a job too. Have you been looking around?"

Isaac made an indecipherable noise.

It had been Macklowe who put it into his head to try Aurora. The foundation wasn't far from work—he liked to stop by sometimes, dream in front of those big blank canvases, hunks of riveted steel. Sit in the coffee bar and draw pictures. They had money—maybe they could use another strong back to help set up their shows. Macklowe had offered to call up the family who owned the foundation, write him a recommendation. But Isaac was in a hurry. Thought he'd try his luck live. Only idiots are in a hurry. He was getting too old to be stupid.

At six o'clock Acme closed. Sometimes Isaac, the offspring of generations of shopkeepers, stayed on after the others had left. His grandfather had owned a general store in Hebron, New Hampshire, where Isaac as a child spent summers. Practically been conceived in the stockroom of Bolt's Department Store in Gilboa, where his mother was a salesgirl. He felt at home behind a counter; if he could have spent the night in the store he would have, but people could always tell.

Six o'clock. September, and though it was still hot as summer, he could feel the days beginning to draw in, the onset of long nights. Pinched days. Early darkness. The cold.

He headed east, where the broad rich streets of SoHo turned into tenement blocks with cheap fluorescent lighting and fire escapes outside. He liked fire escapes: they broke up the too dwarfening concatenation of verticals. When he drew New York streets, it was always as low tunnel landscapes zigzagged by fire escapes. The fire escapes were a funny kind of symbol, like ladders in a Counter-Reformation Crucifixion. Rusty salvation. Mysterious, the way they crisscrossed Manhattan at crazy diagonals like crooked lightning bolts, like so many Jacob's ladders promising escape, delivering burglars. One guy, summer before last, had let him camp out for a couple of weeks on his fire escape; tough trying to remember not to roll over in his sleep. He'd dreamt that he was still sleeping in his childhood cot at home, his brother, Turner, in the next bed. Isaac had to ration how many times a day he thought about Turner, but in dreams the boy kept creeping back unbidden.

He watched the men and women in the street, couples clinging; laughter, and from an open window on Mulberry Street a blast of bossa nova, the woozy divagations of Stan Getz's tenor sax like a drunk's weave, like a searchlight pulsing through fog right for your heart. Why couldn't you paint music? he wondered. Mussorgsky had put painting to music in his *Pictures at an Exhibition*. Why couldn't he, in turn, paint Bach partitas or bossa nova? Was it easier for time to mimic space than for space to mimic time? A painting turned out different, obviously, depending on whether you'd been listening to Glenn Gould or rockabilly, but that difference was not much more than an undetectable undercoat of influence, like what grass the cow whose milk you drink's been eating. When the Aztecs and the Mayans, when Islamic artists carved and painted pure pattern, then surely art partook of, infringed upon, music's prerogative, which is of all the arts not to be confined to representing the natural world. Chinese brushstrokes held a note.

But in the West, artists had shown no interest in stealing a march on music's lone privilege, had clung stubbornly to the material world of flesh and fields and larders. Even with the rise of abstraction, it was more as if painters and musicians were each responding separately to the spirit of the age. If cubism looked like jazz, or minimalist sculpture like serial music, it was because painters and musicians found similar ways of portraying modern technology's jolting fragmentation of time and space, or the repetitiveness of industry.

He passed a couple sitting on a stoop—a girl in a fuchsia New Look dress, a boy in crew cut and overalls. The overalls, of baggy soft stuff, unstarched, fell in wrinkles over his wiry legs, like the nape of a puppy's fat neck. She, a step higher, gave a loud hoarse laugh and bent to kiss the boy on the top of his shorn head. He wiped off the kiss and grinned up at her, teeth tobacco-rimmed: sin's stain. The boy wasn't wearing a shirt under the overalls; you could see the wisp of hair under his armpits, the foothills of his breastbone, one nipple. The boy was Isaac's age, maybe younger.

It seemed to Isaac, passing, that the whole city was joined in twos, that the very air twittered, hummed, fibrillated with love. He walked behind an older black man who was carrying a paper sheath of flowers, springing along with the expectant gleam of a lover on his way to his beloved. Suddenly Isaac was almost doubled over by envy. Body rebelling against the drummed-in dictum This is not for you. Body protesting, But this is what I'm here for.

A year ago he'd been so deep in the hole it would have relieved him to think that someone else on earth had figured out a way to be happy; sexual envy—the brazenness to think Why him and not me?—was a symptom of convalescence.

Six-ten, and the light already keening away, trailing off, the sky easing unprotesting into darkness.

Most evenings Isaac tried to force himself to work, but today he felt too bruised by his ejection from Aurora to face his naked-bulbed cell in Hell's Kitchen, rocked by the boom of the nightclub downstairs. What were you playing at? You knew you should have called that place and not just showed up. This is New York; you don't just show up.

I'll walk out to Coney Island and stroll on the beach, I'll swim in the great Atlantic Ocean, he ventured, knowing he wouldn't, that he wasn't strong enough yet to leave a pile of clothes in the sand and dive into the saline breast of that phosphorescent mother, origin of life.

I'll stop by Washington Square Park, he thought, rustle up a game of chess. Chess wasn't company exactly, but strenuous joint solitude. I'll play a game of chess, and then head home and try out the oil sticks. It was then that Isaac realized with a twinge of horror that he'd left them— no, he didn't have them when he'd arrived at the frame store; yes, it was that bad—he'd left them in Gebler's office. No help for it, he'd have to go back. One game of chess, and then he'd go back.

Four

"MUSHROOMS."

"Smoke. Smoke."

"Mushrooms."

"Smoke."

"Mushrooms. Mushrooms."

September in Washington Square Park, a granite parade ground— former execution grounds and potter's field, now afrill with fountain, statue to Garibaldi, and triumphal arch to some forgotten war—that pries open the jaws of Greenwich Village, dividing the Greek Revival row houses and inserting between them a screaming circus of merchandise, menace, play.

In one ring, a rodeo of Hispanic boys in baggy jeans doing wheelies on their bucking-bronco bikes. In the second ring, a circus of Jamaican drummers and windblown garbage. In the third, a shirtless man with bird-nest hair and pink molten lava scars down his back like someone escaped from a chain gang had attracted a curious crowd of Italian tourists with a harangue about the U.S. war on Central America.

And in the fourth ring—no, not a ring, a scholarly corridor, sober as a library, aisled by tall plane trees whose leaves were only just crinkling golden—were the chess players. Casey Hanrahan, cycling home through the park, stopped, wheels still spinning, transfixed by the couples seated at the checkered stone tables.

The game was speed chess. Casey marvelled to see how the game of kings—a game designed to be played under the desert canopy by men possessed of memory, cunning, and continents of time in which to sift among, enact, reject a hundred different paths to entrapment—had been bastardized into a quick urban hustle, a scam. Speed chess is chess without memory, contemplation, past—eternity boiled down into a loud, ringing instant. You move your piece, you slam the alarm clock at your side; you delay, you lose. Move, slap, ring; move, slap, ring. One minute per move.

Casey, who remembered with a quiver the infinite boredom of childhood matches with his father, undulated to the calypso beat. Time is civility, haste is barbarism. Everything worth tasting takes a hundred years to cook. Instead of real chess's slow-motion minuet of spider-and-fly, here was the jittery thrill of thinking on the run. Instead of deliberation, improvisation. Democracy. God, he swooned, sometimes New York could be a dream. No place like it. Made everywhere else seem white-bread bland, dull, edgeless.

Casey, drunk on autumnal clarity, the sharp air turning dusky, the syncopated beat of move-slap-ring-shift, watched a grizzled Orthodox Jew in a homburg beat a young black man, watched a West Indian beat a wincing older West Indian, watched money change hands, winners, losers, professionals, customers; was it a scam? Watched an older man, Polish, Russian maybe, losing to a burly blond . . . a . . . a . . . *Hooker*. Nearly fell off his bicycle, joy jostling misgivings supplanted by guilt. Isaac, he said under his breath, and wished he hadn't seen him. It's a simple soul who spotting a friend from a distance doesn't consider crossing the street before it's too late.

Yes, it was Isaac Hooker, looking slobby, don't-touch-me-with-a-bargepole as ever, but different too, older maybe. Thinner. Much thinner. Older. Hadn't seen him in a dog's age–. A year? Two years! Not since kicking him out of the apartment on Vandam Street. Christ–a lifetime ago. My blood brother, but the blood unfortunately had turned to bad blood and not yet been thoroughly regenerated; my unseemly semblable. Was Isaac sore at him? Ike hadn't exactly kept in touch. Were they speaking? Would Isaac ask him for another loan–or worse yet, a bed? Better just pounce, pretend nothing happened. Nothing small or ungenerous about his ex–best friend ex-roommate. Casey dismounted, watched Isaac beat his partner three games running with savage swoops like a bird of prey, shake hands, pocket the outstretched greenbacks, and wait for the next customer. Watched the young man take off his glasses, close his eyes, fold bare arms across his chest. He looked older. He had crow's-feet around his eyes.

"Mr. Hooker, I presume," Casey enunciated. Loudly. The boy was hard of hearing on top of it all. Yes, the words registered. Eyelids fluttered, blue peepers cracked open. A moment's regard, myopic squinting. His beloved farmboy, his own true hick. Casey chuckled. He remembered all of a sudden he loved this boy. Then Isaac too after another pause and squint gave a roar of laughter, lunged up at Casey, and engulfed him, throttled him in sweat, dirt, muscle, a human bear–yes, he had that funny smell you smell in a zoo, discovering to your surprise that animals left to their own devices stink–ham hand landing in Casey's curls, trying, it seemed, to pick him up by the hair, settling for a prolonged rumple.

"You damn devil–you little bogtrotter, you."

Casey, to his consternation, saw that the tears were welling up in his friend's eyes. He bent and picked up Isaac's glasses, which had fallen in the scrimmage of reunion.

"How you doing, man? You look like you just crawled out of a garbage can. Why haven't you called me all this time? I gave up on you, figured you must've headed back to your mom's. Where you living, anyway?"

Isaac gave him a last disrupting squeeze, wiped his nose with the back of his hand. Embarrassed, suddenly. "I don't think you *live* in this city," he amended. "You haunt it, you hunt it, you are haunted and hunted by it. *Not* a good city for a blind man, let me tell you."

"So you're a chess hustler now."

"Noble profession, huh?"

"Yeah, now you mention it, I kinda expected you would have invented relativity by now. You make good money?"

"Enough to buy you a drink."

Casey hesitated, glanced at his watch. "I can't, dude—I got to meet somebody at—well, what the hell. A quick drink. On me—I just got paid."

"No, *my* treat," said Isaac, suddenly imperious.

"All right, all right, big spender, I submit."

They headed east, Casey wheeling the bicycle, Isaac with his arm around Casey's shoulder. They made a peculiar pair: Isaac, a Nordic giant, a charity case, a half-blind blond bear in patched clothes, violent and messy in his attempted tendernesses; Casey elegant, vain, black Irish, a brawny little strutter—shoulders rolling, pelvis thrust forward—and all the cartilage, muscle, sinew, and surface to him groomed and flexed into high definition, polished to a sheen. Blue angel rippling on his forearm. Grinning from the pleasure Lafayette Street must be getting from the sight of hunky him. He was still young enough, too, to feel happy just at being alive and kicking. Isaac, not realizing that the grin was for the crowd, clasped his friend's shoulder, happy back. Hummed to himself, smiled, hummed, squeezed Casey from time to time, bumping into the bicycle and banging it into his friend's thigh.

"Is it you, is it really you, Casey Jones, Casey at the bat? I think I must be hallucinating. I've gotten very old since I saw you last. Have you too? I must be twenty-five by now and I haven't done a blessed thing, I feel useless as a cat in a well."

"When I feel useless, I spend money. I bought this beaut at the crack market over at St. Mark's Place this afternoon, seat still warm from its rightful owner's butt. Whaddaya think? It's a good old racing bike—the scrooge painted it to look crappy so it wouldn't get ripped off. Ha-ha."

Isaac looked at it. "I don't approve."

"Yeah, the green's pretty pukey, but once I've—"

"No. It's indefensible buying stolen goods."

"You just need a decent motorcycle-type lock they can't prize apart," said Casey. "The lock'll cost more than the bike. Forty bucks I paid for it. Not bad, huh? You can't get into a taxi these days without shelling out twenty. Watch out for the Georgians, man—they fix their meters. These guys are into mean monkey business, nothing but hustles."

"How's your girlfriend?" Isaac asked abruptly.

"Which one?"

"The one you were moving in with—Maggie."

"Oh, that's history. She was insane—she wanted a baby. Now she's pregnant by some . . . I was, like, Thank God it's not me. I got two girl-friends at the moment, one live-in, one—"

"Are they also stolen?"

But Casey, instead of being offended, laughed.

They turned into McSorley's pub on Seventh Street. Casey hadn't yet acquired a lock for his machine, so the bartender let him put it in the back. It was happy hour, and the bar was full. They squeezed into a table next to a boy and girl, both with dyed black hair and nose rings.

"Can I have the two-for-two-fifty special, please? Dark," said Casey. "Isaac, you having something to eat? A burger? I'm going to have something to eat. I could eat a . . . Nice juicy burger?"

They ordered two beers, two bacon cheeseburgers, and two orders of fries. Casey winked at his friend. He wanted to do something wonderful for Isaac. He didn't know yet what it was. He wanted to make him rich, loved, grateful. He had to find out what Isaac wanted so he could give it to him.

He was a fixer, that was how he thought of himself—a fixer and an artist, a man whose spreading arteries of appetite, desire were constantly being routed into schemes, lust merging with profit, social benefit: e.g., The girl was not only gorgeous but could probably get his friend Oscar a job. Selfishness justified by becoming collective selfishness. If he'd been born in a less organized country, he would have been a black-marketeer or warlord.

"Happy days." He raised his mug to Isaac's. "*Salud, amor, pesetas, y tiempo para gustarlos.*"

"Happy days." Isaac relaxed, the stale soaked liquorous bar smell of barrels and blue-plate specials shooting to his brain. He stared at the faceted mug of brown ale with its paler brown spume, downed it in one gulp, ordered another round. Outside it was dark, but he for once was ensconced by the hearth. He licked at his mustache of beer froth, looked over his friend lovingly. The hamburgers arrived, Isaac spurted his in fake-blood gobs from a plastic squirter, he liked the way the bun was soggy with rose-colored blood, they smelled like absolute juicy san-guine fullness, an end to hunger. And the thin gold of his fries like winter sunlight, shiny, glistening. He breathed in and out through his nose. Let this moment last forever, he was thinking—red meat, liquor, warmth, companionship. "So how're Number One and Number Two?"

"Who?"

"The new girlfriends."

"Number One's a lawyer. Number Two's dessert. Number One I am more or less shacked up with, which is kind of a drag. You, like, end up talking all the time about who's going to stay home for the cable TV repairman." He gave an exaggerated shudder. "Death by trivialization. Do you ever feel like you're living a life that doesn't belong to you, someone—"

"I'm not living a life at all."

"—Else's life? The company car picks her up at seven, brings her home at midnight, and on weekends she, like, cooks these pretentious four-course dinners—cassoulets and tiramisù and whatnot—and invites all her banker/lawyer friends over. Dinner parties—you know, Jack sits here, and Rosemary next to him, and Shitface you sit here, and oh dear, we're short a girl. It's obscene."

"Is she nice?" Isaac asked, with envy.

Casey, ignoring, continued, "And now she's bugging me to come skiing at Christmas with her parents. I mean, I'm sorry. I tell her, I don't know who brought you up, but where I come from, Christmas is the day that Baby Jesus came into the world to save us from sin, it's not the day you hit the slopes in your Azzedine Alaïa ski suit. So she says—just to teach me—Fine, on Christmas we'll go to Midnight Mass—you know she's the kind of Waspy girl who just chokes on that word. They got church in Colorado. Supposedly. I tell her, It's only September. By Christmas I may be a completely different man in a completely different country."

Isaac, shifting, finally got a word in. "Come off it, Casey, you see the girl's point—she's a wage slave, she's got two weeks off a year, and she wants to know if you'll be with her or not. Have a heart. The point of total freedom isn't to make you close-minded to those who haven't got it."

"Okay, okay, but tell me this. How come every woman considers a man a project for major remodelling?"

Isaac got up abruptly, a funny look on his face.

"Where you going, man? What's the matter?" Casey grabbed hold of Isaac's sleeve, tugged at it.

"Nothing."

"What is it?"

"I forgot how much I despise the way you talk about your– girlfriends."

Casey laughed, not in the least offended. "Oh, if that's all–sit down. I thought you were sick or something. Hold your horses, I gotta split in a minute myself. So what else do you do in this City of Dreadful Night besides hustle chess?"

"I work in a store."

Casey made a face. "What kinda store?"

"What's it matter? Any old store. Nice store."

"For fuck's sake, Hooker, what are you doing working in a store? Why doncha find a real job? I told you to call my friend Carlo back in–"

"I'm allergic to real jobs. Subsistence jobs are what give you time to think and make and be. Anyway," Isaac conceded, "today I did go to see a man about a real job. I lasted about ten seconds before they threw me out."

Casey looked him over. "You look like a basket case, but you're not, you're just unmotivated. You need a manager."

"Manager, manage yourself."

"You writing anything these days?"

"I haven't written anything for years."

"So you work in this store, you hustle chess, you . . ."

"I've been drawing. Painting, making things." Glanced at the clock on the wall. With any luck, Aurora would be closed, and he could pretend to himself he'd done his best to retrieve the oil sticks. It would be worth the thirty-eight dollars they'd cost not to have to set foot again in that fancy mausoleum. . . .

Casey was surprised. "No kidding. You're horning in on my profession? Well, that's great. I'd love to see what you're doing. I mean it. I always thought of you as a man of words, but . . . So when can I see your stuff?"

"No."

"No what?"

"No, you can't see it. It's not ready."

"Come on, Ike, let me take a look at least. Maybe I can put you in my show," he joked. "I'm putting together this major exhibition of young artists—"

Isaac had such a cynical look on his face that Casey interrupted himself, laughing. "You think I'm bullshitting, huh? No bullshit. This is a *major* show, I'm talking big time—I've been asked to curate it for the most important gallery in town, this museum-type gallery run by this megarich family from Chicago. They think I'm God—I've got a hundred thousand dollars and five thousand feet of exhibition space to fill, and the Geblers—"

"The who?"

"The Geblers. That's the name of the family. Her dad owns—"

"Oh. That's where I went today asking for a job."

"Where?"

"Aurora."

"Aurora? Over on Second Street?"

"Mm-hmmmmm."

Casey mimicked a dropped jaw. "This is psychic. I mean, this is karma. I don't see you for a century, and then . . . Why'd you go there? Who told you about them?"

"It's so big and peaceful—I thought working there, even just sweeping the floors, would be like living in a lovely Central European sanatorium. All those glass walls and miles of skylight, all that blank peaceful art on the walls. I heard they were a charity, and hoped I might qualify."

"Who'd you talk to? Andy?"

"No. Mr. Gebler."

"Alfred? You went there today?"

"Yeah, this morning. I left my oil sticks in the office—I mean, I forgot them."

"I musta just missed you. Isn't that wild? We don't lay eyes on each other for three years and then . . ."

"Isn't God wonderful?"

"You went to Aurora dressed like that? No wonder Alfred threw you out. You shoulda told me first. Listen. Listen to your uncle Casey. I tell you what we'll do. I have no idea if they are hiring or not, but first thing tomorrow morning, I'll call up Alfred and put in a word for you. Or else I'll hire you myself for the 'Home' show. But listen, first we gotta do something about your clothes, man. For a start, they don't smell too good, and I'm not even mentioning the stylistic aspect. They got a bathtub where you live? And you showed up at Aurora looking like you just robbed a gravedigger?"

"I'd like to get my oil sticks tonight," said Isaac. An idea, suddenly, of something good to draw. An itch to finger those juicy bars of pigment, thick as ingots.

"Well, hold your horses. Let me talk to Alfred first."

"No, I'd like to go get them right now."

"Will you hold on a minute?" Casey, exasperated, stared at his friend. "You want to me to call him right now, tell him you're coming by? You drive a tough bargain, man."

"It was your idea to call him," said Isaac. "I don't see what good it'll do—he said they weren't hiring. I just want my oil sticks."

Casey looked at Isaac once more. On Isaac's face was that stubborn, ramlike expression, head lowered, that he remembered well. Then with a sigh he rose to his feet, jiggling a quarter. "Well, I'll give him a buzz. I bet everyone's left for the day—it's past seven already."

Five

DOLLY WAS ON the telephone to her mother. Every evening now she rang her mother. Formerly her mother had had a rather telegraphic relation to the phone, as a medium for the speedy transmission of essential information. Arriving on Tuesday on the 5:05, longing to see you—bye, dear. Or Happy Christmas, and love to the children. But Dolly couldn't fly out to Chicago every day to see how her mother was getting along, so the telephone had to answer a new need. And Dolly was almost disappointed by how quickly the remote unworldly old lady had got into the hang of long-distance chatter. Really, old people were a good deal more adaptive than one allowed.

Her mother was quite well. Remarkably well, in fact. Old age suited her. Mittie, the nurse, had told Dolly something curious. In old age, temperaments shift. "If she's a sweetie pie now, you kin be sure in her heyday she was a vicious"—"viscous," she pronounced it—"little cuss. And vice versa." Wasn't that so much with Mother; more that she'd grown more definite, with sharper angles and opinions to her. Not old age but widowhood. The truth was that Daddy had shrunk her, kept her abject from fear of displeasing him, the field of Dolly's father's silent rages being so extensive and their causes so obscure.

Now that Daddy was dead—and there was no doubt that the salt was gone from her mother's life, that she wished for nothing more than their swift reunion—there was a gap-toothed grin on her face from time to time that Dolly didn't remember seeing before, and all kinds of assertions and tastes emerged that she had never previously allowed herself. Dolly had accused her, teasing but tentative—didn't want to frighten her out of her wings. "You're getting uppity, Mother."

"Am I? Well, it's rather pleasant being old. I'm enjoying my privileges. I'm far too old to be contradicted. And if I'm not going to come out with it now, well, when will I?"

Dolly's mother was a New Englander, an outdoors girl. Now she couldn't climb the stairs anymore—rheumatism. They'd had to fix up the library as her bedroom. Worse still, she could no longer get out much into the garden. That was the sad part. It had to come in to her, like Birnam Wood. In pots and vases. Otherwise, a hale widowhood of solitaire and crossword puzzles and being read aloud detective novels— her only complaints Mittie's flat twang and her own loss of taste buds. A tall rake of a woman, now truly skeletal, the flesh curdled about her upper arms. An old mule.

They passed along news.

"I talked to Beatrice," began Dolly.

"Oh," said her mother, discouragingly. Of her three daughters, only Beatrice, the middle child, had stayed in Chicago and made a suitable marriage. Dolly sometimes thought the parable of the prodigal son had caught a cruel constant in the nature of parents—whichever one gets away is the one they adore. Dutiful Beatrice, who came out to Norwood every Sunday lunch, didn't rate a breath of long-distance phone time.

"Have you heard from Sophie, Mother?" Sophie was closer to favorite.

"Yes. I got a postcard from Carmel—she said she's having a ball," said her mother's voice.

"Well, it's lovely out there."

"Do you think so?"

"Well, the beach and ocean . . ."

"I never cared one bit for the Pacific Ocean. I remember the first time I bathed in it with your father when we went to stay with the Haverfords. The ocean bed is so violent—one step, it's up to your knee; the next, it's over your head. And of course I simply loathe pelicans. Always did."

"I knew it—you're not a real Christian," said Dolly triumphantly.

"What's that got to do with it?"

"Oh, you remember—the symbol of Christ. Feeding its young with its heart's blood . . . The other night I sat next to a man at dinner—he's just made a fortune in computers—who asked me who in history I'd most like to meet. He said he'd like to meet Jesus."

A pause. "How very sappy," said her mother's voice.

"That's what I thought. Disgusting."

"What did you say?"

" 'Disgus–' "

"I mean, who did *you* say you wanted to meet?"

"Well, I was stumped, after he'd gone and been so smarmy and teacher's-pettish about it. I said I didn't want to meet anybody—I felt as if I'd already met a damn sight too many people as it was. But I was being disingenuous—I *would* like to lay eyes on Jesus, just to be sure he isn't that golden-haired fairy the Catholics make him out to be. I've always pictured him a small, dark creature with a sort of feral intensity."

Silence.

"Is that blasphemous?"

"I don't know," said her mother. "I find that the closer I get to all that the less it interests me."

Silence.

"She's got a new beau, apparently. A music man," continued her mother's voice.

Sophie. A record executive, to be precise. The last one was a twenty-two-year-old unemployed carpenter. Dolly's heart had sunk, but when she met him—he'd dropped off some Christmas presents for them, having driven back east in his pickup truck to visit his parents in Fishkill—she saw the point instantly. Those lean brown arms, with long flat muscles and golden hairs on them, the loose way he moved, the remote laughing eyes. Pure physical cunning. You'd like to watch him cast a line or even just tie his shoelaces. She'd talked to him long enough to see that he wasn't dumb, either. Huh. Greedy Sophie. Too paranoid she was being taken advantage of to stick with a good thing, a young lick half her age with a body true as gospel, motion like quick-sprung honey, and sly blue eyes that could hold a joke. As if *she* weren't the one taking advantage of him, a much more insidious bloodsucking kind of exploitation than his simply being sick of being broke—nothing corrupt or twisted about the desire for some hard cash. So she'd dumped Duane and now she was stepping out on the town with some facelifted old fraud for no better reason than that he was as ungodly rich as she and therefore could not be accused of "taking advantage" of her. Silly bitch. Wonder what happened to Duane.

"What news have I got for you. . . . The children seem to be settling into school. . . . Leopold has an English teacher he's crazy about."

"Oh good," said her mother's voice with emphatic relief—she herself had always been frightened of school, and seemed to regard it as a peculiarly vindictive punishment Dolly was visiting upon the children.

"I sent you a story Carlotta wrote. Very amusing."

"Oh dear. I'll have to get Mittie to read it to me."

"And what else. . . . An opera we helped sponsor is opening tomorrow night. Very modern. Alfred and I are giving a party afterwards."

"Goodness." Her mother hated opera and parties even worse than school. "Well, goodbye now." Conversations with her mother always ended abruptly, like film of early flight.

"Goodbye. . . ."

The click of separation, the dial tone of loss, a momentary desolation at being deprived of even such imperfect communication, such a false and diminutive presence as a seventy-eight-year-old lady's voice from two thousand miles away. Alfred couldn't have cared less about his mother, whom he'd stuck in some ghastly home in Brooklyn—okay, apparently, because all her friends were there too—then never gone to see her. Quite cross when she died.

Mother. Here she was, forty-six, and still consumed by remorse at

not having loved—which of them had started the not-loving business?—
that lean distant lady. Truth was, all of them—mother and daughters—
had been too caught up by the battle for Dolly's father's favor to regard
one another as anything more than rivals. Not that Mother cared much
anyway for girls—a little rough when three of them is all you've got.
Mother also would have liked Duane.

Or maybe Sophie unloaded Duane just because he had that light-
heeled look to him, and she wanted to get in there first. It takes a kind
of grit to sit around waiting to get dumped.

When she was a child Dolly thought everyone was laughing at her.
Still did.

When she'd finished wondering about Duane, missing her mother,
she got up, straightened her hair. Time to make the children's dinner—it
was Ernestine's night off. Excitement at the prospect of being alone
with them, of having her babies to herself. Laughed out loud remembering Johnny's imitation of Alfred interviewing the new cleaning lady.
Cruel children. How they'd taken in stride having a father they could
sass. Unimaginable to Dolly, who had grown up with chronic knots in
the stomach towards dinnertime and careful scanning of the servants'
faces for clues as to whether Daddy was in One of His Moods. . . .
Spaghetti or yesterday's meatloaf?

"But darling love—

". . . My dear girl—

". . . But I thought—

". . . Yeah, me too. But I thought you wanted to—

". . . Yeah, me too. Zonked. Hmmm. Would you like me to come
pester you just for an hour right now? . . . No, I don't blame you. That's
a much better idea. And how's—?

". . . Yeah, I got to go, too. Well, don't let that ignorant young buck
maul you, you hear? I mean it. I got my hit squads, you know—he might
just end up in a Canarsie disposal.

". . . What are you—? . . . Don't tempt me. Well, I guess I'll see you—
no, I can't see you tomorrow, I've got to go to the—

". . . Goodbye, angel."

Mr. Gebler stared reproachfully at the receiver as if the sievey plastic
had bitten him, replaced it gingerly, and sat down with a sigh that

turned groan. Everyone else in the office had left—even Cecile had been picked up by Mark, and Andy had gone straight home from a meeting.

An animal panic seized Gebler at being alone in the dark, stranded five floors up above the streets. He didn't like heights, because you were afraid you might jump even if you didn't want to. He had never lived above the second floor till he met Dolly. The heights, the heights. Who had invented that phrase "the heights of despair"? He got up, cleared his throat, paced, lit a cigar. Whom could he call? He considered calling back and—abjectly—offering to take her and her date out to an expensive dinner. What did the mortal pain of sexual jealousy matter beside the joy of snuffing at her nesty hair, just a hand's breadth away, hearing her laugh deep in her gullet?

He picked up the phone and played the little song of her number, the secret code to her curly ear—oddly pointed at the tip, like a terrier's, lobeless, tucked aerodynamically close to the skull. No lobes was a sign of criminality. His little jailbait-jailbird. Rang and rang. *Vroom-vroom-vroom.* She wasn't picking up. She knew it was him and she wasn't picking up, and she hadn't put the machine on. He felt hysteria rise in his lungs, the panicky wing-beat of heart, as he let the phone ring fifty, sixty, seventy times. She had no manners. Panic. All alone.

He wondered what his daughters were up to—he pictured them running baths, pattering down the hall barefoot and imperious, doing their homework (unlikely), trying on their new dresses for tomorrow night— and felt cut off from them by his own wolfish desires, by his love.

Couldn't go home just yet, couldn't pitch his disappointed lust into that warm nest—besides, he'd told Dolly he'd be back late because he had an appointment. With whom? Couldn't remember. No, he would sit here till he got a grip on himself, him and the bottle and the cigar, or he would drag himself over to the Emerald Isle and have just one quick slug in its baize-green stewed squalor. But who could he call? For to sit here alone, reconstructing as if he were its sculptor every vertebra along that musky brown column now being clad for someone else to unclad—

The ring of the phone, and Gebler sprang for it like a devouring tiger.

"Hello?" he panted. "Hello? Who is it? Hello?"

Silence. "Hey, Alfred."

"Who's this?"

"It's Casey."

Oh shit. Only Casey. "What's happening, Casey? What are you up to tonight? You want to get together for a—"

"I can't, man, but I got a great friend here. . . ."

"You're back," said Mr. Gebler.

Isaac, rocking from foot to foot, was examining a box suspended from the wall. It was simple but ingenious. A cedar box, open-fronted, with a sheet of midnight-blue cellophane across it. A tiny theater, whose backdrop—through the blue glass—was an engraving of a temple. Not Greek. Assyrian, maybe.

"What is it?"

"Joseph Cornell."

"I mean, what's the picture?"

"I believe it's from an excavation near Baalbek."

"I think it looks more Assyrian."

The light in the office was changed from this morning—whiter. White, but a milkier white than the halogen of Acme. Isaac looked at the ceiling. Yes, it was a fluorescent tube, but not a glary-blue fluorescence: milkier. He had never seen fluorescent light so mild, forgiving. Forgiveness cost.

Now, for the first time, he noted the richness of the office's furnishings, compared with other offices he'd been in. No fake-wood panelling, no bald nylon carpeting, no coffee machines with Styrofoam cups and tiny ridged tartlets of nondairy cream. The contrasting luxury of Aurora aggravated Isaac. With the money should come manners. The fluorescent light didn't glare or hurry you, so why should Gebler? Why hadn't he soaked up some of that slow benignity raining down from above? And something ungenerous in Isaac, too, thinking, If he really hired Casey he's a clown, because no one serious would fall for Casey's jive.

On the elevator ride up, he had been practicing his return—heart catapulting as the lit numbers rose, anger mounting as L turned to 2, 3, 4. Maybe the elevator would get stuck. Maybe it would just be the secretary with the funny way of smacking her lips over the words, of opening her mouth so wide you could see the flaccid tongue as she inhaled for the next sentence.

But the office was empty, and there was Gebler in his chrome armchair, appearing smaller somehow than he had this morning—that's what a day at the office did, it shrunk you, unless it was Isaac's own dismay which at their last encounter had inflated the man into a Thanksgiving Day Parade–sized genie, a banishing Saint Michael–and faced with this more worn and diminished Gebler, his prepared words, proud, chastising, correct, went up in smoke. Just get the oil sticks and get out, because who needs to have these people, these cosseted gasbags, humiliate you . . . Gebler with his silly red beard and his black pearl cuff links, his handmade shoes? Puffball. Just get the box and leave. But Gebler looked sad. Was it hard to be him? Don't bother, just go home.

Gebler had said something which he hadn't caught. Something in a not-unkind tone of voice. Cajoling. Isaac fiddled with the computer chessboard in his pocket with one hand, shifted from one foot to the other. And examining once more the Assyrian temple, reconstituted in its primal grandeur, felt depressed. Why bother to make art, when everything great had already been done so long ago it took bulldozers to extract it from the ground?

"Anyway, nobody cares anymore about art. The moment's gone," he muttered to himself.

Mr. Gebler heard and replied. "True, art is dead, but I must confess I rather relish the small self-righteous melancholy of working a dead street."

Isaac, pleased, considered this a moment. "What's so great about life, anyway?" he agreed, and both men relaxed.

"So what can I do for you?"

"I moronically forgot a package when I came to bother you this morning."

Mr. Gebler raised aloft Isaac's box of oil sticks, then took another peek inside. "Nice."

"Birds of paradise, in the right hands," Isaac agreed. That vouchsafed flash of peacock blue-green cheered him up again. He could already feel the squelchy fatness of oil stick in his fingers. Now all he wanted was his box back and to be gone.

Mr. Gebler evidently felt otherwise. "Let's have a drink," he said, rising. From the kitchenette next door, he brought back a bottle of tequila and two glasses. He poured the shots, handed Isaac a golden brimful. They both downed their tequilas too fast and looked at each other speculatively.

"Isaac Hooker, huh? Are you a Jewish Isaac?"

"No. I'm from Gilboa, New Hampshire."

"New Hampshire!? I don't even know what street New Hampshire's on. Do you know who said that?"

Isaac stared at him unforgivingly over those taped-together two-inch-thick glasses.

"Al Capone. He said it about Canada. But New Hampshire—now you're really talking Nowhere. Just a lot of lakes with summer camps. Right? All those camps with names like Chuggawawa my children refused to go to were always in New Hampshire. Good thing too—last thing you need is your daughters getting deflowered in the bottom of a canoe by some lousy townie. Like you."

Isaac didn't seem to be listening. He had plucked a magazine from the desk and started reading.

"So what can I do for you, Mr. Hooker from New Hampshire? I feel like you're some kind of recording angel from a Frank Capra movie, turning up in my office chair first thing on a Monday morning."

"I told you before—I was looking for a job. I already have a very nice job at a frame store, but now they've lost their lease, so I was hoping you could hire me instead."

"We don't make frames here."

"I know that. You go to my store. That's how I heard about you."

"Which? Acme? Huh . . . I didn't know Acme was going out of business." Mr. Gebler considered. "Well, we're not really hiring these days. What can you do besides make frames?"

"Oh, I can paint like a house on fire. I can lift heavy boxes. I can hang pictures and stretch canvases. I can cook. I've been a security guard . . . a delivery boy . . . a typesetter . . . a newspaper journalist . . . I can work a cash register. I can keep books. I can set type. I can–"

"Hold on a minute. You're giving me a headache. You're like one of those kitchen appliances on late-night television that do ten things none of which one wants done. Anyway, as I told you, we're overstaffed. We won't be hiring anybody new for about forty years—our employees have a longevity problem."

Mr. Gebler drained his glass and stood up, sheltering his eyes against the glow of the fluorescent lighting. "Well, I don't think I can give you a job, but at least let me buy you a square meal."

He put on his jacket, cast around for his briefcase. "Let's go. Do you know any chicks, any girls?"

"No."

"None? Not even a little one? No? What a pity. I hate eating without women. Well, let's eat and talk, and I'll think about whether there's anything we can possibly do with a man so embarrassingly overqualified."

It was five o'clock in the morning, and Gebler and his guest were sitting in Kicky's Topless. His companion, Gebler noticed, had flinched at the flash of bare boobs and seated himself with his back firmly to the sequined jiggling. Maybe he had a hometown girlfriend he was trying overhard to stay true to. Maybe he came from fundamentalists, and didn't approve of the merchandising of mammaries. Later on he had delivered a speech in favor of women's right to prostitute themselves and men's right to seek cheap consolation, but Mr. Gebler wasn't convinced.

Isaac had wolfed down dinner while Gebler checked out the crowd. Last year Kicky's had been a scene, but now it looked past it. Too many expense-account businessmen. And too many Japanese. Business obviously was booming, but the place had lost its chic.

"Casey tells me you were at Harvard together." Gebler, who had never been to college himself, sounded accusatory.

"For about ten minutes. I dropped out."

Mr. Gebler crammed three olives into his mouth. "That's right—Casey said you'd been some kind of—uh—child whiz kid or whatever. Not a past I envy." He binked the sucked-clean olive pits into an ashtray. "No offense, but I had my fill growing up in Brownsville—you heard of Brownsville, Brooklyn? Where all the skinny boys with glasses who couldn't shoot a basket grew up and won the Nobel Prize? Manny Klein. He was the smartest person in our class. Math, physics, chemistry, classics—you name it. Chess. The violin. Ghastly.

"When Manny Klein was sixteen years old, he went to Yale and discovered acid. Last thing I heard he was still—aged forty-five!—hanging around campus with dirty matted hair arguing with undergraduates.

"Listen, let's face it, early brilliance—or what passes for it—is a trap. Better not even learn the alphabet till you're twenty. Myself, I put great store in the social graces." He was warming up now, having dismissed from his mind the revolting specter of the Harvard prodigy. "I have two daughters. They go to dancing class, they take figure skating at Rockefeller Center. Riding in the summers. They speak French, they can't add, they can't spell, they can hold forth for hours on the inferiority of Madonna and the superiority of taffeta, and they can talk to anybody: they are perfect human beings.

"My Carlotta, alas," Gebler continued, "is a closet book-reader. She gobbles up everything from Archie comics to George Eliot. Thank God it hasn't gone so far that she isn't also an Amazon on horseback."

Isaac had perked up at the mention of the daughters, managing to look at once overeager and down at the mouth, like a dog who knows the steak's not for him but can't help hoping. Wild, the stubborn hopefulness of the human heart.

By now, the other customers had gone home, except for one table of young Japanese, and the waiters had turned the chairs upside down and washed the floor, and from time to time the owner would come over and ask if he could get them anything more, and Gebler always said yes.

Terror of deprivation, of the lights going out on him. His wife accused him of having the soul and habits of a seventeen-year-old. Should have been a jazz musician. Being a night owl and gregarious to boot—although "gregarious" was too peaceable a word properly to capture Gebler's frantic efforts never to be alone—was an imperative that acted as a harsh chemical agent on the rest of your life. Not being able to bear admitting the party was over meant you ended up asshole buddies with people you didn't necessarily know or like.

And he had married a woman who had no concept of companionship or even an honest social life, for whom everything was appearances, obeying the most hypocritical and measly Midwestern sense of duty. Six nights a week Dolly had her black-tie galas at the New Museum, special viewings at the Whitney, AIDS benefits, board meetings, you name it. Institutional hell. Dinners at Angelica Broadman's, fixed up two months in advance, the extra women—heartless term—swained by sycophantic curators willing to do who knows how much to weasel a bequest or donation. And Gebler, who liked to be a good Joe, besides being curious to see what people's houses looked like and what kind of pictures they had and what they kept in the medicine cupboard, would allow himself most nights to be dragged along, except that when the party broke up at eleven-thirty, he dropped his wife home and headed on to the Hellfire Club. So everybody was happy. Or should have been, if he hadn't hitched himself to a congenital malcontent.

Tonight he had decided to cleave exclusively to tequila. (It was mixing your drinks that made you feel like suicide next day.) And Gebler was crazy about tequila, which he had completely forgotten about until that very week. Something about cactus that didn't just get you soused but truly bounced you off the walls and ceiling. Mind-altering. No wonder the Aztecs had gone around volunteering to have their beating hearts ripped out. You wouldn't much mind. On tequila it might even seem like a good idea.

Mr. Gebler wondered if he was looking as wild as his drinking mate, who as he got drunker had rolled himself up into a ball. Over the course of the night, Alfred had found himself getting increasingly fond of this strange kid who'd barged into his office. The boy had a handsome face behind the cartoon specs. An oversized Fragonard, all pink and gold. And a good nose—a Roman nose, high-bridged, unexpectedly fancy on this raw-boned farmhand. Pudgy fingers, though.

"I must say you've discovered an unusual way to ask for a job," Gebler teased. "Plumping yourself down in the boss's armchair. I thought you were some kind of tramp who'd busted his way into the building."

"I am a tramp."

"So I see. But—um—as an employment-seeking technique, yours really takes the cake. Don't they teach you anything at these Ivy League colleges? Like, for instance, don't sneak into your prospective employer's office and sit in his chair?"

"To hell with the chair," said Isaac, wiping his glasses. "People shouldn't have to stand on ceremony with each other. We should all be brothers. If I want you to help me, I should be able to come to you without feeling ashamed."

Gebler made a thumbs-down sign. "What kind of commie bullshit is that?" He gestured to the owner to bring them another round of shots. "I didn't come to this city so people could get all touchy-feely with me—you can stay in New Hampshire and cozy up to the cows if that's what you want. I came to the city so I'd never have to know anybody's name or be bothered by strangers. Anonymity. It's the modern religion."

Isaac considered. "Anonymous is all right. Anonymous painted some of the best pictures in the world and wrote some gorgeous poems. But it's not much of a religion, I think. I mean, as compared with Christianity or Judaism or even . . . Shinto, for heaven's sake."

Later he asked, "So will you give me a job?"

"I don't have a job to give you," Gebler repeated. "What do you want a job for, anyway? You're an artist? Go on welfare. And especially if you want to be an artist, don't get a job in the art world. I mean it."

Isaac, who was gazing at the Japanese girl in jodhpurs at the next table, came back to attention. "Why not?"

"It's corrupting for artists to be too conscious of the market. This is my advice to you: Drive a taxi. Keep your independence."

"My mother drives a taxi," said Isaac, laughing. "I came to New York not to drive taxis. Anyway, I don't want to go into the art world. I just want the freedom–the money–to paint pictures."

Mr. Gebler made a razzberry noise. "That's the most arrant piece of hypocritical disingenuity I've ever heard. I don't want to get wet, I just want to go swimming. You want too much, that's your problem. You want a job. You want money. You want freedom. Try being a little more Zen about things. Your generation is too fucking materialistic."

Isaac's smile got even broader.

"What's so funny?"

"I like your shoes, Mr. Gebler," said Isaac slyly. "What are they, crocodile? They're handmade, aren't they? Where did you fly to buy them? And your cuff links also are very fetching. Are those black pearls? I say this as a man who's seriously into things, but maybe since you aren't a materialist, you wouldn't have noticed how nice your shirt is, too."

And Gebler, seeing the joke, burst out laughing too. "By the way," he said. "Remind me, I've got to go buy flowers."

"What's the matter–is your wife mad at you?" Later, Isaac was to remember this first innocently disrespectful reference to Mrs. Gebler.

"You must be clairvoyant. I need three dozen lilies, and that's just for starters."

"She must be hopping."

"Actually, we're giving a party tomorrow night. Whoa–I mean tonight. It's for the opening of an opera."

"Where do you buy flowers at five in the morning?"

"At the flower market. Don't you know anything about this city?" And then a semi-mischievous thought occurred to Gebler. "Why don't you come? I mean, to the opera? I'll invite Casey, too—you boys can flesh out the stag line."

Isaac looked as if he thought he was being made fun of.

"No, I mean it. You can come to the opera, and to dinner at our house afterwards." The more Gebler thought about this idea, the more amusing it seemed. "My wife would be thrilled. She's always complaining that we don't know any straight single men. I must say, I find hostesses' obsession with sexual symmetry a bit daft. After all, we're not traipsing off to Noah's ark to propagate a new and better species, we're just going to the opera. Do you like opera?"

Isaac still hesitated. "I don't know. My kid brother was once in an eighth-grade production of *Pirates of Penzance*."

"Well, this one's pretty pitilessly new wave."

Isaac frowned. "I don't know." Then he stood up, overturning the table.

"Where are you going?"

"Let's go buy flowers." And before Gebler could protest, they were out in the middle of Fourteenth Street and Sixth in a dove-gray half-light, sun not up yet, but the clouds already tinged in expectant readiness. Garbage trucks plowing up Sixth Avenue, and pools of light from the Korean grocers. Silvery barred shutters down on the wholesale garment stores. And a couple of homeless men stirring in their gray cocoons of blanket and newspaper. The city waking up, stretching and yawning. His favorite hour. And Isaac, lungs full of oxygen, happy as a clam. "Come on, Mr. Gebler, where's the market?"

Because Gebler had wilted, gone blurred on him. Confused. "Where's my briefcase? I forgot my . . ."

Isaac waved the chestnut-brown steed of a briefcase, and the two men, rocking slightly on their heels, set off uptown towards Twenty-eighth Street in the clay-colored early-morning light.

Part Two

Six

AJAX WAS BEING PERFORMED at the Space, a red-brick mammoth built in the 1830s as a lending library for workmen, which was then relegated to city archives, marked for demolition at the beginning of the century, and finally, in the 1970s, reclaimed as a center for the performing arts by the nerve and optimism of a Romanian-born theater director. The Geblers were among the Space's chief patrons.

Isaac arrived at the theater early. He had spent a febrile dawn, after dropping off Gebler and the flowers, fretting over whether or not he should go to the opera. The previous twenty-four hours, with their abrupt reversals of fortune, their chance-encounter-with-long-lost friend, their two square restaurant dinners in one night, considered in the dishwater-gray light of his areaway room seemed improbable. That the prospective employer who had kicked him out of his office that morning should be inviting him to the opera next night just wasn't likely. He must have been even drunker than I was. And Casey's re-emergence as an Aurora favorite? What a funny world, if Casey's king of it. And then he recollected that this was just what he had suspected at college, and had concluded priggishly that if the world was arranged for Casey to thrive in it—rewarded bounce, patter, shameless self-promotion—then it wasn't made for him.

And how could he dream of going to the opera—even if Gebler had really meant it—when his clothes were so tattered and dismal, had collectively mutated into some mongrel no-color, gone translucent from too much wear, attached to themselves an ineradicable odor of funk. Surely he would get turned away at the door. Casey was right. Casey knew nothing about art, science, industry, or the ways of God, but clothes were his element. Discovered he owned no shirts at the moment—not even an undershirt—but only a moldy green sweater with the elbows out.

Ten a.m. found Isaac still undecided about whether or not he had been invited, but bent double nonetheless over his trousers, attacking the knee with an iron-on patch purchased from the A&P. If only I hadn't blown my last wad on oil sticks, he caught himself thinking. I won't go, he decided, disgusted by his frivolity, depressed by his drabness.

At noon, the buzzer at Acme rang. "Dude asking for you, guy," said Adam. It was Casey, in wraparound dark glasses and black leather. He couldn't make it to the opera—he had an important business meeting—but he'd drop by the Geblers' afterwards. In the meantime, he and Isaac were going shopping.

"I'm working," said Isaac sternly.

"It's your lunch break, man. Everyone's got a lunch break."

"I don't have any money."

"This one's on me. I'm investing in your future. Isaac Hooker Inc. Social butterfly in the making."

By seven, Isaac was pacing the lobby of the Space in his new suit. There were indeed two tickets in Casey's name waiting at the box office. Self-consciousness yielded to the most violent excitement. He had been remembered!

The theater was rather sere in its furbishings. Here were no seraph-incrusted ceilings, no opera boxes like honeycombed gondolas, no red velvet curtains and shivering chandeliers. Instead, brick and concrete, with wires, pipes, and lighting prominent. The ethic was pointed: at the Space, theater was no conduit for pomp and magic, but strenuous and edifying reality, scornful of illusion.

The opening-night audience for *Ajax*, as it began to trickle through the doors, offered a more consolingly vivid spectacle. The crowd divided into geographical camps. Willa Perkins's main constituency was militantly downtown. There was a honking, hissing gaggle of young men in spatter-painted dinner jackets and military buzz cuts. There was a black boy in a saffron sari and leopard-skin fez talking to a white girl with a shaved head (bumpy) and spandex cyclist's knickers. There were more solemn older men—one Isaac recognized as a painter who was a regular customer at the frame store—in black turtlenecks and gray ponytails. A girl with a Day-Glo-green Mohawk was holding hands with a boy whose hair was sculpted into geometric topiary. There were women dressed in boiler suits, and women dressed like escaped Bedlamites in draped, trailing rags and faded leggings. Isaac, who liked to see women's bodies, regretted this punitive-looking billow. Where were their breasts and bottoms? Dark glasses, wraparound, mirrored. And enough black to blot out the day. Isaac again disapproved. To him, as to a late-medieval painter, money meant color: what did dollars translate into if not the sartorial equivalent of lapis lazuli and gold leaf?

And then there were the very rich, the uptowners disgorged from gleaming limousines. For Willa Perkins, after having spent the seventies performing in basement gyms and the eighties scooping up European commissions for ten-hour spectacles in Stuttgart and Cologne, had at last come home famous, an American phenomenon magnetic enough to attract this small pride of bejewelled lionesses in taffeta and skinny legs, accompanied by husbands wearing double-breasted suits and velvet slippers, men who were wondering why they had allowed their wives to drag them below Fiftieth Street and how soon they could get to bed, for word had already got out that the piece was very long.

And amid this congelation of the very rich and the very hip—many of whom, both uptown and down-, were destined later on for the Geblers' house—sat Isaac, eyes agog, while inside his head questions were crashing, roaring. Why do they all know each other? What are they laughing about? Why don't they shut up and sit down? Do I look like a buffoon? Are they laughing at me? And then nervousness was sedated by that form of ambition we call curiosity. Calm down, cretin. This is the world. I will learn it.

Isaac pushed himself down in his seat until his skull was level with the top of the theater seat, then practiced levitating his feet while balancing the program on his head.

Craning, he saw his host—identifiable at a hundred yards by the curly nest of beard—coming down the aisle with three ladies, blowing kisses. And Isaac, timid, ducked. He didn't want Gebler to feel obliged to say hello just because in a fit of alcoholic largesse he'd invited him. Worse still was the alternative that Gebler might simply stare through him in nonrecognition. I won't go to their house afterwards, he decided.

Why should I? The man had already thrown him out once. It was better just to soak up the sights, to suck at his own isolateness, shrinking and concentrating himself into a pair of overeager, carnivorous eyes. When the lights dimmed, he forgot himself in needling shivery anticipation of the spectacle.

The opera lasted four and a half hours. There was no scenery; the stage was bathed in a radiant whiteness. White, Isaac realized, came in almost as many shades as black. This whiteness wasn't the rosy light of angels and uplift, or the bluish skim-milk pallor of infants' eyeballs, or even the frothy churning dairy plenitude, vanilla-bean richness of ice cream, bridal satin, the chipped viscousness of pearls—no, the white light of *Ajax* was an ammoniac greenish white redolent of penitentiaries and toothache. Into this antiseptic whiteness, the sickly warrish tinge of attrition and gangrenous wounds, came three figures—a council of war consisting of a little boy, a fat black lady, and a sailor. The little boy went chasing after butterflies with a net, the lady got down on all fours and pressed an ear to the ground, the sailor mopped the floor and then departed in scissor leaps. Much later an ancient Chinese Ulysses emerged, bowlegged, robed, wearing a scarlet mask, and sang in a voice that smelled like rotten eggs. There was a ten-foot turkey and an Indian chief and a chorus line wearing Elvis Presley masks, accompanied by a grizzled black man drumming on a washtub. Somewhere along the way Isaac realized that he wasn't sure which of the players was Ulysses and which Agamemnon, and that the one he'd thought was Ajax couldn't be, because he was still alive.

The intervals between action were so long and the action itself so minuscule—it took a good thirty minutes for the Elvises to shake a leg—that people in the audience kept walking out, and each new defection seemed, vacuumlike, to suck other people into the aisles and out the doors. There were hisses and catcalls, too, during each new longueur, met by silencing rebukes. Isaac, vexed as he was by the lack of drama, felt sorry and hoped the director and performers were too busy to notice these mutinies.

It was indeed quite boring, but maybe that was the director's point: war was dull. Especially a war as long as the Trojan War. Most of war wasn't battles but bivouacking: washing clothes, digging trenches, and waiting. Maybe, Isaac thought, seized by the boredom of waiting for more nothing to happen, poetry began not as an accompaniment to religious rite, but like scrimshaw on a whaling voyage—as a way to pass the time between kills.

After almost three hours, there was an intermission. A semaphoric wave of communication passed among the more uptown segment of the Geblers' guests, a broadcast of raised eyebrows, lowered thumbs, apologetic and inquiring smiles, comic grimaces. Congregated outside, they inquired of each other in undertones, Do you like it? Like a trip to the dentist. Would it be terrible if I left? I'm leaving—you can get to Paris in less time and the seats are more comfortable—Alfred says he's leaving too—Alfred's leaving?—Come over to the Geblers' now—So early? Can we?—Al says come over now—Because I'm perfectly happy to sit in a bar for two more hours and meet you—Come over now—Can we go now? Will anybody be there?—We're all going—Is Dolly leaving too?

Alfred now appeared. Al, are you really leaving? You betcha. Want to come? Is Dolly leaving too? Alfred said, ironical but proud, "Would the Pope walk out of mass? No, she's mad for it. She's been sitting there literally white-knuckled with suspense."

"Shouldn't we stay?"

"No, we'll leave the culture vultures to their feast." He, too, was speaking in an undertone, glancing half-guiltily, half-defiantly in his wife's direction. His guests caught some of his uncertainty; some went back to retrieve their coats, but many more decided to stay.

Isaac, pacing up and down the sidewalk outside the theater, chewing over the problems of the opera, didn't notice this flight of departing birds until Mr. Gebler put a hand on his arm.

"How's your head, kiddo?"

Isaac beamed. "How are the flowers?"

"The flowers are a bit droopy and hurt like hell. Listen, young man, I'm leaving, my wife's staying. You're welcome to come back to the house now, if you want a bite to eat. Casey called to say he couldn't make it to the show, but he'd meet you at our place afterwards."

Isaac was surprised. Leaving? Willingly to forsake midway the magnetic glamour of artificial light, cymbals, song, image, the embroidered and perfumed crowd?

When the evening ended and the curtain came down, half the the-

ater was empty and those who remained stood and cheered thunder-
ously. This equivocal thing was triumph. The creator came out on stage,
a puppet-limp young woman with a crew cut and black jeans. A girl!
thought Isaac. How old? He couldn't see. Maybe not much older than
he. And however arid and pitiful a spectacle she had composed, still you
had to respect her, because she'd known what she wanted and had done
it, and this self-belief made her indomitable, so that everyone in her
wake was carried along too by her tugboat confidence, emptied their
coffers to her and believed. And he? When would he know what he was
after?

The young woman bowed, hand in hand with the conductor—a man
with a ponytail—and the turkey. The Elvises and the Chinese opera
singer took bows, the army of women with rakes. Brava! Brava! Bravo!
Bravi! The young woman didn't smile. Brava! A clotted carpet of roses
landed at her feet—she bent unsmiling to pick them up and handed
them out to her company. Another flower bomb catapulted onto stage.
Even though he hadn't liked the performance, Isaac wished he too had
flowers to throw. He stayed until the theater was empty, still feeling as if
something finally were going to happen. Then he found the subway.

Seven

UPTOWN IN THE Geblers' apartment was settled the circle of guests
who had sneaked away from the performance early. The group consisted
of Benoit Goldschmidt, a Swiss industrialist whom Dolly was contemplating getting on Aurora's board of trustees; Benoit's Italian girlfriend,
Delfina, who was a philosophy professor at Columbia; and various
layabouts, including Alfred's best friend from childhood—this is how
Dolly described Bobby Wasserman, rather as if childhood were a town
in New Jersey—who was now a top lawyer, and Bobby's wife, Sarah.

Bobby had married upscale the second time; where Gebler and Bobby came from, girls were called Sharon and Heidi, not Sarah—their parents hadn't yet realized roots were cool. Sarah came from a Massachusetts Bay Colony family that three hundred years ago had gone in for burning witches and Quakers and now went in for golf—you could tell she was upper-crust just from the hair, which was heavy and straight, a thick changeable tawny gold, held back by a band of black velvet. Sarah was a partner at Davis Polk—worked even longer hours than Bobby. She was underfed and intense, and her voice shot up touchingly when she got excited—one of those girls who can't sit in their seats but come canting over almost into your lap from sheer enthusiasm. Sarah had brought along her younger sister, who made paper clothes. Gebler liked the sister, who had clearly taken one look at the competition and chosen to opt for goofiness.

Gebler went out to the kitchen to get a bottle of champagne and warn the hired hands that some guests had arrived early. The waiters and waitresses, all unemployed actors, were sitting around glumly, like children waiting to be entertained. Gebler told Molly, a sturdy blonde, to bring out some hors d'oeuvres. "The bruschetta and the chicken satay—oh, and how about some olives." I meant to tell her not to wear that ridiculous tuxedo, he thought—women in bow ties look like dressed-up mice.

For the first half-hour the guests had talked about where everyone had been that summer: the Rosenblums had gone to stay with the Sheehys in Tuscany, which was divine; Bobby and Sarah had just finished renovating their place in East Hampton and had spent August there, their kids were eight and ten and loved to sail; the Swiss, like all businessmen who are so successful that they want to prove to you not how hard they work but how little, made much of his three weeks' idling along the Aegean coast of Turkey, but then held forth too pedantically about the flaws of the Austrian reconstruction of the library at Ephesus. And only now were they beginning to deliberate on *Ajax*'s merits, a jury of ten determined to come to a unanimous verdict.

At first everyone hung back, a little guilty at having deserted midway, uncertain of the general opinion, shy of being either too damning or too laudatory. It was opening night, after all; there was no critic to fall back upon, no accepted wisdom to repeat or to take issue with. If the work was later deemed a masterpiece, you didn't want to have missed the boat. And then again, there was an inhibiting politeness: since the Geblers' foundation had helped kick in for the production, no one wanted to say it stank.

"I have to admit, I find her work rather . . . long," said Delfina.

"You said it." Bobby, leaning back on the sofa, put his tasselled feet on the coffee table. "Four hours of dancing turkeys is *not* what you need after a long day at the office."

"Robert!" chided his wife. "You're the one who's always complaining about the children's ten-second attention span."

"Time is money, honey," smirked Bobby. "We work harder than our kids. Somebody ought to teach that woman about sound bites. If you can't say it in fifteen minutes . . ."

"But will someone please tell me what it's got to do with Greek tragedy?" demanded the Swiss, mock-pathetic. "Why is it that any director who considers himself artistic has to adopt . . . gimmicks? It reminds me of little children who think it's amusing to dress up their cat in the baby's bonnet. Please, next time give me a nice Sophocles tragedy with togas and wailing choruses, and not a Thanksgiving dinner at Graceland."

Everybody laughed.

"Listen, you're way ahead of me," said Bobby. "All I want to know is, Is this woman kidding or what?"

"No, no, she's dead serious, solemn as . . . She couldn't do it if she didn't mean it," said Delfina.

"You are wrong, I suspect," said Benoit. "That little chihuahua girl is utterly cynical. Believe me."

There was something intensely irritating about the peeled pinkness of the Swiss's face, the manicured nails, the watch-me-be-provocative self-satisfaction with which he sank back into the sofa after delivering his opinion. As if he were under the delusion of thinking he had become rich and powerful because his opinions were interesting and not the other way around.

"If Willa doesn't mean it, then Joan of Arc didn't mean it. Wait till you meet Willa—you'll see she means it all right." Gebler topped everybody's fluted glass and went out to get a new bottle of Laurent Perrier, which he had decided was really almost as good as his old favorite, Roederer.

The apartment looked goddesslike. The flowers had turned out just right. He and Isaac had borne away from the market the summer's last crop of lilies–Gebler had splurged on three dozen Stargazers and three dozen Rothschild lilies, and the rooms were filled as well with mixed bouquets of larkspur, delphinium, bleeding heart, and columbine. He had allowed Morris, too, to talk him into three dozen mauve roses, which he'd placed around the living room in silver pitchers. Gebler didn't usually like roses–seasonless, provenanceless, manufactured, almost as vulgar as carnations or gladioli–but he had to admit that these ones' shade, the livid gloaming of a three-day-old black eye, was pretty delirious. The guests were well enough; why had Dolly got herself into such a panic about not enough men? There were too many men in the world, that was the trouble. All of them with mouths open, squawk, squawk, squawk.

Now, just after midnight, the first wave of opera-goers who had stayed to the end began to pour into the apartment in elevator loads of three and four, faces illuminate with the blind, self-righteous elation of the martyr, the long-distance runner. The newcomers smiled in exhaustion, and confronted by such gratified zeal, the truants began to feel not only ashamed, but cheated, like people who have turned back down the mountain just before reaching the view. Opinion and language perceptibly shifted; the deserters found themselves backtracking.

"Why did you leave?"

"What can I say?" Gebler shrugged apologetically. "I've got a short attention span. Was the second act wonderful?"

"Beautiful. Such purity."

"Oh, it got better and better."

"We shouldn't have left," said the maker of paper clothes to her brother-in-law.

"Oh, can it, honey. If you really mean it, I'll buy you a ticket for tomorrow night. One-way."

Now Dolly Gebler came in, accompanied by her daughters and a pale man in a green velvet suit. Gebler seemed to shrink when he saw his wife.

Stout and solid, forward-canting like a ship's prow, with strong arms, a massive bust, and shapely legs, Mrs. Gebler was a formidable figure. She had a crown of mahogany-black hair, a russet-brown skin, faintly freckled, and blazing black eyes set close on either side of a big beaky nose, eyes that expressed a fury out of proportion to daily life. This combination of regal matronliness and the savagery of a wild boar, this strange union of public stateliness and barely controlled passion, gave her the look of a Hellenistic matriarch—perhaps one of those mothers who poisoned husbands and sons to seize the throne for themselves. You had seen such faces among rows of Egyptian tomb portraits from El Faiyûm, in which the burning voraciousness of one individual's stare seems to raise an arm from the grave to pull you in.

She was wearing (as if conscious of her classical bearing) a yellow tunic that seemed almost wilfully unbecoming, accentuating her stoutness, in some private penance against vanity. She came swiftly up to Gebler on tiny feet. "You *left*, Alfred? You left before the end?" A low throaty voice, occluded, broken, at times, by emotion.

Gebler hemmed and hawed. "Oh, darling, you know I'm just not constitutionally capable of high art."

His wife looked at him uncomfortably long before turning away. "It *was* high art, wasn't it. Free of all impurities." She was addressing the green velvet man at her side. "It was as if she were stripping layer after layer until she reached some small pure heart. I'm anxious, naturally, to go back as soon as possible."

"Anytime, Dolly. Just call the office and let me know—I'd love to see it again with you."

And then, scathingly, to her husband, "Did you eat all the food?"

"*No*, you mistrustful minx. I resent that question. We showed earth-shattering restraint, didn't we, children?"

"You *are* a child. And sometimes I get awfully tired of being married to a . . . an infant."

Gebler, chastised, went off to tell Molly that the waiters could begin laying out supper in the dining room. He watched the blond men and women in dinner jackets bring out platter after platter. A salmon wearing a pale-green chain mail of marinated cucumbers; a lacquered Muscovy duck arrayed in glistening golden armor. An arsenal of steamed baby squashes, yellow and green, like tiny hand grenades. A late summer feast such as you might see chinked in mosaic on the floors of a Pompeiian villa. Then there were the cheeses—Stilton blue-bowelled, smelly, ribald and corrupt as a Chaucerian cleric; Tommes swaddled in grape leaves and stippled in pips; goat cheeses chimney-swept in ash or rinded in white chalkiness; a millstone of Parmesan—a fifteen-pound hunk of it—dry, flaky, granular, the color of rats' teeth, yet almost crystalline on the tongue, dissolving in thrilling sharpnesses: *it* ate *you*. He had purposely bought enough Parmesan so that there would be mountains left over—nothing so magical as having heedless gulletsful of a delicacy you were used only to rationed grams of.

On his way back to the living room, Gebler was assailed by Enzo De Felice, an Italian composer who had just celebrated his eightieth birthday and wanted to discuss politics.

"This savings and loans scandal is a real disgrace. Your Reagan, we all know, was a criminal. He should have gone to jail for his illegal wars in Central America—"

"He should go to jail for his stupidity," interjected De Felice's seventy-five-year-old girlfriend, Graziella.

"But your new President, Mr. . . ."

"Bush," supplied Gebler.

". . . is even worse. Why didn't the American people refuse to vote for a man who was lackey to that senile liar? How can you elect President a head of the CIA, a man who is paid to lie and murder?"

Mr. Gebler smiled affectionately at the old man, to whom he had never dared confess that he'd voted twice for Reagan, and gestured behind Enzo's back that Molly was to tell the guests to go help themselves from the buffet.

"Come, let's get something to eat and find a table," he said, ushering Enzo and Graziella towards the dining room.

"And now these bank scandals . . . Such brazenness, bailing out the crooked banks at public expense. Such brazenness," persisted De Felice, who was a lifelong communist. "Tell me, why doesn't your Congress demand a straight answer about how much the savings and loans business is going to cost? . . . Three hundred *billion* dollars, they say, just to save the skins of the crooked bankers. Really, your Republicans make Italian politicians look honest."

"But Enzo, surely you don't want us to have an honest President, do you?" Gebler teased. "They're the most dangerous of all. Last time we had an honest Joe in the White House there was a civil war and two hundred thousand Americans died in each other's cornfields."

"You should have a civil war once more," retorted Enzo fiercely.

"You should have a real revolution this time. Then you would stop funding death squads in everyone else's countries."

Tired by his outburst, the old man sat down at the table Gebler had gestured him to. Gebler patted Enzo's hand. "Let me get you something to eat." When he returned from the buffet with plates of food for Enzo and Graziella, the old man was sitting upright, staring vacant as a parrot with the curtain over his cage.

"Did you like the opera?" Gebler asked him. This man who in his youth had been a disciple of Varèse's in Paris—how tame this electronic humming must seem to him . . .

"Musically, it's not much, but rather attractive visually, I would say."

Gebler smiled, remembering one of his favorite Enzo stories—he and Enzo at a dinner party given by Murray Fisher, the director of the Lyceum and an audio maniac. After dinner, Fisher'd shown off for his guests' delectation his latest twenty-thousand-dollar sound system, putting on a digitally remastered version of a 1952 recording of Toscanini conducting Beethoven's Ninth Symphony. Everybody had oohed and aahed as the room blossomed into luscious golden sound, except for Enzo.

"Well, Enzo," Fisher had prodded, "just like being in the old Carnegie Hall, isn't it?"

And Enzo, politely, had conceded, "Yes, it is very nice. It is almost as nice as reading the score."

"You know, Alfred, he insisted on taking the bus downtown to the theater tonight," Graziella beamed at her boyfriend in mock reproof.

"He's amazing," agreed Gebler, and hating himself for sounding condescending, turned to his friend. "What a skinflint, Enzo. Can't you treat your girlfriend to a taxi?"

Enzo sat, blinking behind his thick eyeglasses, uninterested in badinage.

"When will we hear the new piece?"

But just then Enzo continued, "Really I am very upset about this savings and loans fiasco. Nobody cares. Nobody seems to understand the scale of it. Why is it? Because numbers are boring? Even the journalists yawn. It is the sign of a really and truly politically ignorant people that the bankers can rob the public of three hundred billion dollars to pay for their bad loans and nobody makes a peep. Nobody is voted out of office, nobody asks a question, nobody—almost—goes to jail. This is not democracy. This is corruption on a scale—on a . . ."

"It's corruption Italian-style," Gebler agreed, laughing.

"No, no—now we must come to you for lessons. Because, with such an uneducated voting population, with such secret cabals within the government that nobody knows a thing about, that break the laws of Congress, democracy cannot survive. Is it democracy when twenty percent of the people vote? There will be fascism very soon, I am sure of it. . . ."

"And what do you think about what's happening in the Soviet Union?" Gebler asked, unable to suppress a malicious grin.

Enzo, who had been sitting blinking rapidly, hurtled back to life. "*Ma che schifo! Che vergogna!*" The party leaders, it turned out, had amassed millions for themselves, gorged on caviar and French champagne in their country estates. Just like savings and loans desperadoes. "They forgot that they were living off the sweat of the workingman!"

So it was the betrayal of the dream of equality that had disillusioned Enzo. To Gebler, it seemed evident that a society had to choose between freedom and equality. The French Revolution's ideal of "liberty, equality, fraternity" was like saying "hot, cold, lukewarm"—three mutually incompatible states of being. (Who was it who had been nattering away at him about brotherhood? Oh yeah, that funny Isaac. Was brotherhood what they taught you at Harvard these days?) Because as soon as things were free, they became unequal, whereas equality could only be achieved through coercion, and brotherhood maintained by main force. Because the only thing you got told as a kid that turned out to be true was the infamous "Life is unfair." And was it really government's business anyway to try to even the odds? Some people got born smart and talented, some dumb losers. Beside that fundamental inequity in the genes, wealth and privilege were chicken feed. The only genuine equalizer, it occurred to Gebler, was capitalist technology, which healed the halt and lame and made every dope with a calculator and a laptop computer smarter than Isaac Newton.

The Party lived off the sweat of the workingman, Gebler repeated to himself. He was curious, too, what Enzo, for whom "artists" had always been workingmen too and who after a sixty-year career was as poor as when he started, made of these slick young painters and sculptors—

many of them sitting at that very moment in the Geblers' apartment—
who were raking in four hundred, five hundred thousand a year. Did it
shock Enzo, the advent of the art businessmen?

De Felice shrugged. "Of course, I want to say this is the fault of Reagan, but for once it is not true. Painters have always been like that. I remember in my young days sharing a room with Satta, long before he
had sold his first work—we were in our twenties and we didn't have even
enough money to buy coffee. The difference between us was that even
then he was saying, When I'm rich and famous I'll do such-and-such.
He knew it would happen, even then. That is what painters are like.
They are materialists; it is the nature of their trade. Us—maybe a violinist dreams of buying a Stradivarius, and that's no mean prize, but then
he is satisfied."

Gebler was pleased. He was pleased to see Bobby, with whom after
thirty-five years he still felt a childish complicity—as if together they'd
succeeded in pulling off the greatest bank heist in history, two boys
from Rockaway Avenue whose fathers, poor working stiffs, could barely
speak English, and here they were, with country houses and Mercedes
station wagons and children fat as young calves from sheer milk-fed
abundance; he was happy to see De Felice, whom he loved dearly; and
as he surveyed the crowd lining up to help themselves at the buffet
table, he noticed many people he hadn't spotted at the opera: Georgia
Rattle and her husband, Bruce Madder; Jennifer James; Celia Rubin;
plus two very cute young San Francisco artists who weren't gay but always went around together. The only trouble with your own parties was
you could never be everywhere at once. . . .

Eight

HE WAS BOBBING. He was floating in a blood-warm silver-and-gold
sea of flesh, jewels, eyes, perfumes. A fur sleeve brushed against him,

someone's crimson double-crescent of lips suctioned onto a neighboring cheek, he was tickled by satin, jostled by velvet, musk ran over him. He was moving through a warm buzzing beehive, honey dripping from his cheeks. He was floating along an ocean floor, brushed by mysterious schools of silver and emerald fish, diaphanous, translucent finned phantoms; octopuses oscillated; nervy scrimmed sea horses fled from him riderless. A pair of white gloves held out a silver tray filled with glass spires of blond foam; Isaac downed another glass and swam into a warmer current of light and sound, floating through a sequence of underwater grottoes. Here the air was darker gold, perfumed, lush. He was a fish, he was a bee. The crowd murmured, swallowed him up, disgorged him into the arms of a white satin miniskirt.

A girl. She, surprised, retreated a step, he advanced, like ballroom dancers. She spoke.

"Are you enjoying yourself?" She was so young, Isaac realized, that she was trying to make grown-up conversation with him. She had long dark-red hair and a big mouth. One of Gebler's sassy daughters.

"I think so. But I'm not a very experienced judge of parties. Last party I went to was Christmas at a men's shelter on the Lower East Side."

The young girl's face clammed up, turning dutiful. Ready to be bored. "Oh. Do you do volunteer work?"

"Yes," said Isaac. "I was volunteering to be a Bowery bum."

A little cry of laughter escaped, one hand over her mouth to bite it back too late. "I'm so sorry. . . ." This time, a different kind of sorriness, not compassion but guilt. "Were you really on the streets?"

"For about ten minutes," said Isaac, embarrassed. Pity seeker, how low will you sink? Just when he wanted to devour this sumptuous cream puff of a Gebler girl, to attach himself like a barnacle to this mother-of-pearl palace and its shimmering inmates. "Anyway, by the time I hit the men's shelter I was legit—four twenty-five an hour for dishing out soup. How's that?"

"Okay, I guess. Kind of skimpy, maybe. I mean, New York's expensive, isn't it?"

"Extortionate." He was wondering if she'd ever been kissed.

"Did you like the opera?"

Isaac realized too late that he had not properly adjusted the volume of his voice. His "No" boomed out massive—heads turned, curious. And out of nowhere, Casey appeared at his side, squeezing him around the waist.

"Oh dear." This from a fat lady with a southern accent. "Young people today are so censorious. You sound just like my son—he's against *everything*."

"Why didn't you like it?" his white satin girl wanted to know. "I thought it was fantastic." She turned to a man in green velvet. "Didn't you think so, Alex?"

"Well, naturally." The green man smiled indulgently.

"It was *very* expressive."

"It didn't express diddly-squat," said Isaac.

"Come on, dude," said Casey, a warning arm on his friend's shoulder. "Let's go get some more chow." But Isaac, gazing at the white girl, was just warming up. "Diddly-squat," he repeated with satisfaction.

The green man smirked at him. "I'm not surprised you thought so. People don't know how to watch avant-garde theater the way they did fifteen, twenty years ago." Turning to the girl, he continued, "You can no longer count on an audience who knows how to read lighting or composition. . . ."

Isaac took umbrage. The green man was trying to steal the white Gebler girl from him. "I'm not the one who doesn't know how to read—that director doesn't." Again he had spoken too loudly.

Mr. Gebler, cruising the party, heard a sudden uproar in the living room. The center of the disturbance was Alex, the director of the Space, who was being shouted at by a big blond man whom Gebler for a befuddled second didn't recognize. Oh yes, of course, Yankee Isaac. Young Frankenstein. Isaac, he now noticed, was outfitted in a flimsy suit of sardine-silvery-black stuff that was a little too tight for his hulk, and already showed dark moons under the armpit. A mistake. In his jeans and flannel shirt he'd had a certain rustic charm; now in the cheap suit he looked like a fallen Hasid—yes, you saw just such blond, red-cheeked, cherry-lipped fat boys in thick black glasses selling computers and diamonds on Forty-seventh Street.

"Come on, dude." Casey was trying to steer Isaac away. "Let's go for a walk."

"But my dear young man," Alex was remonstrating, "surely we've got the right to—"

"No!" interrupted Isaac, suddenly furious. "*Nobody*'s got the right to be so boring and *trivial!* That director had the nerve to take one of the all-time tragic subjects. Mortal jealousy. Achilles' armor is given to Ulysses and not Ajax. Brute strength hogtied by cunning. So what does this person do with Sophocles' tragedy about honor and envy and the aftermath of a ten-year slaughter? She turns it into a comic strip. And for everybody to stand around gushing about the lighting is to accede to her meretricious pretentious *gall* in lobotomizing one of the most heartrending stories in Greek tragedy. I mean, why pick on the Trojan War? Why not make an opera about—uh, about Ajax the bathroom cleanser?"

"That's very funny," said the girl in white satin. "Hey, Mom!" She plucked at the arm of a neighboring woman. The girl's mother, who was talking with a sallow young man, looked around. "What is it, Johnny?" She glanced at Isaac. Their eyes met for a moment, unsmiling.

There is a theory of Jung's that in the first instant strangers meet, they understand everything about each other, and that the next moment they forget it. The subsequent years are spent trying to recover all that lost knowledge.

"What, Johnny?" asked the woman again, impatient now. The young girl repeated with much laughter Isaac's crack. "Mom, this man said Willa should've written an opera about Ajax the bathroom cleanser!"

Her mother cast Isaac a look of contempt. With one hand still on her daughter's shoulder, she resumed her conversation with the sallow young man.

"Did you try some of the ham? A friend brought it back for us from Barcelona." Gebler addressed this last to Angelica Broadman, a fellow art collector from Cincinnati, gawky, blindingly rich, with whom he and Dolly sat on several boards. "It's even better than prosciutto, don't you think? They let it dry in the mountains."

One of the annoying rules of social intercourse: whatever it was you were dying to do or find out was precisely the thing that was forbidden. Gebler would have given a mountain range of pato negro to be able to ask Angelica if it was true she had just paid Benny Krook five million dollars for his Franz Kline.

It was the resale market that was making art prices so crazy. Twenty million dollars at the Sotheby's auction last year for an iffy Jasper Johns—a painter still in his prime—five million for a Kline. . . . Okay if you wanted to unload and didn't care who you sold to, but museums as well as a lot of serious collectors were getting priced out of the market, so that some speculator ended up acquiring as a vanity trophy, to go with his vintage Rolls-Royce collection, a Johns that the Art Institute or MoMA should have had. If the prices kept soaring, the Geblers were going to be reduced to that dismal mathematics by which you can't buy a Rothenburg without first selling a Rauschenberg.

"Oh, I don't think anything's better than prosciutto," said Angelica.

"Well, this pato negro is more gamey . . ."

Emanuele Conti, who was Angelica's date and was just returning with two glasses of wine, shouted with laughter on overhearing this. "Not talking about food again, Alfred! If you were RRRRrrreaally such a glutton as you make out, you'd weigh five hundred pounds and Dolly would have to push you from meal to meal." Everyone laughed, although Gebler didn't think it was funny.

"In fact," said Bernard Ayala, an art dealer whom the Geblers had known forever and were immensely fond of, "I've always suspected that we aren't half as keen on what the eighteenth century called our ruling passions as we pretend. Don Giovanni, for instance, in his heart of hearts, I am sure, preferred the morning's newspaper and a rare beefsteak to the burden of *yet another* . . ." He paused.

"Cranking up of the gonads," finished Gebler.

"Exactly."

Gebler was offended by the unflattering suggestion—apparently accepted by everyone—that his own ruling passion was food rather than, for example, sex. Or even, God forbid, art. Did he in fact have a ruling passion? Wasn't the absence of one his very trouble?

Emanuele, meanwhile, unusually serious, was commenting, "Wouldn't you say that we use these obsessions as a kind of trademark to make ourselves more easily identifiable—"

"While in fact we are much more well-rounded—"

"—or indifferent—"

"—than we pretend."

"In short, we don't really give a fuck about anything," concluded Alfred.

"Don't say that in front of Enzo or he will think that you are accusing him of not being a genuine monomaniac for his work," said
Emanuele, hugging the older man, who was just going past. Emanuele
was tall, chubby, Enzo a tiny sprite.

Enzo, who hadn't followed, tried to escape from Emanuele's grasp.
"Not at all—I love Alfred because I know he believes in art. When I first
met him . . ." They had met through the composer William Orton, the
same year Alfred had met Dolly.

"Believe!" Gebler interrupted. "Give me a break. I don't believe in
art, I just buy it. Isn't that enough?" The group didn't laugh, so Alfred
himself stopped laughing, depressed that prissy Angelica might take him
at face value and think him crass. Had she really paid five million for
Benny Krook's Kline? He had only seen pictures of it. "By the way, let
me urge on you all a second helping of my ruling passion."

"You are not a jealous man," observed Emanuele. "If I loved food so
much I wouldn't let anybody else come near it."

"It's a democratic passion. Unlike love. Anyone can eat, but you
have to be rich or cute to get laid."

Enzo, for whom the conversation had become incomprehensibly
silly, now started telling Gebler about his experiences on the jury of a
composition prize in Bern. All the best candidates were Chinese, Japanese, Korean!

At one a.m. the artist herself arrived, followed by a retinue. A crowd
gathered around her, like fans camped at the barricade awaiting the
transatlantic descent of an early aviatrix, bony, begoggled, descending in
jodhpurs from her rivetted wind-lashed steel steed. Gebler as always felt
discomfited by the sight of her pale high-mindedness. "We're talking
about your opera," he said, kissing her smackingly on both cheeks.
Mwuh-mwuh! "Which was, incidentally, a *triumph*. Sublime. What can
we give you to drink?"

"Can I have a Stolichnaya, straight up?"

A waiter brought the young woman a vodka on the rocks. "I said no
ice," said Willa. Un-iced vodka appeared. She downed it as if it were a
glass of milk.

"Hey, Willa," said Johnny, who was sitting on the arm of her
mother's chair. "There was a guy here who wanted to know—"

"Johnny," said her mother warningly, "I told you not to use the word 'guy.' "

"There was a man who–"

"Why don't you let Willa have something to eat before you start in on her. Your *Ajax*–well, it's–extraordinary. Monumental. But eat first. You must be hungry and exhausted. Let's get you a plate of food right away." In a whisper she ordered the butler to bring Miss Perkins some food.

Johnny took advantage of her mother's distraction. "There was a man here who wanted to know why you didn't do an opera about Ajax the bathroom detergent! Isn't that great?"

Willa considered. "What's the difference?" she said. "This is the modern world. War as hygiene."

"Try some of the pato negro," Gebler urged her.

"The . . . what? What's that? Oh, ham? I don't eat meat. Thanks, but . . . In the United States, we use the same kind of chemicals to wipe out illiterate Third World peasants that we do to get a spotless toilet."

At the end of the evening, Mr. Gebler put on a Nat King Cole record. He sang along to "Jambalaya," wiggling a hip, and grabbed Joan Chavez, a sculptress who was well into her seventies but a beautiful dancer. She met his embrace calmly, readily–an old-fashioned girl. The pair glided about the floor, Gebler with an arm around Joan's narrow waist, whirling and dipping his partner. Smiling, they gazed into each other's eyes, like an old couple who have shared a lot of jokes. Bobby, watching his friend, now said to Sarah affectionately, "Come on, girl, let's work off our dinner," and the two of them joined Alfred and Joan on the parquet floor.

Mrs. Gebler watched, biting her lip at the sight of her husband's arm so snug and proprietary around that shameless old courtesan's waist. Trying not to look self-conscious. Then, catching sight of her eleven-year-old son, Leopold, standing in the doorway in his pajamas, she went over to him. "What are you doing up so late, sweetheart? Couldn't you get to sleep?"

Ernestine had put Leopold to bed hours ago.

She noticed her son's brow, heavily furrowed like a baby's. He tried to smile back at her, but failed. She squeezed his hand. "I think it's bed-time, my sweet."

"The music's so loud."

"Try to go back to sleep, darling. I'll tell Daddy to turn down the music."

And Leopold, in one of those deceptions that are so frequent and involuntary as to be almost physiological, acquiesced in passing off his misery as sleepiness and, rubbing his eyes and yawning, allowed himself to be led to his room.

For how could he begin to tell his mother how he hated the sound of drunken laughter and the sight of his father standing in the middle of the floor, rubbing hips with a woman who wasn't Leopold's mother?

It seemed to Leopold that when he got married, he would not forbid his wife to dance with other men, but that if she wanted to, he would feel as if something were wrong between them, because the very definition of love was not wanting to dance with anyone else. He had tried to explain this idea to Carlotta, but Carlotta, although she thought Daddy looked pretty dumb wiggling his ass at Joan Chavez, was scornful that Leo should ever have been looking to their ill-matched parents as a standard.

Nine

WHEN MRS. GEBLER finally got to bed—it was almost three—her daughter Johnny was curled up under her parents' eiderdown, waiting to talk.

Johnny watched while her mother, seated at the vanity table in nightgown and wrapper, scrubbed her face with oatmeal wash and witchhazel, smeared it in lotion, and brushed out her hair in swift punitive strokes. When Dolly was done, she scuffed off her slippers, climbed into bed, and began to braid her daughter's hair, while Johnny snuggled up to her. Johnny required almost as much animal warmth as Leopold, and yet each time Johnny appeared in her parents' bed for a cuddle and talk, Dolly couldn't help thinking how unimaginable such proximity with her own mother would have been. That was what one hired nannies for.

"Did you have fun tonight, darling?"

A nod.

"Who did you talk to?"

"Oh, I don't know. Nobody much." There was something else her daughter wanted to discuss. "Mom, I met a man Sunday."

"Did you, sweetheart? Where?"

"In the park. He was following me around. We kept stopping and looking at the model boats, except *he* was watching *me*."

"What kind of man?"

"Dark . . . kind of ratty."

"And what happened, darling?"

"Nothing really. He was just watching me. But he followed me out of the park, and when we came to a traffic light he started whispering in my ear. . . ."

"What did he say?" Terror. Blind unreasoning animal terror. That you can't protect them. The helplessness of it.

"Oh, I don't know, Mom. Gross stuff. Really creepy."

"Like what?"

"I don't want to say it. . . ."

"And what did you do?"

"I ignored him. . . . It was kind of scary, though."

"Did he follow you home?"

"No, he just kind of disappeared."

Mrs. Gebler exhaled in relief that it hadn't been worse than that, and then a moment's anxiety that maybe there was more her daughter wasn't telling her.

Mrs. Gebler's own mother had been the last person she could ever talk to, and the idea of confiding in one's parents about sex was still amazing to her.

"How come men are so *disgusting*, Mom? I mean, can you imagine a woman following around a guy whispering dirty stuff at him? How come they're like that?"

Now it was Mrs. Gebler's turn to pause, a flood of possible answers coming into her head.

"And the boys at Interschool are even worse. I mean, in a completely different way. Obviously. They can't even get it together to . . ." She jerked free of her mother's braiding to look over her shoulder. "Am I really going to have to go to bed with one of those dweebs half my height?"

"Well, why don't you cool your jets till you meet one who's bearable, at least? And stop encouraging perverts to follow you in the street. I'm serious, Johnny. It's dangerous."

Already quite a few of Johnny's pals had boyfriends. The summer after ninth grade half the class, as if by prior agreement, had come back laid. Now Johnny, poor thing, was feeling the pressure. . . .

"You know what? I think I'm gonna become a nun, Mom. I'm gonna enter a convent and spend the next seventy years embroidering knobby white bedspreads for other people's wedding nights. I think all men are disgusting except for Jesus and Michael Jackson. Just kidding, Mom. Then sometimes I think I'd like to get married *now* so I—"

"Do you want to leave us that badly, darling?"

"—don't have to worry about getting into college, and then I think, well, who?"

"Exactly."

"I think Emanuele is pretty glam. Don't you, Mom?" Johnny was in a panic about who she was going to ask to the eleventh-grade dance.

"Emanuele?" Mrs. Gebler considered.

"Doncha think Emanuele's pretty glam?"

"Yes, I do. Too glam by half. I don't think I want you to have a glam boyfriend. In fact, no need to have a boyfriend at all. Just wait till you meet someone you really care about."

"What about the weirdo Daddy brought?" Johnny interrupted energetically, eyes alight. "The one who got mad at Alex about the Trojan War? Maybe I should ask him to Disco Night."

They both laughed.

"Didn't you think he was kinda cute?"

"Cute? I certainly did not. I thought he was a fool."

"Well, at least he'd read Sophocles, right? I mean, unlike everybody else in the room."

Dolly, finished braiding Johnny's hair, fished around for a rubber band.

"He said he'd been homeless on the Bowery."

"Who?"

"Daddy's friend."

"Oh lord, I thought you meant the man who followed you. . . . Who? That idiot friend of Daddy's?"

"I thought he was kind of cute, in a goofy kind of way. Didn't you, Mom? I mean, at least he'd heard of the Trojan War. . . ."

"Great idea, Johnny–go get a homeless boyfriend. That would be very socially . . . concerned of you. Good lord. Are you sure you've exhausted those shrimpy Collegiate boys?"

Alfred came in around quarter to four–he'd taken Joan Chavez home in a taxi, and then finished washing the last of the glasses and ashtrays himself. He loved clearing up after a party.

Having returned a half-asleep Johnny to her own bed, he noticed to his pleasure that his wife was still wide awake and, like him, keyed up with after-party elation. Not cross anymore about his leaving *Ajax* early, about his not having gotten home till seven the previous morning, or whatever other items on her grievance list had mounted since they'd last had a chance to talk.

"Smash hit," he pronounced, hanging up his jacket on the clotheshorse, unravelling his tie.

"It was, wasn't it?"

"Fabulous party. I think everyone had a wonderful time."

"They certainly didn't seem to want to go home. And the flowers looked marvellous," she conceded.

The opera too had been a success, in its sparky way. Alfred had spotted the *Times* critic, who was already a Willa fan, and a writer from the *Village Voice* who was doing a big piece about Willa. And Alex had said that Dutch television was coming tomorrow night to film. . . .

"Is Willa a lesbian?" Gebler asked suddenly.

"Why–are you interested?"

"Are you kidding?" said Gebler, not realizing that she was kidding. "That scrawny chicken? No, I was just wondering."

"She lives with John Hanlon." Hanlon was one of the hottest young artists of the decade–three SoHo galleries had gone into a bidding war over him and finally agreed to represent him jointly, thus proving that dealers could be as big fools as anybody. "They've been together since RISD. Didn't you know that?"

Gebler felt obscurely piqued, the way you do when hearing that even someone you don't much like is happily entangled with someone who isn't you. He had wondered earlier what Hanlon was doing in his apartment—a slender epicene boy with a curly mouth, like an Aubrey Beardsley ephebe. The idea of those two pale skinny hard creatures coupled was unexpectedly stirring.

"By the way," he said, "that blouse of Carlotta's is a knockout. Did you pick it out or did she?"

"She, of course. I nearly throttled the child, I must say. . . . You cancel all appointments to take her shopping at the last minute—at her request—to buy her an extremely expensive outfit, and she acts as if you're taking her to the guillotine."

"I hope you kept your temper." Dolly and Carlotta could get a little dicey sometimes.

"I was a saint. But I could have strangled her. By the way, what exactly was going through your head bringing home a Bowery bum?"

Mr. Gebler looked for one moment utterly confused, stricken with instinctive guilt. "I beg your pardon?"

"That man who brought home the flowers with you. Johnny says he told her he's homeless on the Bowery."

Mr. Gebler shook his head, relieved. "That Isaac's a riot. He'll say *anything*. I love it. That kid's no Bowery bum, he's a Harvard graduate who works at the most expensive framer in Manhattan."

Mrs. Gebler laughed, chortling almost.

"By the way, Benoit Goldschmidt is a *nightmare*, don't you think?"

"Insufferable," Dolly agreed.

Gebler was pleased his wife agreed. Sometimes she didn't, just to be perverse. "What a self-satisfied little . . . What's the matter?"

She had doubled up. Cramp in her foot. She'd gotten cramps since she was a child, always at night. Used to wake up screaming. In the old days—back at Norwood—her nurse used to come to her bed and pummel her foot. Now Alfred did the job.

Gebler, in his pajamas, sat down and took her naked foot in his hands, kneading the kinks out of it. He looked at his wife, her masses of dark hair spread out on the pale bank of pillow and an unseeing inward glaze to her black eyes that reminded him of the blind gaze of sated pleasure, and kissed her foot, which had been resting in his lap, surprised, suddenly, to find himself aroused.

It was in a state of elation bordering on fever that Isaac arrived home that night. He was far too excited to contemplate sleep, but stretched out on his army cot, fully clothed, hugging himself tight, almost asphyxiated by the rush of joy that filled his lungs. A joy so compacted, so bursting he didn't know what to do with it, but thought he must fly out of the window and up into the soft gray night sky. Explode.

It no longer mattered that he hadn't liked the opera, that he'd acted like a jerk, and that everyone had looked askance at him. It had (now that he was home) been the most glorious night of his life.

Lying on his bed, wide awake, breathless, at five o'clock on a Wednesday morning, the rumble and roar of garbage trucks patrolling the empty streets outside his window, he recollected solemnly every separate instant of the evening.

He was in love. He was in love with all of them, he was in love with the white satin girl and with Alfred Gebler and with Alfred Gebler's wife and even with Casey. He was in love with the Gebler family at large, and by extension with their friends (except for the green velvet bogeyman) and with every cigarette box on their table. He recounted to himself their various attributes: Alfred Gebler's auburn beard and long veined hands and high patriarchal nose and cavernous ironical gray-green eyes, pink-rimmed, like a white rabbit's, and his velvet slippers, which gave him the look not of a New York art mogul but maybe of a German professor of philology; Mr. Gebler's wife with her impatient intonations, her majesty, her glare. He was in love with that half-impudent, half-guilty white satin girl and the obedient unhappy little boy and the ten-foot-tall sister radiant with contempt for the whole world.

And their failings—that Dolly Gebler wore an ugly dress and had put her good name behind a mediocre opera, that Alfred Gebler if you stuck a match to him would combust, that the white satin girl was ungrammatical and inarticulate, that they were richer than human beings had a right to be—only served to bring them back within reach of one's protective pity.

Like a burglar, Isaac crept once again through their apartment, reinspecting pictures, books, replaying conversations. Extracted fragments of sound, slow this time, in order to appreciate their full import. They'd talked about the collapse of communism; they'd talked about art.

"Utterly absurd," Dolly Gebler had said to some old man. "The very idea of . . ." "She's a total loon" (this from White Satin Girl). "Good lord." "I must say . . ." The emphatic intonations, the laughter.

He wondered if the older daughter was still a virgin, and how her breasts and buttocks and thighs underneath the white satin would look. (The tall sister didn't attract him so much and was anyway too young.) He imagined the nipples very pale, the same pale liquid pink of her father's retinas, like a dawn sky at Easter where the pink almost imperceptibly melts into the white. He wondered what they did after school, those girls. Not what sixteen-year-olds he'd known did—help their dads with the livestock, or else work part-time jobs at the Shop N Save. He wondered what they talked about at the dining-room table when there weren't any guests, when it was just them, and the flickery flames thrown by tall wax candles, and the sideboard laden with substances that caught the light and crackled. And Mrs. Gebler, at the head of the table. "Utterly absurd." Did they talk about the fall of communism when there wasn't anyone else around?

For the moment he was satisfied just knowing that the Geblers—a family with three children, who were patrons of modern art and lived in a big apartment on Manhattan's Upper West Side—existed. He had been there and seen it. He had drunk French champagne (for the first time in his life) and he had been to the theater (for the first time in his life) and been waited on by servants with white gloves. And now it was over. And now he would never see them again, because Alfred Gebler did not need anyone else to work at the foundation. And now he would never again see the white satin girl's mischievous smile and the intimate possessive way her mother kept an arm around her, and now he would never hear Gebler laugh too loud at his own jokes. Unless . . .

It was the strenuous proliferation of unlesses that kept Isaac sane, while at work they were packing everything into a city of cardboard boxes, to be carted over to Macklowe's apartment until Macklowe figured out what to do next.

Part Three

Ten

THE MORNING AFTER *Ajax*, Dolly awoke at ten to seven. Late for her. Each year she rose earlier, spring and summers earlier still. Out in the country, she'd get yanked from sleep by the young sun vogueing her, bull's-eye in the middle of the bedroom window.

In the city, facing westward, it was reflected light that penetrated her unconsciousness, the first paling of the sky over Weehawken, and the whole world outside—the natural world, which escaped you when other people were awake—peeking in, inviting you out. The effort to trick the body back into sleep (No, it's only five a.m., you fool) till finally, giving up, you shuffled out to the front hall, in bathrobe and slippers, to see what had happened in the night.

Every early riser knows what it is to feel herself briefly empress of creation, to lord it over the hushed unspoiled hours, before the world gets squalling, importunate. Before children need feeding and dressing and packing off to school, before the hordes pour down into the subways and cars stampede the Cross Bronx and the Bruckner Expressway and the FDR Drive, before alarms and telephones and faxes start to chirrup, clang, and whirr. Before Ernestine showed up, Ernestine with her guileful neediness dressed up as wisdom.

Now, in the hour when four people around her tossed and murmured and pulled sheets higher under the chin in defense against imminent rousing, Dolly put on the coffee and, like a general surveying the unrolled map of the innocent topography he will convert to battlefield, laid out her day—meetings, phone calls, taxes, bank, sickbed visit, two SoHo openings, a seminar at the Museum of Modern Art that Emanuele had bullied her into coming to. The battle was the day: a thoroughly secular engagement. Daytimes, if you stopped to think about why you were here and how, under the circumstances, to acquit yourself decently, you were lost. It was only at night, before she went to sleep—more and more frequently, alone—that Dolly took stock of her soul, wrestled with, interrogated her Maker.

Seven o'clock. Alfred said, "Dolly waits until I get home and then gets up one hour later, just to feel superior." Alfred's unshakeable conviction that virtue and duty were things people practiced solely in order to make other people feel guilty.

And she: "What nonsense. I have no interest whatsoever in what time you decide to come reeling home." Naively revealing her false pride.

What people didn't realize when they said that long-married couples become like sister and brother was what kind of sister and brother they grow to resemble—not fond companions but hair-pulling, tale-bearing brats, rivals locked in a game of one-upmanship that over the decades becomes an unexitable war of attrition. The sense of having been unfairly yoked in life to an alien unwanted twin—a bad imitation who brought out one's worst.

That, surely, must be the prime motive for adultery: to be able once more to see oneself reflected ideally—generous, sexy, dashing. To escape from the war over toothpaste tops. Remembered Sophie—one night last summer, after everyone else had gone to bed—asking her if she'd ever had an affair. As if, if she had, Sophie'd be the one she'd choose as confidant. Do you think Mother ever did? Sophie!! Please, just a scrap of elementary human knowledge. Well, she might have. . . . With whom? With Waggon? Of course, it turned out Sophie was only asking because her latest beau had a wife and two kids. Soph really ought to get married just to learn for herself that marriage was no big deal.

Hearing the familiar succession of slaps in the outside hall, Dolly in white charmeuse dressing gown opened the front door to scoop up *The New York Times*, the *Wall Street Journal*, the *Daily News*—ugly addiction, soap opera for grownups. Glanced at the headlines: Exxon Halts Oil Spill Cleanup. Unemployment Down .1%. Any news about the Helms proposal?

A package outside the door: a shopping bag, tied with a bow, labelled "Mom's." Containing . . . chocolate-covered pretzels. Ugh. What kind of practical joke . . . Attached, her name in Joe's unmistakable calligraphy—capital A's and E's, small d's. Still loitering in the outside hall,

Dolly heard the coffee machine's bubble. She closed the front door, trailed out to the kitchen with papers under one arm and Joe's package under the other, and dumping her cargo of news and pretzels on the kitchen table, poured eight ounces of steaming aromatic brown ink into a glazed white terra-cotta cup. Breakfast.

Sat down, plucked apart the folds of *The New York Times*, and darted through it, back to front, removing the arts section first—No review of *Ajax* yet; the days of critics phoning in their copy at intermission were over—and absentmindedly tearing open the brown paper parcel, popped a chocolate-covered pretzel. Unexpectedly not bad. The chalky salt of the cracker underneath giving bite to the chocolate casing—tasted like a cut-rate version of an English biscuit she was very fond of, Chocolate Olivers. Tried in turn a dark chocolate, a milk chocolate, a white—the white chocolate namby-pamby, oversweet—before feeling utterly sick. Not even eight a.m. and there goes the diet.

Pressed a button on her telephone which automatically dialed the number of Joe's car phone. Joe, who lived out on Long Island, was always in his car. So often did Joe talk to one from his car phone that Alfred liked to pretend the poor man actually lived on the Long Island Expressway.

"Didja get the pretzels?"

"Oh," she feigned, "was that you who dropped on my doorstep those noxious little sugar pessaries? Did you think I was looking too thin? I can tell you they made a much happier breakfast than half a Ruby Red, which was the alternative. Are you trying to sabotage the Gebler family diet? You know I'm going to have to get through this whole bag before Alfred wakes up."

Joe chuckled, well pleased. "Grapefruit sucks."

"It's healthy."

"I'm healthy. If I'm feeling unhealthy, I just pop a multiplex."

"I thought that was a movie theater."

It had taken them a while to figure out how to talk to each other. After founding Aurora—which depended on breaking the trust managed by Dolly's father's Chicago bank—the Geblers had gone through several unsatisfactory investment counselors. It was Bobby, finally, who found them Joe, who had been second-in-command at a small investment company but was looking to go out on his own. Dolly offered him a job managing Aurora's money and her own full-time. He agreed, ambivalently. He knew nothing about the art business, and felt funny at first having a blueblood lady boss, someone you couldn't tell dirty jokes or talk to about sports. Initially, they had communicated through Alfred. Now they managed, partly by her doing, not quite consciously, a semi-imitation of her husband.

"What's the occasion?"

"Well, I went to visit the company yesterday. It's a cute operation, headquarters down in Stroudsburg. Mom Inc."

"And who's Mom?"

"Two old college buddies who like to bake. They started a store in East Stroudsburg. Now they have outlets in malls around Pennsylvania, Maryland, Delaware. I think if they could break into a few supermarkets, it would be Ben and Jerry's all over again. Plus mail-order sales, get out a nice catalogue . . ."

"Is it all cookies?"

"Cookies 'n' cakes."

"The name is shameless enough to work, but the packaging is dreadful."

"I sent you the prospectus and the financial information."

"You don't think the market's overloaded with gimmicky snacks? When do people eat chocolate-covered pretzels? Are they appetizer or dessert?"

"You have teenage kids and you ask me a question like that?"

"They're too expensive for teenagers, aren't they?"

"Not for their parents. Anyway, you just told me yourself, you eat 'em for breakfast."

"I noticed you unloaded our shares in La Menorca."

"Yeah, I thought it was overextended. I swapped it for Bundesbank bonds."

"That's exciting."

"I don't wancha to have excitable stocks."

Joe was level-headed—two years ago he'd been unhappy enough with the stock-market boom to have got them mostly into gold mines, government bonds, and the Pacific Rim by Black Monday, when the market dropped over five hundred points in a day.

"Tell Leo I got an extra seat Sunday night at the Rangers game if he's interested."

"Thanks, I will." Actually, it was Carlotta who would probably be more interested. Leopold, who had the makings of an eleven-year-old Tolstoyan, went blank with despair at the idea of men hurting each other on purpose.

The next seven a.m. phone call was from Emanuele, asking if she'd heard the news that Jim Arnold, the director of the Contemporary, was getting canned. Poor Jim. No word on who they wanted to replace him. That museum was really getting itself tied in knots.

Now she called Mr. West. She loved talking to Mr. West, just for the sniff of country pleasures, country rounds, he exuded. Luckily didn't get Mrs. West, who was a talkaholic and would want to gab hours about the burglary. A few days ago someone had tried to break into the Geblers' house on Long Island. Mr. West, the caretaker, had heard the noise and gone to investigate. Obviously frightened the burglar away. Nothing gone, just a broken window in the basement. In fact, they only kept the sort of things at Goose Neck Farm—hardware—they wouldn't miss. Irksome, nonetheless. Were they going to have to get an alarm system? She hoped not. . . .

Her list for the day, in no particular order: Staff meeting at eleven to discuss upcoming exhibitions. Get tickets to *Ivan the Terrible* at the Underground. Prepare for the board meeting on the twenty-fifth, which meant xeroxing press clippings, checking with Andy on ongoing projects. Leo: new sports shoes. Call Germaine to get the telephone number for the allergist she'd mentioned. (She wasn't very happy with Leo's squeeze spray for his asthma. Perhaps going back to shots was the answer, after all?) Order the pear trees for the country. Call: Willa. Mac. BAM. Richard. Edward Banville. Jim Arnold, in case it was true. Who would the Contemporary be likely to appoint in his place?

At least his ouster would amuse Jesse Kraemer, whom she had arranged to go visit after work. AZT had not zapped the malice out of that fine brain. And for God's sake, remember to call first, to check that Jesse was still feeling up to it. She recollected with guilty horror her last visit, when they'd closed a lane on the FDR Drive and she'd arrived half an hour late, only to find Jesse, who'd been all geared up since three, slumped on the sofa ashen, speechless with fatigue, and Michael furious with her.

With a shiver, Dolly addressed herself to the morning's mail—a hefty sheaf of hospitals, cancer societies, political fundraisers, mimeographed notices from various investment banks of Joe's latest stock transactions— You sold 1,500 shares of Fortuna Enterprises, You bought 1,000 of Walker Industries. A postcard from Richard Cruikshank with a picture of the Olympic Village in Estonia, a scrawled letter for Leo from a mysterious pen pal in Jerusalem. Art openings, a school in East Harlem asking her to be on its board. The fiftieth letter that year—forwarded to her by her mother—from a scholar requesting a transparency of her father's Ingres.

The Ingres was the only serious work of art from Charles Diehl's collection that his widow had hung on to, not given to the museum. When she was young, Dolly had found the great naked female insipid. Now, in middle age, she had come to admire wonderfully the enigmatic smile, the nacreous gleam of finished flesh, which betrayed no hint of underlying blood or bone. She understood now her father's taste for Empire— pervading those portraits of generals and courtesans an expression remote, enigmatic, archaic as Etruscan tomb carvings. David's rendition of Napoleon and his family, where even the children look as if they are suspended over an abyss, gazing out into the emptiness of eternity.

Shifting to the bathroom, she unsheathed her body from its wrapper and nightgown. Gross marbly white thighs and stomach, heavy-hanging boobs—at which preening truce in her history of self-hate had Dolly installed such a hard-eyed expanse of bathroom mirror? Damn Mom's chocolate pretzels; why couldn't Joe invest them in a nice chain of Northern California spas? And stepped into the shower, which she took stone cold, to bruit her into shocked alertness. Bracing. Scrubbed at that gross flesh with the loofah as if erasing, hard, a mistake. And reaching for the towel—hot from a radiated rack—wandered into the dressing room, a dark-gray office, mercifully mirrorless, with closets for files. Too much room taken up by Alfred's exercise bike, never used, of course. Now she stepped into her uniform of navy blue dress, shapeless, and a pair of handmade beige kid shoes. Legs not bad. Should start wearing a corset. Matronly.

Seven-thirty-five. Time to get the children out of bed.

When she got to the office, a young man was sitting on the front step. Casey Hanrahan. Lord, another early bird. Wasn't even eight-thirty yet. Probably come straight from clubbing. She found intensely irritating the way the boy couldn't stay still, but hopped around, gabbing non-stop. Callow. Incontinent. The kind of person who probably boasted about all the women he'd slept with only you weren't sure it was true. Was that unfair? Alfred said he wasn't a bad soul.

"What's happening?" he asked, jive-style. A question she found impertinent.

"I might ask the same of you."

"Fine, fine." Knew she didn't like him. "Show's steaming full-speed ahead—I got some beautiful pieces coming in. It's all shaping up real smooth." He reeled off names and projects.

"Well, that's wonderful." She unlocked the door, he filed in after her.

"Where's Constantine?" he asked.

"Costa doesn't get in till about ten, ten-thirty, usually."

An indignant expression crossed Casey's face. "Man, you give these dudes an easy ride. When I have people working for me, I keep their noses *ground*. Nine o'clock sharp, no ifs, ands, or buts. They're begging for boot camp."

She laughed, in spite of herself. "Do you need him badly? You might try him at home. Although I doubt he's up yet."

She moved towards the stairs. "If you decide to wait, do please help yourself to some coffee, whatever you need."

He, learning she didn't plan to sit and chat till Costa showed, made shuffling noises down below, then evidently took off. Had she been inhospitable? After all, he was their guest curator. But he didn't seem capable of acting towards her like a grownup, so what could you do but treat him like a child?

With relief, she settled down at her desk and opened up the *Wall Street Journal*, reimmersing herself in that arch, edifying world of trials and frauds and treaties and mergers, before picking up the telephone.

"Jesse? Did I wake you? . . . How are you feeling? . . . Heavens. I can imagine. Well, are you still up for me to—. . . Good God, of course."

Eleven

In the late sixties, several years after she got out of Wellesley, Dorothea Diehl moved to New York, where she continued to work for her father's foundation. One of her main projects was Bellville, a music festival held every summer at a Victorian Gothic castle up the Hudson.

The festival's founder was Elkanan Grinspan, a Lithuanian-born violinist whom Dolly had first met at her parents' house when he was recording with the Chicago Symphony. Grinspan was a nervous dragonfly of a man, stick thin, all elbows and unmatched socks, who played with a high acuteness of intelligence that to Dolly's mind made other interpreters sound syrupy. As if music weren't mood, but the working through of a theorem about the creation of matter, the composition of the universe.

Bellville consisted of a two-week festival during which musicians came together daily to work out their conceptions of chosen pieces. Elkanan, who favored contemporary composers such as Shostakovich and Berio, made it a jam session for musicians who liked to play music which audiences didn't especially like to hear.

The festival was frustrating to organize: musicians' time is blocked out ages in advance, so that schedules rarely conjoined; and having snagged and pinned down the colleagues Elkanan had set his heart on, they were continually confronted by artists dropping out at the last minute. The aggravations, however, were redeemed by the nobility of the enterprise and by the sympathetic humor of Grinspan himself.

It was at Bellville that Dolly met Alfred Gebler. Alfred, in that particular incarnation, was acting as private secretary to William Orton, whose violin concerto—written for Elkanan—was being premiered at the festival. Orton and Gebler had erupted discordantly upon the dowdy Spartan enclave of musicians and their spouses, devout as patients at a mountain sanatorium. Particular opprobrium attached itself to the gangly redhead in a not very clean seersucker suit, who laughed much too loud while telling dirty jokes to Mrs. Hovannian, the violinist's wife.

Dolly, then twenty-six, thought—so far as she noticed him—that Mr. Orton's sidekick was silly and vulgar. Gebler, a year younger and living by the skin of his teeth, thought . . . well, who knows what he thought. Thought it was time the girl loosen up and stop mooning over a happily married violinist more than twice her age.

Dolly noticed that William Orton's friend in the dirty suit kept seeking her out for conversation. He even had the impertinence to comment on her personal habits, to mimic how she ate her soup or clasped her hands when listening to music. He mocked her for being a bluestocking. She could not imagine what he supposed the two of them had in common that entitled him to such familiarities.

One evening Gebler invited Dolly out to dinner—the cloisteredness of Bellville was getting him down. To Dolly's own surprise, she accepted. They ended up in the dining room of some lugubrious inn in Rhinebeck—the kind of place you eat in only when you've been married thirty years and don't give a damn.

At dinner, they put away two bottles of wine and he recounted with disconcerting frankness the shifts by which a Brooklyn tailor's son had wound up a groupie of the avant-garde. Dolly listened, disapproving but nonetheless laughing, and at six o'clock the next morning Mr. and Mrs. Hovannian on their way out for a walk before breakfast noticed a man with no shoes creeping out of Dorothea Diehl's bedroom. The following morning, the man without shoes left at seven.

Dolly's attraction to Alfred was from the first animated and complicated by revulsion. The whiteness of his flesh, the redness of his lips, his self-satisfaction, struck her as unforgivably ambiguous. For years she had been looking at Elkanan Grinspan, in moth-eaten cardigans and droopy dungarees, as a model of masculine perfection, and Gebler's crocodile shoes and boutonnieres affronted her. Strange to say, it was precisely his creepiness that whetted her appetite: she wanted to correct and master him. He was by no means unintelligent; the maddening thing was that he had no dignity whatsoever. What she did not stop to ask herself was why his clowning should get her into such a rage.

After a couple of years' meeting on the sly, Alfred—who was then ghostwriting Orton's memoirs—moved in with Dolly in New York. Her friends, who had never heard her mention his name, were amazed. She in turn was surprised by her own pleasure, coming home from a trip to Chicago or Paris, at finding him waiting for her. But when Alfred suggested they marry, she said, "You must be joking." Couldn't face telling her parents was Alfred's diagnosis. Unwilling to rouse an outcry over something she refused to believe in herself. Alfred accused her of planning on waiting till her father died.

In truth, her parents remained a chief obstacle. Her father, a stickler for female chastity, never mentioned Dolly's new roommate. Once, however, when a colleague's daughter made an unsuitable marriage, he held forth pointedly on the importance of choosing a mate from a similar background. "Youngsters think love conquers all. But when the going gets tough, it's same values that counts. Basically, people like their own kind—more and more as they get older." Unspoken was the threat of being the prey of fortune hunters. You had to marry a man with money, it seemed, just to be sure he wasn't marrying you for yours.

When she repeated this wisdom to Alfred, he surprised her by agreeing. "He's right—people like their own kind. If they like anybody. Of course, when your old man says 'own kind,' what he means is 'own religion.' "

Dolly denied it, then wondered. It had never occurred to her that her parents might be anti-Semitic, since so many of her father's business and artist friends were Jewish, but clearly there was a tacit difference between listening to one play the violin and marrying one.

Three years after that first summer at Bellville, Dolly and Alfred went to City Hall and got married. Then they wrote their parents.

Even then, Dolly was reluctant to admit that this was what she had done: become Mrs. Gebler, the wife of a lower-middle-class Jew with no job prospects or recognizable talents.

They married; she discovered too late the import of having chosen a husband she did not respect. She found herself comparing him with other men, never to his advantage. Why couldn't she have married an Elkanan, instead of this lightweight who couldn't bear to be alone, this infantile buffoon, this desperate reveller? All her life she'd been surrounded by distinguished men twenty-five, thirty years older. She missed being among grownups, missed gravity, sagacity, intellect. Missed home.

Although Dolly did not, strictly speaking, support her husband, it irked her nonetheless that he did not support her: this violation of the natural order of marriage made the balance of power still more unequal, allowing her too much room to criticize. He went out every night, slept all day: his mania for nonstop companionship, didn't matter whose, roused contempt as well as jealousy. She thought of herself as self-sufficient, rare, a prize. Might he really prefer others to her? Sometimes the very sight of him revolted her: those too big, carnivorous teeth, that facial nest of hair that, rancid, archival, trapped and carried stale smells—cigar stench, pussy, dinner.

She made scenes; she laid into Alfred for days on end for minor offenses, imagined betrayals. Why had he looked so hard at Henrietta Pye? Did he have a lech for underslung jaws? How come he'd made a lunch date with Bobby instead of the three of them having dinner together? No, don't change it—if he wanted to see Bobby without her, by all means she didn't want to stand in his way. She heard him talking on the phone and wondered why he laughed so much with strangers, was so dull with her. Was Delfina Pazzi wittier than she, or was he just being a sycophant?

He, worn down by the twin furies of her jealousy and her scorn, would ask, "If you don't want me around the house, why do you give a shit what time I come home?" She couldn't answer. It sounded too petty to say only that she didn't want to be made ridiculous, that she didn't want her family to hear of it and pity her.

Silence: this had been her father's revenge. Having sent her letter, Dolly sat and waited. She'd imagined her father jumping on the next plane to New York to have the marriage annulled. Producing the hired evidence that Gebler was a draft dodger, a check bouncer, a bigamist. Threatening to cut her off without a penny. What she hadn't imagined was . . . nothing. When she finally summoned the nerve to call home, her father, coldly, asked only if she had visited Anselmi's studio to see his new work. From then on, he treated her as an employee who had abused his trust. Their familial relations were over; her marriage went unmentioned. Dolly, devastated, acquiesced in her own demotion.

It was Alfred who refused to play. When they found out she was pregnant, Alfred decided it was time he meet his in-laws.

Dolly said nothing. A few days of false starts before she got up the nerve to tell her parents they were coming to visit—both of them. A tiny click, as her father hung up.

"Hello? Hello?"

Silence. And then her mother's voice. "Do you really think that's wise?"

The meeting naturally was hell. Horrific. Almost seventeen years later, she couldn't think of that night without a spasm of anger and self-loathing. Her father, who, without looking at him, had held out two fingers for Alfred to shake, maintained a terrible silence, inhibiting everyone else's falters at conversation.

Of course, Mother and Alfred did not have one shred of an interest in common, and although he tried stalwartly to talk to her about gardening, she was too frightened of her husband to be drawn.

In the end, Alfred gave up, and the three lapsed into silence—dead silence, cursed silence, broken only by Alfred's lapping his sorrel soup. The food as usual was dreadful, and the procession of servants made the silence even more self-consciously oppressive.

As soon as dessert had been removed, her father without a word went to his room. Shortly after, Mrs. Diehl excused herself, telling Alfred it had been most enjoyable to meet him and she hoped they had a safe trip back to New York. Dolly still had not told her parents she was having a baby.

Alfred, in a rage, drove Dolly to the hotel downtown, where they spent the night before taking the train back to Grand Central the next morning. She watched him from bed, sprawled in his Y-fronts in the adjoining sitting room of their hotel suite, sipping cognac and glaring into space. There was nothing she could say. It was his fault, really, for forcing her to do it. But for a night, she felt, lying rigid beside him, that they might never speak again, that their marriage was over, that each understood he had made a terrible mistake, and needed only the courage to get out of it. Better to be a single mother than to live with an enemy. It was only once the train passed Albany that they began to fight.

Sometimes Dolly wondered if her father ever would have relented and come around to Alfred. Sometimes she wondered why he never changed his will, which maintained Dolly as favorite daughter, trustee of the Diehl Foundation. As it was, six weeks after Johnny's birth, Charles Diehl had a heart attack at O'Hare airport and died on the way to the hospital. Dolly, unable to endure their parting unreconciled, collapsed. Only eight years of analysis had made her halfway able to mention her father without bursting into tears.

What followed amazed Dolly in retrospect. The long and the short of it was that Alfred—through sheer doggedness and a sneaky kind of intelligence—managed not only to bring Dolly out of her blackness but to worm his way, if not into the affections, at least into the tolerating consciousness of Dolly's remaining family. Sophie was already mad about him, but even Beatrice and her deadly husband decided he was fine.

Dolly's mother had been the last to hold out against Alfred's surprising all-rightness. With her, it appeared to be a physical aversion, the kind you can never entirely overcome. You saw it every time she shook hands with her son-in-law, the involuntary drawing back. Finally she accepted him as an unattractive but well-meaning necessity.

By the time Mrs. Diehl came round to Alfred, there was so much bitterness between husband and wife that love was no longer a question. He could never forgive her for having subjected him, without any support, to this long familial humiliation. For siding with that overrated bastard her old man. For never showing the slightest interest in *his* mother, a little fury who had worked thirty-seven years in a factory turning out women's sweaters and had now taken up residence in an old people's home in Long Beach. She should at least have had the human curiosity to want to know about the history bottled up in this tough life, begun in an eastern province of the collapsing Austro-Hungarian Empire, transported steerage to the New World, and played out in the ILGWU.

Dolly countered her husband's unspoken accusations by saying, You never go to see your mother. But Dolly wasn't that dumb. She should have had the wit to figure that it was his mother who had made Alfred who he was and that his feelings for this woman whom he'd disappointed by squandering his advantages—not going to college, not entering a profession, not being a son whose doings you could boast about—were the most intense and complicated he knew. And for all Gebler's love of luxury, his faith in American capitalism, something atavistic in him despised the Diehls. Believed that Diehl's smug lordliness had come at the expense of Shimon Gebler's root-vegetable pallor and nervous blink, his death at fifty-two. Felt that Mrs. Diehl's passion for her roses was a poor match for Mrs. Gebler Sr.'s passion for the Jews. Felt that even his own lovely daughters could have done with a little of their grandmother's spunk.

Hanging over this marriage—even on their good days—was the feeling It's too late, because it had gone wrong too long, and because each had come to enjoy the sour satisfaction of being locked in an unsatisfactory situation.

Now that *Ajax* was over, Dolly's next concern was the board meeting on the twenty-fifth.

Dolly always got into a state before the trustees' twice-yearly meetings. (The directors, on the other hand, who met twice a month, gave her no trouble.) For several nights before, she wouldn't be able to sleep. If she did, at dawn, manage to teeter into unconsciousness, she would dream that she'd boarded the wrong subway train to work, which then took her miles and miles through unknown suburbs, hours late for the meeting, and no return. She would dream about walking into the trustees' meeting stark naked. Or that she'd forgotten her prepared speech, like a schoolgirl at exams. One night she dreamt the foundation was taken away from her for incompetence and given to her sister Sophie. She woke up still protesting, stammering with indignation.

Alfred, who could never believe that a woman so majestic could get into a panic about what seemed to him a trifle, tried to tease her out of her nerves, but his kidding only angered her. "If you can't be useful, why don't you at least go away and leave me in peace?"

He relented, genuinely surprised. "Come on, darling, what's the problem? You've picked these old farts yourself—they love you, they love Aurora. It's a walk-over. Piece of cake. You can do it in your sleep. Anyway, nobody pays attention, except Lucinda scribbling away in her little notebook." (Lucinda was the director of the Merrimack Foundation.) "You just tell 'em the wonderful things we've been doing, and then we go out to dinner—which is the part they're interested in, anyway." He had booked an upstairs room at Dominick's, and already had been over there several times to discuss the menu with Jed.

Which was more or less what happened.

They had had lunch at "21" that same day with George Mason, the CEO of Diehl, who had flown in from Chicago for the meeting. Alfred found Mason quite a stick. They were fighting a battle with him at the moment to see whether Aurora, in addition to its annual grant, might not dig into the Diehl Foundation's capital for new acquisitions.

The lunch began with Dolly asking Mason about Hemogen, a company Diehl had recently acquired. Hemogen was a small lab out in Southern California whose scientists were developing a blood substitute, contamination-free, from cow's blood. "It's good for us, and it dovetails very nicely with the strong interest we've already got in blood," Mason explained. Count Dracula and Co.

Dolly had read that Upjohn had just taken out a $179 million contract with a rival company which was developing its product from pigs' blood—cheaper, surely. "What does that mean for us?"

"Nothing much. They're a long way off yet, and there's a very good chance we'll get FDA approval in the next year or two. Anyway, even if Upjohn's does work, it's not going to be one product that dominates the market."

The conversation moved on to Diehl's research into clotting agents, and the troubles it was having with its prostate drug, which was supposed to reduce the need for surgery but which had produced some unfortunate side effects in its first, experimental patients. "We're going to have to pay out some money on that one."

Farther down the line was Mason's own pet project, still under development in their research center in New Haven: the manufacture of amino acids that create copper peptides in the body that would heal diabetic ulcers. As he talked about it, his brush cut seemed to stand even higher on end in excitement.

Alfred, over the caramelized banana tart, yawned. Dull work being rich.

Dolly's father had been the kind of boss who ate lunch every day in the company cafeteria and knew the ages of everybody's children. He was often in the field, visiting the laboratories. Liked to switch employees from division to division, make sure everybody stayed on the ball. He was always thinking ten steps ahead—what was the next thing after the next new thing, and how to corner the market in it. U.S. business, to his mind, was too bent on short-term profits, and the FDA was his nemesis.

That kind of charismatic, one-man rule has its limit. When Old Man Diehl died, everyone suddenly noticed he hadn't picked a successor. The board had scratched its head, pondered, fought, and eventually alighted as a compromise on Mason, a former chemical engineer who was the head of their European division. Gebler knew that Diehl himself would never have chosen someone from within the company: he counted highly on fresh perspective.

After sixteen years of Mason's bland rule, Diehl Pharmaceuticals was doing okay. Its net income had grown by more than twenty percent annually, and last year its profits—on revenue of $6 billion—were $400 million. Yet even to Alfred's untrained mind, it seemed apparent that the company had lost its spark, once Mr. Diehl wasn't around to keep everyone jumpy and in love. People who worked at Diehl no longer felt part of a semisacred mission, as if they were out to save humanity and screw the competition all in one go. Now it was just another big multinational drug business, like the others.

After lunch, when they had said goodbye to Mason, Alfred walked Dolly to the corner of Fifth Avenue. "Shall I put you in a cab?"

She looked at him. "Where are you going?"

He squeezed her elbow. "I want to look in on some shows on Fifty-seventh Street."

She was silent while he hailed a taxi and bundled her into it. For a moment, Gebler hesitated, then closed the door. "Don't worry about this evening—we'll bowl 'em over," he told her through the half-open window.

She tried to smile, unsuccessfully. "Will you be sure to be back in plenty of time?"

"Loads." He walked away, west along Fifty-second Street, jaunty, still buzzing from the second bottle of La Doucette, glanced at his watch, and stopped by the nearest public phone. It was occupied by a black boy in spandex shorts, who was sitting on his messenger's bike, receiver tucked under his wagging chin. Gebler tossed a quarter up in the air and caught it, baseball-mitt-style, singing softly to himself: "Johnny you too bad . . . whoa-whoa-whoa. . . ."

Twelve

WHEN A DOG SETTLES DOWN to sleep, it turns around and around again before it lies. Those nervous circlings were how Isaac Hooker thought of his drawings. He was getting ready to paint, but first he needed the skill. So far, his eyes were bigger than his stomach. So he circled and circled, in pencil, in crayon and charcoal—whatever he had the money to buy. Whatever cast-off materials he found. Two years he drew, and then he switched to paint.

His first paintings were on tin, which, if you used it right, gave a delicacy and precision quite different from canvas's thirsty suppleness. On the corner of Tenth Avenue there was a salvage center. Isaac made friends with Manny, who was soon supplying him with regular handouts of scrap metal. What resulted was the Hell's Kitchen bathtub series.

The first scene was a nightscape, by candlelight. The candlelight was churchy, funereal; the bathtub looked like a coffin with feet. His own body grotesquely foreshortened, like Mantegna's sketches of a feet-first Jesus but from the other direction: a Jesus'-eye view of his own body, made wavy, greenish white, by being seen underwater, hairy white legs and prick like a buoy bobbing at the surface.

The water roiled into little whorls and riptides of current, and the candle's flame reflected in shards and trickles, as in a broken mirror. The play of what was real but distorted (i.e., underwater) and what was merely reflected pleased him.

At the center of the composition was the faucet, which in Isaac's figuring had become a fox's head with pointy ears and luminous red eyes. And above the bathtub a square of night sky, in which hung an airplane, dripping flames that turned to blood.

In the second painting, daylight, the colors were brilliant baby blues and crimsons, the bathtub opalescent, gleaming. The bathtub now had become the pond in the woods at Gilboa, and he used the high window as entrance into another, more intricate painting: in the sky-blue window were floating his mother and father.

Isaac's arch-hero was Goya, who with one hand painted courtiers, graceful, greedy, ironic, and with the other sketched nightmare cartoons howling against the depravity of war, the hypocrisy of clerics. Who understood light as lucidly and intimately as a Dutchman.

He had been studying reproductions of Goya's portraits of the Bourbons, in which each family member's fate is already implicit in lips and gaze—the child who will usurp his brother's throne and start the wars, the mother who will make her lover more powerful than her shy husband, who is only interested in horses—and he had intended to charge his portrait of his parents with just such a delicate freight of destiny. He had wanted to make the ratty fur of his mother's coat, a wedding present from her coworkers at the department store, palpable, dense, luscious as ermine. But instead, working from memory, he had been stymied by the more rudimentary riddle of how to fit this ectoplasmic couple into the window frame.

In the last painting, the bathwater had turned to a gray-green sea, and through the window was escaping the soul of his father in a blue suit.

He did one more picture—his favorite: himself on his bed at home, a naked white elf, jerking off. The flying sperm was turning, magically, into garlands of flowers, and among the flowers was the little wooden house where he'd lived with his girlfriend Agnes.

In art class on Henry Street, his teacher, Melissa, had said that he had a dark imagination. He was surprised—in his own family, he had a reputation for almost idiotic cheerfulness. He'd had a dark life, it seemed to him, silly and wasted. To his teacher he replied, "I'm telling the truth as I see it." And then realized that he had repeated verbatim a favorite phrase (one he'd always disliked) of his mother's. Melissa laughed. "I'm not insulting you," she said.

By now he had tired of his own limits—he was not content to look naive. He wanted to make the viewer believe in the flesh and muscle beneath the clothes—to trust that behind the closed door was not canvas or tin but more rooms, a street, a city. He wanted, above all, to learn how to paint light, which was the essence of color. Color was not a thing—not matter—but a vibration, like sound. Each wavelength had its own color, which objects touched by light waves and light particles soaked up and reflected, according to their absorbency.

Painting from live models, studying the anatomy books in order to get good enough so that people would believe what he had to show them. He became fascinated by eighteenth-century medical artists, by the Italian craftsmen who made wax replicas of the human body sliced through to reveal the arteries and internal organs and muscles and sinew. If you wanted to draw a man's head, you started with the medulla oblongata, then the formation of the cranium, which encased it.

Every day Isaac ventured out into the world to look at its colors—fresh-washed grass, gray skies, rough water, the crimson of young branches in winter. Sometimes he went through weeks of painting only clouds on scraps of tin, or clouds seen in puddles. Clouds and sky were a way of spying on heaven; water was magic.

He liked best of all to paint rainy days. The spearlike clash of umbrellas. How rain refracted the cars' headlights. How through the wet store window of Kalamatis Spices on Ninth Avenue you saw the owner with his high belly poised behind sacks of star anise, red chilies, orange lentils, and linden blossoms.

Texture: the matte must of chalk on blackboard. Function: which legs dogs ran with. The structural difference between a horse's leg and a man's. The vertebrae and play of muscles on a woman's naked back.

On weekends, he walked to the Frick and the Metropolitan Museum, parked himself in front of Old Masters, and copied.

His most ambitious work to date was on unstretched canvas, like a circus backdrop. It was a picture of the county fair back home, which here he reconceived as a Roman circus of the saints. First panel, Daniel and the lion. In the second panel Saint Sebastian, attacked by men with darts impressing their girlfriends. The third occupied by Saint Catherine on the wheel—the wheel being an illuminated Ferris wheel–type whirligig.

The colors were candied—aquamarines, hot pinks, marmalades—but the painting, to Isaac's mind, was a failure, because the mix of what he had actually seen and what he had copied from Spanish martyrdoms proved indigestibly stiff.

Before Acme finally closed for good, Isaac went over to Henry Street and visited Melissa. He brought with him a large portfolio containing the work he had done in the last six months.

"These pictures are too melodramatic, too narrative," she said.

"When Caravaggio painted the supper at Emmaus or the Virgin Mary, he didn't have some historical idea in his head. He ganged up his friends—the prostitute at the corner, the blacksmith down the street—and made them pose for him. Look at Rembrandt. That's not history paint-ing, that's the neighbors. You need to flush some of those ideas out of your head, get back to nature."

She said, "You should stop painting narrative for a while. Just try still lifes, or better yet, abstract."

Isaac followed her advice and banished stories from his work. In-stead, he played with color, mixing oils to see which produced what, and discovering that if he concentrated hard enough before he fell asleep, he could dream pure pigment. One night he saw in his dreams a field of yel-low, the luscious lemony yellow of Vermeer's wife's cloak with the chin-chilla collar, where she looks up, surprised, as if she were glad to see him. All that seasoned connubial contentment—the being pleased to see your husband—was contained, it seemed to Isaac, in the yolky custard of Ver-meer's yellow. Another night he dreamed violet. He wanted to be rich so that he didn't have to scrimp with oils, didn't groan inwardly when he used up a whole tube of zinc white on a girl's shoulder.

At ten to six, the first navy-green Mercedes-Benz pulled up outside Au-rora. Others followed. Nine trustees out of twelve had announced that they would be coming: Prescott Bing, who was the head of the Fairfield; Grayden Amory, the former director of the National Gallery; Jerry Mehl, the president of Cal Arts; Lucinda; Bobby; George Mason; Emily and Arnold Bishop, who were important art collectors; Dave Flaxman. Healey had called that morning to say he wouldn't be able to make it since he had to go see the mayor and next time could they please not meet at rush hour? Jewel Winterman never showed up at meetings—they really ought to can her. The third no-show was Ethan Miller, who was about to get indicted for insider trading.

Gebler and Bobby and Flaxman were speculating about how long in the clink Miller was likely to get. A light sentence, probably, since he'd already ratted on his buddies. Been wired for sound, it turned out. Funny how primitive, how mafioso one's morality was: to Gebler, as to the others, evidently, defrauding innocent stockholders was far less queasy a sin than squealing on one's co-conspirators.

Flaxman told Alfred the latest gossip. When Miller heard he was about to be led out of the office in handcuffs—he had a friend in the attorney general's office—apparently he'd vanished for a week. Wife and kids thought he'd jumped off a bridge. Finally he was discovered holed up with the ex-hustler it turned out he'd been keeping all these years in a pied-à-terre on Sutton Place. "You want to know what they'd been doing?" demanded Flaxman.

"I don't know—do I want to know?"

"Ordering take-out pizza and watching *The Wizard of Oz* over and over."

Dolly had from the start been against putting Ethan Miller on the board. She found him physically repulsive. Besides which, she had an irremovable contempt for these eighties financiers who were buying up contemporary art and then dumping it. Why couldn't they go back to racehorses and ballet girls, and not drive up the prices?

Alfred had replied, "Well, he does have one of the most important collections of contemporary art on the East Coast. You ever seen Ethan's Ellsworth Kellys? They make your mouth water."

Dolly had shrugged. "It doesn't take much talent to keep Edward Larrey on commission."

"Think of who he could have hired instead."

Dolly thought if the man had any tact he would resign from their board, but until he decided to do so, they were stuck with him. Gebler, who felt a tiny shiver of there-but-for-the-grace-of-God whenever he heard about the world falling in on somebody, plus a twinge of envy at someone who had almost got away with it, said, "If Ethan had tact, he'd still be poor."

Anyway, the other trustees were going to have to decide whether or not to ask Miller to resign. "Is there any allowance in the bylaws for trustees taking a sabbatical to Sing Sing?" cracked Bobby.

"Actually, as you may know, we've commissioned a project out at Rikers for the 'Home' show. Maybe Ethan can be our man on the scene," said Gebler. "I bet we end up voting *him* a grant—he'll be turning out some of those cute little crucifixes made outa Pepsi cans."

"Crucifixes? I think not. Isn't he also giving some kinda auditorium to Yeshiva University?"

"He got religion, huh?"

"Yeah, but there was some problem—they built it already and he still hasn't coughed up the dough."

"There'll be some pretty sore Jews sitting up in Washington Heights," said Gebler.

While they were kidding around, Gebler caught sight of his wife, who was standing rigid with nerves, and felt a stab of pity. It was weird: with those business genes, you'd think she'd feel at home in a boardroom. Once she said her little set piece, however (she wasn't too good at improvisation), she'd be fine.

Cecile served coffee in bright green art deco cups and passed around a plateful of the little savory cheese straws Mr. Gebler bought at the Italian bakery around the corner—he had noticed that businessmen ate three times as much as most people. More chitchat—whose child had applied to which college, who had been to see the new Oliver Stone movie about Vietnam, the awfulness of the stock market, the wonderfulness of the art market, Bush, Bush, Bush. Dave Flaxman told the latest Quayle joke—this one involved the Vice-President going to a plastic surgeon to get a birthmark put on his head like Gorbachev's. Gebler laughed too loud, even though he'd heard it before. (What was wrong with Dave anyway? Gebler'd thought the only point of working on Wall Street was you heard the new jokes the day they were invented. He wondered if this meant Roth, Flaxman, Sheed was going down the tubes.)

Gebler caught himself observing as if from a great distance the roomful of trustees, the glossy massaged cosseted ease of these men in their pinstripes and Prince of Wales tweeds, their Turnbull & Asser shirts and handmade loafers, their pocket handkerchiefs rising in castellated peaks like egg whites. What a battlefield of wool and linen and finest Egyptian cotton, what tubloads of starch and French soap and Italian cologne and English shoe polish had gone into making these men presentable for the evening's meeting! Did he, Gebler, look as spoiled and complacent, as ass-kissed-from-birth as Prescott Bing or Grayden Amory? Not possible. You had to be rich for at least two generations to accumulate such a crowning air of self-delight, to look as if two manservants were permanently employed in massaging your little toe.

Even Mehl, who twenty years ago would have looked like the West Coast hippie-academic he basically was, was decked out like an arbitrageur in an Armani suit and ostrich-skin cowboy boots. Did that mean the art business really was a business, like microchips or coffee futures? (Could you make billions out of something that *wasn't* a business?) Compared to the men, his wife and Lucinda appeared rather rumpled. And Andy, slack-jawed, slobby in his khakis and shirtsleeves, looked like someone's son home for Thanksgiving.

They took their chairs. Aurora's conference room had been designed to resemble an office in a Hollywood movie from the thirties, when capitalism still had an aura of sinister glamour: a twelve-foot-long Empire table, fruitwood inlaid in ebony with charioteers and sphinxes, held up by griffins, and surrounded by a dozen Empire armchairs fitted in violet leather which gave off a delicious smell of luxury, like a fine cigar. There were violet taffeta curtains: it was the one room in the transparent building you couldn't see into or out of. When he was too hung over, Gebler sometimes snuck up here for a nap.

Beside each place was a bottle of San Pellegrino and a tumbler, a yellow legal pad and a sharpened pencil, and a bright green translucent folder. One leaf of the folder contained last year's grants—slides of some of Aurora's artists' recent projects, reviews their exhibitions or performances had received. The other side contained CVs of artists who were being considered for upcoming grants, along with transparencies of their work. Marjorie, their graphics director, had done a pretty job on the portfolio. Of course, the trustees had already been sent this material; this was just to remind them who was who.

And then to work. Dolly, flushed, blazing-eyed with the fury of the occasion, began. After almost twenty years of living together, even when he was exasperated beyond endurance by everything else about her, Gebler still got a thrill from hearing his wife speak in public. What a deep voice, so throaty it evoked visions of the dark vibrating internal regions, the Wagnerian grottoes it had emerged from. In the old days he used to get a hard-on just hearing her talk.

She thanked them for being there—Jerry for flying in from California and Mason from Chicago. She talked about expenses—last year, they had disbursed $3 million in grants and spent $1.2 million in operating costs. This year was going to be more expensive—plus, they had some stock-market losses.

She outlined the year's accomplishments, the ongoing projects. She talked about the archive they had set up the previous spring for experimental film, the exhibitions at their various spaces; she mentioned the poetry project at St. Luke's, she mentioned the review *Ajax* had gotten in the *Times*—it was in everybody's packet, wildly favorable but rather dim, to Dolly's mind—she explained the general idea behind the "Home" show, which was opening in December, and how Aurora was committed to fostering an urban art that interacted with, commented upon, improved the city in which it operated. Mr. Gebler listened, puffing on his cigar, amazed as always by how his wife, such a purist, could unleash, when addressing businessmen, perfect paragraphs of middlebrow jargon. Where did she pick up words like "fostering" and "interact"? How come she never used such words at home?

Then she passed the floor to Andy, who talked more particularly about the artists who were taking part in the "Home" show and about the accompanying symposium which he was organizing.

Then Marlene Battle, their budget director, discussed expenses for the upcoming year. She mentioned in passing that they were hiring a new bookkeeper, since Edna was retiring (that reminded Alfred, he was going to have to give her a party), and that they had switched their graphics design account from Arc Design to Kaspian. In addition to their operating expenses, they were planning to spend $1.5 million on grants and $3 million on new acquisitions.

This was the important part. Dolly was fighting a tricky battle against Mason. Because of the shaky market, Aurora's income was going to be slightly lower than usual. Dolly, who wanted to be allowed to dip into the Diehl Foundation's capital, once again stated her objective. In the 1950s, her father over a ten-year period had spent $3 million buying art which then had become the backbone of his collection. She wanted the same liberty. Unfortunately, prices had skyrocketed. As a consequence, Aurora's permanent collection of over eight hundred works from 1960 to 1980 had probably trebled in value in the last few years, but correspondingly, art that three years ago cost ten, twelve thousand now couldn't be had for less than seventy-five thousand. She was asking the Diehl Foundation for $20 million in order to build up a first-rate collection of art from the seventies, eighties, and whatever the nineties produced. Mason, however, insisted that Charles Diehl's will stipulated that his foundation's capital be reserved for maintaining the Chicago museum and its permanent collection.

The last item on her list was the annex, to be built on the vacant lot opposite. The board had been going over architects' proposals for the building, which was in effect to be nothing less than a new museum of contemporary art. The question was, how soon, realistically, they could begin construction on this desperately needed space. Mrs. Gebler could not countenance its being completed any later than 1995.

Then it was Gebler's turn to discuss the seven artists their managing directors had selected for that year's larger grants. (They also had a slush fund which distributed smaller monies throughout the year, dependent only upon the approval of their smaller group of directors, which met every two weeks.) Some of them were continuing grants—Richard Cruikshank, for instance, was being given $250,000 to complete a slate pyramid in the Nevada desert. Others were first-timers. Alfred made his pitch, then opened the floor to questions.

Flaxman raised an objection. Flaxman was getting to be a pain in the ass—they had picked him as a counterweight to Mason and the rather stuffy Bing, which he was. Two years ago, however, his marriage had busted up, and now he was dating a woman who kept telling him that Aurora was too establishment, too white male. Last meeting he and Lucinda had joined forces in complaining about there only being one woman on their list of six grant recipients.

Didn't the Geblers feel that they were devoting too much money to—how should he put it—recidivists? Richard Cruikshank, for instance, who belonged to an older generation. Did the world need yet another series of stone planks? Shouldn't they try to be more on the cutting edge, help younger artists who had something to say about the society we live in? Dolly looked furious.

Gebler explained to him how they'd already just explained to him about the "Home" show, almost all of its participants under thirty and lively as a bag of Mexican jumping beans.

"Incidentally," said Mason, "I read in the press clipping about your opera *Ajax* that a considerable portion of—uh—one scene was devoted to doing fairly offensive things with a tampon. Considering that Diehl owns the second largest tampon manufacturer in the country, I'm not sure it's all that constructive to have the company's money going to people who make fun of its products."

Mr. Gebler burst out laughing, imagining his prudish father-in-law confronted with a future in which women's menstrual leavings became the subject of an opera. "You're quite right. Actually, I think it's kind of a good advertisement for the damn things—all kind of uses no one'd ever think of putting them to."

"But she does seem to be implying they're not very environmentally . . . kind," persisted Mason.

"Yes, I see. But what can we do?" said Mr. Gebler. "Perkins is a brilliant artist, and we certainly wouldn't want to cramp . . . um . . . her . . . creative impulses. As long as she isn't explicitly condemning any of the company's products by name . . . Andy, you look as if you were about to say something."

This was a hint. Andy obligingly improvised. "Yes, I was wondering if we could get on to the operating expenses for . . ."

Whew, sighed Gebler silently, digging himself deeper into the violet leather. What a nice day it would be when Mason dropped dead. There was a moment's silence; then Flaxman repeated, as people will do, in almost identical terms what he had just said, how he thought it was important to be more on the cutting edge.

"Well, used Tampax sounds like the blade of the razor itself to me, boy," said Bobby.

There were other questions, other objections. Then they got onto the subject of Benoit Goldschmidt's being made a trustee—if either Winterman or Miller stepped down—before adjourning for dinner at Dominick's.

Thirteen

WHAT MR. GEBLER's board-meeting speech did not include was the news that a young man named Isaac Hooker had been hired as an assistant to Constantine Constantinakis to help set up the winter shows.

A few days after the *Ajax* party, Isaac had once again dropped by

Gebler's office unannounced, this time with a bunch of flowers. He had wanted to leave them with Cecile and go away again, but Cecile insisted on his waiting while she went to see if her boss was busy.

Gebler was busy—he and Andy were in a meeting—but he popped his head around the door of his office just to say hello to the kid. It was a clever bunch of flowers, Alfred saw at once, not the awkward, long-stemmed skyscrapers that oblige you to go scavenging for a tall enough receptacle. The boy instead had chosen just a fistful of poppies that would fit in a coffee mug on someone's desk. Kid with no elbows to his sweaters shouldn't be buying rich people flowers.

Mr. Gebler, who had forgotten about Isaac, looked at him and remembered that he wanted a job, and then that he liked his face. "Are these for me or for my wife? I don't think I've ever been given flowers before by a guy—it makes me feel like I'm sick in the hospital."

He wanted to say thank you for the other night, Isaac explained. Both nights.

Mr. Gebler examined the boy closer. He looked greenish. Not quite his boisterous self of previous visits. "Why don't you leave us your telephone number?"

"I don't have a phone."

"You got anybody takes messages for you? What about where you work, at the framer?"

"Acme's closing this week," said Isaac, shifting from one leg to the other.

Mr. Gebler didn't consider himself a particularly charitable man, and yet his own past and its indignities were still fresh enough in his imagination to make other people's predicaments palpable. "So what are you going to do?"

"I stay in bed," said Isaac. "You don't use up so much energy." His eyes were shining very bright behind the glasses. Beaming. As if he were a saint, overflowing with love for an unfeeling world.

Mr. Gebler pondered. Then he picked up Cecile's phone, pressed a button. "Costa." Pause. "How're you doing?" Pause. "You don't say. Well, I'm sure you'll handle that one just fine. As long as you get us in there by the thirtieth." He listened, then spoke. "Say, Costa, have you got any use for an able-bodied young person, male, name of Isaac, who used to work at the frame store?"

Pause. "Yeah, Acme. It's closing. Apparently we didn't bring them enough business. By the way, did you know the place was folding? . . . Why dincha tell me? . . . No, you didn't. I woulda remembered. . . . Well, I'll send this kid down to you, you can look him over for yourself. I don't know, maybe you need a . . ."

Now, hanging up, he turned to Isaac. "You know, we're so goddamned rich in this place we've got money coming out of our ears. I don't see why we shouldn't hire you. Maybe freelance, to start with." These litigious days, you had to watch who you gave a job. Catch an office boy with his hand in the till and he'd slap you with a million-dollar lawsuit for discrimination against kleptomaniacs. "I mean, all the big galleries have three full-time staffers just licking stamps. I don't see why we shouldn't employ a man soulful enough to throw away his last paycheck on poppies." He winked at Isaac, gestured him away. "Now go see Costa and ask him if he's got anything for you to do. Downstairs. Back of the store. Don't worry, he won't eat you. He's a Buddhist."

Costa was the general manager. Alfred and Costa had been buddies since the sixties, when they met at a party at Allen Ginsberg's. Back then, Costa hadn't been a Buddhist. He was an aspiring filmmaker, an escapee from an uptight Greek family from Gloucester. Costa from Glosta.

Costa's ambition had been nothing less than to make an archive of his own life and times. Wherever he went, Costa kept the camera rolling, so that before long you forgot about it and went about your business, which in those days was monkey business for sure. For years after, Gebler had an ugly suspicion that there existed in some can in Costa's archives footage of a very stoned Alfred fucking Ellery Joyce's wife in the kitchen sink. Luckily Costa was such a perfectionist his films never got finished or shown.

When the Geblers founded Aurora, Costa was the first person they hired. Even though Dolly was snotty about most of Alfred's friends, Costa she couldn't get enough of. Everybody liked Costa. Sage, uninflected, discreet. You could count on him. Which maybe was just another way of saying he was a gent.

In the old days he'd been friskier: the guy simply didn't seem to have any biological need for sleep. Besides which, they'd all had a friend named Jimmy America who manufactured homemade speed, rough stuff, ammoniac, out of a lab in his mother's garage in Hoboken. For two years solid—before he went to work at Aurora—Costa had snorted speed and filmed his sleepless life. He always wore the same old jeans and a white T-shirt and as he was brown as a berry year round, he never looked much the worse for wear. Then one day Costa went to bed and slept for seventy hours straight. When he woke up, he sold his movie camera for a tool chest.

Now, long divorced—he had a daughter who lived with her mother, who was a dancer—Costa seemed content in the evenings just doing his meditations and turning in early. And even though old Costa was nothing if not tolerant, Alfred nonetheless felt shifty with him, as you do with someone who has outgrown vices you still cleave to. Besides which, hard as he tried, Alfred could never get the hang of Buddhism: it simply did not appeal to him, that bland chilly doctrine of detachment and renunciation. An old man's philosophy, maybe.

Downstairs, Isaac and Costa were getting acquainted. Isaac had found Costa in the back, hanging pictures. Costa looked at Isaac and said through a mouthful of metal, "Hey there, Isaac. Do you mind giving me a hand here?"

Isaac took the pencil from him and the picture hooks and together they dotted tiny pencil marks in the wall. Isaac noticed how cleanly Costa drove in the nails, like a golfer teeing off.

When they'd hung the pictures, Costa sat Isaac down with a cup of peppermint tea and they chatted about this and that. They talked about the films they liked and the virtues of Super-8 over video, and they discovered they both were in love with Gena Rowlands, and then Costa explained about the upcoming shows. "How much did Alfred say we were going to pay you?"

"He didn't. I'm not used to getting paid too much. As long as the lunches are hot."

Costa blew on his tea to cool it down. "Well, when we bring in someone freelance, we usually pay 'em seven dollars an hour."

Isaac thought that sounded like a lot. "Do you really need somebody or is he just being kind?" There were people, he'd found, who took pleasure in disciples and people who wanted to do everything themselves, and the latter kind you'd best stay clear of.

"I tell you," said Costa. "I turned forty-nine this year. Don't tell me I don't look it. My point is, forty-nine is old for manual labor. I never even finished high school, let alone got a college degree, so there isn't much soft work I could do. Al's always throwing assistants at me. They stay a couple of years and then as soon as they're any use they leave, so I figured it's easier to do it myself. Recently, though, my neck's started seizing up when I lift things. Anyways, I'll tell you what to do, and you do it, and let's see how we get along."

Costa could tell from the way Isaac moved and the questions he asked that he was going to be about as helpful as a puppy, and he felt a little sore at Alfred for foisting on him another dud assistant, and yet he couldn't help feeling sorry for the kid, who looked as if he had nowhere to go.

It was the end of the day and the light in the front of the gallery had turned to blue ice, the color of the Manhattan Bridge, of glaciers. Nippy out, these days, soon as the sun went down. Isaac didn't feel like leaving, but he forced himself to his feet. "When shall I start?"

"How about Tuesday morning, at ten," said Costa. "That'll give you a few days' liberty."

"Liberty?" said Isaac. "I've been drowning on liberty. Now all I'm after is that hot lunch I mentioned."

Isaac felt blessed by God. On his way home, heart singing, he stopped at the Franciscan church. Only that morning the jaws of penury had opened up to swallow him, and now he had a job starting Tuesday, and not just a job, but a job working for the most divine institution, the most intriguingly heavenly family on earth, whom he already loved with all his heart. He could scarcely breathe for joy when he thought not just of the Geblers, but of Costa, agile and patient, with his clever hands and way of sitting still, still. God was gracious, and it looked as if his luck were turning.

The church, with its scent of molten wax and incense, was almost empty, except for two old ladies and the janitor from the building next to Isaac's. Stretched across a pew was a homeless man in an army overcoat, who had come into the church in search of somewhere quiet and safe to rest. Isaac knew the man, who hung out in front of Port Authority—an anxious-looking bearded fellow with a suitcase, who at first glance might be mistaken for a foreign academic waiting for his bus to Amherst. Isaac had tried to talk to him before, but had realized that the tramp—like a dying person—had already sunk to a place where he couldn't be reached. Another day, Isaac, seeing a laminated-paper coffee cup at his side, had ventured to put some coins in it, whereupon the man, terrified, had shrieked, "What are you putting in my coffee?!" and, jumping to his feet, bounded away. Now he was sleeping, but his face was still furrowed by anxiety.

Isaac looked around for the sacristan, who was his particular friend, but Claude was nowhere to be seen.

Going to the side chapel dedicated to Saint Jude, he knelt in prayer, closing his eyes so tight that when he opened them again, everything was freckled with pink. Then he chose a chubby white candle in a red glass bowl. He lit its wick from the flame of another candle, trying not to extinguish the first candle by pressing his own against it too insistently, and placed his in a field by itself. Watched just long enough to make sure that his own candle was burning surely before slipping out of the church, head lowered, wondering how he could possibly make the hours spin fast enough till Tuesday morning.

That night, sitting down at his table with pen and paper, Isaac worked out exactly how much money and what kind of life seven dollars an hour would bring him. He figured it came to almost fifteen grand a year, and that after rent and gas and electricity, he would be left with a little over eight hundred a month. Once he eliminated two hundred dollars for groceries—every Sunday, Isaac went to the A&P and loaded up on bulk food, spaghetti and potatoes and bacon and greens, for since his first winter in New York he'd had a mania for hot cooked meals—and assuming he managed not to fall sick, that still left six hundred dollars. And oh yes, taxes. Now that he was a real human being again there would be taxes to pay.

Such a sum seemed to Isaac a king's ransom. For a brief moment, he wondered how in God's name he would possibly manage to spend it all. He calculated that on six hundred surplus dollars a month, he could go to the movies and visit the museums whenever he liked. He could drop in on his favorite Holbein at the Frick, or look at the Goyas at the Metropolitan. He could up his monthly money-order home to his mother by an extra hundred bucks. It would be no stretch, either, to buy a CD player, so that he might have proper music to work by in the evenings, instead of a broken-down radio. With music of his own, he could drown out the Turkish nightclub's pesky boom with Glenn Gould fugues. Perhaps—but this was more expensive—he might even be able to get hold of a halogen light, instead of the yellowish glare he now worked by.

More intoxicating still, and more pertinent, was the thought of the art supplies his new fortune would bring. In the past, Isaac had worried that using cheap materials would make his paintings crack and disintegrate. Now he could upgrade from synthetic to cotton canvas. He could buy oils, and not acrylic. Perhaps he could even take a life class, with professional models.

Then he remembered how much canvas and oil paints cost and how much the landlord was threatening to raise his rent, and realized, with a crash, that fifteen thousand dollars a year did not go very far in New York City, the most expensive city in the Western world. And now, he remembered that whereas working at the frame shop he'd had four days a week to himself, at this new job which he had just won, with such cunning, he had sold himself into full-time bondage.

All his exultation, all his dreaming dried up, and he was frightened of being engulfed, diminished by the more magnetically attractive world of the Geblers and their good deeds. How did he know he would be able to do his own work at night? By the end of a day at Aurora, there might be nothing left of him. His ideas of how a CD player and a halogen lamp would solve everything, and his own illicit motive in wanting to work at Aurora so he might see more of the Gebler family, now seemed to him abject. What mattered was not that he pleased others but that he please himself, and as he had got no worthwhile work done since that very first day on which he had visited Alfred Gebler's office, there was not much cause for glee.

This tangle of worries and involuntary joy, of conflicting advantage and hazard, kept Isaac up till dawn. At one point, although he had said to Costa so gaily that he would see him Tuesday morning at ten, he determined that instead he would have to explain to the man that he couldn't take the job after all. But then he remembered Costa's hurt neck, and felt that he would not like to disappoint him.

When daylight blanched his areaway window from dark to paler brown, Isaac, giving up on sleep, walked over to the Hudson River, where he watched the smoke from a factory chimney in New Jersey billow into a lemon-pale sky, and the cars drop the male prostitutes on the pier where they had found them, and then he went to the diner where he used to work as a cook.

The Blue Sky was full of cabdrivers coming off duty, eating breakfast at the counter before they went home to the boroughs. Some of them he recognized—a jolly fellow in a lumber jacket who swaggered in, stuck a toothpick between his front teeth, and plopped himself down on a swivel stool. "Well, look who's here," said the waitress to the lumber-jacket.

"Morning, Merry Sunshine."

"Is it the usual?"

"That's what my mother used to say to me bright and early every school day, when she was trying to drag me outa bed. Good morning, Merry Sunshine, what makes you wake so soon? My mother came top prize in declamation class in junior high."

And Mary to kitchen, "Over easy on a toasted English and a light coffee." When she caught sight of Isaac—Mary who even at five in the morning had a sprayed chestnut bouffant and starched nursey bosom— she let out a "Look who's back! I thought the sharks musta ate you. George, you seen Ikey's here?" Briefly, Isaac was gathered up into that starch and hairspray, like some midwestern church lady's idea of going to heaven.

Disorienting to be plunged from his own caged solitude into this lively world of people bustling, joking, transmitting orders from customers to kitchen, full-volume, as if it were broad daylight and not five o'clock in the morning.

Behind the glass, illuminated, were the same desserts Isaac remembered from when he worked there—baklava and cheesecake and rice pudding and cherry pie, its berries glistening hot-pink—and at the cashier's desk were the stack of *Daily News* and the toothpick dispenser, and the coffee tasted as weak and vile as ever, but there was a new waiter—Hal was gone. In the greasy vaporous kitchen were all his old friends, however, including Sancho, who pretended to ignore him in mock pique because Isaac had not been by in so long.

Although Isaac was very happy to see Sancho and Luis, he realized that whatever happened he did not want to go back to work in the Blue Sky. Leaving through the kitchen door, the coffee still hot in his stomach, he walked out onto the pier, where the early-morning light along the West Side Highway appeared so tremulously silvery, so delicate that it seemed as if the whole world had just been hatched from the thinnest of shells, and that he had no more reason for weariness or mistrust.

He decided to take the train out to Jones Beach for his last swim of the season, and that on Tuesday morning he would start a new life.

Part Four

Fourteen

Costa was like the civil engineer of a city-state that rebuilt itself six times a year. And Isaac was his assistant. Costa's job was to set up installations, which meant not just hanging pictures or painting walls, but often laying down pipes, installing false floors and ceilings. One of Aurora's shows the previous year had called for a miniature waterfall. Another involved tipping the exhibition space at a forty-five-degree angle. And Isaac, when he wasn't working, spied out the lay of the land.

On the top floor were the administrative offices, a chattering terminus of bookkeepers, secretaries, and accountants. Except for the Geblers and Andy, who came by the gallery almost every day, the world of the offices and the world of the exhibition space were separated as by an ocean. Which meant that the exhibition space, which was open Tuesdays to Saturdays, was run with an erratically zealous freedom unknown to the office, whose employees, dressed by the best department stores, arrived at nine-thirty on Monday morning and left again at six on Friday.

The first four floors were Isaac's to range in. On the ground floor were the bookshop and the coffee bar and the admissions desk, overseen by Martha, who had been at Aurora almost as long as Costa. Martha was a tall gaunt woman with dirty-blond hair. She came from a rich East Coast family and had gone to a girls' boarding school where you were allowed to keep horses, and Martha had been a champion rider until she'd discovered acid. There was a rumor around Aurora that Martha was once the mistress of a famous, now-dead rock star, and another rumor of a suicide pact gone wrong, and the doomed death-ridden legends attached to Martha had left her with cavernous eyes with dark circles under them, and an air of mild submissiveness.

Then there was Jane, who had ladders in her stockings and smudged mascara and at night was the bass guitarist in a band called Dogface and the Puking Mothers, which played at Wetlands and CBGB's. Jane ran the bar, whose chief ornament was an Italian espresso machine that looked like an early-model steam engine.

And the bookstore belonged to Ella, who like Martha came from what Costa referred to as a Good Family, although in her case it was the family that had gone bad while she had remained shell-shockedly staid. Even though she was only in her twenties, she and Costa used to talk about Old New York—the New York of the 1970s. Ella would reminisce about Sunday lunch at the Carlyle and tea at the Plaza and dancing school at the Knickerbocker on Park Avenue, and did Costa remember when Eighty-sixth Street was still Germantown, a land of beer halls and *Konditoreien* serving hot chocolate and sauerbraten, and waitresses named Lotte with hair the color of ginger ale, who'd left their homeland before the war when Germany was so poor you had to leave? And Costa, waiting politely for her to finish, would then chime in about the New York of East Village poets and underground filmmakers. Sometimes they would try to meet on common ground, such as which year Lüchow's finally closed. Eventually Isaac, who was suspicious of nostalgia, realized that Costa and Ella rehearsed these block-by-block inventories of a vanished city because time had stopped for Ella in about 1971, when her father went bankrupt and her parents divorced, and because Costa was just being kind.

Between top floor and ground floor was the exhibition space, patrolled by a small force of security guards armed with walkie-talkies, and headed by Pete, whose chief sport, when not making sure that no deranged messiah threw wet paint at the Lohenburgh, was teasing Mr. Martinez, who tended the communal garden across the street.

These were just the full-time staffers at Aurora's headquarters on Second Street—there were also the movers and packers, the neighborhood kids who came in to help out, as well as the employees of Aurora's satellite sites around town—the poetry project, the film archives, the four or five other spaces where the Geblers had installed permanent exhibitions, plus the locations in New Hampshire, upstate New York, Arizona, Nebraska, and New Jersey, of which Isaac knew little.

In the lull times, when there weren't pieces to erect or dismantle,

Isaac would make the round of his colleagues, and as he was cheerful and eager to be loved, everyone soon grew fond of him.

"How's the job?" Gebler asked him one day.

Isaac considered. "Not so demanding. Most of what people do in galleries, it turns out, is talk on the telephone, eat lunch, and try to look busy. In fact, I read a very interesting book on entomology that said that even ants, despite their reputation, spend a good deal of the day milling around, trying to look busy."

Alfred and Costa exchanged looks. "Boy, is this kid ever tactful," said Alfred. "Did *you* hire him?"

"I think it was your idea, Al."

"You mean to tell me, kiddo, you're underworked? Constantine, are you letting this ant mill around all day? Well, that's going to change. Tomorrow morning, six a.m., we'll have you reporting at the salt mines."

Isaac blushed. "I guess I put it badly. What I meant to say was how grateful I am to be working so tirelessly in the service of such a glorious cause."

Except for Costa, who was so much older that he was almost motherly, the chief difference between the frame store and Aurora wasn't the extra money, or the massive scale of the operation, but the contrast between a workplace full of women and a workplace full of men. Working with Frank and Adam had always been edgy, rivalrous. Here things were calmer, and Martha looked after them.

The only disruption was when Casey came around to supervise his upcoming "Home" show. Casey, who got fidgety staying in one place too long, was always thinking up reasons to hijack Ike, whom he considered his private assistant.

Every couple of days, Mrs. Gebler came into the gallery, sometimes to show people around, sometimes by herself to talk to Costa and to see how things looked.

Isaac looked forward to her visits, because she was often in a bad temper. He could tell that she ran at a higher temperature than other people, that every switch in her brain was on, and that operating at a hundred-percent capacity, full-time, you risked some kind of major blowout.

And precisely because she herself ran on a permanent wartime footing, she became easily infuriated by the discovery that other people were not equally alert, but just goofing off, fudging, making do.

Sometimes she asked Isaac to do things for her. She would demand with exaggerated courtesy that he pick up such-and-such a piece and put it over there—no, not there, higher—stop. No, a little to the left. Fine. Thank you. He liked her seeming astonishment that anyone so ignorant as to contemplate hanging the Joseph Beuys box fourteen inches from the ground and not eighteen could actually manage to inhale oxygen or move upright along the ground, let alone be employed by her.

One time, to his surprise, when he'd rehung a whole wall for her, she said, "Thank you, Isaac." He had had no idea that she knew his name (it was Marlene who authorized his paychecks) and wondered if she recognized that it was he who had made a fool of himself in her house after *Ajax*.

He never spoke much in return. He concentrated on obeying her silently, on making himself invisibly efficient, on guessing what she wanted before she herself knew. It was a curious discipline—he'd never tried to obey anybody before.

He found himself waiting almost unconsciously for her to come, the way a cat starts perking up before suppertime. He seemed to have a presentiment—a gnawing in the belly—of when she was about to appear, swift-footed, black eyes beneath their fierce brows racing, searching. If he was wrong, and she didn't come, he felt disappointed.

Just as in childhood he had failed to understand that his parents were married to each other, so now he refused to connect Mr. and Mrs. Gebler. Mrs. Gebler was so remote, Alfred—he was allowed to call him Alfred now—so comically accessible. Isaac often went out drinking after work with Alfred, while Mrs. Gebler remained elsewhere, in some sphere no strain of the imagination would permit him to penetrate.

Isaac was working on a series which when it came right would be a glory to behold. All fall—since he'd come to work at Aurora—he had been afever with fresh images. He had discovered that as he worked deeper, long-submerged memories surfaced. His new pictures, set in his home landscape, combined childhood fragments with episodes and symbols from the Old Testament and the Gospels.

His latest subject was a rooster. Initially, he had been thinking of the rooster whose crowing signals Peter's threefold denial, and then he had thought of his maternal grandfather, whom he had never known.

Whereas Isaac's father's family, the Hookers, had been abstemious churchgoing people of Lancashire stock, the Doucettes, his mother's family, were French Canadian hillbillies, notorious around Jessup County as prodigious drunks and petty thieves. If ever a car was stolen or a knocked-up girl abandoned, you could be sure a Doucette had done it.

Isaac's maternal grandfather died before Isaac could remember him, and his mother, a hard jaunty woman who lived for the future, rawly ambitious, was not given to reminiscence. But out of the blue Isaac had dredged up a story his father once told him about Roger Doucette.

Old Roger had worked as a young man in the mills for a time, and that was his last job. But he had various moneymaking schemes, one of which was raising chickens. Scabrous beasts, full of angry diseases, whims, which were always sneaking off, like young girls breaking curfew, to lay their eggs in places where they wouldn't be confiscated.

The Doucette house stank of chickens, Isaac's father, Sam, complained, and when young Sam came courting, Doucette would dispatch him to crawl through underbrush to retrieve their brittle, pale, still-warm secretings. "Not a dignified position for a suitor, I can tell you."

When Isaac's mother and grandmother complained about the hens, Sam continued, Doucette replied, with a wink at his daughter's beau, "They're a sight better behaved than the hens inside the house. And better looking too."

"He was an old rooster, all right," Isaac's father had said. "A mean old rooster. Cock o' the walk, for sure."

Isaac had used as his model a rooster named El Moro who lived in the co-op garden between Avenues B and C. El Moro was a resplendent bird, and after several weeks' practice, Isaac had finally figured out how to convey his jaunty carriage and lustrous sheen.

Now he was hungry for human models. This was Isaac's latest discovery: life drawing. Get out there and draw what's before your nose. Not in your head, not from a photograph—photographs flatten, that's why we're back in the age of one dimension. It sounded corny but it wasn't. It was something younger artists had been deprived of, because

136

it required intimacy rather than technology, and besides it was expensive. Going backwards was always expensive, and decent models, who knew how to hold a pose, ate up cash.

Then one day, just outside Port Authority, he'd run into Scout, his Antiguan friend from Henry Street, and Scout, a tiny man, very black-skinned, with big crooked white teeth and an intense sense of drama, had agreed to model for twenty-five dollars a day. He was posing Scout as an angel, a job Scout took to like crazy. The only trouble was getting him to stay still.

Sometimes Isaac drew Scout as an angel standing in the middle of his mom's kitchen in Gilboa, and sometimes he drew him as an angel with a sword, standing in Balaam's path. Isaac had always loved the story of Balaam, who, summoned by the pagan king Balak to curse the marching armies of Israel, finds his path barred by an angel whom his she-ass can see but not Balaam. What an adorable interplay of the farcical and the divine—from the fond scolding intimacy between prophet and she-ass, to the voluptuous climax when Balaam on the mountaintop three times opens his mouth to curse Israel's tribes and three times finds not anathema but gorgeous blessings streaming honeyed, helpless from his lips. How goodly are thy tents, O Jacob, thy tabernacles, O Israel.

He would draw the rooms of his parents' house in Gilboa, the empty rooms, in charcoal, watercolor, oil stick, and pastel, and then he would draw Scout as an angel with a flaming sword, and these drawings he would interpose with the rooster and the burning bush. The burning bush was his favorite new subject, after the rooster and the angel, even though in his present rendering it looked not aflame but merely autumnal. The model was a sumac bush from Central Park. Unlike Scout, it at least stayed still. And did not charge twenty-five dollars a peek.

When he had completed twenty, thirty drawings, Isaac would sit with the sheets of paper spread out on the floor like a landscape seen from a plane, and arrange his selections in crossword-puzzle squares, before pasting them onto a backboard. His bedroom in Gilboa, by day, by night, the kitchen, the vegetable garden, the black angel, the red rooster, the kitchen again, his father's funeral, the burning bush. Like tarot cards, almost. And charcoal bouncing off against rich violent oil stick—raw sienna, umber, violet, alizarin. Size always constrained by the straitness of his living quarters. You had to go out into the hall to get anything like a decent gawp at it.

Fifteen

IT WAS A SUNDAY AFTERNOON in early November, and Dolly and Leopold were closeted in the library, Leo's papers spread out across Dolly's desk, while Alfred took the girls off shopping.

Since her children were little, Dolly had been in the habit of over-seeing their schooling. You had to. Because New York schools, even these outrageously overpriced institutions her children went to, were so utterly inept and amoral—fraudulent, really—that you could not count on them to pay any attention whatsoever. If she could have tutored them at home—that is, if her babies weren't under the dire necessity of becoming socialized as well as literate—she would have. But school, alas, was, among other things, escape from home, and so she was forced to relinquish them, seven hours a day, to the teachers' loose and inatten-tive clutches.

In the last decade, even, she could see how the ethic of the private schools had deteriorated. When Johnny had entered kindergarten in the late seventies, the older girls—a mixture of bankers' and doctors' and lawyers' daughters—had seemed to Mrs. Gebler reassuringly scruffy and swottish. Child bluestockings, with hair in messy braids. "Status sym-bol" was a dirty word. Whereas now she could see quite clearly in her daughters and their friends the rise and triumph of a new glitziness, a false grownupness. Carlotta and her set no longer looked like normal tenth-graders but like aspiring models—Marci, Carlotta's best friend, re-sembled nothing so much as the newest wife of an elderly tycoon, all legs and yawns and designer labels. The queen of the class was no longer the girl who knew the most cantos of *Paradise Lost* by heart, but the one whose parents had a Lear jet and threw parties at Limelight, a disco-theque she forbade her daughters to go to because it was in a church and made tasteless use of crucifixes. Of course, everyone knew that children, like dogs, were snobs, but it seemed to Dolly that the field of snobbery had become depressingly straightforward.

And even in Leopold's dullish boys' school, by sixth grade the rivalry appeared to be who had amassed the most Calvin Klein and Ralph Lauren. Pathetic, this boy foppishness. They were no better, these children of privilege, than their ghetto cohorts who blew each other's brains out for a pair of sneakers: the same empty name-brand acquisitiveness, the same worship of a garbage culture.

Meanwhile, there was nobody in charge who seemed to give a damn whether you could read or write. Those thousands of dollars' tuition apparently went into the meretricious fluff of extracurricularism, into goods that impressed prospective parents and donors—videocam courses and photography darkrooms and a squash court and state-of-the-art computers—instead of smaller classes, more reading, more grammar. Mrs. Gebler, reading Leopold's teachers' comments on his papers, was appalled to find a mess of dangling modifiers and split infinitives and lazy meaningless jargon. No wonder her poor son had such trouble. Last summer he'd retaken biology and French, and already this year he'd failed a crucial social studies test. Dolly had lined up extra tutoring, but even so . . .

This afternoon, she was helping Leopold with his classics paper, which he had chosen to do about Aristotle. This, to Mrs. Gebler, summed up everything that was obscene about her children's schooling. At Leo's school, "classics" consisted not of spending seven years learning the basic elements of Latin or Greek, but rather of a few weeks reading American translations of the greatest hits—an immersion that apparently entitled an eleven-year-old to sound off about Aristotle. (In fact, Mrs. Gebler was quite certain that the chief reason Leopold had chosen Aristotle from the list of topics was that their neighbors the Blums had a tabby cat by that name.) The presumptuousness and frivolity were staggering. And Leopold naturally felt ashamed, shrank from the undeserved largeness of the task.

"What do we know about Aristotle, darling?" She had always liked Aristotle, compared to totalitarian Plato. He was more American, more pragmatic.

Leo, red and miserable, stuttered to a silence.

"Do you know anything about Aristotle's life? Where was he born?"

"He came—he came . . . I can't remember. Um . . . um . . . Where did he come from . . . from Greece?"

Mrs. Gebler felt the familiar boil of impatience rising. Down. Calm down. Don't lose your temper. "That's right, darling. Well, more specifically, Macedonia." Aristotle's grandfather had been physician to the king of Macedonia. The king of Macedonia's grandson was Alexander the Great. Aristotle, who had been Plato's student, became Alexander's teacher. A conduit between knowledge and power.

Leopold was making unhappy scratches with his pencil on the paper. The scratches weren't words so much as doodles designed to make his mother think he was taking notes. Leopold owned a box of colored Caran D'Ache pencils, each of which he kept sharpened to micro-pointiness. Leopold's class notes, fantailed across his mother's table, were a peacock's plumage of sky blue, ultramarine, bitter orange. Dolly suspected that Leopold spent so long deciding which color to use for which piece of information that he missed most of what was said in class.

"Darling, do you really need to copy down everything in a different color? Now which aspect of Aristotle did Mrs. Lambert want you to write about?"

Leopold, head lowered. Yellow pencil. Invisible writing. Silence.

"Well, you read some of the *Ethics* in class, didn't you?" Voice sharpening despite herself.

An indeterminate mumble.

"Did you like them?"

"Mmmm." Yes.

"Did you understand what he was saying?"

"Mmm." No.

"Well, maybe we might go over together what you read. Was there any particular aspect of Aristotle Mrs. Lambert wanted you to write your paper about?"

Yes.

"Which one?"

More mumbling.

"What did you say, darling?"

"She—um—she—uh—gave us a photocopy of some pages and—um—some questions for us to answer."

"Could I please see what she gave you?"

Leopold at this point became very intent upon his drawing.

"Leopold, come on. Put away those silly crayons. I'd like to see what she wants you to write about."

"I don't have it."

"You don't have your homework assigment? Where is it?"

"I left it at school." Head ducked low.

Mrs. Gebler's fingers began drumming the desk. She got up and paced the room, trying not to speak till she had calmed down. But could not remain silent. "For Christ's sake, Leopold," she burst out. "Every single time you have a test or paper due, you come home from school empty-handed. Will you please tell me what's going through your head? Are you determined to fail every course? What are we going to do with you? Your paper is due tomorrow."

She went and stared out the window. And by the time they'd gone around to the school to see if they could chase up the janitor to let them in to retrieve Leopold's Aristotle assignment . . . It was her fault. She should have asked Ernestine to check as soon as Leopold got home Friday afternoon that he had brought everything he needed for the weekend.

She turned around and saw Leopold, head lowered, kicking the desk leg hard with his toe. Telltale sign. Next, a small muffled sound. Relenting, Mrs. Gebler rushed across the room and, kneeling before her son, bundled him into her arms, pressing his head tight against her chest. She covered him in guilty kisses, while he sobbed. "Sweetheart, sweetheart, don't cry." But by now he was convulsed by sobs.

When he had subsided, they agreed to break for an hour and sort out Aristotle later in the day. She gave him one last kiss and straightened his sweater, which had gotten hiked up over his pudgy stomach. "Let's go see what's in the kitchen. Shall we have some tea?"

"We baked a cake," said Leo, and now a note of self-composure, even pride, had crept into his voice.

"Who did?"

"Me and Ernestine. Yesterday afternoon. A coconut cake. With, you know, coconut icing."

"Yummy . . ."

Ernestine was retiring next month: she'd bought herself a house and some land back in Trinidad and was planning to lord it over her home village, terrorize the aunts and brothers and sisters and nephews she'd been supporting all these years. And who would take over from Ernestine? Carmen, whom Leopold already adored, could certainly stand in till Dolly found someone who spoke decent English. Ernestine had been wonderful when the children were little, but now they needed someone younger, more cultured. She had meant to ask her secretary, Jamie, if Jamie's niece, who had a graduate degree in education, was still looking for a job. Sad. Sad that Ernestine was leaving. Leopold had barely been able to crawl when Ernestine had come to work for them. . . .

"Do you want some cake?"

"I'm afraid I do."

"It turned out kinda burnt on one side, but we covered it in the icing."

They moved out to the kitchen, Leopold still shaken.

"I wonder what it's like out at Goose Neck," said Dolly, bringing cups and teapot from the pantry.

And Leopold, who alone in the family loved the house on Long Island as much as she, brightened instantly. He was a country child. He should have been brought up scooping for oysters in the creek and tending his vegetable garden. Going off in the mornings to the local junior high. This New York competitive hustle, which affected even eleven-year-olds, was not for him.

"Do you think the leaves are up still, darling?"

"I guess so. Unless it's rained too bad."

"Mr. West told me the nights have been below freezing this week. I wonder if we could sneak out there for a few days before Thanksgiving." (They were planning to go out to Chicago for Thanksgiving, to see Dolly's mother, who was recovering from a broken hip.) "Would you like that, darling? Shall we try to go out to Goose Neck next weekend, just the two of us?"

Leopold nodded, eyes shining.

It had always been the Geblers' habit to split up the children occasionally, giving each separate treats. Dolly remembered well her own childish frustration at never getting her parents alone, but being regarded as part of an indivisible trinity, invoked by her father as object of his hard work and sacrifices. It was only once Dolly had shown an interest in the fine arts that she had won a little free time with her father, a privilege her sisters never earned. She had been determined not to make the same mistake with her babies. But without realizing it, Dolly was duplicating her father's habit of rewarding the child who shared his own tastes.

Sixteen

Sunday afternoon in Brooklyn, a shiny blue November day with the sky gleaming like a scrubbed china mug and the white light—a transparent, silvery light New York had on its better days—tripping along the sidewalk, tickling the eyelids of babies in their carriages, and the high wind whisking away the last rumpled leaves from the trees. The wind along the Brighton Beach boardwalk animating old newspaper, plastic bags, into fierce rodents, scurrying mammals seized by fits of dancing. The high wind that scours your heart pure, rids you of the stored-up sourness and defeat. The high wind from the North.

Isaac and Casey and Casey's friend Gina were out in Brighton Beach, enjoying the fine fall weather. Gina was a powerful-looking black girl with greenish eyes and a mop of bleached blond hair, and Isaac found himself peeking at her with the surreptitious raptness of a man looking over someone else's shoulder at a pinup magazine. Not that there was anything dirty about Gina, she was splendid, and in any case well accustomed to being gaped at.

That morning, Isaac, who the previous night had begun an oil painting on tin of the rooster, had stuck his head round the canvas that blocked his window, peeked skywards up the air shaft to claim the guileless blue, and realized he didn't want to work. It was one of Casey's charms that if you felt like a frolic, Casey was the first thing you thought of. Consequently, after his second cup of coffee, third squint at what he'd done the night before—equivocal—and four quick games of chess outside the Public Library, Isaac at eleven a.m. had found himself ringing the bell of the apartment on Fifteenth Street. Emma, Casey's lawyer girlfriend, was out of town, but there in the sunny kitchen instead was this sprawled pantheress, lapping up milky coffee and daintily picking apart French crullers from a box of Dunkin' Donuts while watching the morning cartoons. And Casey, happily, was watching her.

"This is Gina," explained Casey, and so evidently it was. "Gina knows all about you, Ike—remember, Gina, this is my college buddy who works with me now at Aurora."

Gina licked her thumb of the last residue of sugar icing, while regarding Isaac. "That old rat trap. You look like you work at Aurora."

"How come?" said Isaac. "First time I went there asking for a job they didn't seem to think I looked like I worked there."

"I don't know. Someone in that place got a thing for well-fed blond boys. Who's that other one you introduced me to?"

"Andy," said Casey.

"Oh, Andy."

Isaac put his feet up on the counter and started reading the paperback he'd picked up on the street for fifty cents: Arthur Waley's translations of Chinese poetry. "Listen to this," he said.

> "My people have married me
> In a far corner of earth:
> Sent me away to a strange land,
> To the king of the Wu-sun.
> A tent is my house,
> Of felt are my walls;
> Raw flesh my food
> With mare's milk to drink.
> Always thinking of my own country,
> My heart sad within.
> Would I were a yellow stork
> And could fly to my old home!"

"What's that?" Gina asked, mollified.

"It's a lament, written in 110 B.C. by a Chinese princess married off to a Central Asian nomad."

Casey, it turned out, had a project for the day. Casey these days was very goal-oriented. No longer did he sit around on a weekend watching the Knicks game—now he was always heading off to the Brooklyn Museum to look at their Egyptian collection or investigating a Gypsy community out in Flushing. Last week he had asked Isaac if they could go track down some of his former associates from Henry Street to make a video for the "Home" show. Isaac, gruffly, had refused.

Today Casey wanted to go out to Brighton Beach, to Little Odessa, where the latest wave of Russian émigrés had settled. All fall the Soviet bloc had been disintegrating, and even here, in faraway America, you felt exhilarated shock waves. It was the end of communism, the end of the Cold War, and Casey wanted to see how the new immigrants were taking it. "Besides," he said, "there are some awesome restaurants out there." Casey was feeling expansive, having just been told by a dealer friend that the painting his friend Danuta Schomberg had given him five years ago was now worth fifteen thousand dollars. "Man, we are going to get us some fish eggs and *splurge*."

They had climbed into Casey's Jeep and barrelled across the Brooklyn Bridge, past the silent shipyards and along the rim of the Belt Parkway, past the Verrazano Bridge, past the faded Ferris wheels and water slides and aquarium of Coney Island, and parked near the sea. Brighton Beach in the rapid dancing autumnal sunlight—leather-jacketed men with gold teeth playing dominoes on the boardwalk, strolling women in leopard-skin skirts tight and shiny as a mermaid's scales, old ladies in furs sitting on benches, staring out to Europe. The scent of knishes and steamed sausage. Exile. Cyrillic.

When the boardwalk got too cold, they hiked over to Brighton Beach Avenue to Primorskii, a Georgian nightclub aglitter with mirrored lights, each table laden with twin bottles of vodka and Pepsi-Cola. Automobile-sized speakers wailing a song whose English-language lyrics went, "A million million million scarlet roses." The restaurant jammed full of families with fat pallid children.

"Man, it's just like Moscow," said Casey, who had been to Russia on a high-school exchange program. "What do they want to come to America for, just to listen to that same crappy music they had at home?"

"I don't think people move five thousand miles because they don't like the music," protested Isaac.

Casey poured the Stolichnaya. "To life."

Gina, it turned out, drank only Pepsi.

"To the land of the free."

"To dollars, more like it."

"To the end of the Cold War. To happiness."

"And riches and fame."

"To Gina."

The vodka rough but clean in Isaac's throat. The flash of a neighboring customer's teeth, two rows of gold. And tattoos on every knuckle, waving hi to the blue angel on Casey's shoulder.

"These Russians, man, they may still be listening to that shitty music, but they are glomming onto the American dream like nobody's business," Casey pronounced. "You never seen such natural-born tycoons. Soon as they get rid of that Marxist-Leninist crap, you'll see."

"God, I wouldn't be in such a hurry to get rid of a system with free education, free health care," said Gina. "They want to be like us, where people starve in the streets or get shoved in prison because they're the wrong color?"

"Man, there everybody's poor, and the whole fucking country's a prison. You wait and see, Isaac, there's gonna be a bridge between Siberia and Alaska good as the Golden Gate, and they'll be running IBM and General Motors in no time."

"I doubt it," said Isaac. "communism's harder than that to get out of the blood. Seventy years of lying and being lied to, that long stultifying culture of intimidation and evasion . . . Remember, the Third Reich only lasted twelve years, and that took military defeat and denazification, plus the Marshall Plan, to get the country back to normal."

"If you call Germany normal . . ."

"Hey, people adapt faster now."

Casey ordered. Plates and plates of food, pickled and skewered and broiled and pressed and fried. Lamb kebab and cheese pie and caviar and chicken with walnut preserves and smoked sturgeon and eggplant salad and unleavened bread. And Isaac stuffed his face till he was full, while the other two flirted and squabbled.

Winter in the air, bringing an almost physiological grief that could only be assuaged by gorging on hot food, human voices. Every day now, he passed bundled bodies huddled under a bridge, cardboard encampments with shopping carts, outstretched cups propping up handwritten signs proclaiming the author a Vietnam vet, AIDS victim, released mental patient. Hungry. Cold. Sick. Unemployed. Far from home.

"Where you going for Thanksgiving, Ike?"

Isaac, startled, wiped his glasses. "To the Blue Sky Diner, I guess.

They cook a hot turkey sandwich that makes you radiant with thankful-
ness to've been hatched on American shores. How about you?"

"I'm going back to Cambridge. Gotta check out my dad's new girlfriend. Why don't you come too? My dad loves you. I guess he doesn't
know you very well." Casey's father was a poet, a follower of Lowell's.

"I have to work," said Isaac. "What are you doing, Gina? Are you an
orphan, too?"

"She's not an orphan—her old man owns half of Haiti."

"You're so full of it, Casey. What are you shooting your mouth
about now?"

"Your rich daddy, hon."

"My rich daddy, *hon*, is a sociology teacher. How's that for rich?"

"Yeah, he just happens to deal in oil and elephant tusks on the side."

"They don't have oil and elephants in Haiti, they just have AIDS
and secret police," Isaac intervened. "My father was a teacher, too. So
are you going to go to Haiti?"

"What Haiti? I haven't seen my dad since I was fifteen years old.
Anyway, Thanksgiving isn't my holiday."

"We just had your holiday, Gina—Halloween," Casey teased.

After leaving the Primorskii—Isaac and Casey having almost succeeded in polishing off the Stolichnaya between them—they wandered
back to the beach in the high wind. The two boys stood watching while
Gina danced down to the gray water's edge, dipping one toe into the
snarling foam, before retreating. A dimpled grin on her face.

"She's something, isn't she?" said Casey.

"She's beautiful."

"She's a wild animal. And she doesn't let me get away with anything."

"I think letting you court her while you're living with another
woman is letting you get away with plenty."

"Aaah, she doesn't want me full-time. God forbid . . ." said Casey, as
a wet-footed Gina came running up to join them.

Back in Manhattan, they dropped Gina at a friend's house on
Ninety-sixth Street. Riding down Central Park West, the afternoon light
fleeing and the air glacial now that the sun was gone. At the bottom of
the park, the craggy silver-and-gold of the fine hotels, the office towers—
all those etched and jostling peaks of prowess and success. Capitalism.

The Hitachi sign telling you it was 38 degrees and time to get back indoors.

"Pleasant day," Isaac said. Looking with grudging affection at Casey's sculptured head, the way his small ears clung to the skull, the crow's-feet around the eyes, the faint scowl now of concentration—near-sighted, and too lazy to wear lenses. His friend. It was the first Sunday in months Isaac hadn't worked. The liquor was wearing off, and he felt ex-hausted suddenly by the day's festiveness, the glittering mirrors, the spiced meats, the lovely girl, the fat Russian children, the confusion of having been reminded what he—and they—had come to New York to find. Exhausted, and at the same time not wanting it to end.

"Where shall we go now?" asked Casey.

"I guess I'll go home."

"Which street are you on?" Casey glanced at his watch. "Maybe I'll come up for a minute. If I can find a parking place. I still got time to kill before my next appointment."

Isaac panic-stricken.

"What's the matter, man? You can give me a cup of tea and show me your pictures."

And it was as simple as that. The first person except for Melissa whom Isaac allowed to see his work, the first visitor to his apartment ex-cept for models. Not that he exactly allowed Casey. Casey simply bull-dozed in, under the assumption that everyone felt just as pleased by his company as he did.

Seventeen

DOLLY, HAVING FETCHED Leo's homework from school and having made a start on Aristotle's vision of the good life, had taken a moment to finish a letter to her mother. It was almost dark out, and she couldn't think of what to write. Although the week had been a frenzy of appointments, dinners, meetings, nothing had happened that would amuse the old lady. No residue. Just anxiety and a fretful weariness in the bones, a desire to stop.

Yesterday morning Dolly had gone to see Jesse, who had been feeling too godawful from the medication to put up any pretenses at conversation. Left her wondering, as usual, why she—forty-six years old and with little to offer the world—was so vulgarly robust, while he, barely thirty and riven by intelligence and desire and ambition, was about to go. Kicking and screaming all these months, but finally now subdued by the nausea his medication caused. And Michael's face a mask of obstinate gentleness, having long ago accepted with pride, even, the transformation from lover to nurse. Not exactly a subject she could raise in a letter to her mother, who regarded homosexuality itself as a disease.

That night they were going to dinner at the Bishops'—an invitation Dolly had accepted months ago, knowing she would regret it when the time came. The fall season was going full swing, and they were booked five nights a week till Christmas. She felt trapped every time she glanced at her Filofax and saw the pale gray weeks ahead already fenced in, darkened by engagements that should not have been accepted and once accepted could not be broken. Lunatic how one's days became a web of imaginary obligations manufactured to distract one from one's true callings. When on a Sunday night all she wanted to do was be home with the children, not piling into a penthouse in Beekman Place for yet another evening of art gossip—everyone buzzing over the upcoming auctions and whether it was true that Piero Ancona had stolen Vince Newman from the Lunar Gallery with a half-a-million-dollar bonus.

Walking around SoHo, you smelled the tall money in the streets. The other day, as she was coming out of a show at Mary Boone, someone, leaning out the window of a double-parked BMW, had called her name. It had taken her a moment to recognize Walter Corman, formerly a mousy little sculptor who taught at a girls' school in Brooklyn. Nice to see you, Dolly, I don't often get to the city these days. Where are you living now, Walter? Oh, I got a ranch out in Montana, next to—here he named a famous Hollywoood producer. I just couldn't take the New York rat race.

This was the reason Dolly was curious about tonight: Jim Arnold, who was now working as a private dealer after his ouster from the Contemporary, was sure to be there, and she wanted to sound him out about a Rothko she had her eye on.

Jason and Elena Goodman were putting up their collection at Sotheby's, and on Friday afternoon Dolly for the second time had stopped by to look at their Rothko. It was a beautiful thing from 1951, steeped in color like bull's blood, that ran from a plummy purple-black up to flame orange. In the late sixties—when Rothko was still alive—she had tried to persuade her father to buy one of his paintings, but he thought the price too high. Back then a Rothko went for fifty thousand. Now Sotheby's estimate—available only on request—was $1 million. Would they get it? she wondered. If she missed this chance, there wouldn't be another. But could she afford it? And who else was interested?

Every collector is a Don Giovanni, lust quickened by love of the chase. Try as she might, for the last twenty-four hours she'd been able to think of little else but those radiant bands of dark soaked heat. Now, as if switching from Don Giovanni to his half-protesting, half-succumbing Zerlina, she'd told herself, I mustn't, the price will be too high. *Vorrei ma non vorrei*, I mustn't lose my head. I won't even go to the auction. I must put it out of my mind.

But the picture pulsated in her brain, and when she'd gone back to Sotheby's a third time on the way uptown from seeing Jesse, who'd told her, Buy it, buy it, the canvas was every bit as mysterious and darkly resplendent as she'd remembered.

Of course, she could drum up justification: it was important for their collection. And with prices way beyond the museums' budgets, it had become almost a patriotic duty to buy American, keep our artistic heritage at home and visible. If Dolly didn't snag the Rothko, it would get whisked off to the boardroom of some Japanese bank, and no one would ever see it again. But then she thought of how much a Rothko would hike up Aurora's insurance, and groaned.

While her pen was hovering over the half-written letter to her mother, with its banal awkward news, she heard her husband creep into the room almost on tiptoe, grab something from the closet, and start to sneak away again.

"Are you going out?" Dolly asked over her shoulder. "It's almost seven. You know we were asked for eight."

Alfred, coat in hand, looked undisguisedly agog.

"You do remember, don't you, that we're going to the Bishops' tonight?" As he started to protest his ignorance, she cut him off. "I've told you a million times. We just talked about it yesterday morning."

"No, we didn't. I thought we were staying home with the children."

"If you thought we were staying home, then how come you're about to go out? They asked us ages ago." As if an invitation of a month ago exerted a claim more absolute than last week's.

For a moment Mr. and Mrs. Gebler glared at each other. Then Dolly spoke. "Tell her you'll meet her after dinner."

Alfred threw his coat on the bed, leaving the door half-open as he stalked out. For a moment, stomach knots tightening, she thought he was leaving; then she heard the sound of the bathwater running, and relief turned to annoyance. For Alfred, once ensconced in the tub, was translated to pure algae, became a mass of marine vegetable matter. You could get from New York to Boston in less time than it took Alfred to get out of the bath. Her husband, lolling in perfumed water, like a great white slug. And now they'd be late, by the time she'd taken a bath herself, and the letter still unwritten, stuck in a lame description of the weather, and everything on her mind unsayable.

The fall auctions did in fact bring in more than even the keenest speculators had dreamed of. The estimated prices were in many cases exceeded doublefold, and the collectors and dealers were euphoric. Dolly, at the opening night of the contemporary sales at Christie's, watching men in black tie vie to pay millions for acquisitions that struck her as dubious, felt almost frightened. It was the floor of the stock exchange at the outbreak of war, a circus complete with paparazzi and closed-circuit television. Even Joseph Beuys hit a new record, when Benoit Goldschmidt bought his *Backrest for a Fire-Limbed Person, Hare Type* for $375,000. The Geblers, infected too by the buying frenzy, ended up with two smaller Beuys pieces—a pair of hair clippers wrapped in felt and two bronze bones bound by rubber in a box.

But Dolly, who then went on to Sotheby's with Emanuele Conti, did not get her Rothko. From the very start it was clear that there were two interested buyers—one was Jim Arnold, acting for Daniel Altschuler, and the other a mystery telephone bidder—who were willing to pay any amount. In a matter of minutes, it was out of Aurora's league, and Dolly, disgusted that Jim had not told her he was an interested party when she had quizzed him the other night, dropped out at $1.5 million.

Now the real battle commenced. Tension so high that the room fell quiet except for the lithe auctioneer's teasing. How briskly, with what an instinct for pace, he reeled his twin fish from million to million. Gasps from the audience as Jim, then telephone bidder, telephone bidder, then Jim, bellied up to the bait, higher and higher. The auctioneer sprightly. Jim expressionless, with Daniel Altschuler like a devil at his shoulder. Up and up, higher and higher, till telephone bidder lost courage and broke free, returning to the sunless depths, and the painting was Altschuler's, for $3.5 million—plus Sotheby's commission.

Then, round the room, a burst of awed applause for Altschuler. An uproar. As if spending your father's money were an athletic feat.

And Dolly, over a plate of pasta at Palio with Emanuele, meditated on her loss and wondered, Was the Rothko worth it? Artists themselves—the matter-of-fact ones—always told you that a painting was only worth as much as its sale price, but even so she could not but believe that there was something like a true level in each age and that today's prices were unnatural. A one-bedroom apartment in Manhattan was not worth $250,000, and nor was a Rothko worth $3.5 million. But Emanuele, who went to dinner once a week at the Altschulers', told her not to be a prude.

All in all, the fall auctions at Sotheby's and Christie's brought in a new record for contemporary art, and the art world was overjoyed.

The day after the Rothko, Dolly picked up Leo from school and drove him out to the country for a long weekend.

Clear light, serene banks of clouds tinged with blue-gray. Isaac, sitting on a park bench in Union Square, watched a mother and daughter waiting at the curb for the traffic light to turn green. The child, maybe eight or nine years old, gesticulating, angry. The mother, a sweet imploring expression on her face, holding out her hand to the little girl. But the little girl, refusing to take it, shoved her own hands deep into the pockets of her parochial-school blazer. Isaac felt, for a moment, crushed by the look of helpless hurt on the face of the mother, who still stretched out her hand, hoping in vain for the answering clasp of those little fingers. He remembered an identical look of hurt on his father's face when a teenaged Isaac, drunk on school prizes, already planning his escape into the real world of cities and fame, first began to cold-shoulder him, to condescend.

On Thanksgiving Day, Isaac had stopped by Costa's place. He liked going to see Costa, who lived in a big room on Jane Street. Costa had fed him enchiladas and told him about the tiny pair of hair clippers by Joseph Beuys that Dolly and Alfred had bought at auction for fifteen thousand dollars. Isaac was scandalized.

What was the matter with people? How could an artist in his right mind wrap a pair of hair clippers in felt and think he'd added something to the sum of human knowledge? How frivolous and crabbed could one get? And why hadn't contemporary artists addressed themselves more assiduously to world events?

The old painters Isaac admired had taken upon themselves the largest social questions. Géricault, chronicling Napoleon's Russian campaign, had revealed the futility of war. Later, his portraits of caged lunatics, by forcing you to acknowledge their subjects' overpowering individuality, made you revolt against the inhuman conditions of their lodgment. Even artists plying, within the constraints of church commissions, a fixed repertoire of saints and miracles conveyed political points: for some, the evangelists were shrewd men of the world, companions to bishops, popes, and donors; for some they were blacksmiths, beggars, hired hands. Whether Saint Peter was in broadcloth or brocade was a message as to how to live one's life. And van Gogh could make one broken shoe preach a gospel of universal brotherhood, demanding that both he and his subject be loved *as is*, all gnarled, humpbacked, wormy.

But why had twentieth-century painters—except for the communists like Picasso or Diego Rivera—avoided world war, the concentration camps, poverty, revolution, dictatorships?

Costa had had a very simple, if interested, answer. Those earlier painters Isaac mentioned were modern men using whatever means were at their disposal. Were they alive today, they would be filmmakers. Because movies were a far more effective medium for battles, crowds, history, or polemics than paint. How Tarkovsky had rendered the Mongol invasion of Russia in *Andrei Rublev* or Rossellini the Nazi occupation in *Open City* would have been corny, heavy-handed on a contemporary canvas. (Only cartoonists–stationary moviemakers–had found a sly way of dealing with politics and history.)

Isaac had been stumped. Of course Costa was right. But if film had really taken over so many of painting's customary tasks, then artists of the still image should confine themselves to doing what could be done only in pencil or paint. And what was that?

All day he had been puzzling, as he tried to paint his rooster. The answers he'd come up with were unsatisfactory, and his inability to solve the picture's background–a scrappy urban Garden of Eden– became one in his mind with his inability to justify his own work, which God knows no one could accuse of having any social relevance. Why paint roosters in a world bursting with sin and sorrow?

Now, sitting under the plane tree in Union Square, watching the vendors from the farmers' market load tubs of unsold apples back into their vans and remembering how he and his brother, Turner, around this time of year used to help the Ostriches pick orchardsful of Macouns and Jonathans and Northern Spies, Isaac understood. What he was setting out to do was show how revelation impinged on ordinary life, to cast light on those little rents in the veil of the everyday through which we escape into, catch glimpses of, the Other World. Of God. He was learning to paint in a way that showed the faith, the tenderness, the suffering in things. To capture the inner radiance. Which meant learning how to see with the heart's inward eye. Painting to make people believe.

Eighteen

"I DIDN'T TELL YOU I finally went to see Polya yesterday–no, not yesterday, Tuesday," Dolly said, over the noise of running water. They were

cooking dinner, several days after returning from Thanksgiving at Norwood.

Dolly had dreaded this last visit to her mother. It was too wretched,
the way old age had colonized the proud woman. Most days Dolly had
sat reading aloud to her in the library-turned-sickroom—a room Dolly
remembered chiefly as the place where the Diehl daughters' beaux were
obliged to have a drink with their father, until the girls, done primping,
descended. The smell of sickness where once you sniffed whisky, old
leather, her father's cigars, teen-aged suitors' nervous brilliantine. Saddest of all, the garden was running to seed without Mrs. Diehl's supervi-
sion. Dolly, remembering her childhood's stately company of gardeners
and cooks and butlers and kitchen maids and chauffeurs and nannies,
now found the house quite ghostly.

The servants. They were an extinct breed, those men who knew how
to espalier quinces and women who knew how to darn, who either
didn't have mates and children of their own or were prepared to sacri-
fice them to the service. Brides not of Christ but of the rich. Well, the
rich, worst luck, would always be with us, but who—which new rasher of
the world's poor—was going to wait on them?

Dolly's mother, reduced in her old age to a round-the-clock sprinkling of giddy young nurses who did little more than heat up TV dinners, in undemocratic moments sometimes let out a sigh for people
who knew how to polish silver or wait on table properly. What Dolly
missed, however, was not the handiwork but the stories. How much of
her family's self-confirming histories had been manufactured, preserved,
passed on backstairs—by Waggon, who had first come to work for
Dolly's great-grandmother Mrs. Albertson, or by Grace, a latecomer
who had only arrived in '40 but eventually clocked up a memorious
thirty-five years of Diehl doings? In whose but Grace's or Caddie's
imagination would Cousin Arthur, who'd got so tipsy he'd driven his
mother's Packard right through the icehouse, live on so gay and bold
and commanding? Or Mrs. Diehl's long succession of terriers, from Flo,
who had a circus seal's talent for scarfing up joints of beef ledged on
sideboards four times her height, to Gordon, who became so flatulent
he had to be kept out in the stables, to Rag, whom Dolly's father once
sicced on a creepy boyfriend of Beatrice's?

And as for the Geblers, Dolly wondered, who would remember

their stories? Who would there be to memorize the miserable procession of unsuitable suitors that soon would be calling for Johnny and Carlotta or to turn into merry epic Leopold's first souse?

Her mother was clearly so fragile that it was wrenching to say goodbye. Abandoning her to that rancid regimen of daytime television, Dolly felt as dastardly as Mrs. Diehl herself must have felt long ago, bundling her daughter onto the train back east to boarding school at the end of vacation.

Alfred had been an angel. Helped straighten out Lusandra, who was always picking fights with Mittie. Even suffered his unbearable brother-in-law Edwin's business advice.

"I can't hear you while the sink's running," said Alfred. "You went where?"

"I went to visit Polya on Tuesday."

"You went to see Polya, huh?" Alfred raised his eyebrows, maliciously intrigued. "No kidding. How's the old tart, anyway?" Polya was the widow of Dolly's first love, the violinist Elkanan Grinspan. It was a visit Dolly had been postponing since the summer.

After all these years Dolly still felt uneasy with the ancient blinking redhead—the great man's widow, Alfred called her. "You know about the widows of great men," Alfred said. "Doesn't matter how many girls he fucked, or loved, or tried to leave her for: she's still the wife."

Had Elkanan played around much? How I miss him, Dolly thought: the avid pallor, the big glasses and long antenna-fingers, jerky motion, high clear demon-clever sound—the shining glee of him, the gladness. Miraculously undiminished by the bitter women who loved him.

Sometimes she felt as if there were getting to be more dead people she loved than live ones. Perhaps it was the balance tipping far enough in the dead's favor—when everyone you cared about was in the grave and only the pipsqueaks were left walking the streets—that reconciled you to dying, like one of those parties you don't much want to go to, where the hostess calls up and says, But so-and-so and so-and-so and so-and-so—all your best friends—will be there. Nobody fun left alive.

Alfred, strangely, was jealous of Elkanan. The never-quite-answered question: Had she or hadn't she?

"How's tricks?"

"Well, she's still after me about the recital of Elkanan's work. I've

got to do something, I suppose. They're issuing a new recording–
Deutsche Grammophon. All Bartók."

"That's nice. What else did she have to say?"

"She was talking about their youth in Vilna–very cynical, incidentally, about Baltic independence. She said last time was just a fight over
who got to beat up the Jews–the Lithuanians or the Poles. All the political sects–the Bundists and the Zionists and the communists and God
knows what else. She'd had a pro-Bolshevik boyfriend she was crazy
about, before Elkanan. Couldn't figure out how anybody could be indifferent to politics, the way we are here. She said coming to America
where nobody lived in history was like moving to a country without
weather." Now Dolly tried to imitate Polya Grinspan but gave up. "She
told me she'd always stayed a Labor Zionist, after sixty years in America.
I felt rather envious of her . . . belief."

"What do you want to believe in? Bundism? That would be timely."
Gebler, amused by his wife's not realizing she was a believer.

"Oh, I don't know–God . . . or man. But God, it seems, doesn't
really need our help, and man's impossible, out of the question. The
answer is, I don't know."

"Only misanthropists believe in man in the aggregate. I think I read
that somewhere."

"Aren't I a misanthropist?" she asked, a little coyly.

"Yes, you are."

She balked now, wanting to bend the harsh judgment. A lot of people considered her a philanthropist. "But there are plenty of people I
love. . . ."

"Name 'em."

"Costa. Martha. Ernestine. The Wests. The children."

"Sometimes."

"No, always."

"When they're good."

"No, always."

"And I don't think people you pay count."

"I don't know any people I don't pay," she deadpanned, uncustomarily frivolous.

Gebler shook a warning finger at her. "You're asking for it, my lady.
Watch your step. You are treading on *very* thin ice. Anyway, speaking of
people you pay . . . I think you ought to give Isaac a studio visit."

She looked so mystified that Gebler mimicked thick glasses and a funny walk. "Remember? Isaac, your favorite employee?"

Mrs. Gebler, who was chopping onions, stopped midslice. "*Why*? I didn't even know he was an artist."

"Yes, your human curiosity really is stunning."

"A studio visit," she wondered to herself, trying to decode this strange request, and concluded that Alfred must be using Isaac to get him girls. "Oh damn, I knew I'd forgot something—the pancetta. How could I have been so stupid? I walked right past Zabar's this afternoon."

"That's okay—we've got regular bacon, don't we? Talk to Casey about his work—Casey's pretty enthusiastic. He even wanted to sneak Isaac in the 'Home' show."

"Have you seen anything he's done?"

"Just Polaroids."

She slid the olive oil—wonderfully green—around the skillet, and pitched in one fingernail-scrap of onion to see if the oil was hot enough. She pictured Isaac and tried to reconcile the image—a big brute with chubby hands that waved in the air when he talked—with artistic talent. She didn't quite believe it, but prepared herself mentally just in case. It was like looking at a flat ugly landscape and being told that it contained mineral or oil reserves.

"I have to admit I was intrigued—from as much as you can tell from a Polaroid. It's not our kind of stuff, by any means, but I think you'd find it interesting, nonetheless." Gebler was always accusing his wife of being too doctrinaire and narrow.

"Well, maybe," she said dubiously. Unlike Alfred, who loved nothing better than to poke around painters' lofts shmoozing, Dolly was made uncomfortable by studio visits. Some childhood residue of feeling you had to say something polite about what you were shown—plus the inhibiting knowledge that the artist was praying for you to be his big break. All the more awkward if you had to face the person back in the office the next day. And how did Alfred know the man even *wanted* her to see his work? Wasn't it presumptuous to suggest point-blank to your employee, I'm going to barge into your apartment to look at your pictures and you are expected to be very honored? Like those stories of Oriental kings showing up unannounced in some peasant's house—the involuntary host obviously knowing if he didn't look thrilled he'd get garrotted. "If you really think it's necessary, maybe you should go instead."

"He'd be more pleased if it were you."

Mrs. Gebler reflected. The more she thought about it, the more awkward it seemed. But since Alfred had asked her to, for whatever reason, it stuck in her head, like a telephone call one puts off from day to day.

Costa had asked Isaac to deliver some paintings uptown to the Geblers' apartment. An Agnes Martin retrospective out in Cleveland had just closed; two paintings had come from the Geblers' private collection. "Take the Black Maria," Costa said. The Black Maria was the foundation's station wagon. Isaac, who had never bothered to tell Costa that he didn't have a driver's license, grabbed the car keys and headed off in high spirits.

It was a rainy winter day. Early December, and the whole world exploding into revolution. A week after Isaac's trip to Brighton Beach with Casey and Gina, the Berlin Wall had come down, and now, for the first time, Isaac felt as if he were living in the most exciting era in human history. Every morning you opened up the newspaper and there, the Poles had thrown out the communist generals and Lech Wałesa was running the government. In Hungary, a free republic had been declared. In Berlin, hundreds of thousands of East Germans were flooding through to the West. The Bulgarians, too. An autumn of freedom. Freedom, dear and exultant. Soon there would be no more tyranny in the East, no more walls. And the Soviet Union just standing by, shrugging. Yesterday Isaac had gone out and bought a tape of *Fidelio* and blasted sky-high its hymn to liberation. The scene in which the prisoners were released, as always, made him cry.

He felt more optimistic now than when he and Casey had argued out at Brighton Beach. Yes, it would take time to convert ex-slaves to citizens, and many would keep hankering after those government-dole fleshpots. But what a glorious undertaking! And how could the West best welcome these brave newcomers to the free world? Didn't it make our own institutions look a little shopworn, in need of brightening to be worthy of people who had fought so hard to partake of them?

Isaac felt as if he too were among the sprung prisoners. For much of his life, he'd been down a deep pit, hearing other people's feet march over his head, craning up at the patch of unreachable blue. For the first time since his father died, for the first time since he'd left Gilboa, Isaac was almost lighthearted. Now he was no longer too much of a basket case to buy a loaf of bread, a cup of coffee, no longer an outcast, no longer insane. Now he had joined the lit world and as a consequence felt strong as an ox, heart pounding with love, ready for anything.

Isaac raced next door to the garage, skipping through a puddle which soaked his thin canvas sneakers, letting in the wet through the hole in each toe, and snuffing up joyously the smells released by the downpour: the smell of soaked sidewalks, the doggy smell of damp hair and wet wool. Of earth, even. He had always liked rain better than any other kind of weather. He had first learned to draw on rainy days, on the tin surface of his mother's kitchen table—page after page of crayoned battlements and turrets. Because the gray smoked out colors keener, because the slick surfaces and puddles refracted light and created odd reflections, gray-brown landscapes, rain was a painter's magnifying glass. The sky as seen by a puddle.

He watched the men and women who had been caught in the storm huddling under awnings, and in doorways, as if a group of timid children were playing Prisoners' Base. From the drainpipe of a funeral home, the rain was gushing forth in torrents. Gutters became rivers.

Sailing up the West Side Highway, he felt like a seaman whose tugboat was breasting, dividing the waters. Across the river, the wooded bluffs of the Palisades were blurry against the darker yellow-gray of sky (the yellowness like the pus in a wound), against the gunmetal dullness of the water. It was raining so hard, now, that it had become dark as nighttime, the thunderclouds had squeezed the light from the sky, and rain came bouncing up off the road, even as high as his windshield. He passed the neon glare of the Blue Sky Diner, which appeared like a Noah's ark in the flood. Truly we were living in the world after the flood, with everything to be re-created from scratch. Freedom, freedom, he sang to himself. And how to be worthy of it, the East's liberation.

> *Blush from West to East*
> *Blush from East to West*
> *Till the West is East*
> *Blush it thro' the West.*

What was that silly ditty? Oh, Tennyson, from *Maud*. The first winter he and Agnes had lived together, he'd read her *Maud* two evenings running. Freedom, and with it, the menace of a hundred new wars. For how was it that just as the new was being born, history was also simultaneously running backwards, as if communism had preserved the East in aspic, had left a dozen nations of clockwork soldiers reanimated, just where they had left off, mid-battle? As if the Ottoman and Austro-Hungarian empires had suddenly been revived in their sectarian prides and hatreds, Armenians warring with Azeri Turks, Georgians killing Ossetians, Albanians glaring at Greeks, Romanians lambasting Hungarians.

And us, what will we do without Them to eyeball? Because freedom can only be self-aware in opposition to unfreedom, otherwise it's just daily life, how to pay your bills and what to eat for breakfast.

Exiting the West Side Highway by the Seventy-ninth Street Boat Basin, he drew up beside an orange school bus. The traffic coming off the highway was backed up because of flooding. Several cars began to honk. Peering out from a window of the school bus was a child's face, five or six years old, Hispanic, with big wild features too large, too sensual for their tiny frame. The child, seated in the warm bus, watching the rain, had just made a discovery: if he breathed on the windowpane, it fogged up. Several times, he breathed and then wiped the pane clear with his palm. Then, in the clouded glass, he made shapes with his finger. Isaac, waiting for the traffic to move, watched the boy fog up his patch of pane, and then, tentatively, with his forefinger, begin to write. Large letter E's.

Isaac remembered his own alphabetic adventures, how he had taught himself to read from an Agway catalog of seeds he and his mother planted in their vegetable garden, leaving him with the impression that the letters of the alphabet could be sown and eaten. Now the traffic began to move, and the pane of oxygenated E's wheeled away, and Isaac made a right turn onto Broadway.

The doorman allowed him to pull up in the courtyard to make his delivery. On the twelfth floor, outside the Geblers' door, Isaac rested his dripping burden against a wall and stepped out of his sodden sneakers, leaving them in a puddle on the doormat.

It was Mrs. Gebler who answered. She was wearing a white wool dress. Short-sleeved. Bare arms, the wiry dark hairs on them standing out against the freckled skin. Her legs were thin, with sinewy calves; the feet narrow in their suede loafers. Rich people had thin legs. Skinny legs and big bellies, like Flemish Adams and Eves. There were freckles on the bridge of her beaky nose. Thick dark eyebrows. And her breasts were very large. The V-neck of the dress showed her cleavage. Sometimes he thought she must have been handsome as a child; sometimes he guessed she was better-looking now. She was talking on a cellular phone and, while she wound up her conversation, stuck out a free hand to him—a vigorous businesslike shake. Without thinking about it, Isaac turned over the hand that had been presented him. Callused palms, like a workman's. His action was so swift that she didn't have time to retreat.

"Gardening," she explained. She noticed his bare feet. "Is it pouring? Where did you leave your shoes?"

Isaac gestured with a jerk of his head.

A very short Hispanic lady in white uniform appeared—on Mrs. Gebler's instructions, bearing a sheaf of newspaper for Isaac's drenched sneakers, as if they were unhousebroken pets. Mrs. Gebler introduced Isaac to Carmen.

Isaac hefted the slim crates of pictures into the front hall, one by one. "Have you got some pliers?"

Mrs. Gebler, followed by Isaac, went out into the kitchen. He watched her rifle the drawers in search of pliers, and opened one himself, just to see. It contained only half a dozen packets of tiny peppermint-striped birthday candles. It was this detail, strangely, that made him feel most acutely the gulf that separated him from the Geblers. He could imagine—barely—being rich, but he could not imagine having one drawer devoted to birthday-cake candles.

It was Carmen who found the tool cabinet under the sink. Then Isaac unhusked the Agnes Martin paintings from their sheaths of plywood and hung them on the picture hooks, where two rectangular patches on the white-white paint had complained of their absence. The Agnes Martins were a pair—one white on white, one palest beige on white, both punctuated by a pencilled gridwork of tiny squares. Mrs. Gebler stood back and watched.

"Are you pleased?" Isaac asked her.

"Yes . . . it's always a bit of a worry—I've lived with them for so long I forget what they look like. Like when your children have been away for a while. You miss them terribly and then, just as they're coming through the door, a moment's sinking spell. Oh dear, is that what my son looks like? Maybe it's just the haircut. . . ." Then, briskly, she added, "This time it's quite all right. Splendid pictures—simply glorious. I think Agnes Martin is one of our greatest American artists. It's her meditative simplicity—really like music, like a kind of Eastern chant."

He looked, for politeness's sake—he didn't really see the point.

"You're too young. Perhaps you need a lot of patience to feel how good she is. You float in it, she makes you contemplate the silent harmony of creation. You realize she must have suffered, too, to have arrived at such calm. It's good to remember that art doesn't have to be a struggle—restorative to watch someone who's survived that struggle, and come through sane and peaceful."

Isaac nodded. It had never occurred to him that art needed to be a struggle—painting was just another way of seeing, a way of telling things that could be told no other way. It was only the artist's imperfectness that made it hard to get every part of the picture up to scratch.

"Would you like something hot to drink? Some tea? Did you get chilled from the rain? I really should offer you a bath." She was looking at him for the first time—even while they were shaking hands, her head had glanced sideways, slightly averted. Almost before he'd answered, she was off telling the maid to bring them a pot of tea, and then, sticking her head back through the kitchen door, "India or China?"

"Huh?"

"What kind of tea would you like?"

"Hot," said Isaac. His bare white toes on the golden yellow parquet floor. Oak, maybe.

"And Carmen, is there any of that lemon cake left?"

She came back and gestured to him to sit down. "No, not that chair. It's unbearable. Someone accused us of having the most uncomfortable chairs in New York. I always thought my parents' chairs were the worst—they were what my friend Jesse Kraemer calls Louis the Terrible—but apparently modernist furniture is even more punitive. Why don't you sit on the sofa? No, sit—I have a bad back, so I usually stand."

In fact, she paced, while Isaac, worried about getting it wet, plumped himself down on a white sailcloth sofa big as an elephant. Now once again Carmen appeared, this time with a tray bearing a teapot, two cups, a strainer, a sugar bowl, a pitcher of milk, a plate of sliced lemon, and a new-moon sliver of cake.

Mrs. Gebler cast an eye over the contents—obviously the result of much training of Carmen—then got up and brought back two teaspoons, a cake knife, and a dessert fork. "I see the children have been at it," she said of the cake. "My husband and I haven't much talent for timing. We've managed to have *three* simultaneously adolescent children. I don't know what happens to them at school, but they come home every afternoon like a plague of locusts, devouring everything we'd planned to serve for dinner."

Isaac nodded and sipped. Then he dug into the cake with a fork too small and curvaceous for the job. He was wondering what was wrong with Mrs. Gebler. Why was she making tea-party conversation? Didn't she remember he was the guy she ordered, No, stick the nail in two inches higher, dummy?

He craned his head, looking around the living room with its varying shades of whiteness, almost empty except for a few abstract paintings. He felt disappointed. To him, these pale geometric canvases appeared smug, trivial, out of the fray. He took their blankness at face value: they were blank because their creators couldn't think of anything to say. And he felt almost protective of Mrs. Gebler for having been duped by such bland unimpressive stuff.

"How come all your pictures are beige?"

She looked annoyed. "It depends what you're looking for in art."

Isaac stopped. He had been addressing himself to the cake, which, crumbly, refused to remain intact during the ride from plate to mouth. A landslide cascaded onto the sofa. One especially large chunk fell onto his crotch, trapped between his legs. He couldn't decide, under Mrs. Gebler's indirect but nonetheless hawklike gaze, whether it was better to extricate it or to let it be. Worse still, the noise of his munching seemed to him stereophonically audible. Reluctantly, he decided it was easier not to eat in front of her.

"How about beauty, for a start?"

She drew her eyebrows together. " 'Beauty' is a rather retrograde concept at the moment."

Isaac, exasperated by these big dull speechless paintings that were sitting around the Geblers' living room so pompously, by being forced to eat crumbly cake with a child's fork, by the recollection of the fifteen-thousand-dollar pair of Joseph Beuys hair clippers his employers had just purchased, lost his temper. "Why shouldn't art be beautiful? What else is it good for? Maybe you have enough gorgeous things on your back and around your neck so you don't care, and can pretend a hunk of brown plastic is beautiful too, but that's just slumming. For the rest of everybody else ugliness is where you're fighting to get out of. Into the world of gold leaf."

She started to protest, but he interrupted her. "I know what I'm talking about. I happen to have grown up in a pretty . . . undernourished part of the country. Landscape that looks like something pulled out of the void a little premature—maybe on the day *before* creation. Mucky lakes. Pine trees like eczema. I was raised on this thin gruel, this pale northern broth of beauty—so since I came here, to the city, I don't want to look at *that*"—he gestured at Agnes Martin's calm pallor. "I want colors that lead your eyes up to heaven, that make you feast on being—downpours of purple and crimson and gold. Ultramarine. You know what van Gogh says about color? That what in the old days haloes used to symbolize—that emanation of the eternal—today painters can only show by the radiance and vibrancy of their colors. I don't see any radiance in your living room. Looks to me like the dog puked up most of your pictures. I went to the Frick last Sunday. I go to the Frick three, four times a month," he confided. "Why can't people paint velvet and pearls like Titian? I want to look at colors like emperors in armor, not . . . beige grids, like the insides of computers. There's too much banality already."

"You're mad," said Mrs. Gebler, offended. "I don't know what your . . . work looks like, but it's absurd to want to paint like Titian four hundred years later. It's reactionary. You can't uninvent modernism. Maybe you don't like some of its results—I sometimes agree—but it's impossible to imagine yourself living in sixteenth-century Venice. It's pretentious. It doesn't work. It just comes across as empty heroics. Of course, I'd have to see what you do in order to judge, but my feeling is, it doesn't work."

"But luckily I'm dead broke, so I make my empires out of postage stamps and matchboxes. We do what we can—what we have room for."

"What are you working on now?"

"An altarpiece."

Her eyebrows shot up.

"For a small altar. This big." He gestured. "A shoebox altar."

"Are you religious?" Not pryingly, but more as if she'd been won-

dering about these matters herself and was curious what position someone else had arrived at.

"Am I religious? Like a trained bear. But still I can't imagine putting
one foot in front of the other without–that. I wouldn't accept this bad
bargain of living without it."

"Without what? Without–you mean, the consolation of believing?"

"It's no consolation. Only a spiritual imbecile thinks it's consolation. It's a goad, it's like . . . somebody sewed you up with thorns in the
stomach. It's torment, mostly, because the doubts are so unremitting, so
unmanning."

She frowned. "Well, in any case, I meant it–I would like to see your
work."

"It's disruptive showing it," said Isaac.

"I'm sure," said Mrs. Gebler.

"I hate showing it," said Isaac.

"I don't blame you a bit," said Mrs. Gebler.

"But why not? I mean, why shouldn't you see it? Yes, why not, yes,
I would like very much for you to see it," said Isaac. "How about this afternoon?" In fact, he hadn't been able to do a blessed thing since Casey
had come by. Like a mother bird that abandons her chicks once an alien
hand's been in the nest.

"I can't, unfortunately–I've got to . . . I've got a million things to
do. But we must make a date for sometime very soon."

Mrs. Gebler moved towards the hall, and Isaac got up, realizing that
his audience had come to an end. She opened the front door. "Have
your shoes dried yet? Thank you for putting up the pictures. Even if you
hate them. Especially if you hate them. This was really an errand of
altruism."

That night, Mrs. Gebler and her husband were lying in bed, after coming home from dinner at the Ayalas'. Dolly, reading, said over her shoulder, "That Isaac of yours is quite a case."

"He is, isn't he?" Alfred was flipping the silent channels. "Fuck, it's
nothing but Puerto Rican and Chinese TV. Look, Doll, doesn't this look
just like Willa's opera?" He gestured to a screen on which two kimonoed
opera stars in rice-white faces were gently undulating. He blasted a moment's screeching at her, then pressed Mute. Thoroughly pleased with

himself, mimicked the screeching in imaginary Chinese. "Waaah-waaa—shoo-pooo."

"Oh, dry up. First that Isaac, now you."

"What'd Ikey do to you?"

"He said our art looked like vomit. He wanted to know why Agnes Martin couldn't paint popes in velvet, instead of making all those ugly beige squares."

Alfred laughed. "Anyway, he sure beats Santiago."

"What's that got to do with anything?"

Santiago, a former office boy, had looted the bookstore cash register and stolen money from the secretaries' purses. In the end, Gebler had gotten Andy to persuade him to quit—he couldn't face it himself, the silly kid had a wife and a newborn baby.

Nineteen

ISAAC'S ROOM WAS on Thirty-ninth Street and Ninth Avenue. It was a neighborhood that had been built for the poor and never inhabited by anyone but the poor, for no amount of speculators' gentrifying could ever transform its pinched jerry-built warrens into anything but slums.

Even so, Isaac had decided that his apartment had been originally intended as a broom closet, but then the brooms had got rich and moved somewhere bigger.

The room had one coffin-shaped window facing onto an air shaft. Isaac had blocked up the window with his canvases. When he moved in, it had looked into the bedroom, three yards away, of a middle-aged Hispanic man, who lived in the welfare hotel that abutted Isaac's building. Every night the man stood in front of his window and masturbated. Isaac was sorry to deprive the man of his only audience, but he needed the space—there was nowhere else to stack his canvases, except on the loft bed, which was, unfortunately, where he slept.

In addition to the loft bed, a particularly aggressive contractor had managed to foist a burner and sink upon the studio's ten by thirteen feet. No closet—he hung his clothes on a pipe that emerged from behind the burner. The floor space was entirely taken up by Isaac's worktable. To get to the burner you practically had to climb up into the loft.

Only above the aluminum sink, where you would expect a mirror, was there room, as over a prisoner's bunk, for a small square of personal effects. Here he had tacked up a Byzantine mosaic from Ravenna of the Empress Theodosia, who Isaac thought resembled Mrs. Gebler. Black-and-white photographs of a Siberian log cabin with bearded peasants outside, of painted wooden churches; a photograph taken in a forest of a teen-aged Balthus, still in short pants, with his mother and Rilke. Rembrandt's *Bathsheba*, Dürer's sister dressed as a nun. A postcard of a horse by Géricault. But today his amulets had gone dull on him, forgotten as high-school crushes.

Isaac had risen at six and gone out in search of pastries for Mrs. Gebler, and since then he had been scrubbing walls and floor, but it wasn't the kind of place that even a tidy person could make clean—the decades of crud were too encrusted. Besides, his own work necessitated such a profusion of handleless cups for mixing paints and broken saucers turned palettes, of jars in whose stagnant water brushes soaked, of turp-drenched rags and newspaper, that there wasn't much possibility of cleanliness. Even his drafting table, a child's school desk with broken legs, was splattered in dried paint like pigeon droppings. He was ashamed for people to visit, and especially ashamed for Mrs. Gebler to see it, as if she were walking in on him when he was sick in a dirty pair of pajamas. He wished he'd had the presence of mind to tell her not to come. He wished he had the money to move somewhere decent, and it made him angry at himself that he hadn't. A grown man and still living like a rat in a hole. Then he remembered how very recently he had been living nowhere at all, and he remembered how before that he had been living cozy as a squirrel in winter with a woman he had promised to love forever and how he had left her for no reason, and felt abashed.

Why did Mrs. Gebler want to come, anyway? To feel charitable, that was why. And suddenly her high-mindedness, which previously he had admired—there must be plenty of rich people who frittered their jack on private planes and jewelry—appeared to him an imposition. She was disrupting his work, just so she could feel she'd done a good deed. And for how long after she left would he remain too het up to work?

Now the downstairs buzzer rang, and Isaac, who had been sitting bolt upright, opening and closing, opening and closing his hands in a trance of angry agitation, started. Rose and, hesitating, lunged down the stairs, smelling as if for the first time their stench of stale urine and cockroach-exterminator fluid.

At the curb were two prostitutes arguing with a taxi driver. A few paces away was Mrs. Gebler, carrying purse and shopping bags. He stared at her feet in their handmade shoes, flimsy as ballet slippers on the garbage-strewn sidewalk. How could he have wanted for even a moment to show his work to someone who only admired big neutral-colored abstract nothings or tweezers wrapped in felt? Not only did he not respect her taste, but she would never for a moment understand what he was trying, however lamely, to do.

"Hello there." Isaac stood immovable in the doorway. Looking as if maybe she were a Jehovah's Witness who'd come on the wrong day.

She, gathering that he didn't mean to invite her in, put down her shopping bags. "Lovely morning."

Her politeness depressed Isaac even further. "Listen," he said. "Why don't we just go to the zoo or something, forget about the pictures. Or maybe you have another appointment."

Now for the first time he looked at her. She was also looking not quite at him directly, but rather off down the street, and the expression on her face was veiled. "Of course, whatever you like."

And her refusal to push, her chivalrous pretense of being at his disposal, obscurely soothed him. He took a deep breath. In, out. "I don't know why I dragged you here. I've only been making pictures two years. It's—nonsense. But if you really *do* want to look at the pictures . . . do you mind if I–I don't think I can be there while you look."

He handed her the keys. "Two A. All the canvases and notebooks are laid out already, on the floor. They aren't too heavy. I guess you can handle them by yourself, with your strong gardener's arms. And some paintings on metal, too. Anything you find you can look at. And do you see that coffee shop across the street? When you're done, that's where you'll find me. In the Cupcake."

It took Dolly several nights to figure out what she thought. At odd moments they would come back to her—the empty rooms, the black angel with his sword of fire, the burning bush, the dead man in the blue suit flying through the window. The naked boy in the coffinlike bathtub. The harsh images branded themselves in her brain. They were as vivid in their dreamlike violence and sexuality as some horrible tale from the Brothers Grimm. Vivid, but anachronistic. Wrong. She remembered what she had felt when she first saw Romanesque churches—Yes, I can see this is good, but it's what I hate. It made her think about what she did value in art. Purity, intelligence, rationality: in the sculptures of Brancusi or even Richard Serra, you felt that the artist with considerable discrimination, rigor was insisting upon the benign and uplifting possibilities of modernity, and that after the piled atrocities of our century, still to see beauty in technology, harmony in industrial objects, or permanence in nature—to indulge even in a kind of abstract and limited utopianism—was a brave act. Isaac's dream pictures, willfully reactionary, seemed to be turning their back on the modern world, plunging deep into some dark primeval forest. And yet hadn't her hero Joseph Beuys plumbed primal sources of energy, Celtic myths; hadn't he exhibited a postcard of the World Trade Center labelling the twin towers after those staples of every quattrocento painter Cosmas and Damian? Why couldn't you, if you liked, paint saints in 1989?

She asked Isaac, almost hurt, "Why do you choose such subjects? Why do you see the world like that?"

"I paint what I know. My bedroom, my father, the woods behind our house, the stories I grew up with. I paint what I carry with me, what I see when I turn out the light."

"It's spooky," she complained, childishly.

"Really? I find my work pretty cheerful. Homey."

She shook her head, bemused. And asked him again, "Are you religious? All that biblical imagery in your pictures . . . You know, for most of us nowadays, well, the Bible just is not common currency."

"Nonsense," said Isaac. "You might as well say, just because you're perched up there on the twelfth floor, that most people don't know what the ground looks like. The Bible is our mother's milk. Still. Maybe not in the art world, but in the real world. This is a very religious country."

"As far as I can see—from the twelfth floor—MTV and soap-opera scandal is our mother's milk," Mrs. Gebler retorted. But then, a moment later, more conciliatory, "You know, I've always regretted that I don't know the Bible better. I haven't really read it since I was a child. Well, certainly not from cover to cover. . . ."

"I'm not a zealot, incidentally—I just happened to spend a winter in a house in the hills with nothing but the Vulgate for entertainment. I was mightily entertained."

"Isn't it very barbaric—the Old Testament, I mean?"

"You mean, unlike life? Unlike New York City?"

"Well, shouldn't religion be better than life?"

"No," said Isaac. "It should be lifelike. Otherwise it's dead. Is the Old Testament barbaric? Yes, it's certainly barbaric to have a religion with laws against stealing young birds from the nest in front of their mother. Or exempting a bridegroom from war until he's been married a year. Or to have a God who describes his chosen people as a foundling, left bloody in a field, whom he's nursed and swaddled and brought up in finery to be his wife. . . ."

In a funny way, she felt jealous of him for being able to concentrate so furiously upon his own private, familial iconography: it made minimalist art seem generic. And yet just when you thought you were about to suffocate from the claustrophobia inside his head, then he opened the window and let you up into the sky with its sailing majestic clouds. Very confusing. "I paint clouds to clear my palette," he explained. "You know, I read somewhere something an artist you've got on your wall said. Frank Stella. He said he tried to keep the paint as good as it looked in the can."

Mrs. Gebler grinned.

"Yes, it's funny, but it's pathetic. A man can't do what a machine does as well as the machine does it. Why go to so much trouble to create with your own hands something that will look industrial, synthetic—untouched by your own experience? He uses 'humanistic' as a dirty word. He boasts that what you see on the wall is *all* that's there. I think I'm trying to do the opposite—to suggest the invisible, the ineffable, through something very flawed and provisional. Handmade."

He was stronger now that she'd seen his work, even if she resisted it, didn't like it. Her seeing it had strengthened him.

Twenty

ALFRED HAD LEFT for California, where Richard Cruikshank had a museum opening. Sunday morning Dolly woke to a sun emblazoning the onion domes of the Orthodox church across the river, and felt revived. She decided to take the children out to Long Island City, where the foundation had installed a sculpture garden of Richard Cruikshank's work. (He had another permanent installation in a former shirt factory in Greenpoint, which consisted of an acre of cedar shavings. When she'd last taken the children to that one, Leopold had asked sadly, "What happened to the trees?" while Carlotta's comment had been "It smells like a hamster's cage in here." Now they were older, thank God.)

Richard Cruikshank was a California artist who had begun working in the late fifties. He was one of Dolly's favorite men in the world. He had been doing his own thing for decades and didn't care whether anyone liked it or not. Every couple of years Dolly would go out to San Diego to see him and they would drive around, cruising shopping malls, or sitting in the parked car by the ocean: he liked to look at the water from the car, sipping Nestea from the can, talking about inner harmonies and tectonic plates and how the freeways converged. He regarded the most hideous man-made creations as if they were geological formations.

She had felt a pang of envy at Alfred's getting to go see Richard, without her. Lucky stiff. It seemed especially unfair since Alfred always pretended to consider Richard an old fart. Jealous maybe because Richard was working on his third wife, a long-legged, straight-backed twenty-eight-year-old. Dolly didn't object to the Babe as much as she might have because Anne was so damn serious. An expert in recycling for the county. Alfred thought it very funny that this recycling expert should have latched on to Richard, who was quite a devourer of natural resources—sort of like a health inspector marrying a cockroach.

Dolly had flown into a temper at her husband's calling Richard a cockroach.

"It was a *metaphor*, for fuck's sake."

"A simile," she had corrected.

The children were crabby, fighting. It was one of those days when together they congealed into a red-faced ball of petty resentment and recrimination, even Johnny regressing into brattiness. The fight was raging up and down the halls, from one bedroom to the next. Johnny was throwing a fit because Leo had borrowed a pair of her jeans.

"Who knows what he did in them, the little jerk-off. He doesn't wear any underpants. I don't want his dick drool all over my jeans. Besides, he's got such a fat butt he'll stretch them."

Leo, meanwhile, biting his lip, on the verge of tears.

"Be quiet, Johnny," her mother said sharply.

"But he didn't even ask—he just sneaked them. Why does he want to wear my jeans? They don't fit him—he's too short and fat."

"He's not fat." Mrs. Gebler riven by the heartbreaking inequity behind this episode—Leo wanting to wear his sister's jeans because he loved her, in some magic-animism wanted to *be* her, Johnny not wanting him to because she thought he was repulsive and totally retarded.

She wondered often if they would be friends when they were older. This, surely, was one of a parent's chief tasks—allowing your children to disengage from you and attach to each other. So far not so good.

Carlotta, who was reading *National Velvet* and refused to budge, wanted to know if she could stay behind. Mrs. Gebler said no. More sulking. Finally, when everyone else was long ready to go, Carlotta appeared, book in hand. She resumed reading while they waited for the elevator. Leo still looked as if he were trying hard not to cry. Mrs. Gebler, putting her arms around him from behind, dug her fingers into his curls.

"Oh, what an angel boy," she said, kissing his ear until he giggled and squirmed. "Do you realize I spent my entire youth wishing I had curly golden locks just like you?"

Leo laughed hiccuppy tearful giggles. Now the two girls, with their Indian-straight hair, looked at him curiously.

"Won't you let me have just one or two?" she asked, bending her head down and twisting a curl to her own forehead, so he could see in the hall mirror. This was a game her bald father had played with his daughters. Now the girls too laughed.

"You look like Harpo Marx!" said Johnny.

They took the car out to Astoria and had lunch at Samatya, a Greek restaurant with red vinyl booths and, overhead, trellises laden with plastic grapes. Afterwards, they wandered across the street to the pastry shop, where Mrs. Gebler allowed the children to pick out a whole tray full of sticky things with pistachio shavings on top and walnuts and shredded wheat below. Remembered the inedible syrup-drenched Middle Eastern goodies Isaac had laid out for her the day she came to see his work. What an odd boy.

The children were explaining to her about a cartoon in which everyone's hair stuck on end and which had developed its own kind of slang, which explained why for the last month they'd been telling her every time she asked them to do their homework, "Mom, don't have a cow." Then Carlotta delivered on how Madonna was completely uncool. Carlotta liked Chucky Dee the best of the rappers. Leo liked Vanilla Ice, but Carlotta thought he was totally bogus—a white suburban dweeb pretending to be black. The children began arguing about hip-hop.

"It's too violent, I don't think it's right for singers to tell people to kill policemen," said Leo, stammering.

Johnny and Carlotta jumped on this, naturally, and said people should be allowed to sing whatever they want. Hadn't he ever heard of the First Amendment?

Mrs. Gebler at this point intervened. "Now that is an utter non sequitur and you know it. Just because you've got legal rights doesn't mean I can't criticize your judgment."

"Do you or don't you think cops are racist?" Carlotta demanded.

"I don't like that kind of ugly generalization. But," Mrs. Gebler allowed, "even, let's say that certain white policemen think young black males on the whole are more likely to commit crimes—" How boring to be a parent.

"And are therefore gonna jump on any innocent black person they see walking down the street," interjected Johnny.

"Or shoot him in the back," added Carlotta grimly.

"—does that mean musicians should be telling their audiences to go out and kill—"

"Mom, come on. That's not what anybody's saying."

"Mom, look around you. How can you *not* think America is a racist society?"

"Look at your own gallery. You don't show any black artists."

Mrs. Gebler gave up, depressed. This is what they heard at school. Everywhere. Too frazzled to argue that she wasn't going to pick her artists by race. That America should become *less* color-conscious, not more so.

Carlotta by now had gone back to reading *National Velvet*—she was supposed to be reading *As You Like It* and *Le Misanthrope*; she had a part in the Molière play the tenth grade put on every year in French.

Mrs. Gebler got the bill and found herself hoping Alfred wasn't going to stay in California too long.

The children by then had decided they didn't like modern art, they wanted to go to the movies. "Why don't *you* go to the sculpture garden and *we'll* go to the movies," said Johnny, all sweet reasonableness.

"Because there'll be civil war over what movie to go to, that's why. It's much simpler if we do something all three of you agree you hate."

The sculpture garden, down by the waterfront, was empty, except for a boy with a racing bike, sunning himself and writing a letter. The ground was paved in massive slabs of reddish brown slate brought from the Sierras. In the center—aligned with Mars in July or something—were three dolmens, resting on each other: a giant's table. Across the silver water, Manhattan, like a taller, skinnier cluster of dolmens, hewn from sandstone, granite, and blue glass.

Carlotta sat down on the ground and went back to reading Enid Bagnold. Dolly, on the point of ordering the child to her feet, remembered that this was exactly what Richard had intended people to do in the garden—to read, meditate, take a nap, generally hang out.

When they left, Carlotta, who had gotten into conversation with the boy with the racing bike, was in a better mood. Back in the car, she said, grinning wide, "He wanted to know if I was Winona Ryder."

Johnny mimicked a dropped jaw. Everybody knew that Carlotta was pretty, but that was going some. "That's nothing—a guy last week wanted to know if I was Marilyn Monroe." Then, "Did you get his phone number?"

"He asked for mine."

"Did you give it to him?"

Mrs. Gebler stiffened to alert. The children had been told a hundred times never, under any circumstances, to give strangers their address or phone number. "I gave him Miss Amber's number!" yelled Carlotta, and now both daughters collapsed into shrieks of laughter. Miss Amber was their biology teacher, whom the girls insisted was mentally retarded. "Plus she has BO. I mean it, Mom, it's so gross—she wears the same white turtleneck every day, even in the summer, and the underarms are caked *yellow*!"

"Girls, will you cut it out. No more bitchiness. It doesn't matter whether the woman washes or not."

"Then how come you keep on having a cow whenever Leo won't take a bath?"

"What did you think of the sculpture?" Dolly asked her children.

They reflected. "I thought it was beautiful," said Johnny. "Mysterious."

"What's it supposed to mean?" Leo wanted to know.

Carlotta was still thinking. "I thought it was kind of bogus."

"How come?"

"Well, here we are right in the middle of Queens. You can't just crate in a bunch of big rocks and make people think it's the Grand Canyon. It's, like, a gimmick. I mean, Mom, how much did you give that guy to crate in those rocks? It's just a gimmick. It doesn't say anything."

"It's not supposed to say anything. It's just *there*."

"Well, they got rocks like that in Central Park and Riverside Park and they belong there, it's kind of neat. They're real bedrock. But those rocks you crated in—they're just sitting there. On top of—nothing. It's like one of those dumb third-grade science projects where you grow clover in a little dish and hey, wow, amazing, we're in the middle of Manhattan and here's a real live clover plant. . . . If you want people to see nature, buy 'em a bus ticket to Bear Mountain for the day." She sounded frighteningly like her father in a contrary mood.

That night they went to the movies. Dolly was feeling puzzled. In some peculiar way she too had had Carlotta's gypped feeling this time around. In the old days, she had often driven out to Queens by herself to find solace in the craggy beauty of Richard's dolmens, the way you might visit a Japanese rock garden. Long Island City's answer to Ryoan-ji. Peaceful, unalterable. This time its weathered outcroppings hadn't spoken to her—the concept seemed academic, sterile, its claim to permanence overblown, and her inability to respond was as devastating as falling out of love. I'll go back in a couple of weeks, she promised herself. It was probably just that she was worn out by the children's squabbling. . . .

She wished she'd have been the one who'd gone to California, to get reinfused by Richard's thoughtful equability. When she talked to Alfred on the phone that night she tried to explain her quandary. "Carlotta said she thought it was a con, and I couldn't say why it wasn't."

Alfred laughed.

"No, I'm serious, Alfred. I couldn't justify it."

"Why should you? Anyway, she's right, every artist's a con artist. We just happen to be co-conspirators. All we have to do is get our stories straight."

"How's Richard?"

"Great. He's been asked by Peter Redpath—will you get a load of this—to construct a *shopping mall* for them in Matamoros. Can you believe it? A shopping mall! He's over the moon. He showed me his sketches. Pretty nifty."

Dolly was not reassured. That night she lay in bed—how big and crisply starched it seemed with Alfred away—reading Joseph Campbell on mythology and thinking idly about Isaac's paintings. At least he knew his Bible. She worried that her children didn't know the Bible—somehow she'd relegated this duty to Alfred, scared that she might infect the children with some Christianness he'd resent. Or else maybe she'd thought they'd pick the Bible up somewhere along the way by themselves, the way you expect them by the age of fourteen to go brush their teeths . . . I mean teeth . . . before they go to . . . Just before she fell asleep, an image of an angel brandishing a flaming sword.

Twenty-one

SEVERAL DAYS AFTER the trip to Long Island City, Mrs. Gebler stopped by the exhibition space to have a word with Costa. Costa and Isaac were dismantling the Lohenburgh exhibition. Isaac was sitting on the floor, swaddling a metal frame in yards of bubble wrap. "Oh, I was thinking about you," Dolly blurted out.

Isaac beamed. "Good. I've been thinking about you, too."

"I was meaning to ask if you had any Polaroids of your work. I wanted to see if it really was . . . as unsightly as I remembered."

"I don't. But it is—as unsightly, I mean."

"Sure you do, man," Costa intervened. "I got some slides in the back."

Isaac continued wrapping the frames, while Dolly and Costa went into the backroom.

Costa, producing a small manila package from his desk, took out the slides and examined each one himself before passing it on to her. Dolly looked at Costa's big brown hands turning over the slides, at the narrowing of his luscious brown eyes, and felt suffused by love for him. Sometimes she felt as if Costa were the one of the few people in the world she could talk to. Even if they didn't exchange a word for months, there was a fullness to his silence that made other people's conversation like barnyard cackling. Was it really true she only trusted people she paid?

After Costa had looked at each slide, he passed it on to Dolly. This time her reaction to Isaac's work was quite different.

So underground is the nature of conversion, so invisibly willful the process of altering one's taste to absorb the alien, that Dolly, without having seen again these pictures which ten days ago had struck her as barbarous, was determined this time to find them beautiful. Her judgment had shifted by that same subterranean process of assimilation that makes us look at a text before we go to sleep and wake up in the morning with it memorized. Thus, by secret unconscious increments, and not by blinding revelation, is how most spiritual, amorous, or aesthetic conversions take place.

"What do you think?" she asked Costa.

"He's a visionary."

Dolly nodded. This word, "visionary," encapsulated what she too had been thinking. A visionary was somebody rude, perhaps untaught, but with an inner spirituality that translated itself into a powerful symbolic landscape. "Formally, he leaves something to be desired."

"He's not much of a draftsman, yet," Costa acknowledged. "But he's getting better. Anyways, there are a lot of good draftsmen around who don't have anything to say." He named a few postmodernist painters neither of them liked.

Dolly nodded vehemently. "I couldn't agree more. I always think that's the greatest problem facing artists today: no subject matter. There's no consensus anymore in society about what's important."

Most artists who weren't absolute loners and freaks needed outside direction, shared symbols. No wonder that after artists got sick of making urinals just to thumb their noses at there being nothing sacred, nothing "painterly" left anymore, they couldn't think of anything to do but rip off Rubens. She remembered Jesse remarking, with characteristic flippancy, that AIDS was the best thing to have hit the art world since the Annunciation—finally a cause worth getting cranked up about.

"In any case, Isaac's sure found himself a subject," said Costa.

"Yes. It's not quite my thing, obviously, but . . ."

"Why not?" said Costa. "He's painting about the same experiences as Rothko or Gorky, isn't he? He's just more upfront about it."

"Well, do you think the art world is ready for Bible stories?"

"I don't think he gives a darn. He's going to keep on plugging away whether anyone likes it or even sees it."

Dolly picked up once again the slide of the angel standing in the middle of the kitchen. A skinny black angel with a big grin and bare legs and worn-out boots. And the sunlight streaming in through the kitchen window. "Have you shown these slides to anyone else?"

"I took 'em around to some dealer friends, a lady friend of mine at Bloom-Kopeck."

"And?"

"They weren't biting. Too weird. Deborah wanted to know what you and Alfred thought of his stuff, and which other galleries were interested. When I said no one, she couldn't get me out the door fast enough."

Dolly clicked her tongue impatiently. Bunch of sheep. That's how the art world was these days, like junior-high-school boys who wouldn't be caught dead looking at a girl unless the other boys were after her, too. No self-trust—only wanting what was already certifiably hot.

"Deborah passed me on to a dealer who's getting up some big show on outsider art—Robert Jenkins. So I called him up, messengered him the slides—he was kinda interested, wanted to know where I'd got hold of this Isaac Hooker from. I said, He works for us. He works for you at Aurora? Man, was that fellow pissed off. He said, You know, I think we need some clarification here of the term 'outsider.' Apparently, 'outsider' nowadays just means artists in prison or in mental hospitals. I said, He's self-taught. He says, That's not enough."

"What a racket. Look, he's unfinished, still—in a not altogether good way. I think the compositions need some work, and the figures and space need defining—but he's certainly got something wonderful there. Odd, but wonderful."

"He'll get there. I tell him, Just keep on plugging away."

Isaac noticed that when he bumped into Mrs. Gebler now, which seemed to happen more often than before, the timbre of her voice was changed. It had grown softer, burry, and she addressed him in a tone almost of deference. It was a voice in which you could not say, "Hang that picture a little higher" or "Isaac, do you mind mopping up the floor."

She wanted now to talk to him about his work, and to make sure that he had everything he needed. The intent of this low, respectful tone evidently was to make Isaac feel that she was his servant and not he hers. But he resisted. It made him uncomfortable. He had got used to her being cranky and imperious, and her sudden deference struck him as artificial. He'd grown up among strong women who didn't bother to hide it, and the geisha-girl manners left him cold. But he liked the chance to talk to her more, especially about his work, and quite soon he became accustomed to the solicitousness.

Part Five

Twenty-two

ALFRED LOVED THE wintertime because it was the season of the best parties. College kids were home, and on Friday nights the streets were jammed with half-baked beauties raring to have fun. He remembered going to Italy for the first time as a young man and seeing the nightly *passeggiata*, when swarms of teenagers, tanned, bejewelled, immaculately elegant, strolled down Victor Emanuel or Via Cavour, laughing and flirting and gossiping. The sight of such sleek amplitude had filled him with retrospective anguish, bringing back his own dingy adolescence, spent in the school cafeteria with David Lefkowitz and Manny Pleshka, talking about basketball and classical music and trying not to think about girls.

Today it seemed to Alfred that America at last matched Europe in teen glamour, and that the girls pouring out of the Tunnel and the Ottoman Club and the Runaround Lounge had legs up to their ears and the boys looked self-assured, whereas his own contemporaries had just been hot and drunk and bothered.

This Christmas season was even bouncier than usual. At work, the "Home" show was only a week from opening–and now most days the artists themselves stopped by the gallery to supervise the setting up of their installations or just to say hi.

And Gebler too found as many excuses as possible to hang around. As soon as the office cleared out, he would head down to the third floor, where things would only just be hotting up. There was an atmosphere of festive emergency that amused him, everybody pitching in as if a gallery opening were Manhattan's equivalent of a barn raising. Jane's boyfriend, Dogface, would drop by on his way home from his job as an engineer in a sound studio; kids from the neighborhood attracted by the lights and noise would come help out. They would work till nine or ten or even later, stopping only for takeout pizza, and then, most nights, Gebler would head off to the Ottoman or the Red Light or the Runaround with Casey and Isaac and Jane and Dogface and some of the artists–whoever he happened to telephone or whoever had come by the office that day. End up at the after-hours joints.

One night Alfred took everybody to a party of Molly Kellaway's. Molly was the daughter of Alfred's old friend Redmond Kellaway, who had been a downtown poet and a lover of William Burroughs before he married a society girl. And Molly took more after her mother than her dad. She was a fundraiser for the Brooklyn Academy of Music, and sat on the junior committees of well-bred New York causes–Save the Library and Save the Park and Save the Democratic Party–and she lived in a posh brownstone on Charles Street, which on this particular night was decked out with waiters in white gloves and boys she'd been at Brown with, snotty beanpoles in bow ties who worked at the *Paris Review* or *Esquire*. No sooner did Alfred get there than he started wanting to get out, but Casey–who had just broken up with his lawyer girlfriend, Emma– was obviously happy as a sandboy and had immediately squirreled himself in a corner with a girl in hot-pink velvet who looked like Kim Novak.

Alfred was standing in the doorway with Isaac, avuncular behind Coke-bottle specs.

"Goodness, what Christmas cheer," said Isaac, rubbing his red hands together and beaming. It was true. Molly, who was nothing if not a ham, had made the house look positively Dickensian: shoulder-high Christmas trees erupting in gilt angels, mistletoe wreaths, bowls of eggnog, and Nativity crèches, as if to make up for the intractable unfamilialness of the unmarried thirty-year-olds who were her friends.

A dancer named Kevin had brought his pug dog to the party, and the two men watched, riveted, as their hostess–clad in a microscopic miniskirt–got down on her hands and knees and began conversing with the dog in barks. Pressed her little pink button nose right against the pug's wrinkled black one and waggled her head. The dog seemed to be enjoying it, but Kevin giggled nervously.

"Hermione!"

Still on hands and knees, Molly smiled up at Kevin, baring big white teeth. Guileless. "Jemima will smell your dog on me and know

I've been *unfaithful* to her," underlining the adjective with solemn emphasis as if she were quoting from a foreign language.

"I didn't know you had a dog, Molly," said Kevin's other date.

"Oh, didn't you know? Really? Oh, Jerry, are you sure you didn't know? Yes, of course I do, Jemima's a"—Molly then uttered a sound like the name of an African tribe that was all clicks and exclamation points and glottal stops. And now, good hostess, she wanted to draw everyone into her circle. "Isn't she adorable?" she appealed to Isaac. "Her-mi-o-nee. See, she knows her name. Don't you just love dogs?"

"No," said Isaac. "I think pets are an invention more debased than daytime television."

"I know just what you mean—I feel so guilty about keeping a pet when I think about all the homeless people begging for food who don't have enough money for a meal."

"Don't let it sweat you—most homeless people don't like to eat dogs."

"Are you an artist too?"

"I'm a hunger artist," he joked.

Molly looked at him intently. "I know we've met somewhere. It'll come to me in a week, out of the blue. Doesn't he look familiar, Kevin? You're not from New York, are you? You're not—you're too idealistic, I can tell."

"I'm from New Hampshire." Isaac, basking in the attention.

"Oh, I know lots of people with houses in New Hampshire. Do you know the Pappases?"

When Isaac didn't, a small cloud appeared on Molly's brow. "You do, Alfred, don't you? George and Nona. They've got this adorable place in Cornish that used to be a schoolhouse. You know, right where Saint-Gaudens lived? Nona restored it herself."

But she wouldn't let Isaac go. "I know we've met—I never forget."

"You probably remember Isaac from Harvard," Alfred helped her out. "You knew most of the football team, didn't you, Molly?"

"Alfred, that's so mean." She laughed. "You know, I'm *very* intellectual." She put a quick arm on Isaac's shoulder. "You're not a football player, I hope. . . . Oh, that's good."

That was Molly's redeeming charm, she was a good sport.

"So you went to Harvard." She had readdressed herself to the problem of Isaac. Something about him obviously set off an alarm, jarred with the homogeneity of her party. "Did you know Lucinda and Ashley? . . . *No?* What about John Stoddard—he's a great pal of mine. . . . Really?" With each missed connection, Molly looked more worried. She gave a last try. "How about Henry Holbrook? Everybody knows Henry."

At this name, Isaac bent and nodded.

Molly laughed in relief. "Isn't Henry adorable? He's one of my favorite—"

"He's so adorable I once kicked him down three flights of stairs," said Isaac. "It was all right," he reassured her. "He didn't have any bones in his body—I was just checking."

It was at this point that Alfred had a brainstorm. As Isaac was snagging another drink, Alfred seized Molly under the elbow and led her away.

"What a delightful place you have, sweetheart. Who did it up for you?"

"Do you really like it, Alfred? You're not just saying that?"

"Sure, I love trompe l'oeil." And indeed, to Alfred it seemed nothing short of miraculous that Redmond Kellaway, who had once spent an entire year sleeping on Alfred's floor, should have wound up with a daughter with pagodas hand-painted on her wall by some fake-French decorator.

"Where's Dolly? You should have brought her tonight. I love Dolly—she's so motherly. Are your daughters very close to her?"

And as soon as they were out of earshot, he began. "Look, I didn't want to say it in front of him—that's Isaac Hooker you were talking to."

Molly wrinkled her brow.

"You know, the Hooker family. They own one of the largest newspaper chains in the country. Isaac's the only son and heir."

"Really?"

"Yes, really. I'm surprised you don't know them, Molly. Isaac is—well, he's an eccentric. To put it mildly. Nice, but incredibly paranoid about people taking advantage of him for his money."

"Alfred, you're so mean. He didn't look paranoid to me—I thought he was dear. Isaac is his name? Really natural and unaffected."

"Oh, that he is. . . ."

But now, having played this prank on his friend's fancy daughter,

Alfred was eager to get away and recount it to as many people as possible.

Casey, unfortunately, was in no hurry to leave, and when Alfred came to see if Isaac wanted to go, he found the boy sitting on the library sofa with a plate of smoked goose and loganberry sauce on his lap and Molly at his elbow. Molly looked up at Alfred with a big happy smile. "I'm trying to get Isaac to give me his telephone number, but he's swearing he hasn't got a phone. Go on, Alfred, tell him I'm not the big bad wolf."

It was almost one o'clock when Alfred finally managed to drag his companions away with the promise that there was a much better party that night at the Bluebird.

"Will it still be going?" Casey asked suspiciously.

"Sure—trust me, we're talking East Village, it's not like these uptight West Village dos where everyone's got to get home to walk the dog, for Christ's sake."

Leaving Molly's, Alfred slipped on the icy steps outside and nearly cracked his skull open. Isaac caught him just in time. Scrofulous old fart—that's what came of having downed four cups of eggnog, two bourbons, and three plates of sliced goose and beef stew in rapid succession. You lost your former sprightliness, your equilibrium, your élan. He was a bottom fish, that's what he was, a garbage-eating eel. This Christmas season, to prove it, his potbelly was already sailing way out over his jeans. So fat he had to sling his trousers down below his hips, and another week left till Christmas. If he kept on like this, by New Year's he wouldn't be able to see his own cock in the flesh.

"Where shall we go, gilded youths?"

"I thought you said we were going to the Bluebird," Casey reminded him, pissed off at having been torn away from Kim Novak, who at the last moment had decided not to come, although another friend of Casey's, called Heather, had joined them.

It was a real New York winter—the city frozen to glass, under skies pure as ether. As if clouds had never been invented. And tonight the coldest yet. A North Pole night, wind ripping flurries of ice off the rooftops. So cold you could hardly breathe, and the stars, peering through the chinks between buildings, like brighter chunks of ice, glittery cold. It must be zero, Gebler thought. At the corner of Sixth Avenue, waiting for the light to change, they were approached by a woman wrapped in a ragged blanket, her half-naked arms and legs swollen.

"Mister, can you help me out? Spare a little change?"

Mr. Gebler performed the usual deprecatory mutter and shuffle, but the lady, not to be dissuaded, sang on loud and clear. "My baby's sick and I haven't had a bite all day. . . ."

Just as Alfred—cornered, feeling everyone's eyes on him—was being shamed into scrounging around in his pocket, if he could even jam his hand into his pocket after that last gulp of eggnog (why did these damn street people put you on the spot? it was malice, wasn't it?), Isaac caught up and pressed into the woman's hand a crumpled wad of bills.

"Man," said Casey, as they moved on down the street, "what'd you give that lady all your money for? I've seen her in this neighborhood before—she's not homeless, she's a real pro. Probably makes more than you do."

"I don't think it's such a great idea to give the homeless money," said Heather. "I usually carry around an orange or an extra sandwich, so at least they get some nutrition."

"Yeah, dude, otherwise they just blow it on booze."

"Well, booze is what I blow my money on, too," said Isaac, wiping his nose angrily. "Would you deprive the wretched of any consolation?"

"I thought you were putting on an exhibition about the plight of the homeless, Casey," Gebler said.

"Damn right. About the government's failure to act. If you give 'em money out of your own pocket, Isaac, you're just encouraging the government to opt out of the whole problem."

"Will you ruthless little Republicans please stop picking on this tenderhearted boy?" Alfred intervened. "First of all, he saves me from breaking my neck. Then he rescues an upright young woman from cannibalizing her baby from hunger."

"That's right—you're a hero, Ike. Forget I ever said anything."

"Oh, shut up now."

They piled into a taxi, Isaac up front, and unloaded at the Bluebird, where the party was winding down. Bluebird herself waved them over to a table where she was sitting with the guest of honor, a dress designer friend from London.

Bluebird—or the Japanese mafia who funded her—had had the smart idea that what people wanted today was a low-key club, with quiet corners where you could sit and talk. No more strobe lights and shuddering disco. Home away from home. She was right. They had decorated the place with dark-green taffeta swag and billiard tables and big leather sofas, and every night it was packed.

Mr. Gebler had a soft spot for Bluebird, who had hair like albino cotton candy and was really just a down-home Cockney who liked to boast about her daughter's grades. "How are you, Alfie?"

Alfred leaned over and gave her a big kiss. "Better for seeing you, doll. How's tricks?"

"We had a great party tonight—Lacey here showed her latest fashions. Lots of leather corsets—pretty kinky. I'm knackered, tell you the truth. The varicose veins are catching up on me."

"We're getting on, sweetheart. Mutton dressed as lamb."

Gebler ordered a round of drinks. "How's Lola?" Bluebird's daughter was two years older than Johnny.

"Honestly, Alfie, I'm a bit pissed off with her at the moment. I think it's the generation gap kicking in. She's up in Cambridge, with a job waitressing. I told her I'd pay her twice as much but she didn't want anything to do with it. She's frightfully disapproving of her old mum."

"What for?"

"Oh, it's the new puritanism. All the kids are like that. They think we've got bad values. You know, single mother, all that. She's fearfully cross at me now for not having found myself a husband who'd bring her up in a nice house with a picket fence and all. After I thought I'd done rather well by her, considering. She's got this dreadful boyfriend, he's a sophomore at MIT who's this dyed-in-the-wool Republican *nerd*. No sense of humor whatsoever. It's the loopiest position to be in as a mother—telling your own teenage daughter to loosen up. I don't think they even sleep together—they just sit around talking about family values."

Mr. Gebler, dismayed, wondered if his children disapproved of him. Leopold, maybe, but the girls?

"I can't bear James," Bluebird wound up, "but Lola thinks he's a genius. I'm just scared she's going to drop out of college and marry the little creep, since they don't seem to believe in premarital hanky-panky."

"Let's find her a new boyfriend. I'll have a talk with her."

"No way. We're all a bunch of left-wing pot-smoking degenerates, she won't hear a word against James, damn his piggy face."

"What about Casey here? Why don't we introduce her to Casey? Or Isaac? Fine upstanding youth?"

Bluebird took one look at the boys and burst out laughing. "What are you drinking, love?"

Gebler, having ordered another Souza Gold, turned reflective. He found himself depressed by the story of Bluebird and her disapproving daughter. Poor Bluebird, who was so mad about her Lola and who'd fought her damnedest for those ridiculous free-love values only to have them betrayed from within. He'd seen Lola last summer—looked like Brigitte Bardot. Arctic-blond hair and a dear pouty face. Didn't quite have Bluebird's punch, though. Of course Bluebird had never told a soul who Lola's old man was. Parthenogenetic—whatever the word was. Probably some Dutch hitchhiker she'd picked up, who hadn't a clue he was dad to the prettiest bimbo under twenty. Children needed fathers. No wonder Lola was impatient with sixties looseness.

"Why don't we fix you up with Lola, Ike?" Gebler asked. "She's a real doll."

"I'm too broke to take girls out," said Isaac.

"What do you mean—for the money you just blew on that panhandler, you coulda bought some nice girl a glass of water at the Bluebird."

"Besides, that's bullshit," Bluebird intervened. "It's a complete myth that women are mercenary. I've kept more men than I can count."

"Get a nice older girlfriend—some thirty-eight-year-old investment banker," said Gebler. "Everywhere you go in this city, you see single women just longing for a loving fellow."

"I'm married to my work," said Isaac.

"Oh yeah?" Gebler grinned. "Well, nothing wrong with an open marriage. I don't understand what it is with my employees—you, Andy, Ella, Martha—it's a goddamn monastery. The only one who's working overtime is Casey here."

"In fact," Isaac volunteered, unexpectedly, "my ambition in life is to find a wife."

Everyone laughed.

"No, I mean it," he insisted. "I would chop off both arms to have—"

"Will you give me a commission if I find you one?" Bluebird inquired. "A few fingers, perhaps?"

Then Alfred turned serious. "*Don't* get married. This is the most serious advice I can give you. Remain single. Right, Birdy? Marriage is a pit. I mean it. A pit. The only somewhat redemptive aspect is children, but then they're bound to disappoint by too discomfiting a resemblance to you. Or her. Anyway, there are a hundred bad reasons to get married and almost no good ones."

"Now, Alfred—that's going too far," said Bluebird. "I'm sure Isaac here—"

"No, I'm quite serious. Somebody at a dinner recently asked my wife why she married me. She said, I married Alfred because he made me laugh."

He looked around the table to check the general reaction. "I thought, What a ball-buster thing to say. To marry a clown, someone you don't have to take seriously? For both parties, it's hell. She could at least have said, because I was a good lay. Anyway, it's a lie. My wife married me because I seemed to be having a good time, and she wanted to put a stop to it. If there's one thing women can't bear it's men having fun. As soon as a woman sees a man who seems to be having a halfway decent time, she thinks, I'm going to marry that one and put a stop to it."

Bluebird, backed by Lacey and Heather, raised a storm of protest. "What a load of crap! And what about you men? Who invented the chastity belt, I'd like to know? Who invented the—what's it called—that burning the widows on the pyre they do in India? Or female circumcision? If that's not men spoiling women's fun, what is?"

Mid the outcry, Isaac asked quietly, "And why did you marry her?"

And Gebler deadpanned, "For her money.

"My God, I almost forgot!" He clapped a hand to his forehead. "I spent a large part of this evening actually trying to finagle you a wife. Get a load of this. . . ." And now Alfred, chortling, was able to recount to the whole table how he'd convinced Molly Kellaway that Isaac was an eccentric billionaire, and how saucerlike her eyes had grown, and how she had decided that Isaac—whom before she'd obviously deemed a total creep—was absolutely fascinating.

Casey and Heather and Bluebird, who had known Molly forever, roared with laughter at the story.

"Lacey, you've never met this lovely girl. She's charming, we all adore her, don't we, Alfred, but she's got a bit of a thing for the rich and famous."

Only Isaac said nothing, but, head lowered, tore his pink-and-white-striped cocktail straw into tiny shreds. Alfred, noticing that his friend was not amused, squeezed the young man's knee. "What's the matter, Ike? Don't you appreciate all the trouble we're going to, to find you a suitable girl?"

"Why don't you just give me ten million dollars," Isaac said through clenched teeth. "That will really fool her."

Gebler, taken aback, then laughed even louder. Later on, when he retold the story, it was Isaac's rejoinder that became the punch line. But Isaac (who, Alfred gathered, had developed quite a soft spot for Molly, with her round eyes and propensity to bark) was evidently pissed off by the revealed venality of this who-do-you-know, how-much-money world he had entered.

When you got Isaac drunk, he was a scream. But on his nondrinking nights, he could seem disapproving. Rightly or not, on these occasions the kid made Alfred feel his age, appeared to him in the guise of a conscience.

Twenty-three

CARMEN WAS IN TEARS. Gasping, shuddering sobs. Mrs. Gebler offered awkwardly a cradling arm while the story came out in torn jerks. Trying not to look at the kitchen clock which was doing its damnedest to tell her she had twelve minutes left to get downtown for a dentist's appointment.

Carmen was pregnant. It was a pregnancy she and her husband had been working at a year now. Dolly found inadvertently comical the way couples nowadays informed you they were trying to get pregnant, as if fornication were a chore. Even Alfred had known for some time that Carmen and her husband were hard at it, trying to have a baby.

"The first baby, my son, he come by accident. We were so surprise!! This time is not so easy. I want a little girl! My son is already big–already when I hug him, he push me away. No, Mommy. He want to play with his friends." Carmen's husband, who was manager of a restaurant on Jackson Avenue, wasn't sure if they could afford a second child. But he had allowed himself to be persuaded. "All year we try, we try. Every month, no luck. Nothing."

Now, at last, Carmen was pregnant. Imagine the motherly love, the sense of completion welling up in her, how eagerly she looked forward to informing her young husband the glad news.

The day she found out, a cousin of her husband's named Fermina stopped by the apartment. They chatted about Fermina's children and about Carmen's wild incorrigible Rigoberto (named after her husband). Then Fermina said, "And Jose too is getting to be a very big boy."

Carmen, puzzled. "Who is José?"

"Who is José? Why, José is your husband's other son." Fermina, seeing Carmen's face, clapped her hand over her mouth. "You mean you don't know?"

And then it came out. That Rigoberto had a girlfriend–a Puerto Rican woman who had a lucrative and prestigious job as a cleaner in an office building in Rockefeller Center. That Rigoberto's family knew the woman and approved of the match and that they had had a son together who was only a year younger than Carmen's son.

This had happened three weeks ago. Since then, night after night, Carmen and Rigoberto had had screaming fights, until finally he'd gone to stay at his brother's. And all along she knew that she was going to keep the baby and all along she knew that Rigoberto was going to keep the Puerto Rican woman.

"I tell him, I don't want no hypocrisy. I don't stand no hypocrisy in our house. Don't lie to me and sneak around."

And Dolly, mid her uprush of pity, was impressed. Where did Carmen, straight from a Central American pueblo, get this worldly contempt for hypocrisy? And how sophisticated–far more sophisticated than Dolly's own set–were these Hondurans' social arrangements, where the mistress and the wife visited the parents-in-law on alternate days and the mistress was preferred.

Dolly tried to comfort her, but Carmen had already picked up a pile of freshly ironed clothes and was making off down the hall to the children's rooms. And Dolly wondered whether Alfred's friends also preferred the nameless girlfriend who she was convinced must exist, who was growing in her imagination like a fetus fully formed, with ten tiny fingernails and toenails, kicking, kicking, and growing slowly by the day—almost a little person. And she wondered whether she too in the end had the courage to scorn lies and deception.

Casey, half-kidding, had asked Isaac to do a picture for his "Home" exhibition. Isaac, to Casey's surprise, had not shown much interest. One evening after work, Casey dropped by his apartment. "You got anything I can put in my show?"

"I thought your show closed already."

"I always got room for new talent."

Isaac in response handed him a small painting on scrap metal. It was El Moro, with plumage iridescent as an oil slick. The purple-russet rooster, with leg daintily lifted and indignant beady eye, was placed against a pale blue background, and beneath him, in scarlet capitals, "DENY ME." The picture, Casey readily conceded, was stunning, much the best thing Isaac had undertaken so far: the paint had been laid on all shimmering, in little whipped-egg peaks, so that each feather stood out in luxuriant bristling vanity. And yet it was impossible.

"What's this got to do with the price of eggs?"

"It's not a hen, Casey, it's a rooster."

"So I see. My show—it's about New York City. Remember? Home, homelessness, urban blight. You can't put a picture of a fucking rooster in it."

"But the rooster's from the city—Alphabet City. If that's not a New Yorker, who is?"

Casey in answer put his two hands around Isaac's neck and gently squeezed. "You try to help the dude and he acts like he's doing *you* a favor," he complained. "Does Dolly Gebler like this barnyard shit?" Casey, some combination of proud and jealous, kept harping on the fact that Isaac, his joke discovery, had now been picked up by the big time. "So she's real interested in your work, huh?" he persisted, too guileless to disguise his amazement.

Isaac shrugged. "Interested? She's given me some kind advice. Let's say her interest at the moment is fairly prophetic."

Casey was nosing in Isaac's sketchbook. "Hey, what have we got here?"

"Those? Those are just sketches."

"They look interesting—why don't you work me up one of these?"

The book that Casey had unearthed was full of drawings of Luther. Luther, Isaac's latest model, was another habitué of Henry Street, whom he had remet through his Antiguan buddy Scout. Luther was a model worthy of a Renaissance anatomist, a knotted marbly Moses with massive back and belly and legs.

Casey was entranced by Isaac's Luther notebook. Why didn't Isaac do a picture of Luther on the streets?

But Isaac refused. "I haven't cracked him properly. Why don't you use the rooster?"

Casey blew his top. "You can't paint *animals* and expect people to sit up and notice. You have to be socially relevant, man. You gotta have the balls to get up there and tell the world what you think about racism, sexism, AIDS, the destruction of the rain forest—you gotta have the vision to take on the big issues."

Isaac listened politely and thanked Casey for having invited him to be in his show. When you disagreed so diametrically with someone, there was no point arguing. The central unspoken fact between him and Casey was that he did not consider Casey to be an artist, he considered him a mere booster, a publicist. In the end they dropped the idea that Isaac would submit a picture for the show, but Casey remained as sore as if Ike had tried to screw him over from sheer arrogance. The lesson Isaac drew from his nonexhibition was not that from now on he should take on socially relevant subjects but that he should never even think of painting anything that did not come from his own private lexicon, his creed.

In the meantime, he had begun work on a new series of drawings.

The series was to be entitled *The Sons of Heaven Meet the Daughters of the Earth.* Isaac was thinking of the portion of Genesis that describes the world before Noah's Flood. In those early days, man was constantly overreaching his boundaries and threatening God with insurrection. What was the Tower of Babel but a battering ram with which to besiege, sack, invade the very heavens? Depressed by these outbursts of human corruption and overweening, God periodically got sorry He'd made us and decided to scorch the earth, saving one wholesome starter-seed from the old stock. That annihilated race before the Flood, of whom only Noah and his family were preserved, had gotten up to singular misdoings. According to the Bible, which was quite terse in these early chapters, the sons of God had been coming down and coupling with the daughters of men. "And it came to pass, when men began to multiply on the face of the earth, and daughters were born unto them, that the sons of God saw the daughters of men that they were fair; and they took them wives of all which they chose. . . . There were giants in the earth in those days; and also after that, when the sons of God came in unto the daughters of men . . . And God saw that the wickedness of man was great in the earth, and that every imagination of the thoughts of his heart was only evil continually."

Isaac's new series was an attempt at depicting that primitive brood of Adamites' abrupt and orgiastic minglings with the violent divine. The first scene was in charcoal and ink, made with a combination of quills and Chinese brushes. Thick paper that stood up to the wet without blotting. The sons of God coming down from the sky. The background of it was brownish, as if enveloped in a brown coal-smoke so dense you couldn't tell land from sky, and the shape of the hill seemed hunkered down against a storm. Crosshatched. The beeches, maples, and birch trees ragged, spindly from craning for the light.

In the top corner of the page, descending diagonally from upper left, was a pink nimbus such as you see on the night horizon when a city lies ahead, and in this nimbus could be seen, falling like soft rain, the bodies of men, whose limbs and wings were furled like buds not yet open. In the upper-left-hand corner, a face—rather like the old-fashioned depictions of the winds in a map's compass—peering down at their descent. Isaac worked on this picture, in different forms, through the first half of December. In the end, he blotted out the face in the corner. Then he moved on to the second scene.

In the second, the daughters of the earth were portrayed as big blowsy shepherdesses, herding their flocks along a road which led into a city. The sheep he painted in watercolor very deliciously, with a tactile sense of the matted squiggly frizz of their golden-gray pelts. The edge of the city was a cluster of tall gray towers, from which rose that same livid sulfurous pink light that heralded the sons of heaven's descent. One of the shepherdesses was lying on a bank by the side of the road, her skirt hiked up over her naked limbs. Her legs were spread so wide you could see, flanked by parallel aisles of dark mat, the dark red mouth of her pussy, like a baby bird waiting for its worm. A yellow-eyed ram with terrifying horns and low-hanging balls was backing away from her.

The third scene was to be an orgy that would almost be like a battlefield. He was thinking of those long mythological friezes by Piero di Cosimo—perverse allegories charting a twilit pagan world in which the men and women were still sticky, bruised, glowing from encounters with gods or centaurs. It was this primeval conjunction of the human with the bestial semidivine that Isaac wanted to capture. He prepared for this picture with many small pencil drawings of the sons and daughters rutting, limbs bunched up, limbs splayed, contorted.

The most successful piece was of the shepherdess giving birth. From her bloody vagina was emerging the head of a lamb with curly horns.

The last picture was a drawing in ink and wash called *And the Bow Shall Be in the Cloud*. A silent empty sea, with little outcroppings of tower from the water, like pinnacled reefs—the city after the Flood—and arching over it, a pale watery rainbow.

All these tableaux had come to him in one ecstatic, sleepless weekend. Now they only required embodying. The physical and financial requirements were heady: he would need plenty of good brushes and oils, and he would need canvas and stretchers, and he would need live models. And he would need sea and woods, and acres of free hours. Most of all, however, he needed to learn to paint better than so far he could even dream of painting. Until he had assembled all that he required, Isaac worked fitfully, from the imagination.

Twenty-four

DOLLY WAS QUITE RIGHT in her suspicions about her husband. Gebler was in love. He had been in love now for almost two years, but instead of settling into a parallel domesticity, the affair was driving him to distraction.

They say the women that get under your skin are the women that aren't your type. So it had been with Gebler and Gina. They had met at the Fragonard exhibition at the Metropolitan Museum. Not a very likely place for Gina to be. Gebler had always found museums erotic. It had to do with a certain kind of watching. It wasn't like the beach or a café, which some people preferred. In a museum, all you were there to do was look, but it was a particular kind of loose, dreamy looking, concentrated, but full of floating associations, fantasy, and you were moving slowly from room to room with other people, strangers, also looking—that joint, anonymous floating concentration, that abandonment to the meditatively sensual, to the absorption of color, texture, gesture—except that sometimes instead of looking at the pictures you looked at each other. And the looking was of necessity—since you were both facing the same way—an oblique sly sidelong sort of looking.

So it was on Fragonard day. He had stopped off at the show after lunch with the curator of the Met's contemporary wing and she, Gina, who it later turned out wasn't much interested in mainstream European painting anyway, let alone eighteenth-century frippery, was there because she had had a fight with her boyfriend and couldn't think what else to do. Except he didn't know that then; she was just an outrageous-looking black girl with hair dyed blond and eyebrows like circumflexes who, he noticed sort of subliminally, was scowling at the Fragonards like an atheist at Mass.

He was floating from canvas to canvas in which dimpled frothy nymphs with mounds of flesh like clotted cream, jammy lips, hair of butter were engaged in lusts so prolific and polymorphous as to be almost innocent—in one picture, a girl in bed actually appeared to be being masturbated by her lap dog—and just when Gebler was wanting to immerse himself wholeheartedly in this lustrous painted world, in the brushstrokes like an elegant kind of fucking, he noticed that they had become aware of each other, he and the black-blond girl, that they were moving in synchrony, like dancers. That he was aware of her was no surprise—the whole museum seemed to be rocking from the shock of her—but why was she, with her sidelong gaze, her inviting butt, registering him so brazenly that he felt interestingly violated?

She was not his type—not that she was a type he'd ever had a chance either to choose or to reject. She was not tall, but hard and wiry, with that mop of bleached blond hair, a ripe brown skin, and hazel eyes, and she was dressed like a high-fashion construction worker in a man's sleeveless undershirt, jeans cut off at the crotch, and a pair of shiny black Doc Martens.

They moved in unison from painting to painting, and now they didn't look at each other but stood very close, so close he could hear her breathing, so close he himself held his breath. At one point his lips almost brushed her crimpy peroxide hair. She was planted firmly, legs apart, and her calves were knotty as a bicycle racer's, and her ass jutted out like a geological shelf. The muscles frightened him. And then, before a picnic of undressed shepherdesses, he finally spoke. Into her ear, which was small and high and pointed. And had no lobe.

"That Fragonard flesh," he said. "Looks bruised, somehow. All those livid purples. Do you think he beat his models?"

And she, not looking back, replied, "I sure beat mine."

So she was a painter.

"Oh yeah? Do you eat 'em too?"

"No, they eat me."

The sense of danger, in a crowd. And she—impossible she, quite terrifying—said nothing, but drew a pointed pink tongue around her lips. And he, uncertain how to proceed, since she was obviously trying to bluff him, scare him off—a novel alternative to simply ignoring importunate seducers—followed, heart racing, blood soaring, weak, woozy, pullulating with desire, until, accidentally, they bumped into each other, and he held on to her hips to steady her and said, "Let's go," and she shrugged and—every man's dream—they went.

He remembered their first coming together, in all its poignant clownishness. She had stood him up for dinner several times, and at last he'd succeeded in nabbing her. They went to some French restaurant in the Village. Painfully obvious that it was somewhere—i.e., pokey, dark, unfrequented—you went when you didn't want to be seen. Afterwards he walked her home, depressed by their not having had anything to say. No common culture. It was quite clear she didn't want him to come upstairs; best write off a lame evening and get an early night's sleep.

"Listen," said Gebler, last try. "I want to smoke a joint."

She let him up, reluctantly. It was a dingy top-floor studio on Mulberry Street, prison green. Feminist literature, stink of absent cats. A sublet. Shag carpet. Later Gebler's knees and spine were thankful for that putrid shag. He lit up, they smoked. He was watching her elbows, her knees—four lone outposts of vulnerability. Then suddenly he reached out and stroked the knees and she shivered like a horse dislodging a flea, and he pounced. Set the tone for their future couplings that left them both black-and-blue, swollen-bitten-kiss-stung-lipped, a mess of raw flesh, sores in the mouth, contusions. She fought him, till he squeezed her tit so hard she screamed. Fucked her with his finger through her trousers. She wouldn't let him in that time. Wouldn't let him in, wouldn't let him out. Just let him suck her through the pants, let him fret her with his fingers through her damn trousers, her gripping him too short-reined by a hank of hair and yelling like a banshee. A trousered hump because she wouldn't let him in, because she didn't want it to happen, not with an old married slob, and him flinching his neck away from her lips so she wouldn't leave a mark.

They were rolling over the cruddy little daybed, rolling over the floor, ramming and butting and chewing up each other's ears and noses and chins, as pent up and murderous with desire as prisoners on parole, a dogfight with no clear winner, a tussle, my one and only love my madness my dear dear death my only girl my heart and liver and kidneys and lungs my wild thing my mercy give in and let me in my mine until they fell asleep on the floor and woke up rabid. . . . Because she'd come on so tough with him, because she was a jock who boxed and ran track and played Saturdays on a women's basketball team, because she still had that adolescent-bully thing about physical strength, because—except for her stepfather—she'd never slept with a man older than twenty-six, but was accustomed to biceps and triceps and permanent hard-ons, he had had to be quite brutal with her at first. They were at that stage still when everything is hanging in the balance, when any tiff could provoke from either of them a That's it, I'm out of here. When every time they saw each other might be the last.

His meanness with her covered most areas of life. He devoted an extraordinary amount of energy, those early days, to persuading her she was ignorant (she was), that she painted like shit (she did), and that she was bad in bed (she wasn't).

"You sound like a gospel revival meeting when you come," he'd complained, plunging into her deeper and deeper, her clever monkey-supple legs up around his ears. And she just laughed and wouldn't be made self-conscious, because she knew it was what she was born for. The painting–like bad Matisse, like loud music–was secondary, another kind of physical activity. What she really did–did for a living–was teach art out at Rikers Island to women prisoners. Juveniles. She got up at five every morning to take the bus to Rikers, and by the end of the day she was so drained by what she'd mastered and endured, by the mutinies she'd put down, that she went to bed at ten.

"I work with big cats," she'd said when he asked her how she paid the rent, asked if he could pay.

"No, what do you really do?"

"I'm a civil servant." And both were true.

Most of Gina's work problems were unspectacular: hating her boss, who was a Jehovah's Witness and out to get Gina; having her art supplies impounded as possible weapons–no scissors, naturally, and the girls always trying to get high on the rubber cement. But some days when she sounded ready to get into bed and not come out again, it was because her favorite student, Shavawn, had rabbit-punched in the kidneys her least favorite student, Yolanda, with knuckle dusters honed from a garbage-can handle for hitting on Shavawn's girlfriend. They all mated like rabbits, apparently, just a bunch of horny teenage girls with no man in sight. Constant lovers' quarrels getting out of hand. Romeyette and Juliet.

Gina didn't like to know what the girls were in there for. One day she found out by accident that Shavawn was waiting trial for drowning her sister's baby. She doubted it was true. She said, "Listen, in Shavawn's house, the things that are going down are so wild you can't get the truth out of *anybody*. I mean, since I worked at Rikers I realized you gotta have an income of at least twenty thousand a year before there is even such a thing as truth. A hundred thousand for justice.

"You see it with the Legal Aid lawyers trying to find out where was Shavawn at eight o'clock and did this happen on Monday or on Tuesday and where were you living, and they're not lying, they just don't understand the questions. I mean, the hours, the days, who's coming, who's going, it's like having a lawyer cross-examine you about what you dreamt last night. You try to find out where Shavawn was living. What's your address? Well, sometimes she's with her boyfriend at his mom's apartment in the project and sometimes she's with *her* mom. So where does *her* mom live? Well, her mom's a crack addict who's been evicted from public housing. So she's always crashing at someone else's place, but mostly they're at Shavawn's grandmother. So on the night of the third where were you? At the gramma's. And who else was there? Well, Troy was staying there that night, too. Who's Troy? He's the father of her sister's oldest child. Was he there at eight p.m.? No, he'd gone out, but he came back later with five friends. So you gotta track down Troy, whose name isn't really Troy, and his five friends, except one of them's already dead and each of these remaining five got such chaos in his head, I mean, the hours and days are not consecutive, they are all just rolling around like crazy. How can you talk about facts when it's like a real loose pinball machine in there, some galaxy whose gravity's losing its bounce?"

Alfred loved to hear stories about Rikers and she spilled them out compulsively, even though she knew he took them not as exemplars of social injustice but as tourism, a glimpse into an exotic hell.

When Gebler took up with Gina, he'd romantically assumed—even though he'd met her looking at eighteenth-century French paintings at the Metropolitan Museum—that she herself had sprung from this steamy ghetto she commuted to every day. Of course, it turned out, she'd been raised richer than he. Gina's father was Haitian—he'd taken off early, and had a new wife and set of kids—but her mother was Jewish (of course) and she'd grown up in Cobble Hill and gone to a progressive school. Her mother was a playwright who'd had some success in the sixties and now taught at community college.

She was only twenty-five, and had dropped out of school after eleventh grade, but she'd read a lot, in an undisciplined way, and had an okay mind once she stopped arguing.

The problem was she had other boyfriends—she was, in fact, suavely promiscuous, a regular Casanova. Gebler was at first relieved that Gina had other irons in the fire, and wouldn't be pressuring him to make impossible commitments (most of his previous girlfriends had been married); but gradually it had become unbearable—if for no other reason than that her taste in men seemed to run mostly to ex–gang leaders on parole.

He had tried to put his foot down. Even if she had no sense of self-preservation, he was damned if he was going to die of some foul disease just because her pants were on fire. He went on to tell her she was just a middle-class Jewish girl who was slumming. She, furious, said the only person she was slumming with was him. It was one of their first major fights, and he was aware of being on shaky ground.

If he was going to exact something approaching fidelity from her, then he was staking a claim. That she was to be his. Which meant that he was hers. Which, it appeared, he was.

Except that Gina refused to bite.

This failure to secure her marked a turning point in Gebler's love, which from then on was fraught with a jealous clinginess that he knew she found as trying as he did, a ceaseless campaign to extend the borders of his rights to her, to see her more often than the once a week or so she allowed him. Mostly, he tried to drive away the rival wolves by avalanching her with presents. For this Christmas, he had picked out for her a pair of emerald pendant earrings that had belonged to a Russian countess.

It was all a bit confusing for Alfred, whose last girlfriend had been a happily married museum curator with a house in Connecticut and two small sons.

Twenty-five

IT WAS DARK WHEN Mr. Gebler awoke, and for a moment he felt befuddled. Was it day or night? Why was he alone in bed? Casting a dopey eye sideways, he saw the electric clock shining four-twenty-five–had his wife risen already, the assiduous bitch? Then, stupidly, he came to. He had nipped uptown for a nap before the opening this evening, and now it was well past time to haul his butt back down to Second Street express. For a moment Mr. Gebler, in Jockey shorts and socks, slumped slack-jawed on the edge of the bed, gaping into space as into the bottom of a well.

Every awakening for one harsh instant reveals to us at its very meanest our spiritual condition, our station in life. Then we forget. Forgetting is optimism. If we didn't forget, we wouldn't be able to go on living. That's what Mr. Gebler thought, sitting in the dusk on a late-December afternoon. Focused his eyes out the window at the pink lights cast from New Jersey into the Hudson River, and felt even more depressed. Winter darkness, and outside cold as an icebox, so cold it would freeze the snot up your nose. The only consolation being that tonight he would get to see Gina in a room full of people, including Dolly. Would they be able to talk? Would she be wearing the pale green mousseline Christian Lacroix dress he'd bought her? Should he have given her the earrings now, to go with the dress, or was he right to have chosen to wait till Christmas Eve? More important, would he be able to keep his eyes from eating her alive, his hands from climbing inside of her, right in front of all those brittle critics and uptown matrons? Who will tell the story of our terrible love? Once again, he dialed her number, and again no answer. She was an unsociable soul, at heart. It drove him mad, how she could just sit there in her apartment and listen to the phone ring twenty, thirty times without picking up.

Besides, she was sore at him. Gebler had introduced Gina to Casey, in the hopes that he might be interested in her Rikers Island work. He was. Casey had commissioned Gina and her students to make a big collaborative painting for the "Home" show. Last week, the piece had arrived in the gallery. It was pretty fetching: a vast plywood frieze of Adam Clayton Powell Boulevard on a fall day, hair salons and African magic stores and Kentucky Fried Chicken and Pentacostalist churches and sidewalk Muslim preachers combined with magical-realist flourishes of flying crocodiles and trees on fire, and Gina had been longing to get her students out on leave for the opening. Who could get more of a kick out of tonight's jamboree than these rambunctious teenagers who'd been locked up eight, nine months in a stinking zoo?

The Department of Correction had refused—prisoners at Rikers hadn't even been sentenced yet, they were just the unfortunates who were too poor or dangerous to make bail. In the end, Gebler had promised Gina to put up the bail for her three chief apprentices. But it had been a hectic month, and by the time Alfred had gotten around to it, Gina had been told that the court couldn't possibly schedule bail hearings until well after Christmas. Gina, furious, had accused Alfred of having stalled on purpose so as to avoid the embarrassment of a bunch of high-spirited yowling Harlem homegirls stepping on the toes of his Park Avenue guests.

Sighing, he heaved himself out of bed and, opening the door to his walk-in closet, perused the suits, tightly arrayed as a male chorus line in a Fred Astaire movie, before selecting a charcoal-gray worsted with a red-chalk stripe, made for him in London. Worthy of Fred himself–Gebler's childhood god. Everything he had wanted to be–not a chubby Jewish boy but the debonaire gambler in perfect tails, living in a hotel suite off cocktails and canapés. And the raspberry shirt?

He started to run a bath, and addressed himself, while waiting, to the question of a tie. Preposterous garments, like long flaccid dicks hanging from your throat. A piece of clothing to get garrotted by. And why were clothes so refractory, altogether? Or was it simply his own congenital refusal to admit that he would never again be thirty inches around the waist or weigh a hundred and forty-five?

In truth, he was quite worn out from the last week or so, during which everybody–meaning he, Costa, Andy, Martha, Casey, et al.–had worked every day till midnight setting up the show. Well as he felt he knew most of his employees, he was always intrigued to see how each one deployed his or her strength, how the long hours under pressure revealed unexpected talents and flaws.

Andy, who burned at a low even temperature and was ruffled by nothing, had held up the best of them. And Martha, loose-limbed, lanky as a six-foot rag doll, although she did not have much practical knowhow and needed to be told what went where, kept the others sane. Plus she was a kind of safety valve for Costa, who was too uptight to vent his furies directly–whether at Alfred or at Casey, who never seemed to know what he wanted, but demanded the impossible and then changed his mind.

Three weeks before opening, Casey had presented Alfred with a guest list for the opening-night dinner he wanted them to throw at their house. Apparently, the Geblers were expected to be lining up Casey's next half-dozen jobs. His chief catch was a Russian impresario who'd opened a gallery on Crosby Street showing artists from Moscow and Leningrad. What Alfred had seen so far of the new Russians were knock-offs of Andy Warhol. For the Russians, apparently, who had been cut off for so long from their own heritage and had never anyway been known for visual refinement, kitsch wasn't just an attitude but the only language in the land. But Casey, who, God help him, was convinced that the Soviet Union was going to be New York in the fifties all over again, was anxious to make some kind of deal with Khazin.

Alfred had offered instead to have a buffet at the gallery. For several days, Casey had stomped around in a rage. "Why are they screwing me over?" he'd demanded of Martha. "They did it for Willa Perkins, how come they're treating me like a stepchild?"

More harmful, Casey was forever dissing Costa, whom he portrayed in his jokes as fussy, unimaginative, a stick-in-the-mud. By opening week, the two men were barely speaking.

And the artists were at a loss, not knowing whom to look to. If Casey was difficult, they were impossible. Alfred had worked with plenty of art-world megastars, but those had been retiring compared to the pretensions of these punky little neophytes. Each of them was as temperamental as if it were his solo show, a museum retrospective, and there was no end to the jockeying for position, the rivalry, the infighting, the appeals to authority. Again, it was Martha to whom the artists instinctively came for reassurance and support.

This vacuum, to Gebler's mind, had come about because Dolly had made herself so scarce. It was not her show, she made all too clear, and her indifference the others found demoralizing. What Dolly never realized was that so addictive was her intensity that its withdrawal could be quite unmanning.

And Isaac, at the moment, Gebler's rescued tramp, Aurora's gofer, was her new genius, beneficiary of that throaty brooding worshipfulness. Well, at least you couldn't call her a snob. But it did not do wonders for Isaac's performance at work, which seemed to consist mostly of hanging around smiling and waiting to be told what to do.

By opening day—despite these grumblings—the show looked very snappy. There had been the usual slew of last-minute hitches. Steve Santo had claimed that his Plexiglas igloo had got scratched and was contemplating legal action, Killian Baker and Sally Francise were threatening to withdraw their collaborative work—a thirty-foot-long chart of

Manhattan development and the decay of city-owned properties—because it had been hung too high, while the printer appeared to have lost an accompanying text. A guerrilla group nobody had ever heard of had called up that morning, announcing they were going to stage a "raid" on the exhibition to protest the exclusion of artists of color, who as a matter of fact had not been excluded, and nobody was quite sure what if anything to do about it. Some blankets mysteriously were missing from the beds in the homeless shelter. And just that Monday Carole Fitzgerald's foundry had gone out of business, absconding with her bronze. Miraculous Costa had managed to track down the Sri Lankan owner, who was in the process of selling off his artists' work in order to buy a ticket back to Colombo. Costa was a diplomat—Alfred had once watched him persuade a gang of teen pickpockets to return his then-wife's wallet—and Carole Fitzgerald's *Slum King*, too, had miraculously reappeared intact.

And McGuinness had been in the gallery since noon, getting drunker and drunker. Gebler had borne him awhile, then slipped Andy eighty bucks to take McGuinness out to lunch, while he himself sneaked uptown for a quick nap.

Washed and dressed now, scented, beard trimmed, resplendent in a navy blue suit—the charcoal, he had decided, would be too hot in a room boiling with artists' nerves—Alfred wandered into the back of the apartment.

Carmen and the kids were glued to the teat of television, the girls wrapped together in a big armchair like two kittens and Leopold stretched on his stomach in front of the set. Some dreary sitcom with a canned laugh track. Carmen flashed him her golden smile.

"Good night, darlings. Leo, you got plumber's butt."

Leopold screwed around, not knowing whether to be worried or flattered.

"What's plumber's butt?" all three children asked at once.

Alfred in answer snapped the waistband of his son's underpants, which underlined a good three inches of white ass between T-shirt and jeans. A butterball, just like his dad. No Fred Astaires in the Gebler family.

"Are you doing everything Carmen tells you, my chickens?"

Carmen grinned appreciatively. He liked Carmen—grounded and worldly. Much more fun than that crazy old witch Ernestine, who'd finally hightailed it back to the islands. Carmen was a realist—women were, that's why they had such pitying contempt for men. Mr. Gebler always felt that the creation story was back to front: women were made of the earth, and men formed from the woman's rib—an incomplete, wanting appendage.

"Are you leaving now?" asked Johnny. "Have a good opening."

"Thanks. Wish me luck—they're threatening to picket the show because we don't have enough minorities in it!"

"Why don't you?" asked Carlotta, knitting her lovely brow sternly. Miss P.C. The Torquemada of tenth grade.

" 'Cause minorities can't paint!" And with that provocation he stepped out into the front hall of the building, cashmere overcoat on his arm, with a belated fumble to check for wallet and keys as the door swung shut. What had Dolly asked him to bring downtown for her? Lipstick? Compact? Too late. Nodded at the pasty young lawyer who had moved into 12C, and pressed the elevator button hard.

It was five-thirty when Alfred got out of a taxi in front of the gallery, and the first sight that met his eyes was Isaac Hooker carrying a bathtub over his head.

"What's the big idea? You look like—uh—some postmodern version of Diogenes or something. Or Saint Christopher. Didn't you ever read the story right? You're supposed to carry the baby, not the bathwater."

"We ran out of room again for all the ice AAA delivered. I borrowed it from Mr. Martinez—he plants his flowers in it in the spring."

Alfred watched Isaac and Costa plug the bathtub hole with putty and pile the tub high with bags of ice and bottles of white wine and beer. "Ingenious," Alfred admitted. "Costa, you doing all right? Where's McGuinness? He sleeping it off?"

"Oh, his wife came and picked him up about an hour ago."

"There been any more excitement?"

Costa looked exhausted. "One of the waiters called in sick. I got Jordan to fill in for him." Jordan was a bouncy, sweet-spoken kid from the neighborhood whom they all wanted to adopt. "He's wearing his school uniform—that okay by you? I promised his mom we'd deliver him home by eleven—he's got school tomorrow."

In Costa's back office, the waiters were changing from their street clothes into black tie. A moment later, the New Jersey fireman, the un-employed actress, the private detective, the gay model, the kung fu mas-ter, and the social studies teacher emerged from the backroom a uniform team. And Jordan. "You filled out, Jordan—what's your mom been feeding you? Look at those shoulders, man. You must be tall as your brothers now."

"Just about, but they still stronger." Jordan, a mother's boy who by her fierce providence managed to stay out of trouble, avoid gangs, sing in the church choir, come straight home from school. An honor stu-dent—how his teachers must lap him up—too radiantly shy, almost, to say much.

"Do you know how to pass a plate, Jordan? Do they teach you that in church? Let me show you." Gebler, showing off, grabbed a tray from the sideboard and whirled it under Jordan's eyes. "Now you got to hold it steady while the gluttons help themselves. Molly here will show you how. . . ."

At six o'clock the first guests arrived—a mousy youngish couple, each carrying a briefcase, who turned out to be the parents of Sally Fran-cise. Gebler felt old.

The opening had begun.

The guests congregated in knots about the third-floor gallery, eyeing the works from a distance. In one corner, Casey and Isaac, Casey talking low in Isaac's ear. Gebler, curious, veered over to them. "What kind of coup are you two plotting?"

"I'm telling him who's who," said Casey, a protective arm around his Friend from the Provinces' shoulder. Gebler eavesdropped.

"That lady in black—"

"Which lady? They're all in black!"

"The one with purple hair—writes for *Konsept*, her boyfriend used to do land art, now he's into neo-geo, he shows with Mary Boone. That's David Flaxman—he's a collector who's on Aurora's board. That's Joan Chavez, she's a sculptress, she works with found objects; that's my friend Joaquin, he used to have a gallery in the East Village, he was the first guy to show Basquiat. That's Celia Rubin, she's got a gallery on West Broadway, she was big in the seventies, she used to be married to Patrick Rubin. That's John Hanlon—oh my God, there's the *Times* critic, I better go kiss her ass." And Casey was off like a bat.

"What do you think?" Gebler asked Isaac, jerking his head at the crowd.

"I think I'd better start driving a taxi, as you once suggested." He was looking rather glum, it seemed to Gebler. Probably pissed off at himself for having turned down Casey's offer to be among this stellar selection.

It was a good and varied crowd. On top of the usual art-world professionals and Aurora supporters, there were Casey's friends, girls in thick black stockings and combat boots and dyed black hair, boys with multiple nose rings, all of whom were determined to stay as late and to put away as much food and drink as possible. Nowhere was the dichotomy between patrons and artists more apparent than in the coatcheck, one half of which was hung in sable coats and chesterfields, the other half in mangy thrift-shop lumber jackets. Of course, Alfred noted, this being the art world, the lumber jackets were probably making more money than the sables.

The artists themselves could be distinguished from their friends and supporters by the peculiar expressions on their faces—in some cases of nervous suffering gloom, in others of the enraptured obliviousness of the bridegroom, the winning athlete who has the TV microphone thrust to her mouth and chatters top-speed without knowing a word of what she's said.

Except for McGuinness. No sooner had Alfred deposited his young employee in the arms of Joan Chavez than he had been seized once more by McGuinness, who wanted to talk about Steve Santo's piece. To his captive, it seemed as if McGuinness's commentary was bullhorn loud and that everybody in the room was listening aghast. Jesus Christ, thought Gebler, to think I was dreading Gina's girl prisoners!

"This—this transparent turd"—McGuinness tapped at the hulk of Plexiglas with dollars embedded inside—"is unrelieved garbage. Frankly, desperately, unutterably meretricious. Don't you agree, my love? Don't you agree, Alfie? Meretricious. *C'est tout. On ne peut pas dire plus.*"

"Let's go sit in the back for a bit, have a talk." Alfred wedged a propelling arm under McGuinness's elbow, wondering whom he could find to baby-sit the old monster, but McGuinness resisted being hauled away. For now he had skated into the stage of drunkenness that gets extremely sober, and he wanted to talk right there. "Why did you put me in this fry-up, Alfie? I do assume it was you and not Peter Pan over there. I can't say I feel at home. Despite the show's title."

Alfred cleared his throat, wondering if he hadn't been wrong to include the old bully: an amusing idea that didn't work. "I wanted to remind the little buggers what greatness is," he said.

McGuinness seemed touched, his old man's vulnerability somewhat reassured. "Now tell me your honest opinion. They are a bunch of preachy little kiss-asses, aren't they? You can tell me the truth. I grew up in a cold-water tenement in Red Hook, I got my first job on the docks, I've worn this city like a glove, like a blister, so I can tell very well they none of them give a damn about urban decay or the city poor or any of it. They wouldn't know the city if it sat on them—all they know is their careers and their commissions."

"Well, we each have our own version of New York—" Gebler began.

But McGuinness interrupted. "You can't manufacture a cause, you've got to feel it here," and he thumped his heart through his checked Viyella shirt.

At this point, Dave Flaxman came up to the two men, putting his arm around Alfred. "Hey, Al, what's happening?"

"Dave, you know Bill McGuinness? One of our artists."

"Well, congratulations to both of you, then. From my heart." Dave placed a sun-tanned hand on his chest to emphasize his sincerity. Where did they teach businessmen body language, anyway? No bond trader that didn't come over like a crooner with religion. "What a show. Beautiful, absolutely beautiful. I was talking to a critic over there, and we were talking about how essential it is to have shows like this, just to try to reclaim our city—to make the politicians sit up and realize that artists and other working people are being driven out of our public spaces by greedy developers. . . ."

"McGuinness here should know, he moved out to—"

"I didn't leave the city because of greedy developers," McGuinness protested. "I left because I was tired of getting bonked over the head by greedy muggers. I put in for a gun permit, but the only ones allowed to bear weapons in this city are the criminals. Of course, out in Port Washington I've got a lovely collection of pistols and shotguns—you should come sample my selection, Alfie—and not a soul to use 'em on, unless I decide it's time to send Ruthie to her just reward. . . ."

"Let me warn you, Bill, you're talking to–Dave, not me–one of the pillars of the ACLU."

"Oh, so you're sweet on the criminals, are you, Dave? You must be a very rich man. It takes millions to be a liberal in this city. Where do you live, Park Avenue? Oh, *Fifth* Avenue–that's a nice public space. . . ."

"There's no need to be hostile." Dave looked genuinely injured.

"You think the show's a success, Dave?" Gebler interrupted.

"It's super. Very timely. Lorraine sends her best–she was sorry she couldn't be here, she's got her class tonight."

"Good, good–Bill, Dave, excuse me, please–I got to go catch Joan before she leaves."

Upstairs, Casey and Isaac were seated at a table with John Hanlon and an artist called David Stacey. John, David, and Casey were gossiping about an art dealer they all knew.

"So I'm, like, bringing some friends into the gallery–this collector of mine from L.A.," David Stacey was saying, "and Edward is like, Who are these people? Get them out of here. And I'm like, Whoa now. These are friends of mine. And he's like, In the future, David, I would appreciate it if you would *advise* me ahead of time before you come into the gallery."

"Get outa here!" said John Hanlon and Casey.

"Well, my jaw was down to my knees. And I'm like, Edward, this is my show. These are my pictures you got hanging on the wall. And you're telling me I don't have the right to bring in my own friends to look at my own pictures? You mean, I'm, like, barred from this gallery where you've chosen to exhibit my work?"

"You know why he does it, right?" Hanlon said.

"Sure. He wants the collectors for himself. He doesn't want me making any independent connections."

" 'Course, he's been bankrupt more times than we been laid. That cat got ninety lives," Casey interjected. "And I don't think he's staying in that space long."

"No?"

"What, in that same building with Mary Krushar and Paul Wiggin? Who is he kidding?"

"Well, it depends who's backing him this time. Somebody told me it was Daniel Altschuler. Could be true—there's something about Edward, people keep on saving his bacon."

"Sure, he's got taste—he shows us, right? Even Helmut's got a soft spot for Edward."

At this point Gina sauntered over. "You boys still gossiping about dealers?"

Isaac, who hadn't seen Gina since Brighton Beach, lit up.

"Grab a plate, honey, and join the fun," Casey said. "We're just trying to figure out who's financing Edward's new gallery."

Gina, undecided, perched on the arm of his chair. He put a hand on her hip, but she slipped over into a chair of her own. "Shit, you guys are pathetic—everywhere I go, it's Helmut this, Edward that, Werner said my new work has really matured, Werner thinks Edward's a scumbag but Helmut thinks he's . . . All you little dickheads creaming to get noticed by the big boys! I mean, who gives a fuck, it's just dealers. You know? In forty years, who remembers the dealers except boring art historians?"

"You got a gallery yet, Gina?" David Stacey inquired.

"Get outa here, you little bitch."

Gina, it seemed to Isaac, looked unearthly beautiful. She was wearing a pale green dress embroidered with tiny white seashells and a pair of matching pale green velvet stilettos and her eyes were a darker green, like the sea on a rough day.

"You're a mermaid, Gina," said Isaac, lovingly.

"You know, she's right," said John Hanlon. "I mean, let's be honest, women artists, they just get railroaded, right? When Willa and I were coming outa art school, all the dealers were calling me up, and her they just ignored. My pieces were going for ten grand, and hers were seven hundred dollars. And we were living in the same apartment, working together like the Bobbsey Twins. I mean, I couldn't even tell apart my work from hers. So Willa thinks, Fuck this shit. I can't get an even break in painting, I'm gonna get myself some attention. So she gets up on stage and paints herself blue—so what if people are just coming to look at her tits? At least they're paying. I always tell my women-artist friends, Man, if you girls only had dicks, Helmut and Werner and Leonard would be lining up to represent you, you'd be having retrospectives at the Whitney."

"Yeah? You think Willa's outa luck? Try being a black woman artist, see who returns your phone calls," said Gina.

"Look, that's why I decided I was going to put together shows myself, cut out the middleman," said Casey. "One day I sit up and realize, Hey, that's where the power is. Wouldn't it be nice to have people calling me up for a change, wanting something, instead of getting jerked around by people's secretaries?"

"Well, you sold out, that's all."

"I like the control, I admit it, I like being able to give other artists a break instead of watching them get screwed. And I don't miss being treated like shit."

"Do you miss the artwork?" John Hanlon asked.

"Oh, I still work."

"I wouldn't," said John Hanlon. "If I could make the same money another way, I wouldn't. I would give up art like . . . I tell Willa sometimes, I'm gonna quit art and become your manager. That always scares the shit out of her."

The party downstairs was thinning, and now Gebler, McGuinness still in hand, came over to their table. "Hi there, kids—hey, Gina, I was looking all over for you. Save us a seat, will you, I'm just going to check out the chow."

When he returned, it was with Dolly as well as McGuinness, whose eyes got big as baseballs soon as he caught sight of Gina. They sat down, McGuinness practically on Gina's lap, and the table now separated into twos and threes. Mrs. Gebler talked very earnestly with John Hanlon about Willa's new opera, Isaac and David Stacey argued about the homeless, while Casey and Alfred Gebler watched helpless as Gina and McGuinness flirted and wrangled. Then Emanuele Conti came over and put his arm around Mrs. Gebler, and she was drawn away. With Dolly's departure, conversation came to a halt. Gina stopped arguing with McGuinness, and Isaac stopped arguing with David Stacey. Isaac found himself looking after Mrs. Gebler. He turned to Gina and saw that Gina too was staring after her with a fixity of regard that was . . . what?

Gina stood up, smoothing her rucked-up dress over the slim hips, with a surprised, inquiring expression on her face. "Well, I'm out of here."

"Girl, it's only eleven."

"Yeah? I get up at five."

Casey and Gebler both jumped to their feet and started to talk at the same time.

"After you, boss."

"No, really. I just thought I'd put Miss Aubeville in a cab. But if you're—"

"No, no, not at all. I . . ."

"Are you going to let this young she-devil out in the streets alone?" inquired McGuinness, who had turned by now to Hanlon.

In the meantime, Gina walked off by herself. And Gebler and Casey, looking at each other, sat down again.

Twenty-six

As soon as the "Home" show opened, Dolly took the children to the country.

Their departure—Alfred had promised to come out by Christmas Eve—naturally was hell. The days had been spent in a torrent of duties: sending off last-minute presents, winding up office business, plus a weekend trip to Chicago to see her mother, whom she felt remorseful not to be spending Christmas with, and finally, two nights before she left, a couple of hours with Jesse, who had now contracted tuberculosis. Followed as usual by guilt at being hale while these beloveds were suffering. By the end of the week, she was exhausted.

Thursday night—the night before they were due to leave—she stopped by Isaac's studio on the way home from work. He wanted her to see the new series he had just embarked on.

Terrifying, how cold his room was.

"Am I going to come back after New Year's and find you a pillar of ice?"

"I come from New England. This is semitropical. Besides, I've gotten used to sleeping in hat and gloves."

"I think we need to have a talk with your landlord. Why can't you buy an electric heater, at least? A room this minuscule should warm up quickly."

He offered her a glass of whisky and a plateful of tiny Spanish macaroons, and she pored over his new drawings of the sons of heaven and the daughters of the earth. Dolly was stunned. Their rank sexuality flooded her, leaving the limbs weak. "My God," she said, leaning back. "What glory. What glory. What genius. It's sublime. *You're* sublime. How do you get such ideas?"

"I told you already. Genesis. I want it all rich, rich colors," he explained. Until the last panel of the world after the Flood, as if God had drained this reformed creation of the old gaudy jangling palette.

"You should do nothing but make art. I'd like to lock you up in this icy room and not let you out again. . . . I must say, I can't wait to see how they will be fleshed out on canvas. Although even these sketches are magnificent. I want to see what you've done the moment I come back. I can hardly bear going away tomorrow. . . ."

"Why? Where are you going?"

"We're going out to Long Island for Christmas."

"Oh." He looked crestfallen. "But you like them?" He jerked his head towards the sketches.

"I think they leave those roosters and kitchens in the dust. It's a whole new realm you've entered. Less quaint, more terrifying. Magnificent, Isaac. I can't tell you how exciting I find your work—it's like nothing else I've seen. Really."

When she was done looking, she said, "I would like to buy a picture."

Isaac went quiet. For a moment, she wondered if he was offended that she should think that these products of his hand and heart, these bloody love letters to God and the unknown, had dollars and cents stuck to them. He rose, wandered over to the door, raised his fingertips to the ceiling. Then he came up behind her, leaned over her chair.

"They don't have prices."

"You're talking to a businessman's daughter. Everything has a price. We'll decide upon it together, if you like."

"Which one do you want to buy?"

"The circus of the saints, to start with," she said, pointing to the unstretched canvas backdrop of Ferris wheels and Saint Sebastian.

Isaac's lower lip stuck out. "No. That one's so crude—I hadn't figured out yet how to make compositions or lay on the paint—the perspective's all cockeyed."

"Yes, but it's got such power of emotion. And perhaps one of the bathtub pictures—the one where the bathwater's a lake, with your father in the window. And then I want very much to see how this new series turns out.

"I tell you—I'd like to buy these two pictures, but I don't want to take them with me just yet. It's much more important that we get people in to see your work as a whole, that it not get dispersed before it's seen."

Isaac nodded. "Five hundred," he said, pointing to the loose canvas. "Three hundred," pointing to the bathtub painting.

"Fine. We'll hike up your prices next year." She fumbled for her checkbook, which was lodged at the bottom of her handbag. "Have you got a bank account?"

"Mmmm. Costa set me up at Chemical first week of work. You're wrong not to like the house pictures better, by the way," he told her, pocketing the check.

She shrugged. "I love your extremeness, I guess. Those big quilts, they're too cautious."

"But the light is good."

"You'll do better light."

He walked her downstairs to put her in a cab. Outside was throbbing with red neon and ambulance sirens. Along the curb was ranged a trio of whores in short skirts and high heels, daring the passing cars to stop. A Honda with New Jersey plates slowed down, then speeded up. Poor cold girls. Did transsexuals have pimps, too?

Dolly still felt prickle-limbed from the savagery of Isaac's new drawings. Conscious, suddenly, of the tameness of her own existence, in contrast to the huge violent visions that possessed the young man who loped beside her, ungainly, shambling, muttering under his breath a little song that was half hum, half dirge, with a beatifically absent expres-

sion on his rosy blond face. As he put her into a cab, she hesitated before closing the door, not wanting to say goodbye.

He leaned in, smiling. "Shall I take you uptown?"

"No, that would be absurd. Well—well, just *work*. I hope you have a
demonically productive Christmas. Now don't scrimp on materials. You
can't shortchange such strong visions. And please get yourself a heater. I
don't want you freezing to death before you've even started."

As the taxi pulled away and Eighth Avenue fizzled out at Columbus
Circle, Dolly's gaiety faded. She had not realized how little she was
looking forward to the evening to come.

The Geblers were not getting along very well. That morning, Dolly had
said to her husband, "I want to ask you as a special favor to be home for
dinner tonight—the children and I are leaving tomorrow."

Alfred's genial expectant face went cold. "Whatever you say, dear."
For the very voicing of this request—icy, accusing, aggressively guilt-
provoking—had poisoned what he had intended to do as a matter of
course.

These days Dolly and Alfred seemed to be permanently at odds.
She, angry at her husband's absenteeism, found herself pushing him
away even farther, in the hopes that he would spring back to her in loving penitence. But he didn't, and Dolly at times felt appalled by what
strangers they had become, how distant, how barely civil. Why did she
have so much fun with Ayala or Emanuele and so little with Alfred? The
only time they talked was after sex, and it had gotten so that she wondered how they could even bear to touch, except that not to would
mean that really everything was over.

It seemed to her that there was nothing in the world lonelier than a
couple living in apparent intimacy and actual alienation, and that she
would prefer living by herself to this simulacrum of connubiality, whose
anxieties and chronic resentments deprived her of even the peace of
mind, the fruitful meditations, that would come of genuine solitude.
She couldn't spend an evening contentedly reading a book because one
part of her brain was always glancing at the clock, wondering when Alfred was going to come home and furious because it was getting later
and later and she didn't believe him when he told her he had been over
at Costa's, talking about old times.

Worst of all, their battlefields were always so damn petty—never the open country but always some pinched little scullery-sink dispute. Their current conflict was over the car, a Mercedes station wagon which Alfred had insisted on getting because Bobby had one. The car had just come back from the garage for the third time that year, but Paul once again had been unable to account for the rattle in its engine.

"Are you sure you feel comfortable about driving?" asked Alfred after dinner.

"What else am I going to do? Have you seen how many bags the girls are taking? I have to bring out all the Christmas presents. And Mr. West's pear trees."

"You could always take a limo."

"What, be stuck in the country without a car just because you can't get that damned Paul to do his job properly?"

"Well, I don't want you to feel unhappy driving."

"As far as I can see, there's not much choice about it."

Alfred, defeated, went off to watch television with the children, and Dolly read her novel, and did not come to bed until after his light was out.

The underlying quarrel was that Alfred could not bear—was positively allergic to—their house on Long Island. He had no inner resources, needed constant entertainment, and the country was a boring mystery. The only way he could stand it was by behaving exactly as if he were in town: soon as he got out to Goose Neck Farm, he was on the phone fixing Saturday-night dinner at Piero Ancona's over in Sag Harbor, Sunday lunch at Bobby and Sarah's in East Hampton, some artist to go visit in Springs, or taking the children shopping at the Ralph Lauren in Southampton. Spent the entire weekend on the ferry back and forth to the Hamptons, where all his friends lived and where at least there was the ocean, instead of being stuck on a goddamn creek on the more desolate North Fork. The mosquito coast, he called it. Of course, the real reason that he hated Goose Neck Farm was that it was hers and she loved it.

The next morning Alfred, exuding the guilty solicitousness of a man with plans, helped Dolly load up. Pretended unconvincingly that if work went well, he would try to make it by next weekend.

The girls too were looking sulky. They didn't want one bit to be going to the country; it was Christmas and their friends who had gone to boarding school were back in town, and now the Christmas parties were on, and Carlotta, who had a crush on a Hotchkiss boy called Stephen, was sure to miss her chance. Sadly, they had outgrown Goose Neck. Maybe they would come around to it again later, but for now, weekends and vacations, they wanted to hang out on that dismal strip of dismal Upper East Side bars that served underagers, moon over boys who either did or didn't telephone.

At eleven, the car's rear piled high with boxes and paper bags and suitcases and trees, they headed off, the girls in back, Leopold up front with his mother. Leopold, pale and anxious, was clutching his asthma squeeze-spray. His parents' difficulties had communicated themselves to him, and although in ordinary circumstances he would have been overjoyed to be going to the country, he felt it was his fault that his mother was unhappy and that his parents were not getting along. Worse still, he was missing his old friend Ernestine even worse than he'd anticipated. His mother had promised they could go down to Trinidad and see her next Easter, but a visit would not be the same as having her skinny arms around him day in, day out.

As soon as they got onto the Long Island Expressway, however, the glorious sunny blue day made him forget his sorrows, and he and his mother began speculating eagerly about how much snow there would be, and whether they would be able to skate on the pond, and how the chestnut-roasting pan she had bought at Zabar's would work, and what decorations they would make for the tree, and whether they should go to carol singing in Greenport or Cutchogue. Even Johnny and Carlotta, who had been sitting in the back complaining that their feet were cold and that they were feeling sick, soon got caught up in the excitement and joined in.

Twenty-seven

THE WEEK OF CHRISTMAS, Aurora closed, and everybody went away till after New Year's. Gebler, complaining mightily, took a jitney to Long Island, Casey went to Cambridge, Costa took his daughter up to his sister's house in Rockport. Even Jane and Dogface, it turned out, had families.

On the last day of work, Gebler gave the staff their Christmas bonuses. Isaac was astounded. Five hundred dollars! Now, including what Mrs. Gebler had paid for his two pictures, he had thirteen hundred dollars he hadn't counted on. On top of which—the very day after Mrs. Gebler had come to see his drawings of "The Sons of Heaven Meet the Daughters of the Earth," a super-deluxe electric heater had been delivered to his apartment along with two pairs of extra-large silk long johns, a handful of sable brushes, half a dozen small prestretched canvases, and a cedar box of oils.

Isaac sent a money order for five hundred dollars to his mother, with a watercolor of El Moro which he hoped would amuse her, and a pair of waterproof hiking boots for his brother, Turner. Then he bought presents for Luther and Scout. He couldn't remember when he'd last had more fun. The leftover money he would splurge on live models, for he badly needed a female sitter for the shepherdess. A buxom one.

For the past few years, since leaving Gilboa, Isaac had chosen to ignore the holidays. Christmas, anyway, had always struck him as a pagan fake drummed up by department stores—Jesus' birth was nothing to the real business of the Passion. On Christmas Day he would get up at seven as usual, go for a quick walk around the block, just to check out the light, the faces, buy the newspapers, then home again to apply himself straightaway to whatever painterly problem he was tackling at the moment. Take advantage of a few unfettered days. If he thought at all about the holiday, it was only to use it as a jimmy with which to reinsert himself more rapidly into the closed rooms of his past. He would pace the small studio, arms tight behind his back, and conjure up the atmosphere, the appurtenances and customs of that long-ago time, that other country, in which Christmases used to be celebrated.

Mostly it was the cold he remembered, air so thin it burned to breathe and gloves turned to five splayed stalactites, and the pond in the woods froze over, and life was reduced to a huddling around the stove, to sucking in deep the few hours of daylight raw and stinging as surgical spirits. Sometimes he and his father and Turner would go snowshoeing in the woods. Come home in the dusk when the satin pinkish white skins of the slim birch trees looked like a bathhouseful of naked ladies, knee-deep in the grubbier white of snow. That last year, when he was living up in the hills with Agnes, they'd gone to Midnight Mass on Christmas Eve.

Those days were gone. His father was in the grave, his brother didn't answer his letters, and Agnes he had left in the lurch. Each year's turning took him farther from that rackety house he was born in, whose rooms he could re-enter only through the medium of crayon, from the days when the thermometer's mercury never hiked high as zero and the back roads were snowed shut till April, and he and his girlfriend had lived in a shack with no electricity and had had to kiss and hug to keep warm.

This year, his fourth in New York City, had turned out to be Gilboacold: the coldest winter in living memory. Old people were freezing to death in the Midwest; in New Orleans it snowed; and in Maine the temperature hadn't reached twenty since Thanksgiving. In New York City, it was thirty-five below with the wind-chill factor. Burning cold, under ice-blue skies, and the wind like a banshee.

All over the city, men from the country had been unloading Christmas trees from their pickup trucks. Ruddy-faced men, laughing and stomping to keep warm, with reverse vacuums that spat out net wrapping around your captured pine. The wind, like a knife at your back, hurtled you along streets that had been transformed by the Christmas-tree sellers into an aromatic forest-cathedral.

On the way home from shopping for Turner's boots, Isaac saw in the subway a father and son, southern blacks with the country gentility still clinging to them, each carrying a tall conifer. The boy, hoping no one could see, patted his tree, steadying it with a hand on its flank, as you might a nervous mare. "Whoa—whoa there," the boy murmured to his tree. To Isaac, it seemed as if the two trees, father's and son's, were nudging each other, atremble, in secret communion, making their druidical presence known even in the sweaty dank inferno of the underground.

The waning day, high above the pine forest and mountain range of buildings, had narrowed to a tunnel of sunlight, an orange-gold conical glow surrounded by violet blue.

On Christmas Day, Isaac worked in pencil on a small canvas of the shepherdess receiving the ram till almost midnight, and went to bed only to give himself a springboard for a fresher view next day. In the morning, miraculously, it looked grubby but convincing. All except for the shepherdess's legs, up in the air as she lay on her back on the bank—the legs somehow seemed stuck on with glue, whereas what they should be was living gates welcoming the conqueror. By afternoon, he had ruined it again, and left the house, dejected. Darkness was falling, falling, and the streets were empty. Doorways like missing teeth in an ugly jaw, gapes of darkness.

He reached Times Square in a cold sweat of foreboding. Overhead, a flashing neon Scotch bottle and a pack of Camel cigarettes, and a high-definition television screen watchable twelve blocks away, now showing shoppers in pursuit of post-Christmas bargains.

Grotesque, to have a mile-high television screen right in the middle of Times Square—the most exciting street in the universe, and everyone gawking at the TV instead of each other.

Suddenly it seemed to Isaac as if all that modern technology was inventing was ways to avoid human intercourse, to blunt the edges of consciousness. First there'd come television, wall-to-wall television so nobody had to face the empty gut of loneliness within, television providing this artificial human company more vivid and consoling, certainly juicier than real life, plus you in control.

Then there was the telephone, so you never actually had to face your friends—telephones creating the artificial secrecy-intimacy of the confessional box, combined with the irresponsibility, the power of instant exit—Sorry, gotta go, the dog's peeing on my fur coat. He'd heard one of the prostitutes in his neighborhood joke that she was getting put out of business by telephone sex, and even this seemed to Isaac positively tragic. For what was telephone sex but the ultimate expression of our insistence on unreality, our refusal of other human beings?

In the logical future people would dispense with fleshly gropings altogether and stick to artificial insemination. Slot-machine sex. Put in your dime and out comes the individually wrapped packet of White Male Physics Graduate HIV-Free Sperm. This is where our sexual liberation had wound up, in mistrust and alienation, and the discovery that we didn't really like each other all that much. Men and women, whites and blacks, Hatfields and McCoys.

He had wrecked his picture—it was overworked and spiritless now—and there was nothing to be done. Nothing but give up and die, roll over. Stop breathing. Start again.

Overhead, Isaac saw on the Times Square television that the Romanian dictator Ceaușescu and his wife had been shot without trial, and the news filled him with dread. All fall had been the mounting joy of communism's crumbling across the Soviet Union and Eastern Europe, the rebirth of civility and freedom. And now this, the murder of the Ceaușescus, struck him as the first misturning. The humane and gentle revolution had shown its bloody face, and chaos or tyranny lay ahead. And the picture was all wrong, because it had lost its freedom, become leaden. The shepherdess's legs somehow, nightmarishly, had turned to trotters. I am a butcher, not an artist. Like the Ceaușescus, who Romanov-style had been shot, awkwardly, messily, by inept guards.

Heading home, he saw that even the triple-X movie theater on his corner was closed for X-X-Xmas. Crestfallen as if only the cast image of spread thighs and eager gaping puss, the sound drop of ludicrously happy grunts and moans, could comfort him in what suddenly he was obliged to acknowledge was acute loneliness.

All the previous months' complicity that came of working long hours side by side, the days of goofing around with Costa and Martha, the nights on the town with Gebler and Casey and their mates, the rolling from bar to bar and party to party in jammed-tight taxis, now seemed a mirage. His quickening semifriendship with Mrs. Gebler, too. All this brightness and foolery had intoxicated him into half-believing, sneakily, My luck is changing, these are my true-destined mates, and I will never feel a misfit again. Now he knew those days were not the ushering in of sweetness but an anomalous break in the unchanging reality of his condition. They—Casey, Costa, Jane, the Geblers—were back where they belonged, with families and lovers, and he was restored to his ordained lot, to his necessary aloneness. Silence, concentration. Patience, patience, and more patience. Your music is not the crashing of cymbals on exquisite sound systems, the rainfall of laughter, but the liquefaction of oils on canvas, the fricative twitter of graphite on paper. I have been wasting time, he told himself. Last week he'd turned twenty-six; next week was a new decade and he had done nothing. Ever since he'd arrived at Aurora he had been meeting painters not much older than he who already possessed dealers, galleries, collectors, reputations. Now he realized that the New York voracity for success applied to him too. I must buckle down to work and accomplish steady things, a slow patient accumulation, a refinement. Not fritter. Only by drawing drawing drawing do you discover. Discover what? The roots of things. Where their weight lies. How they join. The disposition of mass. Out of nowhere he started dreaming of the coiled knotty rivulets of vein in Luther's feet, the yellow-blue horns of his toenails.

Three days after Christmas, Luther came to model, and Isaac set him up on a mattress on the floor, blasted by the supersonic heater. Luther was from Vidalia, Georgia—onion capital of the U.S.A. He had been on the streets eight years, maybe ten. In the old days, his turf had been Grand Central. Now he was living on Henry Street. Had a body like a chest of drawers: massive great rib cage, the upper arms run to fat, and a belly that hung over his loins. And frightening feet, gone purplish gray and a toe missing from sleeping under bridges. Fiery bloodshot eyes, and an overhanging shelf of forehead, creviced in wrinkles, and grizzled beard. The beard was distracting—turned him into a paunchy black saint.

Isaac fed him and gave him twenty-five dollars for the day. Luther was an artist too and had opinions. When Isaac showed him the best of the drawings, Luther almost spat in scorn. "That's not modern—that's a very traditional drawing you done there."

"What's not modern about it?"

"See, in art, the trick is not to tell everything at once. You telling us too much. The story is laid out there bold, you got no cards left in your hand, boy. Didn't you ever court a woman, try to get her interested in you when she got a dozen other dogs after her tail? That's what you got to do with your audience. I never spent a day in art school, but I know that. Mystery is the gates."

"The gates?" repeated Isaac, agog at the rightness of it.

"The *key*. Got to keep your audience guessing."

Isaac drew him over and over, and finally settled on Luther sitting on the floor, knees up to his chin. Luther didn't like the position so much because that was how he used to sit on the streets. He would rather be seen relaxing. He liked to fish, for instance. They argued, and Isaac drew him as he wanted and then drew him as Luther wanted, and then Luther drew Isaac, except what it ended up looking like was broken glass, and Luther ran Isaac's fancy oil sticks into the ground.

All day Isaac drew Luther or worked on the shepherdess and the ram, with a quick walk in the afternoon to get some air. And at night when he'd gone cross-eyed from looking too hard, he read Spinoza on the Old Testament over whisky and a bowl of soup, until he fell asleep.

By the time Aurora was due to reopen, Isaac had grown so fruitful and content in his routine of work and walk and work and soup and whisky that he almost wished he could afford to quit.

Part Six

Twenty-eight

I<small>T WAS THE BEGINNING</small> of February, and Isaac was driving Mrs. Gebler back from the studio of a Catalan artist named Enric Urgell who was living out in Williamsburg. The Geblers had first met the young man in Barcelona: he was the fourth generation in a family of master mosaicists. His great-grandfather had done the mosaics in Barcelona's Teatro del Liceu and the Palau de la Musica, and his grandfather had designed some of the pavements on the Ramblas. As a teenager, Enric helped his father restore the mosaics in a Romanesque monastery in the mountains outside Barcelona. Then he came to America. In the early eighties, Enric Urgell had made conceptual art. Now since he'd moved out to Williamsburg, he'd abandoned piles of burlap and rubber boots and taken to painting. That afternoon, Dolly had bought a canvas, eight feet by ten, on which were scrawled in crimson and purple a chair, a hangman, a house, and then scratched almost illegibly, down at the bottom, the words "Saber es evitar."

"This is Isaac Hooker, he's a very talented artist who works for us at Aurora," Dolly had introduced her companion.

Enric had a shock of brown hair that fell over his eyes. He flicked back his hair like a pony. "What kind of work does he do?"

"Biblical narrative, mostly. Set in his native New England."

Now Enric for the first time looked at Isaac directly. "My God." He laughed. "A few years ago, a friend of mine and I were speculating, Well, here in the New York art world, anything is possible and no one is shockable. But what are the limits? Here in New York the only forbidden subject, we decided, the only thing that would really shock and embarrass the pants off the critics, is religion."

"We'll see," said Dolly.

After leaving Enric's studio, Dolly was eager to take a look around some of the newer galleries that had opened up in the neighborhood, attracted by low rents and large spaces. She and Isaac were a little nervous about leaving the Urgell in the back of the Black Maria, but they figured the car was too dingy to break into or steal.

The last gallery they went to had an installation entitled *Flesh Is Grass*, by a young artist called Rebecca Halberstam. It was an actual golf course, with real grass. Mounds, sand pits. The only thing irregular about it, besides the reduced scale, was that the holes in the green were bright pink replicas of female genitals. There was a sound system of waves breaking, alternating with slurping noises. In the entrance was a TV set with a video of the artist, explaining how the piece was a critique of male ideas of recreation as conquest. The little flags over each tee were phallic symbols representing male attempts to subjugate woman's mystery—how even men's insistence on women's mysteriousness was a way of dismissing women as irrational negligible childish creatures. It was also about how as we destroy the environment, we find ever more expensive artificial ways of re-creating it, establishing our ultimate tyranny over nature through sport.

"God," said Mrs. Gebler, after they got back in the car. "That's what Andy wants us to show, isn't it?"

"He'd better not, " said Isaac. "Do you know how much work it is, maintaining a golf course? Anyway, I didn't come to Manhattan to mow lawns."

They both reflected.

Then Isaac spoke. "I think I'd better quit."

She had almost forgotten he was there, driving her, so intent was she on her own thoughts. She was thinking about her marriage, a subject she found distressing.

The Geblers had been back from the country a month now. Christmas, after all the anticipatory grumbling and fights, the protests and evasions, had ended up being really quite wonderful, uncustomarily benign. At the last minute Sophie had arrived on her way back from Haiti, where she was sponsoring an orphanage for the children of AIDS victims. She had broken up with her record-producer boyfriend, whom she'd discovered in bed with the Philippine houseboy, and had thrown herself into country pleasures—interior, mostly, thanks to the cold—with a vehemence both pitiful and endearing. On the twenty-third Alfred had arrived, with a haunch of venison, and on Christmas Eve they had taken the Greenport ferry over to Shelter Island to have dinner with Cleveland and Berry Heathcot, who lived out there year-round. The ferry moving like an icebreaker through polar waters. The creeks and inlets a new territory of gloaming sludge, precarious platforms of ice. Theirs the only car on the last boat coming home. Christmas Eve on the frozen night-waters, Leopold and the girls half-asleep in the back, and the harbor lights of Greenport glimmering, chattering beyond the dark waves. For the first year Dolly could remember nobody had gotten sick, nobody had sulked.

On Christmas Day, they had eaten chestnut soup and venison that had been marinating two days and Mrs. West's mince pie, and the children had put on a play written by Carlotta, and on New Year's Eve they'd told fortunes: Sophie had brought tarot cards and a kit for dropping molten lead into ice water. Whatever blobby shape emerged was your fate. My future as a lump.

Then, towards midnight, they had all jumped into the hot tub— Alfred's last-year Christmas present. Dolly had loathed the idea of a hot tub, and yet, lolling on her back staring up at the stars like sea salt in the crisp black night, steam rising, the lunatic proximity of near-nakedness and ice, she had indeed succumbed to the majesty, the mystery of it. . . .

She had come back to the city almost optimistic. Even Alfred, insincerely, had complained, "Why can't we stay out here all the time?" The fruit of five days of Sophie's sucking up to him like nobody's business. The poor lamb, though it didn't seem to get her anywhere, still regarded a woman's business to be making men feel good, and even Leopold had emerged sleeker from her ministrations: shiatsu and horoscopes and God knows what else. Talked him into wanting to try acupuncture for the asthma. Dolly said, "If you don't cut it out, Soph, I'm going to stick a pin right into you!"

But already, a month after they were back, the Geblers were fighting again, and their Christmas country cheer had dissipated.

Two weeks ago Alfred had gone down to Miami for the opening of a new contemporary art museum, built by Peretz Kaminer, whom Dolly wanted to design their future annex.

While Alfred was away, something disturbing had happened. Dolly

received a call from Walter Newsome at the bank. He'd been trying unsuccessfully to reach Alfred—they'd just received his check to Visa for
$22,428.56, but unfortunately his account was already way overdrawn.
Was he expecting some new funds, or did Mrs. Gebler want to cover the
difference? Dolly transferred twenty-five thousand dollars from her
Chicago account. Then she looked at Alfred's Visa statement, which was
lying on his desk in a pile of paid bills. In its pages she saw itemized a
succession of restaurants, nightclubs, and shops, day after day of them,
not one of which she recognized.

How had he managed on December 14 to spend twelve thousand
dollars at Barney's? On whom, a day later, had he blown seventy-five
hundred dollars at A La Vieille Russie, an antique-jewelry store on Fifth
Avenue? Somebody had had a very happy Christmas. Who? Who was
the recipient of twenty-eight dollars' worth of booze from Quality
Liquor? Or two hundred and twenty-five dollars' worth of goods from
an in-line skating store? Not his children, that was for sure. And the
American Airlines charge for his last trip out to California was too high
to be a single ticket. No wonder Richard Cruikshank had sounded so
odd when she talked to him on the phone.

It was the life of a stranger. Not only the places but the style was unfamiliar to her. If Carlos had slipped up and delivered her the next-door
neighbors' mail, its chronicle could not have been more alien to her.

There was no longer any avoiding it—this itemized, clocked itinerary
of pleasure and cost confirmed beyond a doubt that Alfred was courting. In her fury, she had been ten times on the verge of tearing open his
telephone bill—they had separate lines—to learn the identity of the unknown miss. She didn't. Because it was unworthy. That he had no scruples about humiliating her utterly, about making a prize fool of her in
public—how could he have taken the woman out to California to meet
Richard!—was all the more reason why she must not sink, not sneak.
She'd had plenty of time while Alfred was in Florida to chew over the
extent of his traitorous vileness, of her own foolhardiness in having married a man who did not respect her, a man without integrity or honor.

For the remainder of his trip, she had refused to answer her husband's phone calls—the children, learning from her grim white face, her
tight voice and writhing hands that something was amiss, had snuck
around the house on tiptoe—and when he returned, she'd had it out
with him.

She had begun with the financial problem. Where did her husband get the right to be so spendthrift, so crassly profligate? She who had the money was frugal, self-denying even (after all, four-fifths of her private income she funnelled each year into the foundation); he who did not have it wasn't. Was she always to be expected to follow him around, cleaning up after his messes because he was too lazy, too infantile, too grossly irresponsible even to keep track of his own wild crude expenditures? Could he add?

Only then had she got onto the real subject. Who's the woman, Alfred? I take it it's a woman. You're not buying your little boyfriend Bobby Fabergé Easter eggs from A La Vieille Russie. Are you? Who is she, Alfred? Do you think in the future, Alfred, you could pay for her yourself?

And Alfred, cornered, had lost his temper. Alfred, who miraculously appeared to consider himself still by dint of his parents' hardships a member of the virtuous working classes, had looked at her with his boppy bloodshot eyes and snarled something about "you people"— meaning the rich. "You're just like your father," he had told her. "You people think you can control everybody with your goddamned purse-strings. Because you think everybody is as greedy and mercenary as you. You know nothing whatsoever about the human heart, you know nothing about the real world. What do you want—do you want a husband or do you want a poodle? Don't you dare try to bust my balls over money, you manipulative cunt who's never worked a day in her life, you spoiled rich daddy's girl."

This conversation dragged out over three nights, and every time Dolly demanded to know who he was sleeping with, Alfred, livid, had lectured her about money, had had the nerve to tell her that if it wasn't for his careful managing she'd be as broke as Sophie, who'd run through half her capital by the age of thirty.

By the fourth morning, they had called each other names that neither was likely to forget. This was ten days ago, longer than they usually went without reconciliation. But this time neither of them seemed to wish for a rapprochement, and when Alfred went out at night, Dolly felt vengefully relieved—bad father, bad husband—not to have to endure the falseness of another evening of his being extra-sugary to the children and extra-cold to her. Something was going to have to give. Dolly had contemplated taking the children out to her mother's—anything to avoid having to share a bed with that liar–but unfortunately there was just too much to do at the office.

Isaac had spoken.

"What did you say, Isaac?"

"I think I'd better quit," he repeated.

She looked at him sharply. "That was a red light you just ran. Quit which?"

"Working at Aurora."

"Why do you want to do that? You've only just started. Heavens, I admit it's not fascinating, but at least . . . Have you got another job?" She knew that John Hanlon, who was looking for a new assistant, had taken a shine to Isaac.

"It's too . . . it's too succulent. I need a barer life. It's distracting, other people's art. I'm scared of being influenced."

"What, you think you might find yourself compulsively producing golf courses? I very much doubt it. Do you need more money? I'm sure we could arrange that. You certainly ought to be living somewhere more salubrious than–"

"No, it's time, not money. It's taking too much time away from my real work. I don't have enough time to dream anymore. It's better to be a night watchman for half the money, and be able to dream."

"Maybe we could see if you could work part-time. I certainly don't want to take you away from *The Daughters of the Earth*."

"Maybe," he said. It was a dismal seasonless afternoon, the city shrouded in white haze. No definition, no cloud outline even, just dank whiteness, the afterbirth of winter, restless and debilitating as convalescence. And the feeling of wanting to be elsewhere. "Maybe it's just the weather. February makes you want to curl up and die." Maybe that alluring square of green grass in the gallery had addled his brain.

She reflected. Even though he seemed to have withdrawn the threat, the idea of Isaac's leaving Aurora was terrible to her. Leaving her to what? The art she sponsored suddenly seemed unappetizing. Her whole life's purpose. Her marriage. All self-delusion, corruption, garbage. She was supposed to go to an opening at the Modern that night, and the prospect of the same foxy curators, smug benefactors, the black ties, the canapés, appalled her. You people. Did Isaac also think of her as "you people"? And the worst of it was, he was right that he should leave.

She had never seen in the raw such a powerful symbolic imagination; he shouldn't be hauling other people's sculptures around a gallery.

"We have the car—let's go somewhere," she said suddenly.

"Where?"

She thought. Then, shocked by the idea, "We could go out to the country."

"What country?" Isaac hadn't yet assimilated the concept of "the country" as signifying somebody's second residence.

"Goose Neck. Our house on Long Island." Having made this proposal, she felt like a locomotive that discovers it doesn't have to run along the tracks but can go careering across fields and valleys. Runaway train.

Isaac hung a left so abrupt she had to grab hold of the door handle not to fall into his lap.

"Where are you going?" She was laughing.

"Long Island."

"Not so fast—I've got at least to check into the office. . . ."

"No, you were right the first time—let's just go."

She was still chuckling from the unexpected daring of it. "My God. How did you ever persuade them to give you a driver's license?"

"I didn't. I don't have a license."

"You don't have a license? Why don't you pull over—I think I'd better drive." When he stopped at a red light, she got out of the car while he slid over to the passenger seat.

The Geblers' house was on the quieter backwater portion of Long Island that branches north at Riverhead. Isaac, glued to the window, watched the scenery change as its underpinnings shifted from black loam to sand. Once past Babylon, Bay Shore, they entered a marine landscape of stunted firs, salt-bleached grasses, petrified forest, scrub. You could sniff the ocean in the air, just beyond the line of houses. Abruptly, the Long Island Expressway ended and they traversed to a rustic two-laner that chugged through half-suburban towns, a bumpy procession of shopping malls with pizza parlors and multiplex cinemas and martial arts schools.

Then, like a musical composition introducing a new motif, the first burst of farmland asserted itself, vying with shopping mall. A clash ensued—plowed field, mall, plowed field, tract homes, with the farmland becoming more pronounced, more insistent, drowning out the once triumphant themes of condominium and shopping plaza, until finally country won and the malls and tract homes were reduced to a subdued undernote. Miles of earthen flatness marked by wheeled irrigators and lone tractors, by shingle farmhouses set way out in the fields. Vineyards—the vines whip-thin, blasted-looking tufts. Villages crowned by eighteenth-century white clapboard churches with graveyards gridded in chipped slate markers, and main streets with only hardware stores and barbers on them. In between the villages, red-brick high schools with big playing fields.

They pulled over at a vineyard on Route 25 and bought a few bottles of Cabernet Sauvignon, just as the store was closing. "All this is new," said Mrs. Gebler. "Fifteen years ago it was nothing but potato fields. Then the farmers figured out that the water they were using for irrigation cost more than the potatoes did, so they switched to grapes. It beats selling out to developers, but I'm not sure if it'll work."

Even out here, you still saw overnight condo-cities rising in what a year ago was farmland, raw infestations with names like Sunset Acres, Golden Time. "Wow," said Isaac. "Just like home."

"You can't imagine how the North Fork has changed," said Mrs. Gebler. "I first started coming here in the sixties. I had a great friend I used to stay with—she's dead now—called Johnny Maine who was a sculptress, lived out in Orient. She used to make things from driftwood, old bicycle parts, rusted hoes, scythes. The most vigorous, uplifting human being I have ever met. We got the house in the seventies. Back then it was just farmland. Now you have to get almost to Greenport before you shake free of all these ghastly jerry-built tract homes."

Isaac was laughing.

"What's so funny?"

"City folk tearing through the countryside always get indignant to discover that the people who actually live there have traded in the ancestral hovels in favor of indoor plumbing."

"Well," muttered Mrs. Gebler, embarrassed. "There is a middle ground. I mean, surely it would be cheaper to install plumbing and central heating in these old farmhouses than go—"

"It wouldn't. Besides, I think working people hit a certain age and figure they've earned some ease. No more staircases, no more drafts, no more scurrying around for pots and pans every time it rains."

"But most of the people who live in those dreadful condos don't even come from the North Fork, they've just retired out here."

"Where did you say you were born, Mrs. Gebler?"

"All right, but at least we didn't go and build one of those—"

"No, you just helped drive up prices so high the farmers had to sell off their land to the developers in order to pay property tax."

Mrs. Gebler subsided, grumbling.

"By the way, I'm not complaining. My mom made a hundred and fifty grand in real estate off people like you. Well, not quite like you. Maybe when you get sick of the North Fork because it's too built up you might do her a favor and turn a kind eye on Jessup County, New Hampshire."

There it was—you people again.

They stopped for a cup of coffee at the diner in Cutchogue. It was almost seven and most of the customers had already left. There was one elderly couple, who were eating the snapper special while each stared absently several inches above the other's head. Finally, the man let out a sigh and picked up the sports page. The cashier was waiting to close up.

Dolly and Isaac sat at the counter and ordered two cups of coffee and a bread pudding from the tired cheerful waitress who called them both "honey."

"I think when they are hiring waitresses, they line them up at audition and say to each one in turn, Say 'honey,' " said Isaac.

"Did you say 'honey' when you worked at the diner?" Dolly inquired, still stinging from their quarrel over development.

Isaac, who had forgotten he'd told her about the Blue Sky, felt pleased that they'd acquired enough history for him to have told her things and forgotten. "How come you know so much more about me than I know about you? I worked in the kitchen—that's very different from up front. No ladies. If you called anyone in the kitchen 'honey,' you'd get slugged. Back in those days, though, I'd have thought it worth a black eye—having someone to call 'honey,' I mean."

"And now?"

"Now I've got a heart of stone. Limestone," he joked. "And 'honey' coming out of my ears—Costa's an affectionate fellow, you know."

"I do know," she said unexpectedly.

"Now I am grateful not to go to sleep any longer with orders of one toasted English and a side of fries ringing in my ears. All jobs are hell, but in the end, I guess I'd rather come home crudded in paint than bacon fat. Anyway, you guys pay better than the Blue Sky. Not that they're begging for me back. . . . Miss, could you please fill it up?"

In Southold they stopped at the IGA, loaded up on groceries. The formal intimacy of her asking him what he liked for breakfast. He couldn't remember anyone ever asking him what he wanted for breakfast. Even sleeping with girls it was never quite so planned—you met in the evening and didn't admit you were still going to be there the next morning.

It was dark by the time they reached the house. The gleam of shocked eyes hitting the headlights in the underbrush along the road. Magic. All the wild creatures out a-roaming that ended up next morning a smear of fur and gore across the macadam.

Mr. West, who lived in the cottage at the foot of the drive, came out to see them in his thermal undershirt. Dolly rolled down the window of the car, leaned out.

"We wunt expecting you again so soon."

"Well, the city was unbearable. Gray two weeks running," she explained.

He nodded, pleased, a countryman's complacency about the horrors of New York.

"How's it been out here?"

"Bit of a thaw. Not too bad."

"This is Isaac."

Mr. West nodded again.

The grounds a loom of darkness, sandy road; the house a squarer, more angled loom, comforted by trees.

"Where are we?"

"You'll see in the morning."

She got out of the car, puzzled to be arriving without suitcases. Isaac brought in the groceries, while Dolly fumbled for lights. "Mr. West wants us to get one of those systems where the lights flood on soon as you come in. It's supposed to frighten away burglars, but I hate floodlights. Not enough darkness left in the world—at nighttime, even out here the countryside's a damn police cell. I think it's part of not admitting you're going to die—a terror of true darkness and silence."

Isaac made another trip to the car and brought in the Urgell painting, while Mrs. Gebler rushed around the house, turning up the thermostats in each room.

They had come into the front hall, which was an enormous rectangle. There was a broad gray-and-yellow parquet floor, a curving staircase leading up. The next room—a living room—was open, unfurnished. Just a wide-planked chestnut-wood floor, a couple of big floppy white sofas, an alabaster fireplace. Isaac put a match to the already laid fire, while Mrs. Gebler fished for more lights.

Together Mrs. Gebler and Isaac examined the Urgell painting, which he had propped up against the wall. So consistent was the Geblers' taste, the painting looked as if it had been made there—a great cream-colored sail with its enigmatic message, "To know is to avoid." To Dolly, it seemed apt. She had spent a lifetime accumulating information, like an A-plus student gone haywire, and learned nothing except for the illusoriness of facts, the indeterminacy of true knowledge. Alfred was right. Ignorant of the human heart.

The living room opened onto a big kitchen with a range the size of a brontosaurus. The kitchen was lined in books. Isaac unpacked the groceries, while Mrs. Gebler gathered the pyres of dead flies that had collected on window ledges and in corners. A few, merely stunned, kicked up a feeble buzz of protest as she swept them into a cocked hat of newspaper.

"It's an old farmhouse," she explained. "A very plain rectangle, good old windows. You'll see in the morning. Of course, they'd tacked on all sorts of idiotic wings and outhouses, most of which we tore down. Everything the eighteenth century knew about proportion, the nineteenth century forgot—a scale of amnesia comparable to what happened in late antiquity, early Christian art, when people simply forgot how to draw a human body."

"Didn't they just have more children and need somewhere to put 'em?" asked Isaac.

"There you go with your damn contrary populism. What's the sense of being an artist and defending tract houses and ugliness? It's just per-

verse. Anyway, no reason to ruin a good house. It was the Gresham family this one belonged to—they owned everything around here. There's
one Miss Gresham left, ninety-three years old, in the nursing home over
by the Sound. Very sprightly, very gay—she dresses up when you come
to see her—lovely flowery print dresses, a little butterfly pin, red shoes.
The rest of 'em live in Florida. Naples. In tract homes, I can assure you.
Florida has done for the Northeast what the potato famine did for
Ireland."

Isaac nodded. "Even where I come from, everyone who can afford
it's packed it in for palm trees."

"I don't blame them for wanting to escape winter, but it leaves
something of a vacuum as far as Yankee grit's concerned. . . . And your
family—does your mother still live up there? In New Hampshire?" She
was shy, always, asking him about his family.

"I guess so. I haven't been home in a while."

"Well, shouldn't you?"

He hesitated; then, smiling broadly: "Last time I saw my mom she
tried to shoot me. I figured after that it was healthier to stick to postcards. I don't hear back, but then she isn't much of a writer."

"My God!" said Mrs. Gebler. "She shot you?!"

"Caught me in the shoulder—just a graze."

"But—why?"

"I think she found me a pest," said Isaac cheerfully.

"My God, I would have thought any mother would die of pride to
have such a son."

Mrs. Gebler showed Isaac the upstairs. Six bedrooms, their walls of
narrow pine planks painted in seaside colors—hot pink, aquamarine, yellow. One closet-sized and very inviting, which he requested for himself.
An enormous bathroom with a claw-footed porcelain tub and a high an-
tique sink. "There are extra toothbrushes and things in the closet." It
was this bathroom, like the drawer full of birthday candles, that reminded him again of the difference between money and no money. By
the sink was a tortoiseshell glass stuffed with a handful of hard-bristled
bone toothbrushes, and a tube of Italian toothpaste made from euca-
lyptus and other strong-tasting herbs. Straddling the tub, a rack bearing
a large sea sponge, a cinnamon-colored lozenge of clove-scented soap,
and a small leather-bound book: Racine's *Phèdre*! When you got out of

the tub, folded across the heated rack were two towels—snowy white, bedspread-sized, thick as rugs—and in the bathroom closet, half a dozen more towels piled high, along with a tower of fresh soaps and toothpaste boxes. Made him feel funny remembering how back in New York he'd punctured his own tube of Crest with a fork to capture the last caked remnants of goo, brushed his teeth with soap all week because he'd spent his paycheck already and didn't have two dollars to buy a tube of toothpaste.

When he came downstairs, Dolly was standing in front of the refrigerator, studying its contents worriedly. "What would you like to eat?"

Isaac, dropping Racine, located pans, bowls, plates, poured her a glass of red wine, and got to work. She watched with evident relief as he produced hash browns, a cheese omelette, a green salad. They sat down to eat at a small table in front of the fire.

"How did you learn to cook?" she asked. "When we were first married, Alfred used to bring home ten people for dinner unannounced and expect me to produce something delicious. Then he finally gave up. How did you learn?"

"I didn't. In our house, my mom was bargain queen. You know, canned beans half-price because they're past the sell-by date. Mutton the farmer was trying to unload. It was only once I came to New York I learned food could taste okay. You didn't know me before—I was sixty pounds heavier maybe, she kept us starved wolves, so I was a real bulk feeder, two-handed, for sure. Then later, sleeping under bridges leaned me down some."

"This doesn't sound like the making of a good cook."

"After I broke my arm, I crashed for a few weeks with this fellow who was a disciple of a Hindu swami. Vacant, but a gorgeous cook. He used to cook these vegetarian feasts every night and I'd watch. Till then, I wouldn't have believed you could be a vegetarian and like food."

"What do you mean?"

"Well, you know, where I come from, vegetables aren't food—plus, you don't see 'em nine months a year. They're not food, they're—oh, I don't know—a free form of Hamburger Helper—you know, something to make the meat last longer. Nine months a year, you don't see 'em, and then they're like flies in September. Mounds and mounds of tomatoes to be disposed of by the human incinerators."

Mrs. Gebler was still considering whether vegetarians could like food. "Perhaps it's simply more of a challenge, like those pianists who play one-handed."

"Wittgenstein's brother. But he at least had the excuse that he'd lost his arm in the war."

"I should think cooking and painting were quite similar. Alchemy. It doesn't surprise me you're a late starter in both."

"I didn't start drawing late. I spent my whole life drawing," said Isaac. "It just never occurred to me you could get paid for it. Not that I do, except by you.

"If I tried to tell you why—well, as a child, it was a kind of conquest over nearsightedness, another way of snatching—of memorizing—of preserving what was just beyond my grasp. As a kid, I drew because I couldn't see and I talked because I couldn't hear. I got waylaid first by words, that's all. Then when words became too tricky, I found the hand and eye had freed up from lying fallow so long. It was a liberation to draw. Plus a way of getting back what I'd lost. Those rooms, that house. That man. Sights that couldn't be put into words."

"And why—I mean—well, why did your mother shoot you?"

Isaac puffed out his lower lip, rocked his chair back on its hind legs. "She's fond of property. Enormously so. She caught me making off with a piece of it she didn't consider mine by rights."

Dolly raised her eyebrows.

"An encyclopedia," he answered. "Of my dead dad's."

"Heavens. You don't make her sound very . . . endearing."

"Then the fault's in my rendition. She's a wild sow, but adorable."

Dolly felt like someone who had escaped from a fire. But she knew her husband was in there burning. Soon she would have to call home and let him know where she was—a novel reversal—but meanwhile she was thinking how much she enjoyed this man's company—you had to feel that kind of physical warmth towards anybody you worked with, otherwise it was impossible—but how pleasant it was to have him sitting opposite her at the dinner table—their first meal together!—burly, ursine, the golden down fuzzy on his cheeks, with those candid blue eyes glowing, exuding heat like a stove. The faint smell of fresh sweat rising from his thin T-shirt, a sweet smell. And his strange sad story.

"How about you?" he asked.

"How about me what?"

"How come you don't like to cook? How can you be a mother and not like to cook?"

"I don't cook because I didn't grow up cooking, and besides, Alfred's so superb at it, I never really felt the need. Where I come from—well, my parents had a friend, Daisy Waterbury. When Mrs. Waterbury's daughter-in-law first came to their house, she said to her mother-in-law, My, the kitchen is lovely. And Mrs. Waterbury said, Oh, really? I've never seen it. It was like that. We didn't cook much in our family."

"What's it like being so rich you don't know where the kitchen is?"

Now it was her turn to flinch—Isaac not knowing or not caring that he was raising a subject friends of thirty years wouldn't dream of broaching—but she'd started it, after all. She pondered.

"It's what I imagine it might be like being a very beautiful woman. Not something you feel within yourself so much as pick up from the way other people treat you. Or—like a head cold. This permanent cotton wadding, this insulation against what normal people come up against. A kind of immunity against reality, against the bumps and shifts and sickening worries.

"It was different for my father—he made his fortune from scratch. He had nothing to feel guilty about—he was a smart man who knew the world and worked like a galley slave till the day he died. Sunday was just the day there weren't quite so many other people milling around the office. I remember a friend of my father's saying after his funeral, Lucky Diehl—he died with his boots on. But as for the next generation, everybody hates you on principle, and quite right, too. I remember our nursemaid pinching us when nobody was looking. Why not? She was the eldest of six children, she'd gone to work at fourteen, she couldn't bear the sight of these petted princesses in velvet coats and patent-leather shoes with their superior snobbish little attitudes, throwing tantrums if their ponies weren't ready on time. That's part of what I mind about money—it makes one very silly and ignorant, being so cut off from reality. Worrisome if one has children. Everyone else in the world is trying to protect their children from harsh reality—I have to work to expose them."

"Why don't you just relax and enjoy it?" Isaac asked. "That's what

I'd do. Buy an island off Nova Scotia, with a seaplane. Laze. Gloat. That's what everyone else would do."

"Well, I don't exactly deprive myself. Anyway, there are more interesting ways to go about it."

"But why should it be a burden?"

She frowned. "It's not a burden. It's a privilege—the greatest freedom imaginable."

"Isn't it a better freedom I've got? The freedom of invisibility. I can disappear. You can't."

"You don't look so invisible to me." She looked him over, laughing. "Look, there are some rich people who genuinely don't like it—who pretend the money's not there, which is even more of a self-delusion. I have to say that I like it. Not because of how people treat you, but because of what you can do."

"Yes, it's true, I guess," Isaac concluded. "Yes, to be a rich American in the second half of the twentieth century—that's the luckiest thing. Lucky, free, secure. You don't even have to fight in wars anymore. Are your parents still alive?"

"Just my mother."

"Does she like Alfred?"

Dolly recoiled, angry for a moment at his impertinence. Then she answered. "So-so. She suffers him, benevolently. And he's amused by her. She's a very grand, formidable old lady."

"Like you."

"Even older."

When they went upstairs to their bedrooms, Isaac took her cold hand in his, as you do to a child's to warm it. She was startled by how her stomach leaped at being encased in that bearish heat. He brought her hand to his lips and kissed it. "Thank you. You've saved me, again."

And Dolly, to her own annoyance, began stuttering, and could say nothing.

That night, when she dialled home just before getting into bed, she felt, almost for the first time in her married life, in the wrong. Alfred answered on the second ring, and Dolly reassumed the frosty voice proper to their estrangement. "I'm out in the country. I got Isaac to drive me."

There was a moment's silence. "Oh? That's quick work." He had flu. He sounded snuffly and sorry for himself, on top of aggrieved. "I guess we'll have to raise his salary. Are you coming back?"

"Of course. I've got a ten o'clock meeting Wednesday morning."

"Meaning you've cancelled everything for tomorrow. Congratulations. Did you crump out on the visit to Urgell too?"

"No."

"Did you buy anything?"

"Yes, I bought a picture. It's here."

"Oh?" His voice sounded even colder. "That's a pity. I would have liked to have seen it."

"Well, I told you—I—and it—will be back tomorrow night."

Because they were fighting, she could not ask him whether or not the children had done their homework and were in bed. Alfred would probably take them clubbing at the Limelight just to punish her. Had the children, too, met Alfred's girlfriend? she wondered, and the question kept her awake till the first birds began to sing.

Twenty-nine

WHEN ISAAC WOKE at eleven the next morning, he saw outside his bedroom window a hickory tree, in which a cardinal and his reddish-brown consort were disporting themselves. The sky—between bare branches—a sheet of pale blue, and beneath it, a park leading down to straw-colored bulrushes, to a stretch of water in which floated two white swans. The air vaporous.

He hoisted open the window, breathed in deep. Poured himself a steaming bath and lolled in the claw-footed tub, reading *Phèdre* and looking out the window at that banner of salty blue. When he emerged to dry land, he found that someone had laid out for him a fresh shirt, socks, a Shetland sweater, and a pair of baggy corduroy trousers—the old-fashioned kind with a metal cinch at the waist. Alfred's? He chose to ignore this offering, to resume his own grubby clothes.

Mrs. Gebler, wearing jeans and a pair of ancient tennis shoes, had already driven into town to pick up the papers, seen the plumber, talked to Mr. West about whether a portion of the roofing needed to be replaced, and was now chatting with Mrs. West, while going through the bills that had accumulated since she'd been there last month. "After breakfast I'll show you the garden."

Isaac, reading the newspaper, wondered what it would be like to be the person who owned the clothes he had just rejected.

Mrs. West looked at him with undisguised curiosity. "A friend of Leo's," she declared to Dolly.

"No, Isaac is a painter. He just looks fourteen years old, that's all."

"Lord, Soviet Union's going to hell in a handbag," announced Isaac merrily. "Hundreds of thousands of people in thirty cities demonstrating for democracy. They've already voted in a multiparty system. Riots in Tajikistan. Free elections in Lithuania. Germany about to be reunified. Well, that's the end of communism for a while. Unless we decide to try it over here."

She laughed. "It's so exciting, isn't it, this marvellous new world being born in Eastern Europe, the Baltics. I talked to a friend from Prague—she says it's an all-night party. I must say, I can't help feeling a little jealous—I always thought of America as being absolutely the center of the action, and now all of a sudden I feel as if we're stuck on the sidelines."

"What a turnaround," Isaac agreed. "Here Czechoslovakia's got this dissident playwright about to become president, and we're the ones landed with the CIA chief."

"We should go there—before it changes," said Dolly boldly. After she'd invited this young stranger to Goose Neck, Prague didn't seem such a leap.

Isaac looked at her. "Do you realize you're talking to someone who's never been farther from home than Coney Island? I want to go *everywhere*."

As soon as he had finished breakfast, Dolly took Isaac out to see what they had passed in the dark the night before. The shingle farmhouse stood in an enclosure of black oaks, locusts, hickory trees, reached by a quarter-mile-long avenue of big old maples, with orchards on either side. Behind the house, a barn, with rusting tractors, the former stables, and the garden. There was a vegetable garden and a flower garden and a walled orchard and an herb garden, but to survey their blasted winter outlines was like piecing together from an archaeological site where baths and amphitheater and temple once stood.

"Emanuele Conti is itching for us to get topiary, with a sundial and all. I think it's too fussy, too Italian-designerish for a house like this, don't you? I mean, this is Suffolk County, for heaven's sake."

Instead, you could see that the place had been arranged with children's pleasures in mind. There was a screened porch at the bay side of the house, with a hammock and a Ping-Pong table, and a splendid treehouse in the crook of an oak. And the barn had been converted into the children's playroom, one room of which—complete with stage and backdrops—they used as a theater. "Carlotta likes to write plays," she explained. At the bottom of the park was a dock with a pagodalike boathouse, in which they kept a rowboat and a small dinghy.

Isaac felt frighteningly at home. Because he was a country boy, he had a far more exact sense of the riches entailed in such a spread than he might have of any Manhattan co-op. And he had never seen anything remotely like this house, these grounds. Even the grandest families around Gilboa—the Driscolls or the Herringshaws—had lived on a scale that was confined by comparison.

After lunch—tomato soup and grilled cheese sandwiches in front of the fire—they went for a stroll on the beach.

Across Peconic Bay you could see Shelter Island, the inlets of East Hampton. It wasn't a harsh landscape, this pale expanse of marshes, creeks, coves, islands—you were always crooked in the land's elbow, sheltered from open Atlantic by the coastal ramblings and undulations. It was instead a benign semi-sequesteredness, a blurred ambidexterity of land and sea.

They walked along the shore in the high wind, picking up driftwood and sea glass and stones. The stones were stained a sulfurous gold, and so were the shells. Isaac split a rock open—like tiger's eye—and found it was splintery pale-gray inside. Quartz, just like Manhattan's innards or Swiss watches.

"What's that for?" he asked, pointing to a tall wooden post in the sand.

"For the ospreys to nest in."

"It looks like a pillar for a stylite. Do they like it?"

"Who—the ospreys? I suppose so. They are very elegant, all black and white, with their curved beaks. Like Parisian ladies. Furious when anyone comes near them."

At the end of the beach—surreally—there was a dead deer. It had been eviscerated, and one foreleg had been picked to the bone. "But how did it get here?" Dolly wondered.

"Maybe it swam," suggested Isaac.

After their walk, Mrs. Gebler served tea and scones by the fire, before they headed back to town in the dusk.

Isaac imagined he could see the yellow columns of toxic fumes rising as they approached New York City. The streets filthy, menacing—worse as they reached his neighborhood and he saw the crackheads and petty hustlers huddled on his corner. He had wished the car would break down, run out of gas, that a freak snowstorm could have kept them country-bound. What stuck in his head, besides the white towels and the soap, was the space of it: acres of rooms, with northern, southern, eastern exposures—big square rooms with tall windows, and the light salt-bleached, vaporous. He had a vision of himself stretched out on the sofa, his head in Mrs. Gebler's lap.

When she pulled over on Thirty-ninth Street, they sat a moment, neither of them wanting to go home.

"I'm glad you took me there."

Mrs. Gebler, embarrassed, suddenly. "Not at all. I'm not sure it's so good an antidote to New York winter, though. Perhaps next time we should . . . accede to public consensus . . . and make it Florida."

"Florida be damned. I want to go to the *real* Naples. Have I told you about my fondness for volcanoes?"

Then he dove out of the car and into the stinking entryway of his building, not looking over his shoulder to see the station wagon pull away.

Thirty

ON A DRIZZLY GRAY AFTERNOON, so dark you had to turn on the electric lights by three, Alfred had arranged to meet an artist friend called Marco Tanner at the Tenth Street baths.

The baths were Alfred's favorite place of the moment. They were open till two a.m., and the food was delicious. You could go and order some borscht, a smoked sturgeon sandwich, a little herring salad. Perfection. As he got older, Alfred grew ever more partial to these harsh briny treats from his ancestral homeland. He pictured his Galician forebears also frequenting the baths for a ritual cleansing, a postcoital scrub. "Roots," as he explained contentedly to Marco, who was far too etiolated and pansyish a Jew to be conscious of any background deeper than Riverdale. And then steam.

It was Gina who had first taken him to the baths, on a Saturday, which was coed day, when everybody wore bathing suits and the young Russian Jewish mafiosi with their hairy backs and bulging Speedos showed off to the girls by plunging into the icy pool with loud yelps. A bunch of Odessan Tarzans.

Before she started working at Rikers, Gina used to go every Wednesday, when it was women's day and the girls with their long legs and high bouncing tits strutted around buck naked. That would be a pretty sight. Gina said it was all young East Village types gabbing about their aromatherapists. God, I'd love to see it, said Gebler, and pictured himself for one erotic moment an Actaeon being torn limb from limb by steamy Artemises.

Whereas today—men-only day—it was just old diamond merchants with paunches. There were pictures on the wall of John Belushi—another greasy fat slob—and a bunch of other comedians from the seventies who'd come to the baths to calm down after shooting coke. The bad old days. Certainly, it was tranquillizing. The tiled walls, the steam.

He and Marco had lunch, television soap opera blaring overhead.

Then, self-consciously, they'd disrobed. Gebler was never entirely comfortable taking his clothes off in front of other men. Somehow the opposite sex was more forgiving. Besides, men's bodies were disgusting. He didn't see how anyone who had a choice about it—anybody, that is, not driven by reproductive necessity—could angle after a pair of hairy balls. Naked men in the winter looked like plucked chickens—white puckered flesh and then the private parts like a packet of giblets, a pouch of purplish odds and ends. Men's feet too were revolting. Scaly. Chicken claws.

Having left their clothes in the lockers, they padded downstairs to the radiant-heat room, which smelled of cedar and sweat. Marco was in a bad mood, needed cheering up.

"I'm not getting anywhere in my work."

Marco was almost fifty and painted stamp-sized watercolors, dainty, vaguely erotic, Indian-miniature-style.

"Why not?"

"I've lost heart, somehow."

"Maybe you need a break. Go back to India for a month."

Marco shrugged.

"What's the matter?"

"I dunno. Life just feels kinda blah at the moment. I don't know why I bother to get out of bed."

"I know why," said Gebler. "For the pleasure of getting back into it." He was sweating hard now, and the oxygen felt as if it were crystallizing into honey in his lungs. He was trying to remember whether steam was good for respiratory troubles or bad, and then he had a rare flash of memory from childhood, of having asthma or bronchitis when they still lived on Clearview Avenue, and his mother sitting him right on top of the kitchen stove, with the kettle boiling, and a towel over his head. He must have been pretty young too, to have fitted on top of their dinky stove. His poor little mother.

And he had passed on to his own boy—was it genetic, the disease, or just the anxiety that caused it?—these same respiratory blues. If he were a good father, he would take Leo to the Russian baths, see if the steam helped his breathing. But the truth was this father-and-son shit gave him the heebie-jeebies. Leo always looking at him half-scared, half-expectant, as if he were waiting to get taken off for camping trips or man-to-man talks. And how come, whenever Dolly pointed out how much Leopold resembled pictures of him as a child, he bridled? His own father he'd hardly ever laid eyes on, the poor stiff was always either working or sleeping. Did he too not see enough of his little ducklings? Would they blame him, would they punish him with neglect when he was old and helpless?

He looked over at Marco, who had no children and wouldn't understand any of these confusions ... and looked again. "What's the matter, man, you look terrible." It wasn't just the heat; big wet teardrops were pouring down Marco's face. "What's the matter?"

Now Marco was sobbing but good, cursing himself and laughing through his tears. If they were anywhere else, he would have put his arm around the guy, but you couldn't do that here—not two naked men, with the old geezers watching.

And Alfred, mid embarrassment, was frightened. Had Marco just found out he had AIDS? Holy Christ, not another one. What could you say to a guy who's just been told he is condemned to imminent and agonizing death?

"Oh shit," bubbled Marco between gasps. The old geezers pretending not to look. Well, fuck them. This was the nineties. Men cried.

Finally Marco calmed down enough to spit it out. "Kevin left me."

"When?"

"Twelve days ago. Just walked out. I can't stand to be in the apartment anymore. It's like somebody died in it."

And Alfred, shaking his head in sympathy, listened to the tale, not sure whom he identified with, the one who walked out or the one who was walked out on. He imagined leaving Dolly and then he imagined Gina leaving him, and his eyes flooded and his breath caught short. "Oh, Marco, I'm so sorry. I'm so, so sorry." The old geezers, narrow-eyed, watching these two naked weeping men and wondering if their favorite haunt was going to the fist-fuckers.

"I don't know what to do with myself. I can't hate him because I love him. So I hate myself. I feel so repulsive I can't bear to look at my own body. I just want to die."

"Well, don't do that. Why doncha hate him instead? I always thought he was a little creep."

"He was a little creep. But he was so loving."

Funny how you talked about people in the past tense, as if as soon as they walked out the door and around the corner, they ceased to exist. Funny to think how everybody you knew, all over the world, in Milan, in Paris, in Texas, wherever, your best buddy from camp, the guy who filled up your car out in Greenport, they were all at that moment busily conducting their respective existences. Whereas you thought they went into suspended animation until you came back and resurrected them into life again. Even faithless Kevin was right now probably having breakfast in bed in an apartment Marco had never seen, sucking on somebody's balls, whatever people did when they were first in love.

"I told him, How can you just walk out on me and Hermione?"

Hermione was the pug dog they had bought together from a breeder on the Jersey shore. Hermione was now eight years old and had bad breath. "He's like, Well, I kin still come'n *visit* her, can't I? And I'm like, No way. You think that was too petty of me? But I *hate* him—I don't want him coming and mauling my pet when I'm not around. Why should he have it both ways?"

Mr. Gebler cleared his throat. He was dying to get out of the radiant-heat room, it was getting too hard to breathe, but he didn't want to disrupt Marco in the middle of his story. "I think you should probably let him see the dog."

"But it would be so *confusing* for her. . . . I hate him. I hate the way they never just walk out honestly, cut and dried, they always kill you off slowly. And then it comes out. So that's why he's been looking at me like I'm a dust ball on the floor for the last six months. That's why he's always too tired to make love. Why can't they come clean, without making you hate yourself first? It's like slow starvation, unplugging the tubes."

Mr. Gebler was gasping now, really unable to breathe. This was the most depressing conversation he had ever had, and there was no getting out of it.

"Well, don't give him the satisfaction of making you hate yourself. You've got to pull yourself together, get up in the morning—"

"I can't get outa bed. This is the first time I've left the house in a week, practically, except to buy dog food."

"Well, you've got to force yourself. Take a shower, get dressed. . . ."

"I don't need a cheerleader pep talk, I need . . . sympathy."

"Of course I feel for you, Marco. I know you must feel like shit."

"I do."

Stilted silence. Then he got up the nerve. "So what happened?"

"What do you mean, what happened?" Marco still cross with him.

"Why'd he leave?" Partly because he was curious: Was Kevin driven crazy at last by the same things Gebler found exasperating about Marco, or was there a whole other set of unbearables Gebler didn't even know about–that Marco snored or wouldn't take out the garbage or was stingy? But mostly because he knew sure as rent day it was going to happen to him. Some days every time Gina opened her mouth or seemed preoccupied, he saw it coming, that she was trying to find a way to break it to him gentle but final. Only question being, Was she going to wait to throw him over till Dolly'd kicked him out too?

And now to his amazement Marco started to laugh. First hollow, mirthless; then hysterical, gulping giggles, hitching up into the out-of-control.

"He's getting married."

"He's *what?*" That light-heeled flit?

"He's getting married. He's met some girl. Loaded. Natch. Something to do with the Rockefellers. And they're getting married. He's always wanted to get married. He wants," said Marco in a voice laden with irony, "to–start–a–family."

And Gebler burst out laughing, too. "Well, what do you know! Fuck me."

"Exactly."

"Have you been careful, Marco? You been checked recently? I mean, these Rockefellers can be pretty . . . You don't want to catch some disease."

"Oh, I'm a total nun. I was always kinda phobic about germs, anyway. Anyway, that's it for sex. I've had it. Never again." Once more the tears coursed down Marco's high-boned cavernous cheeks as he remembered God knows which item of their past love, which blissful cavortings in the hay, which acts never to be repeated. Never again. The saddest words in the language. Never again.

"Don't I know it." But now he was getting gripped by an unbearable anxiety, watching Marco sitting there like a limp rag, utterly beaten, the stuffing knocked out of him, abject with self-loathing, not even able to meet you in the eye—and thinking, That's me. Maybe not today, maybe not next week, but on some unnamed unknowable day, and there isn't a damn thing I can do about it but just wait for it to happen, for the hand of God to come squash me like an ant and that girl to flick her pretty head and march out of my life without a backward glance.... And knowing this made him want to get out of the baths and away from Marco and far far far away. Far into those punishing arms.

Thirty-one

IN THE MORNINGS Isaac rose early and walked up to Central Park before it was light, to draw the oaks and locusts and scaly plane trees emerging from the heavy gray shadow of dawn. Like the way you see cows sometimes looming in a field in the morning dark—surprised, comfortable. Although it was early March, the trees were still winter-naked, but you could see how already the new young branches were shooting forth from the old stumps like pins in a cushion. How even the barest-looking limb was on closer inspection never quite bare but always laden with acorns or nuts, or a few last bone-dry leaves. Or berries. Or a tiny brown bird, a wren or a robin, or a silver-gray squirrel bustling in its hollows.

Old men and women circling the boat pond with their dogs—animals too old to sleep past five.

He was teaching himself to draw, in pencil and ink-and-brush, in a way that pleased him, moving from scratchy, crabbed, overworked, to loose and fluid as a skater's glide. The trick was to concentrate very hard on the essential character of the thing you were drawing, to try to express in each stroke the spirit of the whole. If it was an oak, the brush-strokes themselves were knotty, balled up. A squirrel, at once coil-limbed and sleek. This is what he had learned from studying Japanese prints and Chinese watercolors—that each stroke had an almost mystical value, so that you might deduce the essential nature of oakness from one twig.

These drawings were studies for the forest in which his shepherdess and ram came together.

Something had changed in Dolly's life. When she awoke in the mornings now, instead of the grimness of girding herself for onerous chores, of either talking or not talking to her husband, of the drive downtown, a day of meetings, phone calls, seminars, gallery openings, children's homework, dinner parties, there rose a giddy upsurge of joy, as if the blood were flooding to her head. Why? A moment's puzzlement, and then she would remember. Isaac and his new drawings.

It had been benevolent Costa's idea to set up a studio for Isaac in the basement at Aurora, with his own key so that he might use it after work. Not much natural light, to be sure, but space enough for him to get a decent view without having to go out into the hall, as he did at home.

Now in the mornings Dolly raced through breakfast, tore apart the newspaper, and, for the first time since adolescence, fretted about what she was going to wear. Groaned inwardly at the sight of the vertical carvings between her thick eyebrows (bad-tempered old lady!), at the hairs which sprouted underneath her chin (witch!), at the sight of herself backwards (a waddling duck!). Now she left the house while her children were still half-dressed.

On the way to the office, Dolly was champing to know if Isaac would be in his workroom yet, and whether it would be impertinent of her to look in on him. And really it wasn't, for what propelled her, as he well knew, was the wonder of seeing once again his drawings. She wanted to look in just to see what he'd done in the night, as a kind of reviving touch of the amulet, a brush with the sacred to get her through the day.

When she was a little girl at Norwood, they kept pointers. Her father was fond of shooting, and used occasionally to bring business acquaintances out to the house—nothing fancy, just a tramp through fields and woods, aiming at pheasants, partridges, whatever rose from the underbrush.

The pointers, mother and sons, lived in a kennel behind the gatehouse, with Caleb. Dolly had been there when Queenie gave birth for the first time, and Caleb yanked from Queenie's rear the pallid babes aspicked in yards of slime, and more and more slime after the pups were done—those lumps of eyeless dough that later became Agamemnon and Hercules and Dido, and the rest were given away. She could relive within herself that excitement each morning—the not-being-able-to-stay-in-bed urgency, bundling into clothes while her nurse next door still slept, creeping downstairs in the dark, fiddling with the high bolt on the pantry door, and running in the early-morning chill to the gatehouse to go cuddle the week-old puppies asleep in the straw, to, bury her nose in their freckled bellies, smell their infantine sourish scent and see how they had grown in the night.

This was how she felt about Isaac and his work.

The catch was weekends, when three days of deprivation stretched—for the exhibition space was closed on Mondays—and she would not be able to see him or it till Tuesday morning. Saturday, Sunday, Monday suddenly had a stale itchy dullness. No savor, as if Puritans had rendered them joyless.

She was looking at the larger landscape that was emerging, the slow fruit of several notebooksful of woodland sketches. "Yes, it's beautiful, your forest. Those moss- and ivy-covered trees, very romantic, like a backdrop of *Swan Lake*. Precise, too. The right-hand corner still needs some touching up, though. The ground cover isn't quite right yet. Are you drawing from nature?"

"Well, nature New York City–style. Rats posing as sheep and crack dealers as shepherdesses. I go to Central Park weekend mornings, up by the Ramble where it's wild."

"Oh," said Mrs. Gebler, surprised. "But that's where I go walking." Speed walking being the latest effort to reduce her loathsome bulk. "Perhaps we might meet for breakfast one morning? After you're done work, of course. I worry that you don't eat properly."

The next Sunday, before Alfred or the children were awake, she had come out to the park to find Isaac. At first she couldn't see him anywhere, but had combed the Ramble—gay men cruising, even at that early hour—feeling like a suspicious character, a lunatic, a pervert. Heart sinking. Was she too late? Had he left already?

But there suddenly he was, cross-legged at the root of a tree with a lapful of charcoals, scribbling, scribbling. He must have been there ages already, for his big hands were red and chapped. Dolly walked fast down to Central Park South and back, and when she returned, he stood up, testing his numbed limbs, stamped his feet, shook himself, and said, "Let's eat. Pancakes, bacon, eggs. Hot coffee. The works. Even my pencil's got chilblains."

And indeed she saw that his teeth were chattering.

That morning—having considered and rejected the grand hotels in the neighborhood—she took him to the Nectar, and they bundled into a booth.

"You look different on weekends."

"Do I?"

She was in mufti—cashmere leggings, walking shoes, a heavy parka. "You look like my mom."

"What? The one who shot you for making off with her encyclopedia? Thanks a lot."

"My mom's a fearsomely handsome woman. Even if she is rather stout."

Dolly, wounded, bit her lip. "This is getting better and better."

"You know I think you look like a goddess," said Isaac swiftly, almost under his breath.

"Let's leave it at that—I'd better quit while I'm ahead. Before you tell me you mean the goddess of . . . uh . . . agriculture or . . . um . . . pig-keeping."

It became a habit. Every Sunday for a month or so they met in the park and went to breakfast afterwards at the Nectar. Booths full of divorced fathers with nothing to say to their unhappy children. She was usually back home before her own ducks were up.

Isaac told her stories about his childhood. She loved to hear about his babyish infirmities: how he had been deaf in one ear as a child, fat, bronchial, half-blind—still was, of course; perhaps that was what created the skewed perspective in his painting. And how despite—or because of—these ills, he had nonetheless become an infant polymath who taught himself Latin and read every book from A to Z in the public library. At the age of seventeen, he'd won a scholarship to Harvard. Only to throw it away for love, for Isaac had told her of Agnes, who had been his high-school teacher. Who had got him into Harvard, when he was an adolescent fuckup terrified to leave home, and then got him out of it, so that they might live together as man and wife in rural, unelectrified glory. He told her about his younger brother, Turner—a lean closed ascetic, big on computers and the military, who was too bound up in their domineering mother, too shadowed by his overachieving older brother, to break away. And his father, a fine, sarcastic, frustrated man who had longed for fame and beautiful things and had placed all his hopes in his first-born. And died, disappointed in himself and in his son. He told Dolly how he himself had cracked up after his father's death, and she, astonished, divulged that the same thing had happened to her. Except that instead of spending a season in bed, gibbering mad, she'd whiled away two thousand hours on the couch. And who was now the saner?

He told Dolly, until she felt as if she knew every pizza parlor and boarded-up movie theater, every plumber and contractor and alcoholic housewife in that hilly triangle of red-brick ex–factory towns and colonial-villages-run-to-seed that made up his home country.

And how having wrenched himself away in order to make his fortune in the city—as a historian, a philosopher, a man of letters, who knows what—he had ended up instead broke, jobless, sleeping sometimes on strangers' sofas, sometimes on the street. Wordless. About his relapses into depression, near-lunacy, and his rebirth—halting, botched, perhaps reversible—through images and color, drawing and paint.

The story of Isaac's life, the tale of struggle against afflictions both innate and self-imposed, brought tears to her eyes. It seemed to Dolly that the world was sadly lacking in men and women of character, brave, high-minded. Heroes and heroines. And Isaac—quite aside from his remarkable gifts—was clearly such a man.

Isaac, eyes down, mounted drawbridges of bacon to a battlement of pancake moated by maple-flavored syrup. "I don't know what you're talking about. I see no valor whatsoever in being a basket case."

"Well, I just happen to believe that a battle against obstacles is much nobler than effortless—"

"I couldn't agree less. Let's say you invite two guests to your house. One shows up on the dot, with presents for the children and a big bunch of flowers. The other arrives two weeks late, covered in bandages, telling you, 'I had three car crashes along the way, sent five people to the hospital, broke my arm and leg, lost the address, but here I am—and by the way, will you pay my medical bills, because I'm also busted?'"

"Sounds like a biblical parable."

"Well, is heaven really rooting for the accident-prone? Hope not. I tell you, I would sell my soul to be a little less trouble to myself and others, for ease and a smoother ride. Why did I have to wait to be twenty-three years old to start wanting to be a painter? Why can't a man so abominably nearsighted stick to numbers and words? Did Beethoven wait until he was stone deaf to fall for music? Where will it end—and when? It's too tiring, being a slob and indecisive to boot."

More often they talked about what each had done in the day or two since they last met. Isaac would tell her what he'd worked on or read or listened to the night before—once a week he went to the Public Library at Lincoln Center and brought home a stack of records to play on a portable stereo he'd bought from the corner pawnshop. That winter he'd gone through the entire *Ring* on scratched library borrowings, and now he was learning up Bach's *Art of the Fugue*. He would work till midnight or so, quitting only when his eyes ached too much, and then he would turn out the light and sit in the darkness, singing along to Bach at the top of his lungs.

"The neighbors must love you."

"The neighbors are a Turkish discotheque. I'm trying to become the competition."

He, in turn, questioned her eagerly, wanting to know every scrap of what she'd done and seen and worn and thought. And Dolly, despite his avidity, was ashamed that she went out every night to parties while he sat home alone. An unreflective existence—inadequate, vacuous, unnutritive. Why would a man who had slept under the FDR Drive and spent his nights reading the Old Testament want to hear about these vapid socialites who talked only about whether the skiing was better in Davos or Gstaad?

He replied cheerfully, "I think it's much safer keeping rich people on the ski slope than all the other places they like to poke their noses."

"Such as artists' studios?"

"Or political causes." He was still boiling from her having told him that they had been to a fundraiser for the son of a friend, a millionaire left-winger who was running for Congress in California.

Now she objected. "Why shouldn't the rich be involved in politics as well as anybody else?"

"Because their interests are so unlike anybody else's, and yet their influence is so much greater."

"You're sounding rather Bolshevik this morning."

"Listen, I'm an American. I think everybody in this country should get rich as quick as possible. There's no more honest way of passing the time than in getting money. I just don't like rich people pretending they're not interested in what they've got and in getting more. And that's nothing but New England pig-envy, since I can tell you down to the last bean what I'd do with it when you finally get around to giving me a million billion dollars."

"I'd like nothing in the world better than to give you a million billion dollars."

"I know you would. But you shouldn't be giving money to artists to begin with. Why don't you give your money to the poor, to those who are really suffering in this wretched city, instead of adding to the mountain of middle-class subsidies? . . . What did you do last night?"

"Oh, it's too dreary," she muttered, impatiently. "Some—oh, a dreadful woman, really—gave a party for my old friend David Butler—a Canadian sculptor. It was—" She interrupted herself. "You know, I've started reading the Bible."

"What for?" He was being contrary that morning.

"I want to understand that spirit of mystery and revelation in your work."

"But the Bible's only sometimes about mystery and revelation," he objected. "A lot of the time it's about how much Abraham paid for a plot of land or how many sheep and goats Jacob's amassed, or about how to collect a debt politely—i.e., not in front of the wife and children. That's what's so satisfying about the Bible—it's life itself. Most other religions—or artists—don't understand how debts and revelation live cheek by jowl. Look at El Greco—he wants every day to be Ascension Day. Well, that's too tiring. Most of us don't have the stamina—we need sometimes just to watch the evening news and turn in early, and hope the Messiah shows up another night."

Dolly thought. "But the Dutch are rather good at that, aren't they? I mean, at showing how ordinariness and revelation coexist."

"Yes, exactly," Isaac agreed. "The Dutch—well, all Northern Protestants, I guess—are the *only* ones who realize that to paint a field really and truly you must know how much it cost and how many days' labor it takes to plow. Italians—their landscapes are always too allegorical for my taste. But Breughel, Hobbema, van der Weyden, Constable—even van Gogh—they all have such a respect for the material, for the holiness in worked stuff."

Sometimes, if the children were awake when she was leaving, Dolly brought Leopold or one of the girls to the park to meet Isaac, and then on to the Met or the Frick, to show each other what they loved and why. Isaac melancholy because this—exactly this—was what he and Agnes, who had introduced him to the Old Masters, had dreamed of doing: wandering down the marble halls, hand in hand, like Antony and Cleopatra in hell. Imagining her freckled boniness and sharp teasing tongue, in place of Mrs. Gebler's matriarchal hauteur. Would Agnes like Mrs. Gebler or think her full of airs?

One day, Isaac told Mrs. Gebler that he was done drawing in the park and would no longer be free on Sundays.

Mrs. Gebler visibly flinched. "I quite understand," she said coldly, looking away.

"I'm back to the shepherdess."

"Oh. I see."

"I need a live model. Someone who will sit for hours without a peep."

"I see. Are they hard to come by?" She still sounded distant.

"Harder than gold, the good ones. Who know how to do interesting things with their bodies, not just be lumps and lie there." And he asked her if she would model for him.

There was a moment's silence.

She answered, finally, not looking at him. "You know, I . . . I'm . . . honored. Honestly. But my days are so damned complicated—I don't really have the time or the . . . talent to sit as long as you would need. I'm not very good, anyway, at . . . uh . . . doing interesting things with my body."

"Was it wrong of me to ask?"

She blushed. "No—why?" Too rapidly. "Not at all. Why should it be?"

"Well, I imagine all the great painters must have asked you already—you don't need some two-bit novice pawing you."

"That's not it at all." The truth was, she explained, she couldn't bear so much as having her photograph taken—even magazine pieces about Aurora ended up with spreads of Alfred, without her.

Isaac took this in. Nodded. "Of course. You're used to being boss."

"I suppose."

"Posing for a painter is different from photographs. It's a different time scale."

"But I don't like to be told what to do with my body—that I'm lying like a lump."

"All right," he said again. "It was just that I wanted very much to—" and in a rush, "to see you without your clothes on."

They avoided each other's eyes. She stared hard into her tepid coffee, sipped it. Blushing so hard it was painful. Scared stiff. On the verge of angry.

"Not, of course, that I wanted to see you naked," he continued, cooler now. "Just that because your clothes are so ugly I thought what was underneath might be a relief."

Dolly burst out laughing. Even if they did nothing further about it, they both knew now.

And in fact nothing further happened. They went back to their old ways, as if these words had never been said.

Thirty-two

ALTHOUGH ISAAC HAD BEGUN painting again, he did not at once take on the shepherdess. Initially, he sat in his basement room at Aurora and made simpler things, on copper—a yellow rose dropping its petals. There had been a Zurbarán show at the Met—Mrs. Gebler had bought him the catalogue, and he'd studied it with dawning pleasure, recognition. He was especially taken by a reproduction of a painting of Mary and Jesus sitting at a table. Jesus, undersized in a white nightie, at that age when pretty boys still look girlish, has just pricked himself on a garland of thorns. The adolescent clutches his bleeding finger, while his mother—the future flooding in upon her—stares at him with a world of pain in her eyes.

Isaac liked the painting both because of that fullness of knowledge contained in it, and because the relation between the mother and the son made sense to him—Jesus as mother's boy, capable at housework. Lots of painters forgot about the homeliness of the Gospels, how grounded in a poor rural economy they were, with their parables of animal husbandry and day laborers and their tale of the wedding at which there isn't enough wine for the guests. Isaac, meditating on Zurbarán, painted three yellow roses in a jam jar, the thorns sharp with foreknown suffering.

It was at about this time, too, while painting the roses, that he realized it wasn't necessary always to tell the whole story. A master like Antonello da Messina could, in making an Annunciation, dispense with the folderol of angels and lilies and convey its full import merely by the expression of lucent inwardness on a young woman's face. Throughout the Christian era, painters had worked with a vocabulary so familiar that its merest flicks of the wrist were charged with a received meaning. The Church had become so economical in its shorthand of knowledge and suffering that one raised finger was enough to express the Baptist's consciousness that although he must die a martyr's death, he is but the opening act, a handmaiden to the awaited redeemer.

Was Mrs. Gebler right—that it was because artists today had lost this shared language that everything once more needed to be spelled out, the alphabet reinvented? Was that why he found the art he saw in SoHo crudely overexplicit?

One weekend he got Costa to pose for him, hands laid out on the table. They were big brown hands, too big for his body, ropily veined, with spatulate fingertips and plaster dust under the nails—they were fine hands for a prophet, a river god. Isaac was pleased with his sketches: it was always good to have a pair of hands in reserve. Then he persuaded Mrs. Gebler to sit for a hand study, and filled half a notebook with her wiry, muscular fingers. Small hands, but workmanlike, with only the ragged nails to betray a hint of anguish—the right hands for a Nazarene carpenter's wife or for the woman disciple of a strange hill-country preacher.

Mrs. Gebler was the daughter of a businessman, and business conduct, with its feudal ways of winning allegiance and gaining power, was imbued in her. Like any boss who prefers the infantilizing power play of Christmas "bonuses" to an honest raise, Mrs. Gebler had a passion for giving presents. She was so much the grande dame, drilled in courtesy's habits of submission, its manner of being at everyone else's service, that she remained undiscomfited by the fact that Isaac—this genius, this incipient giant—technically, at least, worked for her. Every morning now she came to Isaac and asked at once, "What can I do for you? Have you enough oils for the moment? I see you're running out of—what is it? Chrome yellow. May I order you a few more tubes? I must say, you're mastering oil techniques magnificently. One would think you'd been working with them since you were a child. . . ."

"No, I haven't cracked oil yet—it takes a lot of experimenting. My art teacher tried to show me, but I see you have to learn it for yourself."

"I want you to get a grant," she muttered, almost to herself. "I mean, when I think of all the perfect ninnies we gave money to this year, I can't bear it. . . . But luckily we've got a kind of slush fund. . . ."

One day a messenger delivered to his apartment a small folk painting of a rooster by Sam Doyle that Mrs. Gebler had picked up at auction. Another day it was a Russian icon with Saint Isaac's Cathedral in the background. Once she stopped by his apartment for Sunday lunch, with a picnic clearly intended to last him through the week—a side of smoked salmon, a loaf of black bread, a wheel of Brie.

Isaac was bemused. He had never in his life been given presents: his mother was stone-stingy, while his father's improvident days had dried up long before marriage had cowed him out of the large gestures that had been youthful escape from New England thrift. Even birthdays were just a cake with candles. The only books Isaac owned, growing up—aside from the ones he had smuggled away from the public library—were school-prize books. Isaac was too busy to think much about how he should regard these presents. He accepted most of them, for the time

being, and stored away in his mind that he must remember later on to
formulate an opinion about whether or not they were permissible.

In the meantime, he drew rather pitiful limits. No, she could not
send him down her Romanian masseur when he complained of a cramp
in his wrist. When the deliveryman appeared with a smoked ham, he
sent the ham back. Isaac had grown up too poor not to take offense at
the charity hamper. Mrs. Gebler apologized, explaining that she and Alfred sent all their friends such presents at Easter and Christmas. It was
the first real awkwardness between them.

She was moody, as he had already discovered, but the intensity of
her concentration was such that Isaac looked forward even to those
more brutal days when she looked in on him not to praise, flatter, se-
duce, but to remark, quite crossly, that he still hadn't a clue as to composition, how to situate a body in real space, let alone two of them. She
was maddened beyond measure by forgetfulness, inattention, clumsi-
ness. When they got into the elevator at work and Isaac pushed the
wrong button by mistake, she could barely contain her impatience.
When he forgot the name of a gallery owner she'd introduced him to,
she berated him.

Isaac had been a child star, coached by father and teacher. To Isaac,
there seemed nothing unusual in having perpetually over his shoulder a
strong woman who appeared to consider it her duty to remove all material obstructions from his path, to act as patron, trainer, and scold to
a promising young slob.

The auburns and dull golds of last fall's leaves, ankle-deep underfoot,
had turned black from the spring rains, this dense sedge decomposing.
Rotting into a kind of granular paste. It was on a bank like this that he
was placing his shepherdess with her skirts hiked up. A redhead. Like
Johnny Gebler: not carroty, not a red with any orange-yellow in it, but a
blackish-purplish crimson, mahogany, a whole tube of white you'd use,
a tube of white, and her skin a redhead's skin, luminous, china white
with just the faintest drop of red—all white and red again, a little blue
even, almost no yellow at all. And the luminous perfect white flesh with
its ruddy sheen like the sheen on white birch, when the outer bark's
shagged away, this gleaming whiteness against the sedgy red-black-
purple of the leaves. The dress hempen, ochre, bringing in a bit of

blond, and the leaves and the hair spread and mashed down, scattered, pressed. And the ram backing off golden-gray, his horns golden-gray, even the rich gold of his pelt would take a little blue in it, his terrible yellow eyes, and blood in the air. He wanted a picture you could smell. Rank, damp. A rape.

The sky was moving fast, fast. A storm rushing by. The hurrying clouds in stacked layers, verging from dirty white and pale gray to an almost cobalt blue with a speck of carmine. What you had to get was how these clouds were not one multicolored bank but moving crowds, some nearer, some very far away, each moving at a different speed, and each of a different density, laden with a different cargo of wetness. The sky and the earth and the water of the boat lake were all in sympathy with each other, each partook of the same mottled piebaldness—earth and trees reddish-brown-gray, and the rucked-up water a murky hazel. Some yellow-greens too—ferns at the foot of trees, and on the underside of the slick black boughs, scummy fungus, the green of oxidized copper.

And now the sun bursting out through a window in the clouds, like a face from a fast-moving train window, white-gold, white-gold, and what it did was cast floodlights on little patches of landscape—a holly bush that briefly turned silver, and the drab olive-grays of dried grass also silvery-lit, sparkish, and the dull gray-brown of the boat lake turned into hacked-up, roiled-up white flame. But all these effects were so thick and mashed you would need to squeeze the tube direct onto the canvas, slosh around in the oils, just squelch 'em and revel in 'em. The mud, gleaming-black like a fat healthy horse's pelt. And the black boughs of the trees where the rain had fallen—thick, thick wet and rotting and yet very much alive and instinct with sly wakefulness and mirth—the black boughs, well, where the light—not even sunlight, just some reflection of sky—caught them they turned pure white.

Dolly had an idea that was taking shape in her mind. She wanted Isaac to move out to Goose Neck for a few months. She loved the place with all her heart—it was to her an image of American uprightness, stalwart abundance. She loved its faded colors and smells. She was as proud of the house as of her children. Like most city dwellers, she thought of the country as curative, purifying, good for the soul. And the idea of Isaac removed from his ghastly little apartment and ensconced there, loving it as she did, and working on his marvellous painting–at peace!–thrilled her beyond measure.

Several years ago, Kay Armistead had stayed at Goose Neck for a winter. That had not worked out so well. Kay had got lonely and bored, her work had gone badly, and Mrs. West complained that Kay treated her like a servant, was always coming around helpless wanting things done. Whiny. But Isaac was a gentleman. And on weekends they could come out to see him–not too often, lest they disturb his work. The thought of driving out to Goose Neck on Fridays and finding him there enthusiastic, radiant, productive . . .

She stopped by Isaac's workroom. "How are you set up here?"

"Fine. Like a thief in a cellar."

"You need natural light, don't you?"

She looked at some of his charcoal studies for the *Daughters of the Earth* series. "*Very* strong. I think my old complaint about the compositions is no longer so valid. They seem more complex to me now. Less naive."

Then she picked up his little painting on sheet metal of the yellow rose. "My God–the color! It looks like a Puerto Rican wedding."

"Dyspeptic, huh? That's what you get from working under electric light. You have to take it out into the street to see what it really looks like."

She came out with it. "Why don't you go use our house for a while? We won't be there until school's out, except maybe the odd weekend, so you'll have the place to yourself. You could set up a studio in one of the upstairs rooms, or the porch if it's not too cold–or else you could take over the barn. . . ."

Isaac paced, humming. "What about work?"

"What, your job? You can take a month's sabbatical."

"What do you mean–leave Costa in the lurch?"

"I'll square it with Costa. You know he thinks as highly of your art as I do. We'll get Ramon to come in full-time."

Isaac walked around the room, pushing the ceiling with the tips of his fingers. He reflected, not liking it that she could treat as superfluous the job he did at Aurora. Was it just welfare? Did Costa too think it was just welfare? Why was she wanting to give him so much, when he had so little to offer in return?

"Really, the house is empty. It would be reassuring for me to know someone was using it. I'd tell Mrs. West to keep out of your way."

In part it was his touchy ingratitude that made her try harder to get him.

Later, she approached him again. "Have you thought about going to stay at Goose Neck? This project you're doing now is so sublime, so monumental, you really need freer working conditions to let your imagination expand."

"I've thought, but not concluded," said Isaac. "I consider my imagination expansionist enough as it is—if you don't watch out, it'll be marching into the Sudetenland."

She expounded on the virtues of country: space and light and quiet.

"I know," he said brusquely. "I grew up in the country."

Nobody to bother him.

"I like being bothered."

It was some days later before Isaac said to her, "Did you mean it when you suggested that I might go to Goose Neck?"

It gave her an odd thrill to hear him call the house by name. "What a question. Of course."

"Well, I guess it might be a good idea to go and work there for a while, if no one is using it just now. . . ."

An expression of pleasure so intense it looked akin to anger came over Mrs. Gebler's face. "I can't tell you how happy it would make me," she said. "And Mrs. West will be absolutely over the moon." Her voice, as always when she was moved or excited, dropped a few bars, and she came up close to him, staring into his eyes as if she wanted to eat him alive. "You must tell me everything you'll need—what you like to eat and drink, any art supplies—there's quite a good store in Greenport—so I can get everything laid in for you. Normally, when there are people in the house, Mrs. West comes in every day to clean and do the laundry and some cooking. But of course you must tell me if she'll be in your way."

Isaac, wondering if he was making a mistake, ducked down his head and was silent until it was over. . . .

Shortly before his departure for Goose Neck, Celia Rubin came over to Isaac's studio. She was a big pale Texan with reddish blond hair and a crumpled face who had a gallery on West Broadway. She was huffing and puffing from the four-story climb and the first thing she said when Isaac opened the door was "Oh dear."

Dolly had decided to let Celia go to Isaac without her. She checked her impulse to tell Isaac to be sure to show Celia his pictures himself and not fuck off to the coffee shop. She was still uncertain as to the extent and pliability of Isaac's worldly ambitions.

Celia chose to drop by at the end of the day. Isaac, who had bought a bottle of sherry—a nice ladylike drink, he figured—had drunk most of it himself by the time Celia arrived, and the two of them polished off the remains. The visit was to Isaac's mind a success; she stayed long enough, anyway.

The next morning when Dolly called Celia to ask her what she thought, Celia talked for the longest time about the trouble she was having getting her contractor to finish the tilework in her bathroom, and finally when Dolly could stand it no longer, Celia said, "Well, I certainly am grateful to you for getting me down to see your assistant's work. He's very intellectual, isn't he?"

"What on earth do you mean?" She pictured to herself Isaac's work, which seemed to her positively kindergartenish.

"He gave me this whole, like, seminar on communism. You know, we were talking about the Berlin Wall and all. . . . I kept on asking him about his pictures, but all he wanted to talk about was, like, labor statistics and party congresses and some Polish economist who'd predicted the . . . I don't know what all. This Soviet astronaut who'd been murdered because he found out . . . well, it was very interesting. I'd love to get him together with Philip. But why are all these kids so conservative, that's what I want to know."

Mrs. Gebler could no longer contain herself. "For heaven's sake, Celia, will you please stop dithering? What did you think of the pictures?"

Celia began, "Well . . ."

"They are hugely powerful, to my mind," Mrs. Gebler interrupted.

"Well . . . I don't know what I was expecting. . . . They're very *spiritual*, aren't they? They're not quite like . . . Well, I thought of some of the Italians. Clemente, maybe? But Clemente's real playful, real *light*. Most of the time, I mean. Well, you know . . . like that one *Hunger*? Or

Enzo Cucchi's drawings, which also are kind of primitive and . . . That's what Isaac's work reminded me of, a little bit. An American Cucchi. You know? Just the drawings. Well, I liked that circus sideshow thing–the one that you bought. And then those ones on tin are . . . Well, I think he's real interesting."

"How interesting?"

"What do you mean?"

"I mean, interesting enough to–"

"I bought one of them."

"You did? Which?" asked Dolly, jealous despite herself. *Her* paintings. She wanted them all.

"A big watercolor. One of the ones where he makes a kinda quilt of all the little rooms and landscapes pasted together."

"How big?"

"Four by four."

"How much?"

"Eight hundred."

"That's a bargain. I would have told him to ask a thousand. Would you consider taking him on?"

"You mean in my gallery?"

"Exactly." Stupid Celia. Why did she think she'd been hauled over to Hell's Kitchen, for heaven's sake?

"Well, I'm not sure he's ready. In my opinion. I mean, do you honestly think he's built up enough of a body of mature work?"

"I think his *Daughters of the Earth* series–did he show you the sketches?–is going to be magnificent, unlike anything we've seen. And an altogether new departure for him. Maybe I've alerted you a little early, Celia, but I thought you would want to be there from the very beginning. Because, really, for me, it's been one of the most exciting experiences since we founded Aurora, to see this fierce, abandoned young visionary just coming into his own. . . ."

"Maybe if he gets together a few more pieces, I might. . . . He's certainly got something very special about him."

Dolly, balancing the telephone between shoulder and ear, ground her teeth in exasperation. Old windbag. She wasn't fit to . . . "I'm glad you think Isaac Hooker is as . . . talented as I do. You should know that if by the end of the year, say, you do decide he's ready and are willing to take him on and give him a show, I'd buy everything before it even went up, and I'd be very happy for you to get the word out that I'd done so."

"What did that lady I got drunk say about me?" Isaac asked Dolly.

"She said you talk too much about Soviet party congresses."

"But I thought you told me she liked parties."

"Very funny. She said you should paint some more pictures."

"Did she say I should invest in a better class of sherry?"

"Sherry? Is that what you gave her? Ugh. No wonder she doesn't want to take you on. Sherry's for cooks' tippling. My father always kept a bottle in the house just so they wouldn't hit the good stuff."

"So she won't take me on?"

"No, she will. Later. After you paint some more big pictures."

"I heard you the first time. So what do *ladies* like to drink?"

She reflected. "It's not your job to please ladies. It's your job to make art. You've been drawing those shepherdesses long enough—it's time to start painting. Do you have all the materials you need? Do you need more canvases? What about brushes? How are you fixed for cash?"

"I just got eight hundred dollars from your friend. What do *you* like to drink?"

"Are you asking me out for a drink? I like bullshots. That's vodka and beef bouillon. They're very tasty. Cold soup. Cold alcoholic soup. Actually, I don't drink much—it puts me to sleep."

"Oh, I was afraid it might make you sentimental," said Isaac crossly.

It was only once he got home that night, after going to the movies with Jane and Dogface, that Isaac registered that an important New York art dealer had bought one of his pictures—his first sale, besides Mrs. Gebler!—and had said she might someday take him on as an artist. Then he quickly put the impossible idea out of his head, afraid that it might distract him from the work he had to do, from the daughters of earth and their seamy callers who had taken up such a monstrous broad residence in his imagination. . . .

Part Seven

Thirty-three

ON AN EARLY SPRING MORNING, Isaac loaded into the hold of the Sunrise Bus four large stretched canvases wrapped in plastic, three smaller canvases, two army surplus bags of paints, pastels, pencils, palette, brushes, knife, turps, oil, beeswax, and a shopping bag full of secondhand schoolbooks. At Southold, outside the luncheonette, the Geblers' Dodge Ram was waiting for him, and when the bus pulled up, Mr. West–gnomelike in watchcap and gumboots–climbed out of the pickup and helped Isaac unload.

"Looks like a travelling circus, huh?"

They drove to the house in near silence, Isaac so joyful to be out of the city he could hardly breathe. Although in Central Park the crocuses and daffodils had already sprouted, in Long Island it was still winter. The fields were straw-stubbly with last year's blasted corn, in the vine-yards the vines were spindly gray sprigs, and a keen north wind came bellowing in from the Connecticut shore.

"How's the team?"

"The what?"

"The Clippers." Mr. West was former coach to the high-school base-ball team.

"The season's not started yet."

"Well, how's it look?"

Mr. West cracked his chapped knuckles as they stopped at a red light. "Lineup's not bad, if you ask me. Some of the old-timers are back again–Mattirolo's the second base, he's a sophomore, Drozecski's a sharp infielder. Then they got a pitcher by the name of Gary Winton transferred over from Mattituck, helped the Indians seal the pennant in '87. I went over to watch 'em practice last week."

Isaac nodded.

"You know they had to drop out of varsity altogether back in '81. The comeback boys. Well, let's see what happens."

"Does your wife like sports, too?"

Mr. West made a sound of derision. Isaac, thinking that was his answer, had gone back to looking out the window, but eventually Mr. West elaborated.

"She likes to watch the ball game with me on TV; she keeps score real nice—I taught her that when we first started going together." Another long pause. "Emily is a bowler. If you call that sport. More like an excuse for six old biddies to get together Thursday nights and spread slander. The Astros, they named their team. The Gastros is what I call 'em."

The sun was just going down when they reached the house. The Geblers' farmhouse stood by itself like a mare in a field, its dark shingles turning ruddy gold, catching fire from the sun's dunking. Isaac had forgotten how bashfully far back the house was set, in a cropped two hundred acres all by itself. Conspicuous even in its nestling of bare-limbed oaks and hickories. You made a big claim when you turned down that avenue of maples; you couldn't slip up on the house unawares as if you'd lost your way, but were exposed as a bridegroom heading for the altar.

Mr. West deposited Isaac in the kitchen, showed him which keys fitted where, the garage where the Geblers' old Volvo sat and where the firewood was neatly stacked, told him how to open the chimney flue. Explained the new recycling system that was local law. On the kitchen counter sat a shepherd's pie left by Mrs. West, with instructions about oven settings. "I see she wasn't too optimistic about my powers of survival."

"She likes to do for people. She'll be in tomorrow morning to see if you've got anything needs washing."

Mr. West racked his brains for more instructions and warnings. Thursdays he went off to the town dump and would take any garbage Isaac might by then have amassed.

"That's all right—I can take it myself if you tell me where it is."

"Off the Old North Road—you'll know it by the pack of seagulls overhead. But you need a sticker, that Volvo's permit's expired, you may as well let me do it, save yourself a trip."

"What else? There's a whole pile a wild cats around here always tryin' to barge their way in. My wife feeds just about every stray east o'

Jamesport, so don't worry that they're hungry. And see that you don't let any of 'em inta the house—it's harder'n a hornet to get 'em out again."

Isaac, left alone in this foreign kingdom of silence, order, glacial emptiness, felt a moment's consternation. He went back outside. On the beach a pair of geese, honking, skidded away from him in alarm. All day long, these first few weeks, this was the noise you heard—the overhead migration of geese returning north, their honks and wing-beats like the creak of a rusty gate. He stood in the half-frozen scurf of last tide's leavings and watched the bluffs of Shelter Island blanch from honey-red to gray-brown, as the dying light departed from them. When it got dark, he came in and lit a fire and explored the house once more. Crept around upstairs, opening closets, sitting on beds, looking at books—children's books, school anthologies, biographies of statesmen and generals and Civil War histories clearly imported from Mr. Diehl's Chicago library. Then, ashamed of his snooping, Isaac parked himself firmly on the living-room sofa, where he sat all evening, unwilling so much as to rumple a pillow, reading a child's biography of Thomas Edison, and stirring only to put more wood on the fire. I think I'll be all right, as long as the books and the firewood last, he thought. Just past midnight, he put out the lights as carefully as someone extinguishing candles, and stuck his head out of doors for a lungful of icy stars, before locking up. Instead of the Sultan Club booming below as if hell were sound, a few dogs barking in the night, cutting their teeth on the huge silence.

In the house on Goose Creek, Isaac found himself for the first time voluntarily alone. His prior life had been so dogged and blighted by loneliness, so harrowed by the tragic sense of the incommunicability of one person's essence to another, that all his efforts had gone into frantically trying to compensate by foisting himself full-time upon any company who would have him. Consequently, Isaac, despite oddities both inbuilt and acquired, had attracted many friends. He had been continuously hedged by an admiring crowd of schoolmates willing to tag along with him all hours, and neighbors, teachers, local elders happy to have him drop by anytime. If you arrange it properly and are not too much of an insomniac, you can go through an entire week with no more than one or two consecutive waking hours burdened by your own solitary company.

After his arrival in New York City, hardship had obliged Isaac to abandon his old stratagems. You come into the world alone, you leave it alone, and in between is just more of the same, so you better get used to it, unillusioned by any dreams of kinship or spiritual union. This, anyway, is what Isaac told himself on coming to the city. Grinding his nose in it, gorging on it, forcing it upon himself precisely because if he hated and feared it that badly it must be good for him. Because if he wasn't going to be with Agnes, then he didn't deserve to be with anybody.

But no sooner was he anchored in the haven of companionableness called Aurora than the cursed condition was once again being urged on him by none other than his adorable patroness. I won't go, said Isaac. He was not ready for occasion to remember what he had left behind and whom he had betrayed. How unhappy his parents' marriage had been and how his father had placed hopes in him which Isaac had then defaulted on. How he'd abandoned his girlfriend, his heart's darling, his wife. Not to mention the undigested catastrophe of his early years in New York City, where he had nearly gone mad or got himself killed through a kind of backhanded and unfruitful remorse.

But finally he consented, simply because he had to trust that his new calling was sufficient antagonist to the old demons. Besides, now he had a body of work to get done, a patroness who believed in him, a Manhattan dealer who might be willing to exhibit his paintings.

He had been right to trust himself. For here, at Goose Neck, solitude was a blessed conjunction of space, light, air, birds, trees. Was liberty. In this square house of the Geblers' with its sofa and books to sink into, its tall windows looking down the park to the bay, its gardens and beach, he felt like the osprey discovering the brave perch that has been commodiously, painstakingly provided for him. Here he might sit in sumptuous contentment, incubating his unhatched babe.

As if the lid had been taken off, and the flooded high changing firmament revealed, and what he formerly believed to be the world was in fact a tight dark box. A lidded coffin.

In the mornings he woke at six and made himself a big breakfast before going up to his studio for the day. He had commandeered the children's playroom—a square, bare-planked room facing east and south, over the cropped golden corridor of park to Peconic Bay. His workroom was icy, but the physical exercise of painting—the pugilistic pounce, thrust, dance of it—kept him warm until the sun left for good.

The light in these spring days was piercing but inconstant. From one moment to the next, the room would fall from brilliance to deep shadow and rise again, like a boat plunging from wave to wave on a rough sea. Each time the light shifted, his picture looked quite different. When he painted in the moving sunlight, it was like talking at a party to a pretty girl whose attention one was nervously trying to monopolize.

In the late afternoons, he went out for a breather. Explored some new portion of creek or wetland, a lighthouse, an abandoned railway depot or old Indian burial ground. He took along a sketchbook to draw the rocks off Horton Point at low tide, some hidebound in shaggy moss, slippery as eels, some grainy, carbuncled. He made watercolors and then sealed them in varnish or honey.

One week he spent learning how to draw fog, which was different from clouds because it was land-bound, sunless. In the end he rubbed wood ash straight onto the paper.

Another rainy afternoon, he came upon a motel at the Port of Egypt that housed the fishermen come up from the south to work the trawlers. Three of the men, who were sitting out on the steps, asked him inside for a game of poker. Isaac, who was fond of cards, agreed.

They played—four of them, and a young girl who didn't play but sat and watched. At the end of the game, Isaac counted up his winnings and the man whose room it was asked if Isaac wanted to take the girl instead, and Isaac said he'd certainly be happy to take her home to her parents, and the girl laughed and said that that would be a long trip. Then the man whose room it was suddenly got angry and said, Who do you think you're doing a favor? This is my wife we're talking about. The other men lent the girl's husband the money—twenty-six dollars—to pay his losses, and Isaac drove home in the hard night rain, nerves still twirling with gaming elation.

That night, he dialled Agnes's old number, then hung up.

Now when he went to town for groceries he could scarcely force himself to buy the newspaper. All those world events, that distant unrolling of freedom, had receded before the preeminence of watching each day the jonquils under the hickory tree raise their pale-green arrowheads and on Cedar Beach the mistrustful osprey take her post. In the brake, the green shoots of the new thorn branches intertwined with the gray-brown dead ones. There were no coffins in nature, last year's leaves lay heavy on pockets of newborn myrtle and young ivy.

Once or twice a week he ate at the counter at the Hellenic Diner, where there was a waitress named Rosy whom he'd persuaded to model for him. Her coloring was wrong—she was a brunette, olive-skinned—but she had a teasing smile and the incipient blowsiness he required. She would bring her five-year-old daughter over with her on Sunday afternoons, and Isaac tried to amuse the little girl while drawing her mother. Rosy thought his picture's subject matter was disgusting and unheard-of.

"Are you sure they never did such things where you came from?" Isaac joked. Rosy's family came from Naples.

"Get out of here! In Sicily, maybe. But Naples? Come on, with men coming out of your ears, what would you need *sheep* for?"

Occasionally, Rosy let him come over to her apartment after her daughter had gone to sleep. Her boyfriend was in the air force and not due home before Easter.

Most evenings, however, he stayed home and worked till his eyes went numb. On clear nights the emerald stars hung above the hickory tree and the moon scattered its cold wares into the Great Peconic Bay, and Isaac liked to sit on the grass in the garden at the bottom of the house and look back at its lit windows, unable to believe his own good fortune that he for once was at the heart of that clasped golden shelter, and not its excluded observer, that at any moment he could race back into that enveloping warmth, and be scooped up by it and baked and comforted.

Every other weekend, Mrs. Gebler came out—once with Alfred, mostly just with Leopold or the girls. And during the week, they talked every day.

Isaac was eighteen before he saw the ocean. And yet there was something about the North Fork that was familiar, for the eastern stretches of Long Island in mores and habits and ways of speech—even, he discovered, in geology—is really a southern outpost of New England: a broad-vowelled, more street-smart cousin to Cape Cod or Martha's Vineyard, and like them, founded by whaling captains and Quakers and ex-pirates.

Its contemporary culture too was the culture Isaac'd grown up with. When he went to the IGA for groceries or for a beer at Pirate's Cove, he recognized with a heart leap of kinship this aimless society of ex-marines with nothing to show but their tattoos, and single mothers with six-inch purple fingernails and sprayed-on jeans, who drove pickups with the wheels so souped up you needed a ladder to climb in, and who met on rainy afternoons in bars and got argumentatively drunk listening to country-western and watching with one eye the Mets beat the Phillies. Life on the police blotter. Familiar, too, was the more self-respecting surrounding community, the Knights of Columbus and the Daughters of the Eastern Star and the Veterans of Foreign Wars, the women who baked for church benefits and the men who were volunteer firemen. On Sunday afternoons the cemetery was packed with families come to visit their parents' graves.

It was back to the briar patch for Isaac.

If he recognized them, they too recognized him, or at any rate weren't inquisitive, for here being a paid-by-the-hour laborer who liked to paint pictures in his spare time was a normal thing for a young fellow. Rosy urged him to submit one of his pictures—not one of the dirty ones, *please*—to the community college, which was having a group exhibition to benefit the lighthouse. Quincy, who was bartender at the Pirate, offered to rustle him up some house-painting jobs—there was a boat owner with a summer place out in Orient might need some work done in mid-June.

And Isaac thought, Why not? Why not rent a room in Greenport or East Marion and earn enough in the summers to do his own work for the rest of the year, without being trammelled with the complications of patronage or exasperated by watching the art-market darlings lauded for filling five thousand square feet of prime SoHo real estate with a pile of teddy bears and rubber tubing, without suffering the insalubrious exigencies of that harsh city, where people lived like scorpions in a bottle? . . . He looked at the ads in the papers and asked around, and learned that such a thing could be done, and kept it in the back of his mind that there was no need to go back to climbing piss-and-cockroach-scented stairs every night to that heart-withering little cubicle with the masturbating Dominican shaking his dick across the way. That it was possible to live somewhere you didn't always have to look over your shoulder in case you were about to get jumped. Where a person could stand up and stretch.

It was getting to be high spring, and his picture was growing. Having completed a dozen or so watercolors and charcoals of each segment—the woodscape, the sky, the ram, the girl, the road with her companions leading their flocks back to the city—Isaac had finally got up nerve to address himself once more to canvas. Six by eight, larger than anything he had yet attempted.

The woodland had gone quite well. He had managed to convey very lushly the treacherous slipperiness of decaying tree trunks, the curling sheen of ivy underfoot, the clayey declivity of the bank. And having completed the bank, he needed now to place his splayed girl more convincingly upon it. The point was to make her look as if she were genuinely lying there, the full weight and mass of her mashed down into moss and leaves, and not just floating ethereally, or slightly askew. And her head, at what angle? Eyes half-closed in that expression most flattering to anxious males, dearer even than desire—the glazed look of satiety? Or still an itinerant, unappeased glint? She had turned out, indeed, a mischievous rowdy big-limbed thing—he was thinking here of Courbet, of Titian's swooning Danaë, of various High Renaissance Europas and Ledas who looked not victims but strapping accessories to the act. Because who knows—despite what Rosy said, maybe a powerful bull or even he-swan or ram made a welcome shift from clumsy boys. . . .

The next feat was to angle the ram so that you could see his body sidelong but also his yellow eyes and horns, could tell he was not approaching but was backing away, the act discharged. There was an antinomianism he enjoyed in having this rank, ambiguous son of God come down to rut with the earthly daughter, taking the shape not of a lamb, but of a ram.

When he got fed up with the daughter of the earth and couldn't see her anymore, he covered the canvas with a sheet and moved on to other things. One week he spent drawing Rosy's brother Peter, who had dyed blond hair, three earrings in one ear, and the coarse wheedling look of a Caravaggio Bacchus. Peter, who played drums in a local band, was lean and wiry, and Isaac, who had done nothing but women for weeks now, was initially baffled by this alien architecture. Whenever Peter moved, a thousand little muscles in his back shivered and eddied, and his haunches were like corrugated sheet metal. Compared to this notched, indented, articulated engine, Rosy's big curves were pure as a cello's.

When she came to his studio in Hell's Kitchen, that great floppy Texaness sent by Mrs. Gebler had asked Isaac if he was making folk art, and the question irked him. Folk art surely was something its maker had no choice about: if you were making it on purpose, then that was over-sophisticated affectation. He had said, "Not at all. It's Goya and Titian and Géricault I'm crazy for—it's just that every time I try to paint a lovely Arabian steed it ends up looking like a bar stool."

Now he recalled that some of his favorite poets, Dylan Thomas and Yeats, William Blake above all, used nursery jingles to achieve poignance or as a kind of psychic pulling-the-bow-tight. How even in Tennyson's *Maud* or Coleridge's *Kubla Khan* the long elegant Hellenic stanzas would unexpectedly disintegrate and hurtle into little jog-trot jingles that mimicked the narrator's descent into madness.

Was Yeats in "Brown Penny" being "primitive," or was he plumbing the deep ardent sources of poetic tradition, deploying some of the most powerful techniques in his arsenal? Wouldn't any poet worth his salt mine nursery riddles as well as sonnets, be as proud to have written "Brown Penny" as "Leda and the Swan"? And when would he, Isaac, be able to complete his own Leda, his latest riff on the chronic question of how—fumblingly, sidelong, or just unrecognized—the divine penetrates our lives?

Mid-June. He had been in the house more than two months—and yet the sole sense he had of time's encroachments, aside from the daylight's clinging till eight, and the landscape's having gone a clamorous monopoly of greens running from the phosphoresent grasshopper-green of the tall grass and the bulrushes' dull silver to the black-oak leaves' inkiness, was Mrs. West's preparing, as for some high jubilee, for Dolly's arrival.

Every morning she had a new task. "I better get the linen closets re-organized before Mrs. Gebler comes out" or "I better see Elwin"—that was Mr. West—"has the car inspected before Mrs. Gebler comes out." And Isaac, muttering, discovered to his consternation that he did not want Mrs. Gebler to move out there for good. Odd weekends were a treat, but permanent residence? Entrenched in his own North Fork ways, he could think only of the liberties the Geblers' presence in their own house would curtail, of the cramping diminution of being reduced to guest. It almost offended him to be reminded that the stray cat he fed or the ladies at the IGA had a precedent relation with the Geblers. Would it be awkward smuggling Rosy into the house, or coming home from her at three a.m.?

Now the shepherdess was almost done. The tones of her flesh he had built up in shimmery luminous layers, so that you almost seemed to see the blood in her veins. A lustrous white, against the black-purple-green of the forest. Against the russet-purple forest between her parted legs. The expression veiled. The rutting ram was sufficiently menacing, the other stream of homegoing sheep and herders had been reduced to a diagonal downpour of heads and blobs of scrubby wool, and now he was determined to get well embarked on his painting of the Flood before the intruders arrived.

Thirty-four

Dolly was showing Ayala around the gallery. He had called her up the day before to ask her for lunch, and even though she was going crazy getting everything fixed before she left for the country, and what's more loathed lunches, Dolly at once agreed. If she had a best friend, Ayala was he. They had known each other thirty years—his father was a French banker friend of Charles Diehl's—and there was no one in the world she was fonder of. The mere thought of his sanguine face sweetly smiling infused her with a sense of holiness, almost.

They arranged to meet at Dominick's at one o'clock, Ayala having offered to come downtown. During lunch, she looked at him closely. His face was drawn, he had lost weight. Was he quite all right? How was his health? Fine, no complaints. And how was Nancy? Dolly was very fond too of Ayala's shy wife, who was often sick.

"Everything is delightful, except business," said Ayala. "Nobody's buying. Nobody. All my old customers have either died or gone bankrupt. I can't get rid of anything. Two years ago, for instance, I bought a charming de Staël at rather a high price. Now I can't sell it. Why? Because Maurice Engelmann has dumped his de Staëls at auction, and if Engelmann is bored by de Staël, nobody else wants to be caught dead with one. This new generation of collectors—during the last ten years, we've depended so much on them that really, we built them up in our imaginations as the new Havemeyers, the new Lehmans. But these people quite reasonably look upon art as a passing fashion, like the latest boat or sports car. If they have no scruples about divorcing last year's wife, why should they hang on to last year's art?"

"Indeed," said Dolly. "So you're in a scrape."

"A mild scrape," said Ayala cheerfully. "Rather, I'm holding my breath to see what the fall auctions bring. And what about you, my darling?"

He took her hand and kissed it, smiling into her eyes. "Who are you planning to show next year? What's in your fall collection? Are skirts going to be above or below the knee, and are we taking our art minimalist or to the max? You know, I envy your position enormously. I would give anything to get out of the buying-and-selling business, and live surrounded by the pictures I love."

Dolly shook her head. "God—if only. We're in for lean times, too, I'm afraid." As it turned out, Diehl had had some serious losses that year. The company had had to abandon its prostate drug, which had caused internal bleeding in its first trial patients, and the lawsuits were beginning to pile up. As a consequence, Aurora's budget was going to have to take a trimming. She had contemplated selling some Diehl stock to raise money, but Mason had persuaded her not to lower the price any further.

"I'm disappointed because I had all sorts of grand plans for next year. We'd been hoping to get started on the new building for our permanent collection—you know, the entire Beuys collection is warehoused at the moment, which I consider absolutely immoral. But I guess we'll have to wait."

"I often think about your father," said Ayala. "I'll never forget his taking me to lunch at his club when I graduated from Princeton. Fifty dollars for the maître d'hôtel, twenty-five for the wine waiter—of course, he knew everyone's name, it was always Gaston this, and My good friend Charles. And this was 1961. Well, you've never seen such smiling faces."

"He certainly operated on the principle that everyone had his price," Dolly said dryly. "I miss him—I miss that expansiveness. When he was in a good mood, he could be more fun than anyone."

"He was a great man."

"The greatest."

"And he loved you. Yes, he did, Dolly. He was so proud of you."

"Until I fucked up and met Alfred."

"Well, parents' rights only extend so far. In any case, I'm very sorry to hear the company is having troubles. So we'll be moving to a cold-water flat in East Harlem together, then? Do you think our friends will visit us?"

"Anyway," said Dolly suddenly. "It's not just money–I'm not as free as you imagine. There's a young artist who's come along–he's still in his twenties and I can see that he's a genius. He works for us. He–he's a working-class boy from New Hampshire, his mother drives a taxi, he's never studied painting in his life, but he's got such vision, such radiance . . . a once-in-a-lifetime painter, what one spends one's career hoping to discover. . . ."

"How marvellous for you. Are you showing him?"

"No. That's the tragedy. I have to get him shown somewhere else first. You know, Aurora has this awkward reputation–I mean, most of the artists we show, unfortunately, are already established, and this child has never exhibited anything in his life. It would look like nepotism, because he works for me. But he paints like an angel, and his paintings just radiate love . . . and mystery. Some of them–they're religious narratives, mostly–are quite terrifying."

"Yes, I see your problem. Aurora, it's like a very grande dame that can't suddenly pick up her skirts and dance the can-can. Do you have any of your young man's work at the gallery?"

Dolly leaned forward eagerly. "Not his most recent work, but . . . Would you come back and take a look? Really, I'd love to know your opinion, Bernard. Alfred thinks I've gone off my rocker."

"How is your bad husband?"

Dolly frowned. "Rotten. He's managed to sprain his ankle–how, I can't imagine, he's not exactly athletic. Anyway, he's laid up at home, cross as two sticks."

"Poor Alfred, I must give him a call. Is he receiving, do you know? Alfred, I say it with great affection, is . . . incorrigible. Thank God. He's a reproach to the rest of us, who have grown so creaky that the idea of staying out past ten or looking in at the newest nightclub is a positive torture. Well, Alfred is our emissary, we are very grateful to him, because he reports back to us about that wicked young world."

"Well, he's out of commission for the moment. Unfortunately. I'd far rather have him out carousing than sulking in his tent."

"Did you know, by the way, that Francis and Joan are getting divorced?"

"My God, Bernard—how awful! What happened?"

"He's fallen in love with another woman. He's left Joan and has moved in with the other one—very young, of course." Ayala looked somber—Joan was a great friend of Nancy Ayala's.

"How sad," repeated Dolly, absently.

After lunch, they went back to the office and Dolly took Ayala downstairs to Isaac's workroom, where he had left five or six earlier paintings and a sheaf of more recent drawings and watercolors. Often during these months while Isaac was away, she'd found herself sneaking down to the basement. His workroom, which previously had been used for storage, now seemed to have taken on the earthy serenity of a dark chapel such as you might find on a remote Mediterranean hillside. A hermit's cave, a badger's lair. She came there to be alone, and to snuff up the leftover scent of Isaac. It was shocking how much she'd missed having him at work. Occasional weekends at Goose Neck only exacerbated her need for him, making Sunday-night returns the grimmer. The city seemed simultaneously overpopulated and empty. Full of fools but devoid of interest.

Home life, too, was quite trying, with everybody underfoot. Carmen's longed-for daughter had been born two months premature, and Carmen had taken the baby to Honduras for the summer. Just when the children were out of school and Dolly most needed help. In the meantime, she'd found Una, a marvellous young Irish woman with a degree in education and two years at a cooking school in Tuscany, but that still left them without a cleaning lady. Carmen had provided a younger sister-in-law, but Carmen's sister-in-law proved singularly lazy. I should fire Lupe and get the agency to find someone decent for the summer, Dolly told herself, but it was as if her sights were set too longingly on Goose Neck to attend to her New York life.

Now, at last, in just another twenty-four hours, she and Isaac would be reunited for the summer in her favorite place in the world.

"What do you think, Bernard? I wish you would see the series he's working on now. These pictures are all quite old."

Ayala turned over the drawings, some of them in charcoal, some in india ink and chalk, some oil stick, some ballpoint and varnish. The varnish made an effect like honey, like translucent beeswax, amber. Then he looked at the tin paintings, the bathtub scenes, the plowed fields and the house, the rooster. The burning bush.

Dolly kneaded her hands in suspense.

Finally Ayala looked up. He said nothing, but joined thumb and forefinger in a gesture of approbation.

Dolly flushed. "Do you really like them? Honestly?"

"Bravo, my girl. You've done it again. And what a surprise. Well, when you said he was a religious painter, of course one thinks of something naive—but no, he is quite finished. Look at his lines, look at his colors. This rooster, for instance, is very cunning. A strong, strong colorist. And humorous. Well, he's a real American, isn't he—bold as can be, and yet quite haunted. I am very admiring, I must say, of these artists who are so rooted in a landscape—it is a great gift."

"He's a wonderful man, too, Bernard. He's had a hard life and suffered a lot."

"One can see it."

"But he has such a warmhearted exuberance and generosity. In fact, you would like him enormously. I must get you two together—he loves to talk politics. He went to Harvard."

Ayala smiled. "I love these rustic geniuses. They've always been to Harvard."

"And you really agree with me about Isaac's work?"

"I think it's very powerful. And how lucky he is to have found you, as a patroness."

"That dreadful word!"

"Still, there are worse things to do with one's—however much reduced—fortune."

Dolly, still soaring, saw Ayala out into the street to say goodbye.

"Well, my girl, have a lovely time in the country, and give a big kiss to the children. Tell Alfred I'll be coming by with the chicken soup and condolences."

Dolly, kissing Ayala on either cheek, said, as they parted, "That's dreadful, by the way, what you told me about Francis Buccam. Joan must be devastated."

Ayala's rosy face darkened. "I must say, I find it very shabby. There's no other word for Francis's behavior. After twenty-five years of marriage, we all know far too much about ourselves and one another for such shabbiness."

Dolly went back upstairs to the office, her euphoria squelched by Ayala's parting words. Startling to hear so harsh and unequivocal a condemnation issue from those sweet lips. It forced her, on the spot, to reappraise her own set's morality, which previously had struck her, in contrast to the world she'd grown up in, as practically nonexistent. In her parents' Chicago society, married people did not split up. It simply wasn't an option. Her father, who everyone knew kept a mistress in town, was so virulent against divorce that he had forbidden Beatrice's first engagement because her fiancé came from a broken family, and when Edwin Buttrick had left his wife and children for Gillian Marshall, Charles Diehl had promptly terminated that thirty-year friendship.

But to Dolly it had always seemed that her parents lived in a different century from the one that she and her husband inhabited. She and Alfred had shacked up in New York, and at once had entered a crowd in which people made pornographic movies and stayed up three nights running whacked out of their minds on acid and lived in apartments that her father would have considered unsuitable for storing grain. Surely, there was no such thing anymore—at least in Dolly's acquaintance—as society, and no more prohibitions. Several years ago, an artist friend of theirs called Garrett Jarvis had murdered his boyfriend when they were both high on angel dust, and everyone they knew had said what a shame, but when Garrett, who pleaded self-defense, got out of prison, there wasn't a museum that didn't show his work or a hostess that didn't welcome him. So there were no more rules, except for the kind without which social life was impossible—i.e., you could murder your lover, but you couldn't no-show a dinner party.

But here was Ayala, not a judgmental scold, saying that for Francis Buccam to leave his wife and do what every man in Middle America was doing was shabby. And suddenly Dolly, the most irreproachable of women and stainless of wives and mothers, realized with a jolt how far she had gone in her imagination towards ending her godawful marriage and felt herself obscurely rebuked. So there were rules after all, and what's more, they were the same rules as always. Today, it turned out, marriage was still a closed city, within which any number of hidden insurrections and massacres might take place, but whose gates were never to be let open.

And Dolly thought, just as she had of her father's midwestern hypocrisy, How stupid. Why should Francis suffer, if he'd fallen in love with someone else and wanted to be happy? For, after all, even Ayala must admit that Joan was rather a stick. Why shouldn't one take a shot at bliss?

Once more the thought entered her head. They could not go on like this. It was too murderous a waste, too soul-destroying. If Alfred insisted on making a fool of her, on lying through his teeth, if things had gotten so bad they no longer even wanted to sleep together, let alone share a breakfast table, if the prospect of him stretched out, swollen with self-pity, on the invalid's chaise longue at home, made her want to run a mile—*if they simply could not bear the sight of each other*—why go on? Why flog a dead horse? It was not the first time that such a thought had lodged itself in her brain—she and Alfred had discussed divorce from time to time—but now it was more persistent.

But once again this word "shabby" entered Dolly's brain, along with the sight of Ayala's cherubic face, and she felt piqued as a cat caught with a paw in the fishbowl.

Thirty-five

MR. WEST WAS TELLING DOLLY all over again about the incompetence of the Clippers' new coach.

Usually Dolly loved to hear Mr. West talk. Now, leaning against the car, she could scarcely contain her impatience to get to the house. Just at the end of the drive, her soul's delight. . . . She snuffed up the early-evening air, heart keening with longing. Sweet, sweet, the scent of new-mown grass—mown doubtless in her honor. "I must say, I've hated being in the city so much. Has everything been all right? Isaac hasn't given you any Armistead trouble, I hope. . . ."

Mr. West still liked to reminisce about the shenanigans of Kay Armistead, the Geblers' last long-term houseguest. "Good lord, no. He's not a city kid, he's a worker. He knows life's a serious business. He tries to give me a hand sometimes, I tell him, You got your job, I got mine."

Now, unable to restrain herself any longer, "Leo!" she called, climbing back into the car, and honking the horn. Mrs. West had taken Leo round the back to look at Millie's kittens, several months old and venturesome.

When they pulled up at the big house, Isaac came bounding out to greet them. Tears of happiness, shamefully, at being smothered once again in all that bearish heat. "How are you, my queen?" he whispered in her ear.

She drew back, still holding his hands, to get a better look at him. "Heavens—you're a different color! Mr. West's been covering up for you—it doesn't look at all as if you've been working."

He was a luscious rosy brown, with a sprinkling of freckles across the high bridge of his Roman nose. His eyes dark as blueberries behind the spectacles. And the shaggy hair almost straw-colored. He was wearing a white shirt she had never seen before—several sizes too big but shockingly clean and starched.

"I got it from a friend out here," said Isaac. "It's my church-going shirt. The person it belongs to's been shipped out to the Middle East."

"You don't say," said Mrs. Gebler, jealous that someone—who?—was intimate enough with Isaac to give him clothes. "Well, judging from the size—if he fits it any better than you do—I hope he's not coming back to claim it too soon."

Isaac stood beaming down at her, and she too found herself grinning like an idiot. Uncontrollable. Leo must think she was mad. She grabbed Leopold now and covered the surprised boy in kisses. "Isn't it the best thing in the world to be here, darling? Finally, one can relax. You have no idea—the city was . . . Well, it's heaven to be here. Have you been well? It looks as if it needs some rain. . . . The lawn's a bit . . ."

Then excitement at Isaac got nudged aside by excitement at the country, and she rushed to inspect the garden. Leopold joined her, and together mother and son walked, hand in hand, down to the bay. It was just after sunset and the air had cooled, but she couldn't resist stripping down to brassiere and underpants and wading out into the water for a swim. Leopold, brows furrowed, watched from the shore, resisting her inviting shouts. Alarmed by his mother's sudden giddiness. When she came bounding out of the water and hugged him, dripping wet, he recoiled. "Ouch! That hurt!"

"Shall we go back to the house?"

Leopold shrunk.

"What's the matter?"

"Aren't you going to put your clothes on?"

"But they'll just get wet."

Leopold looked so appalled that Dolly, relenting, slipped her summer dress on over her sopping underwear. Back at the house, Isaac was waiting for them. He had put flowers in every room, she noticed—brazen handfuls of marigolds, and lanky tiger lilies. And big bowls of peaches, apricots. The living room an explosion of golds.

"I want to see everything you've done."

Isaac looked at her dress. Bikini-shaped archipelagoes of wetness. "Don't you want to change first? You'll catch cold."

"Isaac, I've been . . . deprived for two weeks. You're the ruin of me. You've spoiled my eye. I used to be a woman of taste—now all I'm interested in is your weird religious maunderings. Everyone thinks I'm mad—although they won't for long. But please, please don't keep me waiting any longer. I want to see what I love. Now."

He had hung *The Daughters of the Earth* by a nail on one wall, *The Flood* on the other. Mrs. Gebler stood back and stared, then came up close to read every part in detail.

The Daughters had turned out very satisfactorily, to Isaac's mind. Each portion of the canvas had its own distinct texture. The homegoing herd that trailed diagonally across the lower right hand of the canvas had been formed by scraping away overlying paint, the sheep scrubbed at like tiny Brillo pads. The woman's flesh, except for the gash of pussy, had a smooth glazed sheen, while the ochre dress, hiked high above her thighs, was braided in little knots and peaks of paint that echoed the clotted clouds above. As for the trees and the brambles, for them he had found a varied calligraphy, an intricate alphabet of bark and thorn and leaf. And there, at the foot of the oak, was his porcupine, Chinese in the elongated wispiness of its spines, which Isaac had produced by using the tail end of his brush to scrape through to an undercoat of dark red.

Dolly examined the picture, frowning, eyes raking from side to side, while he, taut, watched her. "I'm overcome," she said at last. "It's rich as a . . . as a . . . Renaissance picture–the landscape is so lush, so jewelled– but the emotional impact of it is . . . barbaric. Really, very disturbing. And masterful."

Then she picked apart for him each bird and leaf, each mound of cloud and speckled patch of filtered forest light. When she was done, quite unexpectedly, she took his hand and kissed it. "My beloved genius, my king, you've done it." She turned to her son. "What do you think, Leo? Do you like it?"

Leopold, embarrassed by the shepherdess's genitalia, nodded.

Isaac, rocking on his heels, breathed in and out. Vindicated. Ecstatic. Ecstasy like an inflamed kind of smothering, like happy asthma. This is why I am, this is what I was born to do. This and only this. And God help me toward the strength to do what I must, and to be worthy of her for thinking that I can. "You said I couldn't paint like Titian," he reminded her.

"Well, you can't–yet. But . . . I want to show it. I must show it. You must make more–five or six, and then I'll show them at Aurora. I don't want Celia to get them, she doesn't deserve this . . . this sublime piece of work, this–" She broke down, laughing.

"It's not finished," said Isaac.

"Of course it's not finished–artists never think their paintings are finished, until they've gone and wrecked them. When we used to show Ed Moscowitz, he'd come sneaking into the gallery with his palette and brush, improving here and there."

"But it's really not finished–look at how blocklike the oak tree is still."

"Nonsense." And then she moved on to the next canvas, in which Isaac had begun painting the calm after the Flood. He explained to her what he meant to do in the picture, which was quite different from anything he had attempted before: a seascape, with no signs of the cultivated human world, and an almost invisible rainbow over the sea.

"It's God's truce with Noah. Remember, He promises He'll never wipe out humankind again, and makes a rainbow as a seal of the covenant. Our second honeymoon. It's a more resigned, jaundiced setup than either Eden or the race before the Flood. It struck me," Isaac continued, "as kind of an allegory of where we stand today, after the fall of communism. Noah's won, his is the only way of life left standing, and so we're faced with this pale and disabused New World to rebuild from reduced foundations. I want a washed-out, prim sort of palette here. . . ."

Dolly stood, arms folded. "Your interpretation is pretty, but I'm not so sure about the picture itself."

"How come?"

"It looks—well, it looks too nineteenth-century to me, that great misty sea and sky. As if you're trying to rehash Turner. I think you're better off sticking to figures."

"Why don't you wait until it's finished?" Isaac suggested.

She shrugged.

That night they ate dinner out on the porch, Isaac, Dolly, and Leo, with citronella candles for light. Isaac grilled tuna steaks and corn on an old broken barbecue which he'd found in the garage and patched up. He felt like the father of a family. That Dolly reminded him of his mother only made him the sadder, retrospectively, at what a barren botch his own family had made of domesticity. Being hard up was no excuse for such comfortlessness. . . . The corn had been picked that afternoon, and the three of them sank their teeth gratefully into the bright-and-pale-yellow-checkered sweetness. Dessert was Mrs. West's blueberry pie, by which time Leopold's head was drooping on his mother's shoulder. "Come on, honey boy, I think it's time to take you to bed."

Upstairs, Dolly sat on the foot of her son's already turned-down bed, while he brushed his teeth and put on his pajamas.

"Isn't it lovely being out here again, darling? What luxury to have all summer. . . . Do you think Isaac will have finished his sea painting by the time we leave?" Visited by a stab of sadness at having thought already of their leaving. "Heavens, you've outgrown your old pajamas!"

She held Leopold by the ankle as he climbed into bed—he had gone through a growing spurt that year and had become almost lanky, his striped pajama bottoms from last summer a good two inches above the anklebone. Soon—maybe by next summer, even—his voice would be breaking. . . .

"It's awesome being here," Leo agreed. "Did you ask Mr. West if the boat's working?"

"No, I forgot. Let's go see first thing tomorrow. And maybe we'll go out to the lighthouse for a picnic, if it's a nice day."

Leo nodded. "Can we put up the flag?"

"Oh, isn't it up yet?"

"You know what? There's a mouse in my bathroom."

"Oh dear, really?"

"It's been gnawing at the soap."

"Well, maybe we'll have to see if Mrs. West will let us have one of her kittens."

"Hey, can we really, Mom? That would be so cool."

"You're not still allergic to cats, are you?"

He shook his head vigorously.

"Not much you're not. Won't it be bliss going barefoot again? You'll be covered in freckles soon—do you remember what you used to call them? You said to me once when you were a little boy, 'Mummy, the stars are out all over my face.' "

But Leo's eyes had closed.

"Leopold's got some projects for the summer," she said to Isaac, who was washing the dishes. "We have to make up some papers from last term. He's got a paper on the Italian Renaissance, and a paper about *Great Expectations*, and I want to prep him in algebra. His school is absolutely absurd. I've brought all these books and . . . I don't know what on earth they expect a twelve-year-old child to come up with about Renaissance humanism—to me, it seems nothing but an invitation to plagiarism."

"Why don't you hand him over to me for a while? Flatter my didactic greed," offered Isaac. "Although I find the Renaissance overrated. Everything revolutionary they came up with had already been figured out in the twelfth century. Minus, of course, the rediscovery of the human figure—but with flesh nowadays positively coming out of one's ears, I think we might do well to put the human body back in the deep freeze for another half-millennium, return to astronomy and the finer points of transubstantiation."

"You're a fine one to talk. Is that transubstantiation going on in that picture of yours upstairs?" said Dolly.

"Well . . . Anyway, what's wrong with American education isn't too much Dickens, it's that some children read Dickens and some get shot."

They were sitting out now on the screened porch, Isaac swinging in the hammock. Stars hanging above the hickory tree, and the scratchy fiddle of crickets.

"I don't know. When I think of what I'd like Leopold to know, I'd much rather he had some practical skills, like how to balance a checkbook and fix a car engine and raise a family. I think it would be far more useful to teach children to be honest and independent and capable than to train them up like toy poodles."

"Vocational training? That's what they used to foist on us country lunks, the ones who obviously weren't going anywhere."

"Well, vocational maybe, but moral really is what I had in mind. The real trouble with this country today is we're too frightened of stepping on somebody's toes to claim any comprehensive morality. Don't you agree? I feel it, above all, as a parent. How are we supposed to teach Leo to be a man when the relations between the sexes have become such a damned minefield? And women—women don't know what they want, they've ended up somehow with the worst of both worlds. . . . Here we've got this wonderful feminist liberation, but the only so-called woman's issues you ever hear about is abortion and . . . date rape.

"And then the only values they do promote are so damned birdbrained. Right before she left, Carlotta and I were talking about the Holocaust, which they'd been learning about in social studies—why they can't call it 'history' anymore, incidentally, is beyond me. Anyway, Carlotta's teacher told the class that there was nothing so special about what the Nazis did to the Jews. Her teacher said, Look at the Holocaust against homosexuals. I was shocked. Don't you agree that's absolutely lunatic?"

"Of course," said Isaac. "What you're describing is the total breakdown of critical discourse, of the ability to judge differences. I don't agree with you about vocational training, incidentally," he added. "I'm a passionate believer in useless knowledge. I think children—all children—should be sent to school to learn Homer and Dante and calculus, not to be taught to repair cars."

Mrs. Gebler was trying to repair a hole in the porch's screen. "Damn." She looked up, sucking a bleeding finger. "Well, Leo's school is somewhere awkwardly in between. As far as I can see, all they are really learning is which is swankier, the Meadow Club or the Bath and

Tennis. I don't know why on earth we enrolled the children in these re-voltingly pretentious schools. You know there's so many assumptions in one's life that go unexamined, that are just pure snobbery when you look at it. I mean, why in this day and age should Johnny and Carlotta be packed off to a Park Avenue dancing school to learn the fox-trot, of all things? To meet boys for them to marry, I suppose. But are these really the boys one wants them marrying—these unreflective snobbish little fops? I often think about moving out here and sending Leo to the local public school, as soon as the girls are in college. I can't believe Southold High would be half so harebrained as to teach about homo-sexual holocausts."

"What makes you think it's such an Elysium out here?" said Isaac. "The human intellect, unlike radio transmissions, doesn't get more lucid as soon as there's no buildings taller than two stories. Or incomes under twenty grand. Let's not do down money—if it doesn't buy com-mon sense, at least it buys learning."

"Yes, but—"

"And broader horizons. Out here's just like my high school up in Gilboa—nothing to do but get stoned all day. Senior year, assuming they've made it that far without dropping out or getting killed driving drunk, the girls get pregnant and the boys join the marines."

"But still I think—"

"Last week a fifteen-year-old girl in Greenport got her arm ampu-tated playing chicken on the train tracks. What else is there to do on a Saturday night? Your children are much safer in the city reading Dickens."

"And learning the fox-trot? Maybe, but I still think there's a more grounded sense of priorities—I mean, having babies and fighting for your country doesn't sound so barbaric to me. Of course, the luckiest thing is to be born with a real vocation, knowing what you want to do in life. I'm very jealous of artists—I think it must be wonderful to be able to believe in something lodged inside you that's somehow bigger than you."

"I'm not so sure," he said. "I think all it teaches you is the same les-son everybody else has to learn—that the only thing that gets you any-where is concentration. Plugging away at the same old thing. You don't have to be Leonardo da Vinci to figure that one out."

"But still—as an artist, you must know more moments of absolute ecstasy, beauty, revelation, than I do, say."

"I doubt it. Anyway, I haven't been at it long enough. And the moments of ecstasy I have known haven't been painting."

They both laughed shyly.

"Have you been happy out here? You look it, I must say. The picture of health."

"Happier than I've ever been in my life, thanks to you."

"Not roaming the train tracks for thrills?"

"Nothing so elevated." And then, after a pause, "I just need to keep my nose to the grindstone. In the city, it seems to want to poke itself everywhere but.

"You know," he said finally, "we both know, there's plenty left to believe in—it just takes a certain thick-skinnedness to restate it, in this age of irony. Look, we've won the war. We—I mean the Western democracies—have finally finished off what we didn't manage to liberate in 1945. Now all we have to do is remind ourselves of what we stand for, and how to live up to it. How to make sure as large a portion of this country and other countries can share in our luck."

When Isaac went to bed that night he felt as if he'd dodged, for the most part, Mrs. Gebler's conversation about the decline of national morality. In the old days it had been one of his favorite rants, and yet today he felt so disqualified by his own sins and suffering that he looked back in wonder at the loud stranger who had loved to hold forth. For a moment he felt almost sorry for Mrs. Gebler, born into this ex–ruling class that no longer had any function, yet still determined to do her duty. But what a cockeyed sort of duty it was, if one of its objects was him.

Thirty-six

WHILE DOLLY AND LEO were out in the country, the Gebler daughters found projects elsewhere. Carlotta went out West to a six-week riding camp with her best friend, Marci, and Johnny stayed in the city with her father. To Dolly's mind, there had been such an unignorable rift between husband and wife that the children, like it or not, must surely be staking their allegiances. Although she had scrupulously shielded the children from their parents' war, she doubted that her husband had the same compunction, and could not help wondering what bad things Alfred might be saying about her to Johnny. She wished that Johnny had come out to Long Island—wished even more that she'd found a worthier excuse for staying in the city.

This summer, Johnny had got herself a job working in the Madison Avenue store of a dress designer named Inez Klein. Inez was an old girlfriend of her father's. In fact, although Alfred never saw her anymore, Inez had been the person responsible for launching him in New York society—or rather to that louche internationale of playboys and starlets and fashion designers and racing-car drivers to which Inez belonged. After his marriage, they lost touch—Dolly thought her bumptious—and during the seventies, Alfred heard it rumored that Inez had become such a dopehead that she was reduced to shooting coke in her clit. For a long time she disappeared, no one had heard a peep from her; and now all of a sudden, thanks to one of those periodic New York resurrections of the dead, she'd shown up with a spanking new store on Madison Avenue and when he dropped by, had greeted him as affectionately as if they had just climbed out of bed that morning.

And Alfred, who felt guilty for not having kept in touch when she'd hit the skids, was mightily pleased to see her. "You look like a million bucks," he said sincerely, kissing her on both cheeks, and swinging her high in the air. And then, plucking a price tag from the row of blazers hanging by the door, added, "My word—two million! Who set you up in this love nest, anyway, sweetheart?"

"A guardian angel." Inez winked.

"No kidding. Can I meet him? Her?"

"You met yours already."

Alfred always felt shifty on the subject of his wife, who refused to have Inez over to the house, even to their largest parties. It was mean, and yet there was nothing he could do about it.

Another afternoon he'd taken Johnny shopping on Madison Avenue for a party dress, and on their way home they'd stopped by Inez's. Inez, who was loud and jolly and had been the mistress of any number of important men and women, had made much of Alfred's pretty daughter. She swept them into the back and opened a bottle of champagne and asked her about college—Johnny was applying to Barnard and Swarthmore and Brown, but wanted to stay in the city—and told her funny stories about her days as a runway model in Paris, and in the end she'd offered her a summer job. If Johnny wanted to help out, she could make a little pocket money, get a discount on the clothes.

"Yes, please, can I really?" the girl's voice had shot up in eagerness. Alfred—who had counted on having the apartment to himself that summer—hoped Johnny would drop the idea. But as they walked back uptown—Johnny had some books to return to the New-York Society Library—she'd said, "I think Inez is the coolest lady I've ever met. Do you think she means it about the job?"

"Why—you really want to spend July and August counting shoes?"

And Johnny, eyes very big, "I'll *die* if I can't work there. I'm *dying* to work there. I think it would be the most fun thing in the world. I'm *dying* to."

"Why?"

"I need the money," she said to make him laugh.

"No, come on. Why?"

"All the famous people who come in. Did you see the picture on the wall of her and Warren Beatty? I think it's one big party. And she's so nice. I think it'd be incredibly incredibly incredibly fun."

"I don't think it would be so fun," said Gebler glumly, his visions of screwing Gina every night on the living-room sofa fast going up in smoke.

"Will you help me talk Mom into it?"

"Sweetheart," said Gebler, much relieved. "There is no way your mom is going to go for it." He gave her hand a squeeze, and they swung their clasped hands as they strolled up Madison Avenue. What a funny girl, his Johnny. What a babe. All his kids had that wide-eyed enthusiasm he loved, that raring-to-go-ness tinged by a certain necessary timidity. Innocents in a big city.

But sweet-talking Johnny somehow managed to talk round her mother, whose watchfulness had grown oddly slack these days. And although Johnny quickly learned that working for Inez was quite different from being a customer, still it was pretty neat getting to meet all the stars who dropped by. One day Paul Simon came in and bought half a dozen cambric shirts.

On his way uptown from work, Alfred would pick up Johnny from the store. Once they took Inez across the street for a martini at the Polo Bar. Another time, Alfred–prefacing the purchases with "Your mom's going to murder me," bought Johnny a cream raw-silk Inez Klein blazer for eight hundred dollars and a crushed red velvet miniskirt for three fifty. Inez, who claimed that Johnny was twice as much fun as her dad had ever been, was always bugging Alfred to let her take the seventeen-year-old along to movie premieres and club openings. Several times, Alfred–swearing his daughter to discretion–consented. Inez had persuaded Johnny to crop her hair in order to show off her neck. Johnny, who had always thought of Carlotta as the looker, lapped up the attention. On the nights Johnny wasn't busy, father and daughter would walk home along Madison, looking in the shop windows, and wander across the park in the late summer light. Pick up a video from the store downstairs, which was run by two gloomy mustachioed Yugoslavs. For dinner, they might eat takeout from Zabar's while watching their movie on the VCR, a medium that Dolly did not exactly forbid–rather, she made it scathingly clear that anybody who had recourse to it was devoid of inner resources.

Once Johnny was in bed, her father went out on the town. Often he didn't come back much before the alarm went off at eight-thirty. No matter how much he enjoyed hanging out with his daughter, no matter how firmly he'd resolved to stay in that night and catch up on sleep so he'd feel like a human being the next morning, somehow he always ended up going out.

Afterwards, Dolly knew that this month at Goose Neck had been the happiest time in her life. How she loved the country at the height of summer, when the corn was high and the garden overflowed. When nature spilled its seed voluptuously, and the rank smell of pollinating greenery hung in the breeze, and the nights clattered with cicadas.

In the mornings, they ate breakfast outside. Then Isaac would go upstairs to his studio, and Dolly, after checking in with the office, would settle down to a couple of hours' tutoring. It seemed to Dolly–not real-

izing that her son was responding to her own uncustomary latitude—
that Leo was no longer quite so petrified a pupil. Relaxed, he listened,
he answered creditably, she no longer lost her temper with him—they
enjoyed themselves.

At the end of the day, when Isaac quit work and Dolly and Leo were
hot and sweaty from gardening, the three of them usually went for an
outing. They would swim off the wildlife preserve at Orient, or bike to
Greenport and take the ferry over to Shelter Island. Or go out in the Sunfish, Isaac sitting immobile as a statue in transport, rigorously evading all
information about winds—he was a mountain man, ferries were passable,
but this tippy fiberglass hat he liked no more than cats or dogs might.

Other evenings, at sundown, Isaac took Leopold fishing for bluefish, with a pair of old rods he'd picked up at a yard sale. There was a so-
ciological division to North Fork fishing. Blacks fished from the bayside
dock at Greenport, Greeks and Italians from the Sound. Leopold and
Isaac traded off. Sound fishing was noisier, more bravura; fishing from
the dock, the kind of slow patient work Leo liked, even if actually catching the little nippers made him blanch. On lucky/unlucky nights they
cooked up three or four sardine-sized bluefish on the barbecue and
Leopold looked at once repentant and proud.

How delectable those nights were, when they sat outside telling stories after supper, or sometimes lay on their backs in the grass, searching
the skies for shooting stars. Conversation loosened by the intimacy of
darkness, and none of them wanting to go to bed.

Leo, after initial uncertainty, now glowed and expanded under the
older man's attention. He was a sensitive boy, and there was something
in the air at Goose Neck that summer—a diffused atmosphere of love—
that was nourishment, after the chronic bickering and sulks that soured
the Geblers' city life.

It was an atmosphere that you couldn't very well miss, dense as hon-
eysuckle. Everyone who came out to Goose Neck remarked upon it:
Never had Dolly Gebler been so radiant, so becalmed of inner demons.
You saw it in her gestures, in her hands—no longer did she chew her
nails anxiously or pace the room like a captain's ghost. To Leo, accustomed to a stormy, sarcastic, fault-finding mother continually laying
into him for picking the grapes one-by-one from the stem or for not
having remembered to call his grandmother, the change was almost
befuddling.

Ayala, who drove over from Southampton for Sunday lunch, was likewise amazed.

"Looks to me like love," said his wife.

"If so, I am very glad for her. But does she know it—that it's love?"

"Well, I guess the real question is, Does *he?* It's such a folie à deux at the moment. Kinda awful to think what'll happen when they come down to earth with a bump."

"When someone points out to him, you mean, that he is a very poor man and she a rich woman twice his age."

"Whatever."

In early July, Johnny called up her mother to say she'd had it with Inez Klein.

"Do you think it's gutless to quit?"

"Darling—not in the least. I mean, she's paying you peanuts. You don't owe her anything."

"I think I'd rather be out in the country with you and Leo."

Although Dolly was longing to know what had gone wrong—Alfred, as usual, hadn't a clue—she held her tongue. Now her contentment—only one duckling still missing—was almost complete. Johnny had climbed down from the Sunrise bus in a frighteningly chic pink vinyl minidress and with her hair chopped off. For a moment Dolly hadn't recognized her own child. Had she acquired a boyfriend along with the haircut, or was this sudden precocity all Inez's doing? Johnny, however, no longer wished to confide in her mother. But after a few days of lying on the porch with fashion magazines, prattling of nightclubs and European resorts and designers, the girl had changed into a pair of shorts that looked like Mr. West's castoffs and had gone fishing with Isaac and Leopold, and from then on she too seemed to have been affected by the general lovingness.

Gebler drove out for the weekend of Dolly's birthday with Gibbie Taylor, a painter friend from San Francisco, and Gebler too noticed the strange new state of affairs. It was nothing you could put your finger on, except that his wife was bloomy as an expectant mother, and that everyone in Gebler's family now looked to Isaac to provide the authority and fun. If a bottle top wouldn't come off, or somebody wanted to know where Ljubljana was, or Johnny suddenly informed Leo mid-poker-game that deuces were wild, it was Isaac they came running to. I guess I haven't been around enough, Gebler concluded, guilt being a more flattering emotion than jealousy. And if Isaac so much as got up to take a leak, suddenly Leo and the women were crawling all over him to come, too. Small wonder that the ex-hick was looking pretty pleased with himself.

Saturday was Dolly's birthday. Alfred, who had brought out a magnum of Roederer Cristal and two pounds of Ossetian caviar, made red-pepper soup and blinis for dinner. Dolly opened her presents between courses: from Johnny, a CD of a bald Irish girl singer named Sinead O'Connor, and from Leopold, unexpectedly, an ivory scrimshaw paper knife carved by some long-dead Greenport sailor.

Next came Isaac's offering, bulky as the man himself and every bit as elegant—wrapped in the *Suffolk Times*. Alfred, clowning, insisted on reading aloud the package's displayed news of church picnics and clambakes. Inside, a picture his wife evidently had not yet seen: a small seascape on mahogany wood that Isaac had painted for her in secret and framed himself. "It's my latest version of the Flood," Isaac said, slyly. In the silvery-green sea, goofy with refracted rainbow, sat a boat, and in the boat—luminous, diminutive, precise as petit-point—the Gebler family: black-browed Dolly as Mrs. Noah at the helm, Alfred Noah with his beard like an autumnal bird's nest, a burning bush, and beside them Leo and Johnny, and last of all Carlotta dragging a languid arm over the boat's edge.

It was adorable. Everybody exclaimed. Everybody, that is, except Dolly. Dolly, habitually uncomfortable with presents, who grieved the children with her ungraciousness because it was so in her grain to give that she didn't know how to be given, sat silent. Isaac must have been wondering if his present had offended her—and then she raised her head and the assembled guests saw that she was in tears. Like the rainbow, she laughed through her tears, and fell onto Isaac's shoulder with a snuffle. "You spoil me," she murmured. "I have never been so spoiled."

"God, I feel terrible," said Gibbie Taylor. "I didn't know it was your birthday, Dolly. Alfred never told me."

"Never mind," said Alfred. "Dolly's right—she's spoiled enough as it is. Oh shit!" he exclaimed. Everyone's attention, half-relievedly, turned from Dolly's drying her tears on Isaac's shoulder. Alfred, while the guests were fussing over Isaac's present, had been addressing himself to the recalcitrant lid of the second tin of caviar—somebody had to do the dirty work around this house. It not budging, he had applied Leopold's birthday paper knife, whose ivory sheath had just splintered under the pressure.

"Oh!" cried Leopold, in involuntary woe.

"Oh, too bad," said Gibbie. "Can it be fixed?"

And Dolly, in one of the sudden transformations that made her fearsome, snapped, "My God, Alfred, what the hell did you think you were doing?" And stalked off to the kitchen, broken paper knife in hand, to pore over the irreparable shards in a stronger light.

In the commotion, Alfred's present—a satin dressing gown from Montenapoleone—had gone almost unremarked.

"Bring a can opener while you're at it, Doll, will you? I'm sorry, kiddo," Alfred said to Leopold. "It was an accident—I didn't think the fucking thing was so fragile. Where'd you get it? I'll buy you another one first thing Monday morning."

"It wasn't mine, it was Mummy's," said Leopold, red in the face but trying his hardest to be civil. "It was from the nineteenth century. There weren't any other ones."

Thirty-seven

ONCE JOHNNY TOOK off for the North Fork, Mr. Gebler was left to his own devices. Dolly hated city heat, but Gebler thrived on the rank savagery of a New York summer, when one-hundred-degree white fog smothered the streets and smells grew pestilent and even the mildest citizen felt stirred to unprovoked homicide.

There was nothing he liked better than to ride the Broadway bus, squeezed and jolted against girls nearly naked in sun dresses, or to watch in the subways young mothers with hairy armpits, dragging along plaintive sons and daughters. In the side streets of the Upper West Side, where yuppies hadn't entirely succeeded in extirpating the old tenement population, Latin music boomed from open windows and entire families sat on the stoops. A throbbing gaiety, the sky-high radio salsas like heat made audible, cooked and seething noise, till even you seemed to be sweating sound. Somebody opened a fire hydrant, and suddenly a dozen tiny soaked children were prancing, shrieking through the fountaining water in their frilly bathing suits and underpants. And sex on everybody's mind, seemingly grabbable before your very eyes.

Months earlier—before Johnny had got her job with Inez—he had announced exultantly to Gina that his wife and children would be out of town for the summer. Worried that Gina, from sheer naughtiness, might take it into her head to disappear, for it was Gina's vacation too.

"Will you be there, honey pie? Will you be my summer valentine?"

"I don't know." Gina was reading a magazine. "I'd been thinking of going somewhere for a change."

Gebler had panicked. Did she expect him to take her somewhere glamorous? After the debacle with the Visa bill, he'd been trying to keep his head down. And how could he leave town when his only excuse not to be out on Long Island with his family was running the office? "Well, we might go away for a weekend. Somewhere cool we could swim."

"I don't know," repeated Gina. "A model friend of mine is living in Paris. She's asked me a million times to come and see her. You know I don't get a whole lotta vacation, and I've never been to Europe."

"I'll take you to Europe," said Gebler.

"Yeah, yeah, I heard you the first time you said that, but maybe I better grab a sure bet, now that my friend Gervase has said she'll show me the sights . . ."

Gebler had chewed his beard, determined not to get agitated. Was he so very unreliable? Hadn't he taken her to Los Angeles and Miami? Finally, he had a thought, suicidally delicious. "Maybe we could go to Paris for the weekend. Thursday night to Monday wouldn't be such a ballbuster."

Why even try to be discreet when his wife didn't seem to care whether he lived or died? Why not blow apart his marriage in style— round-trip Concorde for two, a weekend at the Ritz? But the more lavish Gebler's promises, the more Gina lost interest. Clearly, a trip with a middle-aged lover was a less red-hot proposition than being loose in a foreign city with a twenty-two-year-old girlfriend.

Johnny's decision to get a summer job had nixed his hopes of playing house with Gina or of whisking her away for a weekend transatlantic. But as soon as he'd put Johnny on the bus to Southhold and returned to the apartment, suddenly immense, echoing, Gebler picked up the phone and dialled. "Baby, I'm yours."

And she—his little bundle of complicated joy—had by the grace of God come through.

With Dolly and the children away, Gebler moved into Gina's studio on Mulberry Street. Although beforehand he had promised her excursions to chic restaurants, when it came to the crunch, the pride of being seen in public with this luscious girl was outweighed by hunger to clutch and tumble her. Better to pick at Chinese takeout straight from the shiny white boxes—Gina wasn't much of a housekeeper—in between fucks. Then, as soon as she had laid down her chopsticks, recommended that toss in the sheets, that plunge—like being caught up in the centripetal roll of a salty Atlantic breaker, and thrown, thrown, thrown, until you think you're drowning, suffocating—that tumult, that explosion of omniscient excitation, for which alone he lived. And afterwards, long afterwards, when each body separately had risen, more dead than alive, to the surface of consciousness, they would sit out on the fire escape, with a joint and a carton of Cherry Garcia, and listen to Stan Getz play bossa nova. It was Stan Getz, Stan Getz and dulcet-voiced João Gilberto who to Gebler summed up the abandon of that summer. These times seemed like the sweetest moments of his life and also the most fatal: that hot white pinpoint where love and self-immolation came together. He had been told for years he had a weak heart, and recently he had thought, unforgivably selfish, how delicious it would be to die in her arms, inside her.

Later he would wake up with a start at three, four in the morning, dry-mouthed, the ecstatic mood vanished, wondering what he was doing sleeping on a mattress on the floor, not remembering where the bathroom light was or that he no longer had to be home before the children got up.

Sometimes Dolly would come sit in Isaac's studio and watch him work. She had always been intrigued by the physical act of painting. Most artists she knew were unwilling to be watched—they regarded painting as a kind of cookery whose magic depended on secret ingredients to be guarded from competitors. Isaac was too generous for such alchemical superstitions. And it fascinated her to see how the young man, so ungainly in his secular motions, became at the easel a gliding, fencing demon of furious grace. To see the whirl and pounce of his brushstrokes, the attack of his palette-work, his two-fisted, often, laying on of paint.

To Dolly, witnessing the fancy stepwork of her young artist's lurching creativity seemed an almost sacred privilege, like being at God's shoulder as He formed the sea and the dry land. Did God too dance as He made us—did He dart forward to model a nose and skate back to regard it from a distance with screwed-up eyes? Did He hold the world upside down or look at it in a mirror to see more freely if all the parts held up? At the end of the day's work, Isaac would ask her, "Well, what do you think?" And she was in the position of one who could say, "I think you've made the Sahara too dry." Or, "Do you really think Australia ought to be way off there by itself?"

And Isaac, once over his initial shyness, was quickened by her brooding concentration. Liked to have her curled up on the sofa behind him. Forgot she was watching, except in some corner of his restlessness that was soothed. Thrived on her clever advice and corrections, which ranged from the nitty (That sky is too bland) to the conceptual (It's too soon for you to be painting abstract). She seemed to understand not just what he had done, but what he meant yet to do, and how he might make the work more effulgently itself.

Between long silences, they talked—Isaac over his shoulder, Dolly to his back. Talk freed by not facing each other. "I like your children," he told her once. For it was in Leo and the girls, to Isaac's way of thinking, that you could see how well conceived was the Geblers' seemingly incongruous union—in these graceful gawky children, with bits of each parent folded into them and sticking out at unexpected angles. He saw it most shiningly in Johnny, for just when you were beginning to find Dolly's intensity unrelenting, there in Johnny was that same earnestness egg-whipped and luminized by Alfred's optimism, his appetite, his chatterbox goofiness. Or, conversely, when Alfred's inconsequentiality most grated there was Leopold with his breathy sense of awe.

Dolly lit up. "They *are* divine, aren't they? I hope they'll grow up happy. I think they will, don't you? I'm afraid none of us girls managed to pass on our father's brain—I wish you'd known him, he had such a powerful synthetic intelligence. But I'm not sure that his brand of intelligence makes for happiness."

"Well, maybe your children got some traits equally lustrous from the other side of the family."

She paused. Isaac could see that for a moment she had thought he meant from her mother's side. Then she covered up. "Yes, no doubt. Alfred's mother was a real . . . ball of fire"—a phrase, Isaac could tell, that was her husband's characterization and not her own. "Growing up, I'd never dreamt of marrying or having children. I mean, I was in my thirties when . . . So because I hadn't intended to, they—the babies—well, just do seem to be absolute undeserved grace. I still look at them and can't imagine what I ever did to . . . There's nothing that compares to it—nothing that comes close. Nothing." She was almost inaudible with fervor. "Sometimes I torment Alfred by saying I wish we hadn't stopped at three."

Isaac looked at his sheet of paper and saw that he had scribbled in Dolly as a Near Eastern fertility goddess, all breasts and packed thighs and a dark triangle indelibly triumphant as a geometric theorem. Looked at Dolly in the mirror, wondering if she was still fertile and deciding yes. Still fertile. And found himself intensely excited by the thought, body up and rearing to help sire Number Four.

"What's it like, being pregnant?"

She laughed. "A million things. Like having a Punch and Judy show in your stomach. A kind of pardonable schizophrenia. Stupid-making."

"And labor?"

"Oh God, don't even mention it. Luckily you forget, otherwise the human race would have died out years ago."

"And what's it feel like, having breasts? I mean, big breasts, like yours? Did it make you shy when you first got them? You must have been very surprised."

At first he thought she wouldn't answer, had noticed, even, his excitement. Then, "Horrified. I couldn't bear men looking at me in the street. As a teenager, I slunk around ashamed as . . . a dog with a can tied to its tail. Borrowed all my father's old shirts."

"Are you still conscious of them, usually?"

"No—well, they ache, sometimes. From gravity, I suppose. I imagine it must be a bit like testicles, shrinking with temperature. Gelid. Tender . . ." She frowned, catching him staring at them in the mirror over his easel. Glanced at her watch. "Ah—the fish market's about to close."

And jumping up, stalked out of the room, without asking as usual if he'd like to come too.

It was a few days before she ventured back into his studio.

"My friend Carlos is in town," said Gina. She was sitting on a stool in the kitchen where Gebler was used to seeing Johnny or Carlotta perched. She didn't look much older than his daughters, despite the maquillage. Over her shoulder he could see the late-afternoon sun, dark as egg yolk, lurking above the Orthodox onion domes of New Jersey. And the sky a pukey white-gray from heat. From a sneaky poisonous kind of heat. Summer was when you cut your neighbor's throat because he was getting on your nerves. Had anybody used a New York summer—hotter than love—as a criminal defense?

The night before, sleepless and rolling in sweat, Gina's purple sheets kicked into knots at their feet, and the sounds of the street a personal affront, they had finally hopped a taxi up to Gebler's apartment, packed it in for industrial-strength air conditioning. Astonishing to wake up in his own marital bed, scene of two decades' alienation and unspoken grudges, to find instead his heart's darling curled up like a tawny bear cub by his side.

This evening, in the pink summer light, Gebler was engaged in painting Gina's toenails white-pearl. Lovely brown child's feet, with prehensile toes, wide-splayed, free, and arches you could fit a telephone book under. He pictured, in contrast, Dolly's feet under the breakfast table. Middle-aged feet, horned yellowish nails and cramped toes. Until recently he had never minded Dolly's getting old, in part because she had remained so randy. A hot rabbit. But since she'd begun to withdraw several months ago, he realized for the first time how much of their peace of mind had depended on that engine of her appetite, which had rolled on regardless of their outer froideurs. Undesired, Gebler noticed that his wife had become old. A heavyset, middle-aged, rather mannish woman. Men and women took on each other's attributes in middle age. Women got hairy chins and their voices sank an octave. Men grew breasts. Was his wife's unsexing simply physiological, or had she transferred her ardor elsewhere? Was she fucking Isaac?

Now Gebler sat on the kitchen floor at his Gina's lovely feet, ducking as she waved a leg in the air to make the polish dry faster. "Watch it, baby. Remind me who's Carlos. I lose track of all your lovers." He seized a fluttering limb and kissed the toes, one by one.

Gina's eyes narrowed in pleasure like a cat's. "Oh, honey, I told you about Carlos. Carlos is like my brother. When I ran away from home the time I was fifteen, after my stepfather—you know—it was Carlos's family I went to live with." That was why she loved Gebler, because she could tell him things her other boyfriends would never understand.

"So where's he been all my life?"

"He works out in Chicago now—he runs this program that helps gang members reform."

"When's he leaving? To get back to his work, I mean."

"Well, I just got a message he's staying at Tracey's—that's his step-sister—and everybody's gonna meet at her house tonight."

Gebler abruptly dropped her foot and rose, screwing the top back on the Pearl-Dew. "Are you going?"

"Yeah, I sure am. Do you want to come?"

Gebler chewed his beard. "No, I don't especially. As I already told you, I stopped by Citarella on my way home from work and bought us a mega-striped bass for dinner."

"So we'll have it tomorrow night."

"What? Day-old fish?" And now his fury could be, sneakily, un-loosed. "Don't you know anything, girl? Jesus, I guess takeout chow mein really is your idea of haute cuisine."

Gina, provokingly serene. "Fine, we'll eat early, and *then* go over to see Carlos."

"You can go. I'm not going. I'd rather watch the ball game."

That was how Gebler found himself, ten p.m. on a Saturday summer's night, sardined in an apartment of a project on Avenue C. Two tiny rooms with cardboard walls and shit-green carpeting, full of tough guys and babies. The homeboys seemed to hit the juice a little more freely than Gebler's usual crowd, but as he drank—cleaving to the bottle of tequila he and Gina had brought—he only got hotter. So far he had met Kitty and Suzette and Rock and Mercury and Geraldo. Kitty, who wore cut-off shorts with fishnet stockings, was in a band; Suzette was a coun-sellor with Gina out at Rikers; Geraldo ran a Loisaida cooperative. Rock and Mercury, occupations undisclosed.

"How can you run a cooperative?" Alfred asked to no avail. "I thought the whole point of a cooperative was that no one ran it."

The boys wore bandanas and flannel shirts and baggy chinos, as if it were a cool autumn day. Gebler trying not to go nuts because all he could look at was Gina in the next room sitting practically on the lap of a big square Dominican who had barely bothered to say hello to Gebler. The almost-brother Carlos. The two of them were talking earnestly. Was quasi-fraternal Carlos asking Gina why she was wasting her time on a married man twice her age? Hadn't Gebler quite often asked her the same question? Just as he kept deciding he could no longer stand their pointed discourtesy, that he must go break up the love nest and explain to Gina that if she wanted to hang with these gorillas till dawn, she was on her own, he would find himself re-embroiled in pointless chatter.

His current captor was a kid with a blond goatee who ran a sculpture garden made of found materials on Rivington Street, which he was anxious for Gebler to check out. "It's modelled after the *Inferno*." In the crook of the boy's elbow was a week-old baby.

So far as Gebler could make out, having a newborn baby tucked under your arm was an even better pickup gimmick than walking a cute puppy. Teenaged girls were constantly coming up to pet it. "Wow! Is it a boy or a girl?"

"It doesn't know yet," the father joked.

"How old is it?"

"Eight days."

"Where's June?"

"She's performing at the Garage tonight—the show's on another week, you should catch it, Larissa, it's really wild."

"So you're looking after the baby? Does it sleep?"

"Not much—he's too interested in things, just like his parents."

"You guys must be exhausted."

"Not really." The boy smiled. "We're too interested, too. Every six hours we just, like, pop a black beauty and chill out looking at the kid. We haven't closed our eyes since he was born. June says it's been amazing for her performance."

Gebler regarded the young man with a new interest. "Did you say black beauty? You got drugs on you?"

"Soon as the baby was born, our friend gave us, like, this care package. He says, Don't even think of catching some sleep. It ain't worth it. Might as well stay up and enjoy."

"Do you have any black beauties on you? I haven't tried one of them for years."

The prospect of hauling himself out of his present slough, of being catapultically propelled into a more viable state of being. Proving he could have more fun than Gina, who was so unconscionably ignoring him.

The boy fished around in his overall pocket, took out a plastic ziplock bag, and, as his own hands were occupied, emptied the contents onto Gebler's palm.

"I don't see anything black."

"No, they're not black—man, I forget what all these are. My friend gave them to us when Titus was born. Well, these are the beauties, and these white ones—they're what we're supposed to take to come down without crashing too bad."

"Oh, give me a couple of those." He was already too cranked up for his own good. "What are they, Valium?"

"I don't know, man—they all come from my friend. A gift selection."

Gebler swallowed two white ones and washed them down with tequila. He patted the blond boy on the back, gave the baby a stroke on the cheek. "Cute kid. Welcome to fatherhood. And, hey, thanks for the chemical consolation. What's your name, by the way?"

"Serge," said Serge. "I'd really like you to come round to the sculpture garden sometime."

"Sure—how about tomorrow?" Gebler was smiling now, behind his beard, buoyed by the certainty that suddenly everything was going to be a lot more fun.

At first light, Isaac crept downstairs and out the door, then cantered to the bottom of the garden. The wet grass prickly on his bare feet. On the beach, the fishermen were striking out for clams, and a ferry was leaving from Shelter Island, which was wrapped in mist. The colors pallid, diffuse as in his Flood. Isaac stripped down to underwear and waded. Bobbing in the water, stared back at the farmhouse, the big old trees. Bulrushes, marshland, and rich, rich farms. A region blessed by God, temperate and bountiful.

Back at the house, pleased to have risen before Dolly, Isaac set about making breakfast. Sometimes he got almost frightened by how at home he felt here, by his preposterous good fortune in having burrowed himself into the welcoming heart of this adorable family so unlike his own grim downtrodden relatives. How instinctively he had come to rely on Dolly's judgment and protection. How the sight of her made him laugh with love, and then at other times seized him with fear. What if she stopped liking him all of a sudden? What if she decided she'd made a mistake, that the paintings were not so good? After all, she'd found his work pretty gruesome at first viewing. What kind of *Midsummer Night's Dream* besottedness had seized this queen, to say things about his work that would make an arrogant man blush? When he was only a beginner and knew nothing yet? And if she came to her senses, if she got bored and remembered that machine-cut strips of white plastic and fluorescent tubes were what she liked in art, then he would be out of a job. Back on the street, dreams of accomplishment and recognition fled.

Other times, he felt on the contrary nervous at how proprietary she, with his encouragement, had grown. Several days ago, Dolly had come down to breakfast in a state of high excitement. In the middle of the night, she had had a brainstorm as to how the Flood should be reconfigured. Quickly, she'd sketched it. Isaac was silent. Not only did he find her idea ridiculous, but a tacit boundary had been breached—Mrs. Gebler had crossed over into the unforgivably controlling. Mrs. Gebler had just fallen into the mortal sin of treating his work as their joint property. And he had given her license to do so, by letting her supervise every brushstroke. For an entire day, he was so angry he could not work, but skulked in his room, vowing never to show her a picture again. But his anger did not last long, and by the next afternoon she was back in his studio.

Humming, he dripped honey along a piece of toast, tracing an alphabet that turned out semi-Semitic. Just as he'd formed a creditable camel, the borders contracted and the honey found itself trickling along the table's edge. A creak of footsteps on the stairs, Isaac mopping up guiltily with a dishcloth, and there she was—in city clothes and a suitcase!

"Oh!" he cried out. "What's wrong?" Frightened he'd done something awful, put his foot in it.

Dolly took one look at him and burst into tears. Isaac for a moment was dumbfounded. Then, tears flooding reflexively into his own eyes, he sprung up and put his arms around her. She tried to speak several times but broke down. Finally, she succeeded. A young dealer friend of hers, she had just learned, had died in the night. There was no need to ask how—AIDS had cut such a broad swath through the art world that not a gallery, museum, or circle of artists remained undiminished.

"He died at home, thank God," Dolly said fiercely, blowing her nose. "At least that's something, to escape these utterly corrupt and soul-destroying death corporations that charge you . . ."

She had been to Jesse often in the weeks before leaving for Long Island, each time trying not to register how changed a man he was from even the visit before. Trying not to look at the photographs on his dresser of Jesse last summer, Jesse out at his stepmother's house in East Hampton, Jesse with Michael in Key West—already full-blown sick then, but now by comparison to the sightless wraith looking rosy and chubby as Teddy Roosevelt. "Well, now he's gone. It's utterly sickening, the waste of it—one more brilliant loving sharp-tongued *immensely* accomplished thirty-year-old who's made his parents know the worst pain known to man, that of seeing your child in his coffin, and who's left his mate haunted by . . . I remember Michael telling me until he met Jesse he'd never had anybody to call 'darling' or 'sweetheart,' and now he was just going to have to walk around whispering those names to himself. What do you do with all those feelings?"

Isaac asked her about Jesse and she told him stories that made them both laugh and her cry a bit more. It was eight o'clock now, and she was planning to drive back into the city to help Michael arrange the funeral, for according to Jewish law, Jesse would have to be buried the next day.

"Do you want me to come with you?"

"Goodness, no. I only wish I didn't have to go. I've really come to dread the city—there's something positively malevolent about a New York summer."

"What can I do for you out here?" Isaac asked. "Will the children stay here, or go in with you?"

"Oh, they'd be mad not to stay. I'll tell Mrs. West to come up to the house and look after Leopold."

"What for? I can do it. I think I've figured out the drill by now."

"I'm not sure if a man is tough enough to talk that boy into his bath. He is alarmingly hydrophobic—I know he's going to grow up into one of those men people move away from in subway cars."

"I'll talk him into it, all right. From one nonbather to another."

"Oh, there *is* one thing. . . ." She hesitated, gnawing at a fingernail. Ashamed to expose to Isaac the helplessness, the indignity of her marital position.

"What is it?"

"I haven't been able to reach Alfred. Do you mind trying the house after I leave, just to let him know I'm coming back into the city? I hate to think what kind of . . ."

She crept back upstairs to say goodbye to the children. Leo was awake, lying in bed, his eyes very bright. She sat down beside him. "What are you thinking about?"

"I was wondering what it was like to be a fish," he said. "Do they ever get cold down there? What do they eat when the water's frozen over in the winter?" Then he noticed her clothes. "How come you're all dressed up? Where are you going?"

"I'm going into the city for a couple of days, darling. I want you to stay out here with Mrs. West and Johnny and Isaac. Is that all right?"

"That's fine. Will you bring back my skateboard?"

It was three-thirty when Gina went to sleep in Mr. and Mrs. Gebler's bed, alone and thoroughly pissed off. For Alfred, after having sulked in the kitchen all night at Tracey's house, rudely repulsing any efforts to include him, soon as the party broke up had suddenly insisted that the remnants come over to his place. Carlos and Tracey and the others had long since gone to bed—it was just a few scraggy-looking losers Gina had never seen before and didn't much take to. Friends of Tracey's boyfriend Freddy's, maybe. Gina, who was used to turning in at ten, was already way past beat.

"What do you want everybody over for?" she'd asked him, loud enough for them to hear.

And Al, squeezing her so hard it hurt, had sung out, "Darling, it's our first party! Did you remember to take the hors d'oeuvres out of the freezer?"

He was drunk or stoned, obviously. As usual. She hated people out of control: it was just plain dumb. Standing out in the street at Avenue C were a bunch of people she'd never met before, who also thought it was a cool idea to go over to Alfred's place. The short one called Angel had a car, and Alfred and Gina had followed in a gypsy cab, fighting all the way. Or rather not fighting, since as soon as she'd asked him again what the fuck he wanted these people in his apartment for, he'd grabbed her even tighter and started singing "Monkey Man." "I'm a MONKEY, all my friends are JUNKIES!" he'd screamed all the way up the FDR Drive.

"What are you on, Al?" she'd wondered in vain.

"I'm a MON-KEEEEEY!!!"

Once installed in Alfred's palatial apartment, slapped in the face by that big-name art on the walls and the million-dollar view of the Hudson River and by their host prancing around in velvet slippers with a rocket-sized bottle of champagne, the guests had gone resentfully silent. All but Mercury, who kept on wanting to use the bathroom and the telephone, and Rock, who studied at City College and wanted to pick a fight. Except that Alfred wouldn't play. Every time Rock laid into him, he just rolled over and agreed. Yes, I am a racist capitalist sexist pig; yes, I do oppress the masses and people of color; yes, this art is just a trophy; yes, it is a confirmation of a fascistic society and unfair power system—let me open another bottle, you got any drugs, Rock?

Fucking incontinent.

Angel meanwhile had taken a still more original tack. "Man, my three-year-old niece draws better than this," he'd announced, staring at the pictures around the room. "Man, I could do better than this and I never even went to art school. You pay for this piece here, with the squiggles?"

"No," said Alfred. "Actually, the artist gave it to us."

"Yeah, look like he gave it to you all right. Look like you been had."

Which Alfred, inanely, thought was hilarious.

"It's ugly as shit, you know what I'm saying."

"I agree it's ugly—it's downright hideous."

Several times Gina had asked Alfred if he didn't want her to get these dickheads out of the house so they could go to bed. The first time he'd said he was having fun for once, so why didn't she just relax? The second time, Alfred, to her astonishment, cast her a look of pure hatred. "Jesus, you women are all alike. You sound just like my wife."

So Gina, startled, had marched off to bed by herself, where she lay under the scratchy white linen sheets, the sound of the party drowned out by the air conditioner's rumble, feeling more alone than she could remember feeling.

. . .

It was almost one p.m. when Isaac finally got an answer at the Geblers' apartment. Ring-ring-ring as usual, and then, at last, a pickup.

"Hello? Hello, who is this?" A voice sounding so rabid suspicious that Isaac didn't recognize it.

"It's Isaac—who's this?"

Silence. "Isaac—what do you want? What's going on?"

"Mrs. Gebler told me to call you to say—"

" 'Mrs. Gebler,' huh? Is that what you call her?"

"To say she's coming back to the city today—I mean, I guess she's back already."

"She's what? What's going on?"

"She said to say her friend Jesse died, and she's come back to town for—"

"Where is she? When's she coming?"

"Are you all right, Alfred?"

"Never better—I just don't understand what you're talking about. Where is she?"

"I guess she's gone straight to—ah . . ."

"Oh, to the gay widow's?" An unconvincing chuckle. "And then she's coming here? Well, that's great. Thanks for the message, Isaac. I'll be seeing you, all right?" Gebler hung up, leaving Isaac horribly uneasy.

Gebler and Gina were sitting in the living room. Gina in a man's undershirt, sprawled on the big white sofa. White curtains drawn—ineffectually—to keep out the ghastly toxic gray-whiteness of ninety-six degrees. Air conditioner blasting. Mr. Gebler in his bathrobe, naked legs looking spindly and defenseless underneath. Everything northwards looking worse. And on the wall where formerly the Frank Stella sat, instead was a big off-white stain of paint.

"Nice friends, Gina."

Gina said nothing. She had obviously heard this a few times before.

"Nice company you keep. I thought you slept with two-bit swindlers, but this time, boy, this is a major heist. I got to give it to you, I really misjudged the caliber of your acquaintances—this is a two-million-dollar robbery. Good going, sweetheart. I hope you get a cut."

"So call the police," said Gina for the fifth time, making off now to the bedroom. She was dressing fast, throwing her makeup and toiletries into a knapsack. Alfred followed her. "What's the matter, girl? You don't want to meet my wife? I don't think we're going to let you go quite so easy. Not until we have a full accounting here. . . ."

"What full accounting? I didn't invite those scumbags over. I didn't even . . ."

Alfred looked at her. "What do you mean, peach-plum? You're telling me I wanted all those lowlife boyfriends of yours in my apartment?"

"You were the one was practically inviting them to make off with your art. So call the police. Just call the police and get it over with."

And now, once again, a wave of panic like nausea. At the futility of it all. And memory wiped out. Last night an aching blank, a cavity. Disappeared.

It had been a morning from hell. Waking up on the living-room sofa like a hungover werewolf, with an evil headache screeching against his skull. Only to see a battlefield of leftover glasses from a party he didn't remember and then, after the first cup of coffee, the blank spot on the wall. At first he'd thought Gina had done it as a joke, but she too had gaped. They had hunted all over the apartment, unable to believe that one of those boys whose existence Gebler couldn't remember had actually walked out into nowhere with his 1969 Stella. Unbelievable. Literally. Panic giving way to nausea giving way to fury giving way to horror at how he was going to explain it to his wife. Their two-million-dollar Stella made off with by some stranger he'd–apparently–invited to make off with it. No, no, no, no. Too bad to be true.

He'd made Gina call Tracey, but Tracey knew nothing–Rock and Angel and Mercury were friends of her boyfriend's; she'd check with Freddy and get back to them. No further word. Alfred had made Gina call back in an hour, but Tracey hadn't been able to find Freddy.

"We need addresses of these little hoods, so we can go scare the wits out of them," said Gebler.

Gina looked at him. "Why don't you just go to the police?"

"How come you're so in love with the police all of a sudden? You think I want it in the papers that Alfred Gebler gives all-night parties for teen convicts? Like hell. I got a much better idea. Fight fire with fire. Let's get some of your other chain-gang buddies to go shake 'em down. You might do that for me, at least."

And Gina, tracing loop-the-loops with her naked toe on the floor: "Was it insured?"

"Huh?"

"Well, look, what can they do? They can't sell it, right?"

"Why not?"

"Can you picture Mercury or whoever walking into Leo Castelli with that painting? What's he going to say–like, It doesn't match the decor on my yacht, so I'm trading it in for a Rembrandt? Have you any idea what happens to young black or Hispanic males when they walk into a fancy gallery, even without stolen goods under their arms?"

"They'll know what to do."

"If you don't want to report it as a robbery, maybe you should wait a few days–they'll turn up with it."

"You think they're just taking it for a walk? Come on, girl, we got to get moving. My wife's coming back any minute, we got to get out of this place and find that picture. We got to get the picture." Panic rising. "If we don't get that picture by the end of today . . ." The sentence trailed off. He couldn't think of anything to do but vanish. Disappear. Jump off a bridge. Which was about what he felt like, slumped on the crumpled bed on a muggy afternoon, with last night's poison still sloshing around in his bloodstream, sickened by his own squalid worthless existence. Scared as hell. Depressed by how he and the love of his life were suddenly at each other's throats, like a couple of cons in a heist gone wrong. Was this what their extramarital honeymoon was come to? Accusations over stolen goods?

"What do you plan to do?" she asked him in a tight little voice.

"Find Freddy."

Johnny was out on the water with Isaac and the children–Leopold and a friend of Leopold's called Kent. Kent was Leopold's best friend from school, a Japanese boy, smaller than Leopold and light-boned. Johnny was entranced by the child's long birdlike legs intersected by knobby knees that barely bent as he walked. Kent's father was an architect–his family lived in a concrete bunker with no windows and no furniture over in Sag Harbor.

They had sailed the Sunfish out to the bird preserve at the end of Orient to have a picnic–Isaac still comically skittish as to the boat's workings, demanding only that they not tip over. It was a stormy-looking day, clouds banked up in the east dark gray, while one little patch of sky overhead remained a cherubic blue.

After they ate their sandwiches, the children had wandered off to build a fort, while Isaac and Johnny played chess. A chess set being Isaac's loopy idea of what to take along on a sail, along with the life preservers. Johnny was good at chess, just good enough to keep Isaac from getting bored, but she didn't really enjoy it much. Making her moves fast, so they could get back to talking. Gazing at the water and sky and Isaac, and at her own outstretched limbs. Legs honey-brown, in their cutoff shorts. Pity about the thighs, which were—immense. Thunder thighs. Knees down, they were pretty much okay. Did Isaac too like unshaven legs? Her last week in the city, Johnny had gone over to watch a movie with Inez at her boyfriend Rufus's house. Rufus, whom Johnny thought pretty vacant, was the forty-five-year-old son of a Colorado mining fortune. They had all three climbed on Rufus's bed to watch "Sabrina," and when Inez was out of the room, Rufus had started stroking Johnny's leg. "Honey, you need a shave. That really turns me on, a girl with stubbly legs." As his hand moved higher, Johnny had jumped off the bed and gone to tell Inez she was going home. And Inez, furious, had called her a spoiled brat. Said Johnny was missing a great opportunity, getting her cherry popped by a world-class lover who was even richer than she was.

Now, stretched out on the beach, her head cushioned against the picnic basket, Johnny told Isaac the story. "Don't you think that's totally sleazy, Inez wanting me to go off with her boyfriend?"

"I certainly do," said Isaac, squinting at the chessboard.

"So you think I was right to quit."

"Sure thing." She had always liked Isaac plenty—ever since he'd made such a jerk of himself at their house sounding off about the Trojan War. He was a big beautiful buffoon. Over the last couple of days, though, while he and Johnny had been left alone to look after Leo, things had deepened. She was beginning to understand what a fascinating guy he was, and now whenever he sat near her, like this, so close she could almost feel him inhale, it gave her the shivers.

"Hey, Isaac."

"What?"

"What do you think of women shaving their legs?"

Isaac, pocketing her queen, laughed. "I'm with Rufus."

"How come?"

"More undergrowth, the better."

Johnny contemplated this, thrilled. "Would you ever ask a woman not to shave her legs?"

"Doesn't mean she'd be fool enough to do what I say."

Johnny paused, and then she blurted it out. "I'd do what you say," she confessed—very touchingly, to her own mind. The idea of being bossed around by Isaac being an uncommonly stirring one.

"Well, then you're a fool."

"How come?" asked Johnny, hurt.

"Because there's no reason to do what other people say—except within those very particular relations when it's bliss to relinquish yourself to another. It's a job figuring out what you want in this world, without giving the game up by trying to please."

"How old were you when you lost your virginity?"

"Twenty. I think I was too young."

Johnny laughed appreciatively. "All my friends at school have gotten laid. Even Carlotta's got a boyfriend—he's a junior at Haverford—and she's a year and a half younger than me. She let him screw her one night when his mother was out on a date. She said it was really weird, getting deflowered on the bottom of this, like, little boy's bunk bed with the sheets smelling kinda cheesy. She said it was like going to bed with Leo. I bet Carlotta would tell me I should have given Inez's boyfriend a whirl, just to see if older guys are any better at it."

"Hey, look," said Isaac. "It's not an Olympic sport. Why don't you wait until you happen to be head over heels. Or think you're going to rot from deprivation."

"Are you rotting?" asked Johnny. And leaning over, she pranced her castle wrong way up chess's one-way street.

The apartment was dark when Gebler returned from combing the Lower East Side in search of Mercury or Angel and the Geblers' missing Stella. Empty-handed, exhausted.

His wife was sitting in the darkness of the living room. Not reading, not watching television, just sitting in the dark with a suitcase by her side.

"What's wrong, the lights blew?" He switched on a lamp. "You look terrible." She was greenish white, drawn. Her lips pursed tight and her eyes fixed somewhere over his head. "Jeez, sweetheart, I'm so sorry about Jesse. You must have had a hell of a day. I tried you at Jesse's number, but there was no answer."

"We were at the funeral home," she said in a small cold voice. Still staring somewhere else, somewhere just beyond him.

"Poor you. Poor old Jesse."

Dolly, who knew damn well he couldn't stand Jesse, looked even stonier. He had done his best to be polite to the guy, but it was true, these Upper East Side brats made him want to puke. Gebler was never even sure that Jesse was genuinely gay, or if it wasn't just that homosexuality was what got you ahead in the art world today. Smart career move, poor health choice. In the old days all the smart ambitious kids were Jewish. Now they were not only Jewish but gay. Not only Jewish and gay but *dead*.

"Did you get something to eat? You want me to fix you something?"

And now she looked at him for the first time. "What did you do with the Stella?"

"Oh, you noticed, huh?" He knew she would. Knew she would notice and knew he would flounder as if he'd never anticipated the question. "The frame bust—I took it to be fixed."

She said, "You're lying."

"No, I'm not."

"I know you are. You're revolting."

"Then why did you ask?"

"I wanted to see how badly you'd do it. I thought after all these years' practice, you might be better at it."

Alfred chewed on his beard. "So you know where it is?"

She gestured, almost imperceptibly.

He followed her out to the kitchen. Oh God, and there it was, laid out on the table, their Stella. Once immaculate as a magpie in its black-and-white plumage. Now—holy Jesus, what was this crud all over it, these mud and bloodstained desecrations? Good God, what had he . . . they . . . done, the picture now a foul smear of . . . shit? blood? No, red wine, maybe—drips and splattered pools of red wine, and across one corner, scribbled words in ballpoint pen. Oh God. Had they done it or had he? Oh God.

"Jesus Christ. Where'd you find it."

Long silence. Then she told. "Luis rang the doorbell—he said one of the men found it out with the garbage this morning. Wanted to make sure you meant to throw it away. In the shape it's in now, we may as well."

Gebler slumped, unable even to muster the optimism to get a bowl of soap and water, to mop up his own befoulings.

"Jesus Christ," he said. "I guess I've really hit the skids, huh?" Head between his hands, unable to look.

His wife, staring grimly, didn't answer.

"Holy Christ," Gebler groaned. Lucky Jesse. Jesse at least was dead. Dead and loved. Because even death from a horrible disease would be better than having trashed his wife's Stella. My God. What should I tell and what shouldn't I tell? Should I just spill the beans about Gina, since it's over anyway? An hour ago he'd dropped Gina on her doorstep, both of them knowing that after such acrimony, such mistrust, they were through. Dropped her on her doorstep and rode away—don't look back—knowing, Never again. Never again would he hold her, never again would he undress her, never again would he enter her and be entered. Feel her knees around his ears, soap her in her bath. Half longing for the release of confession, to be shut of it, since it was over anyway. To be scolded and purged. To come home, clean. But Christ, that Stella . . .

"I think it'll come off, mostly—let me go get a . . . let me go call Emanuele and ask him what to . . ."

But Dolly instead rose and picked up her suitcase, as if she'd been waiting there like a passenger whose train has been announced.

She had reached the great age of forty-seven without having experienced many of those dark nights of the soul where life and death hang in the balance, and madness draws in very close. When she was nineteen, her first boyfriend, the son of a neighbor at Norwood, had taken her for a drive, with a bottle of whisky and a shotgun, and threatened to blow out her brains, then his. After that, much as she longed for it, she'd shied away from the all-excluding union that leads to the lightless room in which a man and a woman decide to die together because they surely can't live.

That evening, she left the apartment and walked out onto Broadway with the conviction that she was never coming back, because her husband was a destructive maniac, frighteningly out of control. It was a muggy night, and the streets were crowded. Single businesswomen with

sports bags and briefcases striding home from aerobics class; panhan-
dlers—at her regular post outside the bagel shop stood the anxious
woman with peroxide crew cut and elephantiasis-sized legs who ever
since Dolly could remember had been accosting passersby for change—
and families out window-shopping: for one crazy moment she thought
the bearded man hefting a baby in a Snugli while he peered into the
window of the new gourmet cheese shop was Alfred with the family she
didn't know about. And Dolly, rather than relieved, felt desperate at
being cut adrift in this morass of disagreeable strangers swarming in and
out of garish new restaurants which served the latest Tuscan peasant fare
at Manhattan prices. She wandered down Broadway, suitcase in hand,
staring in ill-concealed disgust at these hustlers and pleasure seekers,
slobbish, self-indulgent, grasping people—and then she thought of her
husband and her mind went blank with horror.

She had no friends, she realized. Nobody except Ayala; and he, she
now knew, would disapprove of what she was about to do.

Sushi bars, two to a block. On what planet had Dolly been living
that she had missed the omnipresence of the sushi bar? What did it say
about New Yorkers that they were lining up to eat seaweed with sticks?
Did Alfred and his mistress eat sushi? What did everyone else in the
world know that she didn't?

She had reached the triangle in the Sixties where Broadway and
Columbus converged, and below them was a more desolate stretch, and
the crowds tapered off into nothing. Empty sidewalk. And below that
was Columbus Circle, and below that nothing but office blocks and
lone coffee shops, and the day's heat still rising from the deserted pavement. Unless she wanted to go sit on a bench in Central Park and howl
at the stars, there wasn't much to walk to. Suddenly exhausted, she entered the lobby of the Empire Hotel, right across the street from Lincoln
Center. A nondescript shabby place she'd walked or driven past a thousand times and never noticed. Where she could sit on a strange bed and
watch out the window concertgoers pour past the fountain of Lincoln
Center on their way home, and the vast splintered orbs of light in each
theater be extinguished one by one. And the world as she knew it end.

As she checked in, using her maiden name, Dolly thought of her
own family—her maternal grandmother, who'd come to New York once
a year with her five children and occupied half a floor at the Plaza; her
father, who, as Ayala had reminded her, had such a winning way with

concierges and maîtres d'hôtel–and cursed herself for lacking the gumption to hop a taxi for somewhere really swell. To one of those grand hotels of her childhood–self-contained metropolises whose lobbies abounded in fountains, chamber orchestras, cigar stores and florists, telegraph offices, boys in gold braid. Now she wanted to revert to those plush innocent days, to sweep away the incriminating detritus of Geblerdom. But there were no more really swell hotels left in New York, there were just businessman hotels. For one delirious moment she imagined going to a hotel with Isaac and where would they go, but all she could think of was far, far away. Barcelona. Vienna. Madras. Mars.

She was lying on a spongy bed on the ninth floor, facing not the Metropolitan Opera but an inner areaway, too exhausted even to take off her shoes, when the knocking began. For a moment she was alarmed, then angry, then indifferent. It was Alfred. Startling how thoroughly she had already expunged him from her thoughts. Alfred, damn him, had followed her, at a respectful distance, all the way along her bewildered march down Broadway. Alfred knocking on her door for what seemed like hours, Dolly trapped inside like a rat, head pounding, until she grew tired of saying go away and just to get some peace had let him in, and there he stood in tears.

"I'm sorry about the Stella, I'm sorry about Jesse."

"I don't want to talk to you," she said. "I'm too tired to talk, just let me go to sleep."

So the two of them had lain fully dressed on that nylon-quilted double bed, side by side, each more miserable than the other. Too miserable for words. Way, way beyond that. The two of them in the not-quite darkness. A clock radio blinking red off and on. And the sound of television blaring from the room next door. Wanting to be dead in order to find true darkness, true silence. But what if–just as blindness wasn't blackness but a colored blur, just as deafness wasn't silence but an aggravating buzz–what if there were no such thing as peace, even there?

At two a.m., she sat upright and thought, I have to get out of here or I'm going out the window. So she had left, and Alfred, wordless, followed. The two of them riding down the elevator, white and bedraggled. She'd headed for Central Park in the two a.m. gloaming, empty except for those who slept there, and when she was done circling the footpaths fiercely, aimlessly, she went and sat in a coffee shop. A party of transvestites, a boothload of German backpackers, and Alfred, still quiet, shoved into the seat opposite. Ordered a club sandwich and devoured it—mortal hungry suddenly, and Alfred, downing a vanilla milk shake, cracked her a timid wink in would-be reconciliation.

"Don't you dare wink at me; I wish I'd never laid eyes on you."

And then, much later, mechanically, not even interested, "Who is she? I might as well know."

He told her. Told her that yes, he had been keeping a girlfriend, but that now it was over, and Dolly felt like someone receiving a once desperately awaited letter that has been lost in the mail, directed and redirected through abandoned addresses, and now arrives long after it has ceased to have any meaning. Yet somehow, between the closing of the coffee shop and the roaring of the first predawn garbage trucks up Amsterdam Avenue, in the oily no-color grayness, still unreconciled but too defeated for the moment to fight, she had agreed not to act immediately, but to think things over.

The next day was the funeral at Riverside Chapel. Late the following afternoon, after a day with Jesse's lawyer, making a start on his papers (she and Michael were his executors), she had driven back out to the country—Alfred threatening to join her at the weekend—muttering over and over to herself all the way down the Long Island Expressway, "God damn your guts. God damn your self-satisfied guts." Not knowing if she was talking about him or herself, married too long, really, to know the difference. Wanting only to get away from this man who'd shat on her, just as he'd shat on the Stella, and back to her babies, and to Isaac, who Dolly realized had become impossibly precious to her, without whom she could not live.

Thirty-eight

Isaac had spent the day playing his favorite game, which required more oils than he usually had to muck with. It was a palette game: how many reds can you make, how many blues, how many yellows, how many blacks. On an ingenious day he could make about forty blacks, which was thirty fewer than van Gogh said Frans Hals could muster. Today it was yellows he was tricking out.

There are yellows that are vegetable (dried linden blossom, mustard, saffron, cinnamon, citrus—that one with a hidden knowledge of blue in it) and there are yellows that are animal (glistening chicken-fat yellow, butter yellow, beaten egg yolk like Mrs. Vermeer's cloak) and mineral yellows (gold, or the sulfuric heaviness of storm clouds). The chief difference among the yellows, as in any color, was of opaqueness versus transparency. Sometimes you wanted density—a thick sheet or brick wall of color. And sometimes you wanted light like a veil, with all the tones you'd built up shining through. The cadmium was flat and heavy, whereas the Indian yellow was deliciously transparent. It was this yellow that you saw in a summer evening's light. That made up the white-white-gauzy yellow of this particular evening sky, melting into a pink like rare pigeon breast where the pink is edged in lavender and gray.

It seemed to Isaac that painters were troglodytic sort of creatures, Vulcans who mine the bowels of the earth. Just look at their tools. The pencils made of carbon, the paints made of crushed minerals or even chemicals whose names you found in the periodic table: cadmium, barium, zinc. The canvas from cotton or linen that grew in the fields, the brushes from animal hair. His old boss Macklowe from the frame store had been a purist; Isaac had watched him, like a chemist in his laboratory, make gesso from calcium carbonate and rabbit-skin glue. How could one hope to use this most stubbornly materialist of the arts to portray the spiritual?

Poetry and literature were made of words—that is, mere breath. Music, more air—brushed, vibrating air. Only art was made of the extracted earth. An artist was a workman—cousin to carpenters or cooks—in a way that a poet or a mathematician or a composer couldn't be, and his work, however often it was reproduced in color magazines and postcards, was closer to a rock than to a novel or a concerto. A crumbly friable rock—a chunk of sandstone, maybe, that wore down, darkened, cracked, was misplaced.

And, paradoxically, this condition of one-of-a-kind irreproducible thingness, this lumpen physicality, was precisely what made art so natural a commodity, a commodity volatile as pork bellies, precious as diamonds, more material than money. You couldn't trade or warehouse a concerto—any performance, score, recording was nothing more than an echo of an original that existed only in the composer's head, only in the heavens. But painting was the thing itself and nothing but.

There were plenty of multimillionaires in America. That the Geblers spent their fortune on acquiring Isaac Hookers—well, maybe not—rather than race cars was what gave the family its highly local prestige. And what did it do to Isaac, being bought? This last, of course, was a baldly modern question. Pre-Renaissance, the Duchess of Gebler would simply have hired Brother Isaac and his disciples to paint hunting scenes in her winter palace or the lives of Saints Ursula and Catherine in her chapel, and there would have been no nonsense about artistic integrity. But today artists were meant to have egos, which was why he felt muscled in on, violated, when Mrs. Gebler told him that no, he should stick to figures and drop the pure landscape of the Flood or, worse yet, came up with suggestions for future works. (How about doing a series on American inventors? Or war?) Even while he thrived on the familiarity and trustful affection that made such a takeover possible.

The last couple of sundowns he and Johnny had driven over to the Sound, to a secluded cove below East Marion. There the beach was made of large polished pebbles that slid and glistened under your feet, some of them a pearl gray, some pink, some apricot. And boulders flecked with mica. The cliffs overhead sage-green and russet. The ocean Prussian blue, and the Connecticut shore brighter, a slip of ultramarine, maybe even cobalt. Johnny, in a dark-blue tank suit that made her look like a metabolized slice of Connecticut, swam off the rocks, while he sat on the beach and read a book.

He had finished the Flood, to his own obstinate satisfaction, and now was fiddling with new prospects. Experimenting with small cartoon-strip watercolor-collages that mixed objects—copper scouring pad, shells, sponge, felt, tinfoil, fur—with drawings and bits of scrolled writing. Using honey, sand, beeswax, nail polish to achieve new textures and finishes.

His best work so far was a large architectural watercolor of a Mesopotamian-style temple, in whose sanctuary was seated a bearded lion with eagle pinions, on a throne of cherubim. The god who makes your children walk through fire. Across the sides of the picture, in scratchy lettering: "To Ba'al Haman, because he has listened to my voice."

Making small pictures, too, that were all calligraphy, all text. Again, using five or six small cartoon-strip panels as the predella for a larger, altarpiece-style subject. Figuring out how to break through, how to insinuate himself into what came next.

Just as he himself was ready to pack up, Johnny came out of the sea, dripping, a big grin on her face, dark hair plastered to the small skull neat as a seal's. A beautiful child.

"Perfect evening to sail," she said mischievously, wrapping herself in a towel.

"To get drowned."

"Come on, Isaac, you know you love it—let's just go for a quick spin before dark."

"Let's play chess."

"No, first let's go sailing."

He lowered his head and, lunging, made as if to butt her. She, shrieking, whirled away. Stopped when he didn't chase her. Ventured back, placing first one naked foot and then the other on top of his two bare feet. Stood on his feet as if they were rungs on a pair of stilts. He clunked forward, Frankenstein-style, with her still keeping balance. Then she fell, laughing.

"Shall I teach you how to dance?"

"No."

"What shall we do tonight?"

"Get drunk?"

"Oh yes, let's. Can we really? I know what, I'll make margaritas. I know how to do it, I've watched Daddy make them a million times. We'll have to get limes on the way home. Let's make a whole thermosful of margaritas, and then we'll take it out sailing."

"Let's not," said Isaac. "I'll die any way but drowning drunk. I'd rather play chess."

Dolly, having unpacked and wandered down to the kitchen to see what she could make for dinner, was gazing out the window as they drove up. She saw Isaac and Johnny in the old car, gaiety bubbling from their mute mouths. What are they giggling about? she wondered, smiling in response, eager—after these soul-curdling city days—to be warmed by their unthinking merriment. Isaac came in first. Face lit up when he saw her. Smacking kiss on the cheek. "Oh good, you're back. Was it awful?"

She nodded, tearful. Old age—made you leaky. "God, it feels as if I've been gone a year," she murmured low.

"Why don't you sit down—I'll get you a drink. Johnny says she's gonna make margaritas."

"Well, that sounds just about right. I think I could use a howling drunk tonight."

Next came Johnny prancing into the house, screen door slamming behind her. Her daughter like a sloppier, puppyish Balinese dancer, towel hitched around her waist, shopping bag under one arm. Mouth opened wide, to tease (probably) her new playmate, and then the mouth, abruptly, clamped shut on seeing her mother behind the young man's shoulder. Stopped dead, and a look came over her face of such undisguisable disappointment, resentment, unwelcome, that Dolly, poised to hug her daughter, to be enveloped in her firstborn child's enthusiastic sympathy, was turned to stone. For a moment, Johnny—transparent girl—stood there glaring. Didn't come kiss her, didn't ask about the funeral. Just stood there, unpacking the bag of limes.

"Oh, you're back. I didn't know you were coming back tonight. How was the city? Is Daddy here too?" Furious, as if about to bawl from vexation at having some special treat spoiled, barged in on. And Dolly too astounded to answer.

"We're about to go out in the Sunfish, Isaac and me."

"Where's Leo?"

"I guess he's still at the Wests. Kimberly's over." Kimberly was the Wests' granddaughter. "Isaac, let's go. Mom, we'll be back in an hour, okay?"

And now Dolly, unable to look at her daughter, addressed Isaac.

"She's dragooned you into sailing, has she? Have you come around yet?" Voice artificial, just barely beginning to register the shock of her daughter's rudeness.

"I have not," said Isaac. "I guess steerage is tattooed into the ancestral coils. Boats, as far as Hookers are concerned, are what you use to escape famine and conscription. Do you feel like a sail?" Looking at her solicitously. "Or shall we have a drink instead?"

She hesitated, pricked by the prospect of wind, salt, the slap of the sail. Purgation. She had been shaken more than she realized by the last few days' marital harrowing. That night on Broadway, she had walked her husband out of her heart, and any reconciliation born of those hours at the Empire seemed to her flimsily expedient. Love had gone, trust was barely memorable—now it was just a question of calling the lawyers, dividing up the property. Although Alfred had said he wanted to come out to the country that weekend, she knew now that she would forbid him. "It's been a tough few days. But God, I'd adore to go for a sail—will you wait for me to change?"

At this, Johnny, unable to control her pique, blew up. "Look, I think we better get going right now, if we're going. You know how long it takes you to decide what to wear—it'll be dark by the time you . . . Can't you come another time, Mom? Let's just go, Isaac."

Which left it up to Isaac. Who plumped himself down on a sofa, picked up Dolly's copy of *The New York Times.* "Hold your horses, girl. What's your hurry, there's a good hour's daylight left."

Johnny flounced out onto the porch, shouting over her shoulder, "Okay, I couldn't care less. If you want to go sailing in the pitch dark, that's fine with me. I didn't think you wanted to sail all that much anyway."

Isaac and Dolly left in the living room, at a loss. Dolly discovering too late that she was beyond the end of her rope. Ready to jump out of her skin from nervous exhaustion. "Why don't you go with her?" she said, voice shaking. "I am going for a drive." She picked up the car keys from the kitchen table and walked out of the house.

Johnny, at the sound of the car, poked her head around the door. "God—now what? Is that woman ever temperamental. I am sick to death of Mom's *scenes.* You wouldn't believe the way she—Isaac, what are you giving me a dirty look for?"

. . .

It was twenty miles out to Johnny Maine's place. The house was untouched, but whoever lived in it now had let the grounds run wild. Dolly parked her car at the foot of the overgrown drive and waded through weeds up to the old farmhouse. No lights on. Nobody home. A swing set on the front lawn. An unhitched horse van in the back. The garden gone.

The house sat on a cliff above the Sound, and in the old days, when Johnny Maine lived there, there were wooden steps tenuous as a rope ladder leading down to the beach below. A rocky inhospitable beach, where every morning and evening, May till October, Johnny Maine and her black Labrador went swimming. Now the steps were eroded. Dolly sat on her ass and slid down the side of the cliff. A juddering ride.

By the time she got to the bottom, she was a bundle of bruises, and the sun had set, and she hurt too much to worry about how she was going to get back up again in the dark.

It was low tide, and she recognized Johnny Maine's rock, well out of the water. Slipping, skinning her shin, scratching her hands on barnacles, Dolly clambered up the side of the rock, settling into its briny saddle, where Johnny Maine used to watch the sun dip into Long Island Sound.

On the coast of Connecticut, the first evening's lights were glimmering. Venus sailing silver into a twilight sky.

She was trying hard not to think, not to imagine. Just concentrating on the breathing. Gasping for oxygen, not too fast. When she felt as if she'd been kicked in the stomach.

What hurt most was the silliest, perhaps. Ever since earliest childhood, her most ravaging experiences were of rebuff. The dread of exposing yourself and being rejected. Of being laughed at. Brushed off. She remembered with shame fresh as paint the day in dancing class thirty-five years ago when Gilbert Angell, sitting in the corner, beckoned to her (she thought), indicating the empty chair beside him, and she, dazzled, made to sit down. Only to have Gilbert gesture over her shoulder towards Serena Beck: "No, no—I want Serena to sit here." The horror. The cringing horror of having mistakenly thought you were wanted. Of waving back at somebody who in fact is smiling at another person behind you. Of being the last to be picked for somebody's team. Of calling someone on the telephone who answers brusquely. Of asking someone to dinner who cannot come. So elaborate a series of defenses constructed to make sure that such things could never possibly happen again–to make sure you got in there with the first blow. Or better yet, never made a move, but waited to be approached, retaining sole power to accept or reject. To be always the one whom others telephoned and caught either at a good time or a bad, had their calls either returned by or not.

Which was why she had sat passive all summer, waiting for Isaac to show her that she was not too old or fat or ridiculous to be loved.

When Dolly gave birth to her first child, she had never anticipated that this scoop of flesh carved out from her own innards might hold the same power to wound as Gilbert Angell. She had supposed that mother hormones rendered you immune to petty social anguishes. Wrong again. Motherhood, it turned out, was one long subjection, without any hope of self-protection or revenge, to those same humiliations, but worse–children having all the manipulativeness of adults plus a cruelty untempered by decency or self-interest. When baby Johnny smiled at the nurse but not her, Dolly tried hard not to be offended. When Johnny, aged two, went through a six-month spell of pushing her mother away, screaming, "I want Daddy," she just about managed not to pack her bags and leave. When Carlotta decided she liked Alfred's mother's apartment better than theirs. When Leo wanted only Ernestine to put him to bed. And so on. Had it ever gotten easier? No. Never. Every time she walked out of the children's playroom and heard laughter following, she was convinced they were making fun of her.

But here, impossibly, was an as-yet-undreamed-of field of maternal humiliation. She was well skilled in fighting Alfred for her children's love. But to find her own daughter competing with her for . . . That Johnny had rejected her mother because she wanted–because she wanted–Isaac to herself. Dolly's guest. Dolly's beloved. Ever since Johnny had got that job with Inez Klein, she'd come back different: harder, defiant. She should never have let her work for that tough floozy. Again and again she replayed the image of Johnny's thwarted pout, her snippy "Isaac and I are going sailing," her flouncing off in a rage when Dolly–idiot that she was–had innocently confessed a desire to come too. To intrude. To barge in, unwanted, on their private treat. And be cast out. Because they wanted to be alone. Because they were–in love? Was that why Isaac had never made a move?

So many areas of her life, suddenly, had become too ugly to think about. In the past, no matter how ghastly relations were with Alfred, her children had remained a sanctuary of golden rightness. Dear, truthful, undefiled. And now it was Johnny whom she did not want to think about. Johnny who had proved her innermost betrayer.

Staring at the rough water raking, raking the rocks, she imagined involuntarily the two of them—Isaac and her daughter—out in the small boat. With a man as large as Isaac, one would be huddled close, knee against knee, thigh against thigh. Felt in her very womb how the waves and wind's angling would throw them into each other—how two young bodies might ache and yearn at the collision of flesh—how they might cling, how salty lips might graze, slippery limbs entwine, in the tumult and forward lunge, the shuddering flight across water. Were they at this very moment hugging, as Isaac had hugged her frighteningly tight so that all that you wanted was to be squeezed airless by his securing bounty? Were they laughing at her? Was Johnny complaining about her mother's awfulness, and Isaac chiming in? Laughing about how Dolly was throwing herself at him? Were they off together laughing at her?

Oh God. How could she have missed it? In fact, she had noticed—it was pretty blatant—that Johnny was developing kind of a crush on Isaac. But Johnny had crushes on so many men. Last summer it was Emanuele, and in the fall it had been her weedy fifty-year-old music teacher—the lone male in a school of six hundred girls—and last winter, believe it or not, it was Marco Tanner's boyfriend, Kevin, who had taken her skating at Rockefeller Center. (Why couldn't she have stuck with faggots, not chosen the one thing that was Dolly's alone—her pride, her Isaac?) So sublimely content had Dolly been these last few weeks, so absorbed in her own wonderment at Isaac, that Johnny's crush had just been part of the general sweetness. Well, she was a grotesque fool. Haven't you looked in the mirror recently? How in Christ's name could it so signally have failed to register that while the mother had declined into a wrinkled, waddling matron—when was the last time a construction worker whistled at you?—the daughter had ripened into a lissome beauty with flesh like a white peach and a laugh that made you want to kiss her, and that seventeen, to a young man in his twenties, was not a child but a lover? Far more likely a lover than a middle-aged hag.

She considered the evidence. Johnny had posed for Isaac. Hadn't he himself told her that you only wanted to paint what you lusted after, wanted to engorge and know, be known by, and that by painting it you loved it inside out? He had painted her daughter, again and again. What more consummate undressing and anatomatizing could there be? He had fucked her with his brush.

Shivering in the darkness on the lonely rock, she contemplated asking Isaac straight out whether he was intending to sleep with her daughter—if he hadn't already, that is. God knows what they hadn't done, these last few steamy summer nights alone. God, what had she been thinking of to appoint Isaac as male baby-sitter for her little ducks while she was at the funeral? Keeping Jesse's ghastly stepfather off Michael's back, chatting up the rabbi while her daughter and Isaac were—what? sprawled in the hammock, his hands unhusking her infantine sweet breasts? fucking in the bottom of the boat? kissing each other to death? Thoughts emptied by a wordless howl of misery and rage. I have nothing, she thought. The world knows my husband's been betraying me, my marriage is a bad joke that has gone on too long, my children hate the very sight of me, I have made a laughingstock of myself over a man who finds me physically repulsive, Jesse is dead. Nothing left except a dull round of worldly duties, expected because I am rich. And then self-pity got drowned out by a quicker fury.

How dare Johnny speak to her mother that way, how dare she be so so spoiled and unfeeling. But Johnny at least was a child. It was Isaac, ten years her senior, who should know better. If he has made any improper advances—if he has betrayed my trust, my kindness to him—I will ask him to leave. I will run him out of town.

He was two-faced, sly. An opportunist. How her friends must be laughing at her—Ayala, to whom it had been painfully evident that Dolly was gaga about her young employee. Christ, I'm worse than Sophie. Less excuse.

Do I ask Isaac to leave? Do I send Johnny back to the city?

It's cold, she realized. The tide is coming in, and I don't know how to get back up the cliff and when I do, I've got nowhere to go. Trapped between not wanting to lay eyes on her daughter and Isaac and not wanting to lay eyes on her husband. Back to the Empire Hotel? Oh God, and on top of it all, Alfred was threatening to come out. Well, let him. Let him come serenade the happy couple. God. Let him bring his girlfriend and join the fun. I'll take Leo away till school starts and leave them to it. Let them turn my house into a pedophiles' bordello.

. . .

When Dolly got home after midnight, the kitchen was lit and she heard the murmur of voices. Animated voices. Her daughter and Isaac. On her way upstairs, she realized that it was just one person talking—a voice she didn't recognize, chirpy, preternaturally excited. As she reached the landing, Isaac came out of the kitchen.

"What happened to you?" he demanded. "I was about to call the cops."

"Where's Johnny?"

He ignored the question. "I went all the way out to Orient, looking for your car. I didn't know whether you'd gone over a cliff or—"

"Where's Johnny?"

"She went to bed early. Before I started getting really spooked."

"Oh. I should have thought you'd go with her. Or weren't you in the mood?"

Isaac's stare expressed such obdurate incomprehension that Dolly's fears were quite dispersed. She paused, abashed. "Oh God, never mind. Forgive me—I am very tired tonight. I didn't mean to worry you, I didn't mean to accuse you."

"Look, I am going to call Alfred and tell him you're all right. I thought maybe you mighta gone back to . . . Why don't you have a drink?" Isaac said politely. "I am just polishing off your bourbon. Any more of your midnight drives and I'll be reduced to paint thinner. Good golly, Miss Dolly, *please* don't disappear again."

Limp with exhaled relief, Dolly followed him into the kitchen. Her assumptions now seemed mad. Of course Isaac was not sleeping with her daughter. That had been no more than a hideous moment of lunacy, a phantasm. Things were exactly as they looked, as they had always been. Isaac was innocent. Isaac was not a calculating rake. Isaac was nothing but a man grateful after long loneliness to be surrounded by loving family. She might as well have suspected him of molesting Leopold. All the more shame on Johnny for throwing herself at a person who had no interest in her, for pestering and distracting a guest of her parents' who was staying in their house in order to complete important work. Isaac had really been too obliging, acting as nursemaid to Dolly's children. Henceforth things must change. In the morning she would have a talk with Johnny, insist that she leave Isaac alone, on pain of being sent back to the city.

But Isaac meanwhile was still keyed up with the anger that follows a groundless fright. Isaac was standing by the kitchen counter, pouring her a glass of Wild Turkey from a gallon jug she hadn't seen since the neo-geo artist James Harris had come to stay. Too upset to meet her eye. She moved to Isaac's side, very close. Snuffing up the wholesome sweat and grime of him. The big childish paint-stained hands. His look of a farmer just in from the fields. His brown throat where he had forgotten to shave, or where curly golden hairs sprung through the gaps in his white flannel shirt. His sweet breath, liquorous, noisy.

"I thought you went over a cliff," Isaac accused, passing her the glass. "I thought you . . ." Then his hand crept into hers, and the sentence, ground to a mutter, trailed away. In that delicious hush, holding Isaac's hand in hers, Dolly now heard the radio, parked on the kitchen table, which was jabbering in the het-up monotone that at first she had mistaken for Isaac and her daughter conversing. "At Fort Benning . . . the Joint Chiefs of Staff . . . General Colin Powell . . . President Bush has summoned his . . . In a statement released today . . ."

Her lips were very close to his face, so close they mouthed the down of his cheek. "Has something happened?"

"Besides your vanishing? Oh yeah. The other excitement of the day." Isaac was trembling as he answered, gasping for breath, kissing her back, tentatively at first. "Iraq's invaded Kuwait. The Iraqi army is marching towards the Saudi Arabian border. . . ." He was kissing her ear now. "And President Bush says we're going to war—he's sending American troops over to kick them out." He drew up the sleeve of her dress and stroked the wiry hairs of her arm so that they stood straight, electrified. Like something he'd been wanting to do for ages. Then kissed her elbow, sucking on its puckery rind of flesh. "It looks like the real thing—it looks like war."

"It does look like the real thing," Dolly agreed, sighing. The familiar surge deep in her belly, as if the womb were turning over. Dissolving, leaping. The fickle womb. The eyes gone glazed, unseeing. As if desire were blind. "Why, that's terrible," said Dolly. "What did you say, Isaac? Iraq has invaded Kuwait? Why, that's awful." She pressed him down into a kitchen chair. Isaac's hands silhouetting her breasts, her hips, her rear. Then more abruptly, he yanked up her loose dress, crooning under his breath a nursery-rhyme gibberish of desire. The womb leaping, the womb leaping like a ram skipping over the hills . . .

Part Eight

Thirty-nine

AFTER THE OPENING OF Isaac Hooker's show at the Celia Rubin Gallery in February, the Geblers held a small party for the artist at their apartment. There were no more than fifty guests, for people had been too caught up by the war—now just ended—to plan extravagant entertainments.

The rooms, warmed by a rich golden light from innumerable candles, were filled with camellia trees and flowering rose bushes; and outside, the night sky, framed by tall windows, looked dusky purple. Far below, on the Hudson River, you saw barges hurrying past in the darkness like warships.

To Alfred's pleasure, Enzo De Felice, who was just out of the hospital after a gallbladder operation, was able to come. Illness had turned him almost translucent. As the rest of him had shrunk to child size, his ears, which glowed like rosy alabaster lit from within, now seemed truly elephantine.

When Alfred met him at the door, Graziella was already bundling the old man out of his overcoat. Enzo, on catching sight of Alfred, pushed her away and seized hold of his host, kissing Alfred with smacking greed. Gebler, touched, pressed the dry bundle of bones to his chest, then drew back to give him another look-over. "How come you only get thinner and I get fatter?"

Enzo, as usual, had no time for banter. "What a scandal, eh?" he piped in his high spindly voice, clutching his host's hand for emphasis. "Your President is as much of a brigand as Saddam Hussein. Why didn't the American soldiers refuse to fight a war over petrol prices?"

Alfred greeted Graziella, who was handing their coats to the waiter. "But Enzo, surely oil's as good an excuse for a war as any other," he teased. "Why's it more obscene to fight a war for economic reasons than for territorial or even religious? Anyway, it all comes down to the same thing."

"Yes, that with the Cold War over, America's global bullying is now unlimited. Without the Soviet Union to keep you honest, your country no longer has any restraint in asserting its hegemony over the *entire universe*," said De Felice excitably. "But I am really very upset about this war. Everybody—my friends who I have agreed with always—have astonished me by supporting Bush. . . ."

"Well, not supporting *Bush*," amended Graziella, straightening the collar of Enzo's jacket.

"Yes, by supporting the war which means the murder of one hundred thousand Iraqi peasants!" cried Enzo, irritably batting his girlfriend away. "This war fever makes me think of 1914, when Mussolini won his great success by breaking rank with the Socialists and chivvying Italy into joining the Allies. . . ."

"How are you feeling, Enzo? You look a little frail. When's your new piece opening, anyway?"

"It is opening at the Weill Recital Hall."

"In April," added Graziella.

"Fantastic, I can't wait. Let me tell Dolly you've arrived—she was thrilled you were coming. You know, the party is for a young painter friend of ours who has just had his first exhibition. Great timing, right? Between the war and the recession . . . I want you to meet Isaac, too. . . ."

He had caught sight of his wife and Isaac framed in the living-room doorway, having just come through from the back hall. She, flushed, had obviously said something that amused the young man, who seized her hand and pressed it to his lips.

Alfred wondered, with unforced admiration, who had dressed Isaac for his great night—not Dolly, surely?—for the young man was wearing a rather amazing pair of moleskin trousers and a Harris tweed jacket. The old taped-together black plastic specs had been replaced by horn-rimmed glasses. Very chic. Who had taken him shopping? Someone with the taste not to go for urban flash—there was Casey, for instance, in motorcycle leathers, and Hanlon in a silvery sharkskin suit and scraggly muttonchop whiskers—but rather to deck him out like the country gentleman he . . . wasn't.

"Come," he said, shepherding his ancient guests. "Let me make some introductions."

Why am I here and how did it happen? It's come too fast, it makes my head spin, it's unreal. Nauseating, almost. It's too fast, it's too much. Like when your frozen hands warm and instead of comfort, pain. Too sharp a contrast. Too much. So recently to have been sleeping on strangers' floors, washing dishes in a homeless shelter, wondering if now was the time to jump off the Brooklyn Bridge. And tonight, candlelight and an ample buffet and ladies in black velvet with foreign accents and kind smiles, and a mistress grand as the Queen of the Indies who loves you . . . There's Molly Kellaway waving and grinning with her rich-girl, years-behind-braces chompers, and if she knew where you'd come from and how much too much this means to you, she'd run a mile. Run, Molly. Some people you knew from then must be dead, and some . . . Remember what you'd not even let yourself dream of, back then. Wonders like a room of your own, an end to the shakes and coughs and chills, *impossible* . . . And he has the nerve, that Alfred, to inveigh against materialism . . . A stack of blankets high as pancakes. A warm bed. Woolen socks. An end to fear of the cold and hunger. A night's sleep. An end.

But tell me this. Why, if luck's come, must it be gorged on like cream puffs in bed, so selfishly? As if you were a foundling with no family, no friends before last week's. Because you did have a past, remember: a hometown, blood relatives. Oh, cretin, did you honestly—yes, you did—expect your mom to come rolling up in her repainted Pinto with Turner in tow? Even if she'd bothered to read the invitation, wouldn't it strike her as more waste of an expensive education? And what would she think of Dolly? You know she hasn't changed address because she still deposits your checks. But Turner? My long-lost, my love, my target, my bony bonny numbskull. Can you spell yet, Turny? Are you still allergic to everything but frozen hot dogs?

"Hello there," said Isaac, slinging an arm around Melissa, his former art teacher from Henry Street. She was as tall as he and straight-backed, more like a riding instructress than a painter, with full red lips and chestnut hair in a ponytail. She had brought her husband, who was a radiologist at Mount Sinai.

"Looking good, Isaac," she kidded, fingering his jacket. "This is really big-time."

"It's obscene, isn't it?" Isaac agreed. Remembering how this rosy-brown girl from Westchester had once been to him so wretchedly lust-provoking, so grotesquely out of his league that he'd wanted to slit her throat. And now, next to Dolly, she looked raw. "I keep expecting to wake up under a bridge."

"Why?" said Melissa, kindly. "You've had an interesting life, that's all."

"Isn't that a Chinese curse?" her husband interjected.

"Yeah—too interesting."

"Well, the paintings are great, Isaac. No shit. I'm proud I knew you before—I'm going to be saying to all my pupils, Sure I gave Isaac Hooker his first art lessons, and they'll be, like, Oh sure."

Isaac shifted his weight from one leg to the other, practiced standing like a crane.

"John's such a riot—he went up to your gallery lady and asked, Are these for sale? Like, have you ever heard of an artist whose work wasn't for sale?"

"I really liked the one of the homeless man sitting at the subway steps."

"That's Luther, right?"

"You remember," said Isaac, pleased. "So what did Celia say?"

"She said they're all sold!"

"Oh!" Isaac looked embarrassed.

"I was disappointed," said John. "We're refurnishing our offices—I really liked that one of the subway station."

"Yeah, ever since we moved out of the city you can look at a subway again without wincing."

"Well," said Isaac, "I got another subway one that's pretty similar, an earlier version, back in the studio, if you guys want to come over some time."

On his way to the living room, Melissa and John in tow, he grabbed hold of Costa and Martha, too—and there was Macklowe from the frame store!—and plumped himself and his friends down on the big white sofa. Energy dissipated, after the long terror of the gallery opening, following upon so many different flavors of fear. For the last week, he had been convinced—despite the hundred and fifty invitations with his name snaking across a color reproduction of *The Sons of Heaven Meet the Daughters of the Earth*—that no one but Alfred and Dolly would show up opening night.

"Nonsense," Dolly had said. "Everybody comes to Celia's openings. Especially nowadays." Celia had found a German backer who had made her hire a snazzier curator, and all season the gallery had been on a roll, turning out one important exhibition after another, beautifully lighted and hung. Trust Celia. Throughout the eighties boom, she'd been a total backwater, and only now that the art market had so spectacularly collapsed had she got her act together. Of course people would come.

Dolly was right. By seven p.m. there hadn't been room in the gallery to sneeze, and Isaac's euphoria was sharpened by curiosity as to who these plausible-looking strangers were. Celia had introduced him around, he had been passed from frosty hand to hand. Why were they here? Men with close-cropped hair and bad teeth who laughed too loud. Women in black who nodded vehemently before you'd finished what you were saying. Lots of artists had brought their babies. Three or four had brought dogs. More people clustered raptly around the latest Dalmatian or prize boxer than around the pictures. A narrow corridor in the middle, and two scrimmages at either end—one where guests were dumping and retrieving coats, the other for the bar, where anemic Chablis was being dribbled into plastic glasses. Celia hawk-eyed for the *Times* critic. "Oh, there you are, Hannah. How lovely you could make it. Here's the artist. Isaac?"

It was Manhattan at the fizzle-end of the twentieth century, it was a SoHo art opening, and across the frozen sludgy city people had been putting on overcoats and leaving their offices—"Pauline? I'm just going to stop by an opening at Celia Rubin's. Want me to pick up anything for dinner?" There were several other openings that night—a group show at Sperone Westwater, and some Czech photographers at the downtown Guggenheim.

So this is success. Too levitated exuberant to bother whether anybody was actually looking at his pictures. You went to openings, he knew by now, not to look but to be looked at, to meet your future buyer, your dealer-to-be, the critic who might write an introduction to your next catalogue. To get ahead. Because it was free liquor and a chance to see your friends. And maybe—just possibly—because, for those alert to trends, biblical naïfs were not what you were used to seeing on West Broadway.

Ayala was telling Dolly about a dinner several nights ago at the Altschulers' house. The Altschulers were newspaper magnates who had built up overnight an enormous collection of contemporary art and just as precipitously dumped it at auction last fall—to Dolly's malicious pleasure, at most disappointing prices. If there was any satisfaction to be drawn from the art market's nosedive, which had just reduced Aurora's collection to half its previous value and was already setting off a string of bankruptcies and foreclosures—every week you heard of a new gallery going out of business—it was that the Altschulers, who specialized in buying up, vulgarizing, and then liquidating once venerable newspapers, had been cheated of a latest windfall.

"Who was at dinner?"

"The Ferreras . . . Marty Wexell . . . the Kaminers. Who else, let me think . . . I sat next to Susannah Dudley, whom I found rather amusing. And I must say, they've hung on to a spectacular selection of art. Sandy says they've unloaded the seventies and eighties and now want to build up a good pop art collection. You know they have those Warhol skulls."

Dolly shifted impatiently. "You like Susannah Dudley? Really? Bernard, I'm surprised at you. I find her *too* mercenary."

"Come, is that fair?"

"Oh, give me a break. She can't be bothered to say hello to anyone without a private plane. . . . It's just too blatant."

"She was very nice to me," Ayala protested. "Anyway, why not? Isn't money, or what it brings, a harmless and very understandable taste? Nobody is shocked if you love Barbados because it's got beautiful beaches, but to say you love the Altschulers because they've got a beautiful house where one dines very well is frowned upon."

They both laughed, but Dolly still demurred.

"Listen," Ayala continued, smiling. "Really what we object to, if you will forgive me, Dolly, is that she is not rich herself. For Altschulers only to like other Altschulers is human nature—for Susannah to like them is snobbery. But you are assuming, most unfairly," he teased, "that the rich are not inherently likable."

"Well, the Altschulers certainly are not. Although I must say if they'd invited me to dinner, I would have gone like a shot. I still kick myself for not having bought those Warhol skulls in '87."

"You would have come to dinner with a pair of cotton gloves and a ski mask and a large shopping bag?"

"Yes, and a submachine gun. I can never forgive what they did to the *Rambler*. Why in God's name buy a prestigious paper just to close it down? They're vandals, that's what."

"Vandals with a delicious cook."

Dolly laid a hand now on Ayala's. "Have you talked to Isaac yet?"

"Well, just to commiserate with him on the terrible embarrassment of having his first show entirely sold out opening night. He hadn't noticed, apparently."

"He's not very interested in the financial end of things," she said lovingly.

Ayala smiled. One generation away from Charlie Diehl and already unworldiness appeared a virtue. How many of the pictures, he wondered, had Dolly herself bought? "Did I tell you I brought the Kohlers down to see it yesterday when they were setting up? George couldn't make it tonight, unfortunately."

"You did tell me—I can't thank you enough, Bernard. You've been an absolute . . . savior. It does look tremendous, doesn't it? I must admit Celia did a splendid job." She squeezed his hand again. "I'm just going to make sure he's all right."

"I see him—he's right over there by the door talking to Dave Flaxman."

"Should we rescue him?"

Ayala was very comfortable chatting on the sofa with his old friend, but seeing how impatiently Dolly's gaze was fixed on Isaac, he agreed. "Yes, by all means—go rescue him."

Alfred again was arguing about the Gulf War, this time with Benoit Goldschmidt, who last fall had become a member of Aurora's board.

Gebler, like a plane lined up for takeoff, was waiting for the Swiss to stop talking so he himself could speak. He nodded rapidly—yeah, yeah—finishing Benoit's sentences for him in order to indicate that since he already knew what the other man was going to say, it was quite unnecessary for Benoit to continue. But the Swiss was very ruthless in

fending off any takeover bids. When shouting down his would-be inter-
rupter didn't work, he would grab Gebler's arm and clutch it tight while
he talked on, having discovered that a person feels constrained from
making you shut up while you are pinioning him in apparent affection.
Meanwhile, Gebler would find again and again that by the time he managed to insert an opinion, the topic had changed.

Finally, he got a chance to make his point. "The real lesson of the
Gulf War," said Alfred, triumphantly, gripping Benoit's arm just in case,
"is that America is still the only show in town. All this garbage about
American decline and the rise of Japan, the new Europe, blah-blah-
blah—well, when it came to the crunch, the Europeans fell apart because
the Germans remembered they were German and the British remembered that they were British, and the Japanese couldn't even get it together to send *bandages*. When it comes to action, the world still looks
to America to get the job done."

"That is true, but it won't be true much longer," said Benoit calmly.
"Take Eastern Europe—when the Eastern Bloc countries wanted a model
of a rich civilized society, they looked to Western Europe, not to America, and that is a very significant change."

"I doubt—"

"No, I assure you, to an outsider, America appears too poor and
violent. Too many problems. Also, you are feeling a bit strapped to remain a great power," continued Benoit. "In the Persian Gulf, America
was rather too much the hired gun. For us, who remember how the GIs
rode through Rome after the war giving candy to the children, who
think of Lend-Lease and the Marshall Plan, there was something rather
sad about America's coming to Europe and Japan asking to be paid to
fight. Then again, there was this feeling that Bush ended the war too
soon because he was terrified of his own people, which is a very bad sign
for a world power. A little like the Russians in Afghanistan."

"I don't exactly see anybody lining up to replace America as super-
power," Gebler objected.

"That's quite true. A leadership vacuum. Very dangerous. The last
time we saw the simultaneous death of two empires, it was called the
First World War."

"Hey, guy," said Casey, high-fiving Isaac.

Isaac hugged him. "Where's Gina?"

"She said to say hi."

"Oh, I was hoping she'd come."

"Well, she didn't. No offense—she's in kind of a pissy mood at the moment. I tell her, Quit the job, go have some fun for a change. She's got this friend in Paris who's, like, begging her to come visit. I tell her, I'd go, if I wasn't waiting to hear if Khazin's money's come through." Casey was hoping to get a job from the Russian art dealer. "Anyway, I brought you Joseph as a consolation prize."

Isaac searched the room eagerly. "Where is he?"

"Probably hiding in the coat closet."

Joseph was a Russian painter friend of Casey's who'd immigrated to the United States in the 1970s. When they first met, Isaac thought Joseph was an arrogant bully, but Casey had explained to him that Joseph was fifteen years older than they were, dirt poor, and doggedly unsuccessful. It had not always been so—not long after his arrival in the U.S., he'd had the glimmerings of success. A reputable gallery had taken him on, he had appeared in a couple of group shows and had a solo exhibition which received good reviews. But nothing had come of it. His gallery went out of business and he had been unable to find another one, sales had dried up, and before long—his girlfriend having left him— he had moved out of his studio on Prince Street and into a rented room in Greenpoint. When you asked Joseph about these early days, he shrugged. I was an asshole then, he said. I drank too much, I fought with my dealer, I blew it. Other artists, subjected to the unrelieved obscurity that followed, might have lost nerve, slipped into a paying profession— Isaac by now had met plenty of former artists who were currently dealers, carpenters, contractors—but Joseph, although he had become indisputably invisible, a genuine underground man, refused to quit. He worked harder than when he had had a career—he painted twelve hours a day, seven days a week, and only with great difficulty could a person manage occasionally to drag him out of his studio in Greenpoint for a decent meal.

On hearing this story, Isaac felt more sympathetic. He had pestered Casey to take him out to Joseph's studio, and had been impressed by the spare scratchy abstracts. He had some cash in his pocket these days, and so found himself in the outlandish position of being able to buy two of Joseph's pictures, which were embarrassingly underpriced. Tonight, touched that Joseph had shown up, he took the older man off

to a corner where they might talk, but no sooner had they made themselves comfortable than Dolly came over, saying she wanted Isaac to
meet somebody in the other room.

When the evening ended at about one o'clock, Alfred and Ayala were
left on the sofa together, smoking cigars. Nancy long ago had departed,
and even Dolly gone to bed. As for the guest of honor, he had made off
with Casey and a gloomy-looking Russian, announcing they were going
in Casey's Jeep to some bar in Brooklyn that served beer at a dollar a
pitcher—an invitation that even Gebler found resistible.

"Alone at last, Bernard."

"As usual, the women have abandoned us."

"Aww, women have no sticking power—they just talk a good show."

The two men leaned back on the sofa, like an old couple too comfortable to make conversation.

"How's business?" asked Gebler, finally.

The question these days was so comical that both men laughed.

"To tell you the truth, as the son of a banker, I went into the art
business—if I can be said to have done anything in my thick-witted
life consciously and deliberately—simply because I thought it wasn't a
business."

"You said it," said Gebler. "Looking at pretty pictures for a living
sounded like nice work if you could get it. One giddy round of shmoozing and parties and studio visits and free booze . . ."

"Not just that. The larger social aspect of painting has always interested me. As a young man I wanted to write like Proust, and when I found
I had no talent except the talent for admiring other people's talent, I decided to be an art dealer, because"—Ayala searched for words—"because
the visual arts, more than literature, seemed to me the truest reflection
of the values, the pleasures, the anxiety, the fashions, of any society. . . .
Well, look at it this way. If you are curious to know what was taking place
in the psyche of seventeenth-century Holland, you look at Hals's portraits of merchants and their wives, who combine material plenty with
such a worried earnestness; or France after 1871 as you see it in Rodin's
Gates of Hell—and, well, one learns as much from Jackson Pollock about
what it means to be an American after the war owning the world—"

"Yeah, and thinking you can piss on it."

"Well, I'm still learning, but I can't say at the moment that I like what I learn. I don't consider myself a conservative, because temperamentally it doesn't suit me. And yet these successful young artists of today—Jeff Koons with his big dolls, his mania for publicity, his glorification of kitsch—if they are holding a mirror up to us, then I don't like us. Maybe the one good result of the art market crash will be to make us rethink our values. . . ."

"I agree with you a hundred percent. Dolly and I have been lucky in being able to find some real talent out there, but a lot of this art's total crap, and most dealers are too corrupt to say so."

Ayala threw up his hands. "For me, it's easy. Everybody I sell is dead—I have no interest in further inflating a Jeff Koons's hot air. But all it took was a drop in the market to make us realize that the art boom of the 1980s has not corresponded to any boom in creativity or genius, any new renaissance, it has been instead simply because we have bred a generation of artists careerist enough to play the big-business game, to blow up another South Sea bubble.

"Your wife, to my mind, puts too much blame on the collectors. . . . Well, collectors are just gamblers. Racehorses are beautiful, but a gambler will as happily bet on how many cigarettes are left in his pack, or—"

"It's also the critics' fault for not . . . I mean, give me a break. I went to an artist's studio last week who Hannah gave a rave—"

Ayala suddenly burst out laughing and patted Gebler on the knee. "Listen to us two old farts—I never dreamed we would become so reactionary! What a fate! And yet of course, in this age as any other—this hardly needs to be said—there are men and women who are pursuing their craft patiently, tenderly, with the old ardor. Look at Isaac—I am not necessarily convinced of his talent, but one recognizes what he's trying to do. I had lunch with him in his new studio last week—I find him very sweet. I don't know about his work, which seems to me rather limited, but he is very sweet. He told me, I am in love with ultramarine. Don't you think, Mr. Ayala, ultramarine is the most beautiful color?

"I asked him what he liked about painting and he said something I liked very much. He told me, When I was young—which I found amusing, as to me he is about twelve years old—all I wanted to do was reach out and grab the whole world in my arms, I had such a greed for experience. But then you go out into the world and you don't know anymore how to express this love. Sometimes you think it's by loving a woman and sometimes you think it's by worshipping God or by dying for your country because life seems too precious to bear. For me, he says, painting is as close as I can come to expressing this love of *everything.*"

"Very sweet," agreed Gebler, and Ayala was too satisfied by his rendition of Isaac's sentiments to notice that his friend sounded sour.

Forty

THE MORNING AFTER his opening, Isaac awoke at eleven to a splitting head. Across the room, the answering machine bleating neon-red with messages he had slept through. I must have drunk too much, he concluded.

He remembered—with a kind of physiological, pain-triggered remembering—his early days in New York, after he broke his arm, when he had nowhere to live, and was just facing up to the realization that he was never going back to Agnes, so that there was no one to be good for. Soon as he'd strung together a couple of dollars, he'd get drunk, but *drunk.* Wake-up-with-two-days-missing-and-no-shoes drunk—that funny game of piecing together what century you've woken up in, what you did while you were out cold, of trying to maneuver your way down the street with a head that feels squishy, as if someone in jackboots had jumped on it. Even after he got to the Blue Sky, every couple of weeks he'd still drunk away his paycheck.

Since those days, he'd been reconstructing himself inch by inch, and sobriety—within limits—had been part of the package. Mostly the pain had been so immense it was all he could do not to crack his skull open against the wall, not to refuse, to say no to, the dinginess of unintoxicated existence. Now he was just beginning to get sane enough to allow himself a little rope.

He thought of the bar in Greenpoint last night, crowded with pasty-faced Poles downing spirits in silence, and thought of Dolly asleep in that big white bed beside her husband.

It was only when the intercom rang that Isaac remembered he'd invited Melissa and John over to his studio to look at some of the pictures that hadn't gone into the show.

And later, it was only when the intercom buzzed a second time—right in the middle of his second sleep of the day—that he realized it must be Dolly coming over after work. Twilight already, the day quite fled! He waited for her by the elevator, rubbing his eyes.

The door slid open, and out she stepped, in an astrakhan coat with a sable collar and cuffs—the kind of coat that caused fake blood to be thrown at you nowadays. Her cheeks, under the sable hat, scarlet from the cold. Isaac kissed her hard, seizing her face in his hands.

"You look like Anna Karenina in your furs."

"They're my mother's."

"What icy cheeks! Did you just get off the train from Petersburg? Why are you out of breath?"

"We got stuck in traffic coming uptown on Eighth. I was so crazy to see you, I got out of the car and . . . trotted the rest of the way."

"My madwoman."

"I resisted calling you all day—I thought you should rest up. But then I got worried."

Of course, Isaac realized, he should have called her. Called, sent flowers. Everything. He was an ungrateful cur. "Let's get you warmed up, my lovely."

He pulled off first her coat and hat and gloves, then her dress and undergarments, stockings, boots, until she stood before him naked. Isaac hung back a moment in admiration, then, seizing her white breasts, plunged his face into them as a person might dash his face into a basin of water.

"So that was Joseph, that lugubrious-looking man you left the party with?"

Dolly, lying in bed, watched Isaac get dressed to take her back uptown. Fending off the moment when she too must dress. Each departure a tearing of limb from limb, and the transition from their private tenderness to her home life—squabbling children, fretful husband—a soul-destroying lie.

Funny how everyone dressed differently: Isaac, bare to the waist, was now lunging blindly into the still-assembled nest of undershirt-shirt-sweatshirt as if clothes were the enemy. Hopping into his sneakers, trampling their backs down. She had been startled when she first saw him naked: an alien male, after twenty years of assuming Alfred a kind of Everyman-Onlyman. Isaac was hairier and burly, the calves and shoulders bulging, veiny, overmuscled. The sweat high as a tomcat's spray, the kisses sweet and milky. (And young. My God, was he young!) It was like coming upon an antlered stag, a wild boar too suddenly, up close: she had needed, despite her own urgency, to back him off for a moment. Now his brawn, his rankness, his cheerful appetite had become her not-so-secret pride.

He liked to talk in bed. They would lie hours, Isaac's arm tight around her, her head in the crook of his shoulder, telling each other stories from childhood. Sometimes he sang to her—"Joe Hill," "Casey Jones," old-fashioned songs he had learned from his father. Then, just when it seemed sweet enough to last forever, when she was thanking God for having granted—in her dotage!!—this life's-dream, a lover whose genius was their joint project, he would balk. Some rich-lady remark she'd uttered, unconsciously, some sting or overbearingness that reminded him of the chasm their generosity and yearning had overleaped. She tried to tell herself, by these regular convulsions, that the romance was temporary, but there was no training yourself for sadness, mid joy.

"Yes, that was Joseph. My gloomy Russian. I'm sorry you didn't get more of a chance to talk to him last night. Let me show you his pictures."

Isaac went next door to get Joseph's two paintings, while Dolly washed.

"You realize, don't you, what a wild success you've had," she shouted over the running water. "Everybody told me how wonderful the pictures were. And Celia telephoned to say lots of people have been in today. I must say, it's been beyond even my wildest dreams, my beloved. I hope you're as proud as I am."

She came out to the studio now, in search of her scattered clothes.

Isaac was holding Joseph's pictures. Dolly looked over his shoulder. Ugly, murky pictures. Just as she'd suspected, taking an instinctive dislike to the Russian. Like abstract Rouault. And what did this sour character want from her Isaac?

She glanced away. "Goodness, your walls look bare."

"They're about to look even barer."

"Oh?"

"I sold another picture this afternoon."

"Which one? Who to?" she asked, too quickly, slipping now into stockings and boots.

Isaac indicated.

It was only that fall, at Dolly's urging, that Isaac had begun to paint the city, as if, having partially exorcised himself of his childhood land-scape, he were now ready for the traumas of his first New York years. What emerged was a sequence of small oil paintings on wood, many of them with captions in red script.

In the painting which Melissa's husband had just bought, Luther was sitting by the entrance to a subway station, massive head lowered, knees to his chin. You saw feet tramping along the sidewalk—high heels, boots—and men and women going up and down the subway stairs. Its lighting and composition—an infernal descent into cavey darkness—deliberately played off Renaissance Descents into Limbo. Except that Christ, instead of, like a midwife, tugging Adam and Eve from the mucky womb, was here slumped despairing on the sidewalk, head in one hand, and the other, long-wristed, held out empty. The title of this picture was *They Only Spend It on Drugs*.

He had painted others, too, of Luther and Scout and Del, of the dormitory at the men's shelter, of himself being beaten up on a dark side street by the robbers who'd broken his arm, and a lovely nightscape of men under a bridge, dancing around a trashcan bonfire, while across the river the pink neon lights of the Domino sugar factory shone gay as a distant amusement park, but hellish, too. That one was called *Why Can't They Get Jobs?*

When Casey had seen Isaac's new series, he had been half tri-umphant, half piqued. "See? What'd I tell you? I told you a year ago, when I wanted you to be in my 'Home' show, Make art about the home-less. And you laughed at me. I told you a year ago. You ought to listen to your Uncle Casey."

"I wasn't ready a year ago," said Isaac.

Although Dolly suspected this might prove Isaac's best work yet, she had been against his including the city series in the February exhibition. She was a purist: she had urged him instead to choose four or five biblical pictures, with some dramatic unity. But Isaac, whose bias was towards flawed surplus, had prevailed, with a big messy array of twelve paintings, some of Gilboa, some biblical, some city. With the best versions of *The Sons of Heaven Meet the Daughters of the Earth* and of *And the Bow Shall Be in the Cloud* as the centerpieces. When she had protested once more against the latter as second-rate Turner, he had pointedly not answered her calls for several days.

Dolly, seeing Isaac gesture to the Luther picture, exclaimed, "You sold that? You can't have sold it!"

"What's the matter?"

"Good God, what on earth was going through your head? It's already sold. You can't sell it twice." She put on her coat and hat, searched for her briefcase, trying to master her nervous anger. "What a disaster! Who did you sell it to?"

"Melissa."

"Who?"

"My old art teacher."

"For God's sake, Isaac, I told you a dozen times I wanted Arnold Bishop to have it."

"We'll give him another one."

"No, we will not," and then, realizing she'd spoken too sharply, retreated to a more coaxing tone. "You're incorrigible. It's that picture he asked for, my angel, and I promised it to him. Don't you remember? You must understand what it means to have a work in the Bishop collection. You have to tell your art teacher you made a mistake, that she can have another one."

Isaac looked stubborn. "You never told me."

"I did—" she began, then broke off. "Never mind. We'll work something out. But really, in future, my dreamer, you must be more attentive. Or better yet, leave these mundane matters to me."

Isaac, pacing, stopped to stare out the window. Night was already settled in, and he could see men and women in umbrellas and galoshes on their way home from work, high-stepping dainty through the sludge. The stuffy, hungover feeling of having slept, housebound, through a winter's day. Waste and more waste, for he'd done nothing for the last month but fret about which picture hung where. Hadn't worked on anything new since November. Did an opening always leave you so fidgety and blue? So "opened," in fact, and thoroughly scooped out?

"Let me take you uptown," he said, finally.

The place Dolly visited that February evening was not his old room in Hell's Kitchen. His emergence from that pinched rathole had been swift, and yet it had resulted in certain ambivalences that still rankled.

The previous fall, after their return from the North Fork, Dolly had told Isaac she had a surprise for him. She wanted to take him somewhere after work. These days, Dolly often took him places after work. They went down to Battery Park or up to Fort Tryon and walked by the river. They had cocktails at the Bemelmans Bar or the Oak Room, or went to art openings on Fifty-seventh Street. Once or twice, Dolly had checked them into a room at the St. Moritz or the Pierre—one of the gilded hotels with horses and carriages at the curb and bellboys in braid and big views over the park. And although Isaac felt like some old tycoon's call girl, still he could not resist these wayward autumn afternoons decanting into evening. The delectable melancholy of lying on crumpled hotel sheets, watching ever-diminishing reflections of Dolly in the bath, and wondering if he couldn't fuck her once more before he dropped her home.

This time, when they reached First Avenue, she hailed a cab and, trained now, Isaac opened the door for her to get in.

She told the driver an address in the West Twenties.

Isaac, from habit, checked out the driver's photo license. Ouedagon Ouemanoue. "From Burkina Faso, formerly Upper Volta," he told Dolly, squeezing her happily. Lovely New York, the accommodating confluence of a million tangled rivers, the indifferent receptacle of every nation's discharge. Sometimes it seemed to him that New Hampshire was a farther place to have come from than Asia, Europe, Africa. He chattered to her about Upper Volta and its various incarnations, until he noticed that she wasn't listening.

They got out on a street of red-brick warehouses, and Dolly produced a key which unlocked a freight elevator. Five flights up, the metal door opened onto empty space. It was the top floor, and there was a skylight. A large room, with high windows on three sides. White walls, golden floors. The autumn sunlight, flickering sharply on the floorboards, turned the room into a high-vaulted cave of ice. The light was like stalactites. In the back, a smaller room.

"It's heavenly," Isaac pronounced. "Is this our new honeymoon suite?" He seized her from behind, pulling her to him.

"It's your new studio," she said, black eyes glowing. "I want you to move in." She bent to pick up a crumpled piece of newspaper. "We bought the building back in '76—the bottom floor's rehearsal space, and the top four floors are artists' lofts. Kay Armistead—your perpetual predecessor—was living in this one, but now she's moving out to Austin with her boyfriend."

Isaac had gone down to the far end of the room and was poking around the stove.

"Of course, it looks rather moldy at the moment, it needs a proper bathroom and kitchen, but that's easy. Wladek—our contractor—is just finishing up a job for us in Long Island City, we'll have him come over this weekend, maybe, and tell him what you'd like done...." She trailed off, anxious for his reaction.

Isaac was pacing. "Wait a second," he said, finally. "You're going to put me in this loft and fix it up and then . . . You want me to live here?"

"Live here, work here—as you like."

"How much is the rent?"

"What rent? We own it."

"But . . . I mean, a space like this would cost—what? Three thousand a month? I couldn't be in a place like this on my own. . . . Maybe if I find another artist to share it with me, to split the rent . . ."

"My angel, what on earth are you going on about? We own this building. We use it for artists. The foundation owns it. You understand? Aurora pays for it whether anyone's in it or not. If you don't need the space, it'll . . . Eric Cassirer lives on the floor below—actually, we might go look at his place sometime to see if you like what he's done to it. Don't go proud on me, for heaven's sake. This is hardly nepotism. I've just been waiting for a studio to clear."

"I can't." His face was quite red. "I mean, to stay all summer at Goose Neck was bad enough, and . . . um . . . letting you fork out for hotel rooms . . . but . . . you're going to pay my rent?"

"Aurora will." She looked at him hard, trying to divine the source of his discomfort, and then spoke, with difficulty. "You understand, no matter what becomes of us, this is your studio. I've cleared it with the board. It's a business matter—I want you set up properly. Do you like the place or not? The neighborhood's rather remote, but . . ."

"It's not remote—the Blue Sky's around the corner. But it's too big for me—it must be almost the size of my mom's house."

Isaac, having paced the front room—just shy of two thousand square feet, by his reckoning—discovered a ladder in a smaller backroom, leading to a trap door. He ascended, dislodging the lid with his head, and emerged onto a tarred rooftop. Looked out at the Hudson River and the Palisades of New Jersey, with their Russian Orthodox domes. Almost the same view as the Geblers' a few miles upstream. He stared up the river to the George Washington Bridge with its broad spokes, its trickle of cars.

When he came back down, his face was determinedly cheerful. "I like it enormously. I'd like to live here. Very much. So this is where you'll come see me?"

"Well, only if you invite me."

"Then let's keep it the way it is. No fixing up."

"Oh, I do think we should at least put in a real kitchen." Then, seeing his stubborn look, "Well, let's not quarrel."

As the freight elevator lowered them past hanks of rusty cables, decades of chipped paint, he said, formal, "You're much too good to me."

"Heavens, darling—don't say that. This isn't goodness, it's part of my job. The pleasurable part."

They stood at the corner of Tenth Avenue, their faces tight, set. The wonderful surprise had ended up instead a source of unspoken contention.

Isaac was confused. He was an extremely grateful man. So few people had done anything for him in his life that those who had, from his hometown librarian on, were enshrined in his heart, remembered in his daily prayers. A welcoming heart you went down on your knees to God for, and to have found in Dolly a lover he could talk to without shame or reticence, whose complex intelligence, whose fleshly cunning and abandon were his daily bread—this was grace abounding. But their relations were painfully unequal, and Dolly's bounty—the stream of expensive favors, the merchandise, the real estate—made him feel the more unworthy.

Dolly, by contrast, appeared unequivocally exultant. She made little effort to hide their new relations: she would tell her husband she was taking Isaac to the theater, to dinner, to Goose Neck for a last autumn weekend—she had even tried to persuade him to come to Amsterdam for Willa's opening—and Alfred apparently acquiesced. Why then was Isaac riddled with misgivings and minute revulsions, unable to look Alfred or even Costa in the eye, half-regretful for those simpler days of being the Gebler family's pup?

With the studio, other things had come into his life, most of them— like the studio—disarmingly pleasant. Shortly after Isaac's return from Goose Neck, Celia had come to see his new work. He had finished three of the *Sons of Heaven* oil paintings by now, and there were twelve small variants in wood. Celia looked around and asked questions, and several weeks later she'd called to say that she would take him on, and that she would try to give him a show some time next year—either include him in a group show, if she could think of one that might be suitable, or even possibly give him a solo exhibition. Isaac was over the moon, but Dolly at once phoned Celia. "What do you mean, next year? Can you really not arrange something sooner?" Celia outlined her schedule for the next couple of seasons, and although Dolly grumbled, secretly she was well pleased. Her bet that Celia's gallery, for the last decade considered dowdy and passé, would once again revive appeared to be right on the money. Isaac was in good company.

In the meantime, Dolly bought five more pieces of Isaac's, two of which she hung at Aurora, one of which went in their dining room at home. The remaining two she told Isaac to keep: she wanted them to be seen.

Several weeks after her studio visit, Celia left a message on Isaac's answering machine. Her February exhibition of Jane Raskin had been cancelled. Would he be able to fill in?

As soon as the exhibition news came through, Isaac quit his job at Aurora so that he might concentrate upon his own work full-time.

Forty-one

H E W A S S I T T I N G in the Geblers' living room, balancing a cup of tea on his lap. Isaac's exhibition had just closed, and they had returned from ice-skating in the park–Isaac, Dolly, and the girls.

After a decade under construction, the Central Park rink was back in business, thanks to the real-estate magnate it was now renamed for. The Gebler women were fanatical skaters, and all three had their own skates, tender white booties with serrated-tipped blades keen as a kitten's incisors. Isaac rented a pair of cruder, scuffed black hockey skates which satisfied him mightily. In skating, to Isaac's mind, the point was to fly fast as the wind. Tearing around the rink, he glanced back in masculine amusement at his companions' frilly turns and almost stationary pirouettes. That was civilization for you–bent on making a fun thing fussy. Then he grabbed hold of Dolly and the girls, and the four of them, hand in hand, cracked the whip, screaming with laughter. He had not skated since he was a child, when he and Turner and their friends used to race on the pond behind the Hanesworths' house, and the sensation brought back recollections too acridly dear to risk tasting.

End of day, and the rink appeared a silvery ellipse of tumbling children and waltz music, a tiny ice-planet surrounded by a darker orbit of trees, while all around them the golden mountain ranges of Central Park South, Fifth Avenue, and Central Park West were bladed radiant against a crimson sky.

When the rink was cleared of skaters so that the now choppy sludge might be reconfigured into perfect glass, Isaac suggested that they grab a cup of hot chocolate in the cafeteria. "I'm sure the food here is vile," Dolly said. "Why don't you come home with us, Isaac, and have some tea?"

Isaac agreed, content, despite himself, to be once again with Dolly and her children.

They walked in the falling dusk alongside the Sheep Meadow, as if the West Side were a village separated by open country from the East Side. The women with their skates tied by the laces around their necks.

A big black dog off its leash came bounding over to them, and Carlotta buried her face in its neck, while Johnny—genuinely timid or maybe just to make her mother mad—hid behind Isaac's protective bulk.

Back home, Dolly served tea and crumpets, and Isaac stretched out on the white sofa where little more than a year ago he had delivered his diatribe against the Geblers' Agnes Martins. This time he was satisfied just to lean back and listen to Johnny and Carlotta do imitations of Shelley Markowitz, a classmate of Carlotta's who was such a fantasist she'd convinced everyone she was secretly married to River Phoenix.

After tea, Dolly ordered the girls to go finish their homework. Carlotta opened her mouth in protest, but Dolly silenced her with a look.

"Let's go, Lo, Mom wants to be alone with her boyfriend," smirked Johnny, already halfway through the door. Carlotta followed before her mother could say a word.

Formerly Dolly would never have let pass such insolence, but nowadays she felt in no position to make a scene. After all, it was she, not her children, who had changed, and her daughters' frequent sassing was no more than a plea to be told where they stood. Johnny no longer climbed into her mother's bed to cuddle and confide. Next fall she was going off to Swarthmore, and so strained were their relations that Dolly was almost relieved to be rid of her. Worse still was Leopold, who, refusing to meet her eye, acted as if an alien were inhabiting his mom's familiar body.

As soon as her daughters were gone, Dolly, exhaling a great sigh, sat down beside Isaac on the sofa. She took his hand—huge-handed as Odysseus, Isaac was—and traced the lifeline on its callused palm. Wondering if she were no more than a little crosshatch high in the long deep river that carved its way around to the base of his thumb. Wishing she could inscribe herself indelibly in his fate.

It was almost a week since she and Isaac had last met. Isaac had said that he needed solitude to start thinking about a next project, and Dolly reluctantly acceded. It was their longest separation since the summer, and Dolly had found herself unable to sleep, digest, read, concentrate without him.

"You know, you've had a very strange effect on me," she said, suddenly. "Everything I've always prized the highest has lost its savor. Orin Jubal came by on Friday to be taken out to lunch—we've just given him three hundred more acres up in Wolfeboro—and really, he must have thought I was mad. I could barely summon up the interest to ask him about the new project. All I wanted to know was what he thought about your show, which the idiot didn't even have the grace to mention. It's as if all my love for art has been funneled into you and your glorious work. As for home—well, I'm frankly astounded by my own delinquence." She made a gesture to dismiss the unwelcome subject. "How was your weekend? Did you manage to work yesterday?"

"No," said Isaac. "Another blank day. I ended up going to a party with Casey."

Dolly made a face. "I know he's your best friend, but I simply cannot understand what you see in Casey. I find him so tinny, somehow, so . . . vulgar."

Isaac grinned. "And how do I strike you, my beauty? Don't you find *me* pretty vulgar? I never thought about such a thing, and now I'm thinking, Thank God for vulgarity." It was quite true—in his own family, his mother had been mammothly vulgar, his schoolmaster father fastidious, and look what happened to them: his father had dropped dead at the age of forty-six, while his mother was raging unstoppable.

Dolly smiled too, but not genuinely. "You have to be careful, you know, Isaac. You're having a remarkable success, very fast, but I don't want it to upset your art. You need to husband your strength. I wish we could hole up together at Goose Neck until you'd painted twenty more pictures. It's too tempting for a young artist to be swept into this flattering New York world of nightclubs and drugs and . . . But I won't have it. If you're not going to be with me, I'd like at least to feel you're working. We have to start thinking about your next show, you realize. Have you had any ideas?"

"No," said Isaac. "Not the merest minnow of a clue."

They sat in silence, Dolly's brow still knit in anguish, and all the things each was thinking left unsaid.

It was quite true that Isaac was having a distinct success. Since his February show, word had begun getting around that Celia Rubin had taken on an unschooled New Englander not yet out of his twenties, and that Aurora was his prime sponsor.

What resulted was a combination of connections and good timing, for, as it happened, Isaac Hooker—in a minor way—was just the man the art world was looking for.

Ayala, who had a clear eye for trends, explained it. A new decade had begun, and the art market's collapse, which had brought down the prices—and to a lesser degree, the reputations—of some of the eighties' stars, bore a message to New York tastemakers: Glitz was out; the nineties were to be an age of scale-back and retrenchment. Of authenticity. Home virtues. Regionalism, folk art, outsider art even—works by unlettered sharecroppers, by asylum inmates, by street people—were being touted as the next new thing. The reviews of Isaac's show made much of the fact that Aurora's protégé was not only a rustic from New Hampshire but a former kitchen hand in a homeless shelter. A new American primitive. A white Basquiat.

One week there was a piece in the Sunday *Times* style supplement about Celia Rubin's Chelsea townhouse, which was decorated with Shaker furniture and cigar-store Indians and featured a tin Isaac Hooker in the bathroom. Suddenly Isaac was getting phone calls from Celia saying she had clients who wanted to stop by the studio. He could tell from the visitors' gingerly approach that he was half-expected to leap on a box and announce that the Day of Judgment was at hand. That he'd attended Harvard was evidently not part of his CV.

One day it was a couple from St. Louis. Another time it was a woman who owned a chain of taco parlors in the Southwest. And then a German. Isaac, unused to visitors, was eager to see what the buyers looked like and learn what they did. From California! From Arizona! Even from Europe! Isaac asked the German a million questions about reunification and the Lander system. Heiner said that Isaac would have to come visit him in Cologne. Isaac learned to stock a better brand of white wine.

Some of these clients, Celia explained, were desirable collectors, some not so hot. It wasn't an open market; you allowed your picture into certain homes and not into others. Some already had collections of Old Master drawings or Chinese porcelain and knew far more about contemporary art than either Isaac or Celia, and others were novices, anxious to be told by Celia what they should like.

One buyer had made a fortune publishing a newsletter offering businessmen tips about everything from Eastern religion's effects on the arteries to the country's best boatyards. Mr. Gardner owned a penthouse on East End Avenue full of conceptual art from the early eighties, but was sick of his LCD messages and giant slide rules. "I like something with a little soul," he explained. He bought a rooster drawing because his grandfather, too, had raised chickens.

Most of the visitors favored his series of Scout as the angel. Isaac was displeased, since these came from a time when he still couldn't draw very well.

In the meantime, Celia kept urging Isaac to paint bigger. He tried to explain to her that subjects had a natural size and couldn't be inflated like a balloon, but she explained back that it was in his own interest, because bigger size brought bigger prices. It was touchingly simple—as with cloth or office space, you paid by the footage.

With so many interruptions and so much advice, Isaac was finding it tricky to concentrate. Life had become too interesting. He would get up in the morning, and as soon as he got down to work the telephone would start ringing, or he would remember that there was an exhibition at the Drawing Center that he must go see, or that he'd forgotten to buy glue. On coming into some money, Isaac had discovered this celestial new activity: shopping. One of his first acquisitions had been a fancy sound system, and often Isaac, who before had barely broken work long enough to pee, caught himself smack in the middle of the day seated on the floor at Tower Records, musing over which set of Shostakovich quartets to buy.

And although Dolly was adamant that he get on with his art, in fact she was always wanting him to come to lunch at "21" with Arnold Bishop or to Pace to look at a de Kooning drawing she had her eye on.

And when they weren't looking at pictures or meeting for lunch, he was wanting to be with her so badly that he had to telephone and say, Come over now, right now.

Although one of the charms of the new loft had been that now he could stay home at night, in fact on the evenings when Dolly couldn't see him, Isaac was always too sad or restless to be alone.

Most nights he went carousing with Casey. Gina had finally quit her job at Rikers and taken off for Paris; Casey had latched onto Isaac as his surrogate date. Sometimes they met up with other artists—David Stacey or Dolly's friend Enric Urgell or John Hanlon, who as soon as he forgot he was the new Jackson Pollock reverted to being a modest guy fond of Irish bars and Rangers games. They would go to openings together and on to Lucky Strike or the Bluebird and hang out till two or three. And this art scene, with its hustlers, poseurs, and impresarios, was really too curious to pass up.

One evening Hanlon took Isaac to an abattoir in Brooklyn, where there was a show by a photographer called Evanston McCloud. McCloud specialized in Victorian-style daguerrotypes of naked boys against a studio backdrop of potted palms and murals of Vesuvius. The first thing you encountered coming through the door of the abattoir was the artist himself, suspended from a meat hook, in a nightshirt and red socks, offering ten dollars to anyone who would suck him off. John Hanlon sneaked up to the hanging photographer, but instead of obliging, carefully removed one red sock.

Casey was relieved that Isaac was no longer so savage about the shows they went to see. His critical faculties had gone into a necessary hibernation. And yet, there was some pocket of Isaac's brain in which he separated William McGuinness, say, from these flimsy hipsters he liked to drink with.

Sometimes—after dropping off Dolly in the early evenings, or coming home from a party when it was already light outside—Isaac's elation dissipated and he realized that he had got nothing done since the fall. He was getting no new ideas, and the old ones left him cold. He caught himself dreaming about Gilboa—not as subject for more art, but as the place where perhaps he'd lived most intensely. Revisiting its narrow valleys and red barns and lucid northern skies; blanking out asphalt and cocktail parties and art gossip. He would think, First snowfall by now, or, Almost time for the maple sap to be flowing, for the sugarhouses to warm up. He would picture his young lanky father, bundled in an army jacket, sawing wood, or, pale eyes narrowed against the smoke of his cherrywood pipe, remaining silently derisive as his son held forth about World War III or the joys of terza rima. Would his father envy Isaac's Manhattan glamours or would he find them shallow? Would he be amazed by how ignorant rich people were?

Or Isaac would re-enter the shack near Mount Elmo where he and Agnes lived, his last year—no telephone, no electricity, no heat. Plenty of lust, awed intimacy. After a day's work—she was teaching school in Menasseh, he was setting type at a printer's—they would spring into bed as if they hadn't loved for a century. Wake up when it was dark and cold, and the gas lantern had to be lit. Tease about whose turn it was to get out from under the eiderdown to put more wood in the stove, make supper. And after supper, Isaac would sit up reading till two, three in the morning.

Compared to the primal sweetness, the borderless intimacy merging into deliquescent oneness he had known with Agnes, Isaac's love for Dolly—barbed, wary, contaminated by guilt and money—looked like a bad deal. He was misleading her; she shouldn't be putting so much stock in him. And he, meanwhile, was getting nothing done.

Maybe he would never get back to painting. Maybe he had run out of ideas. Maybe he was through, as abruptly as he had begun. Maybe Dolly was right—he should hole up in the country. I will stop drinking and going to parties, I will stay home and work at night, he vowed. No more meat hooks. But somehow Casey or John always coaxed him out in the end, or if he managed to stay in he would fritter away the evening talking on the telephone or listening to music.

Forty-two

SUNDAY-NIGHT DINNER at the Geblers' house. Willa Perkins, who was just back from Amsterdam after *Democracy*'s closing, had brought along a conceptual artist called Dan Kelly. Celia was there with Philip, her son by her first marriage. Isaac had asked if he could bring his friend Joseph.

It was a blustery March night. Alfred served roasted artichokes, Italian-Jewish style, and afterwards spaghetti alle vongole. He had hesitated between Pouilly-Fumé—his favorite—and an Orvieto, then decided to go all-Italian. A very sexy dinner. The tiny cherrystones were just coming into Citarella's, and he had been experimenting all week boiling the pasta and the clams together in fish stock instead of water. Tonight's brew, the steeped extract of several pounds of cod carcasses, was so potent that even the spaghetti seemed drunk and reeling from it. Alfred ladled out the sauce, while Isaac served.

Gebler felt differently about Isaac now, and could not speak to him without sounding either cold or falsely jolly. It was Dolly he blamed for this new constraint. He used to love the boy, and now he couldn't even say his name. His wife had forced his awareness by how nervous she got when Isaac was coming to the house, how unnaturally excited she became in his presence, how unapproachable afterwards. Whereas Isaac was if anything more affectionate with him than before, was always practically trying to climb into his lap. Was it only Gebler's paranoia that made him see condescension, even contempt in Isaac's affectionateness?

And it was doubly unfair because he was not and had never been a jealous man. Indeed, it was not the possibility that his wife loved Isaac that made him uncomfortable, because love could never be a bad thing. It was that this love—if it was love—skewed her judgment, made her furious with her husband, indifferent to her children, led her professionally to espouse art that previously she would have laughed at.

Despite this undercurrent of unease, the evening was cozy. Gebler was touched by seeing Celia with her son, a pale twenty-five-year-old, tall as a poplar, very grave, who was studying foreign relations at Georgetown and who leaned over his mother with not just fondness but a kind of delight. It seemed almost impossible that this long boy in his baggy corduroys, hands in pockets, shock of fair hair already thinning, full of considered opinions, had once emerged from Celia's little cunt, and this reminded him of the mysteriousness of life, which no matter how you looked at it centered so obstinately around these versatile caves of flesh, which men spent their lives either coming out of, red and squalling, or going into, red and squalling. And how odd—like theater doors that are barred from the inside—that the one you came out of is the one you alone are never allowed back into.

Dan Kelly was revealing the latest installment of a romance they were all intrigued by. Hannah Greenberg, the art critic, who was Dan's best buddy, last summer had fallen for a bartender up in Martha's Vineyard and had brought him back to the city. The romance had now soured, according to Dan, because Hannah resented the young man's moving in on her friends.

"She says to me, Dan, I've worked like a dog these last ten years, developing my network. Jason's only been in town since November, and already he's going to Knicks games with Alex Hirschhorn! She says to me, she says, He's acquired all my friends—don't you think that's the tackiest move? I mean, just because he met Alex once at my house . . ."

Dan said, "And I'm, like, Hannah, that Rolodex of yours weighs more than you do. Maybe he just wants something a little more substantial to get his arms around."

Everybody laughed.

"Only in New York—right?—does a Rolodex come before sex."

Willa, who was in an unusually expansive mood, told them about her wrangles with the Brooklyn Academy of Music, which had promised to bring *Democracy* to the U.S. next year, but now wasn't sure if they could afford it. Gebler knew that his wife was considering a co-sponsorship with BAM.

At the other end of the table, Isaac and Joseph were huddled in conversation with Dan. Gebler, bored, called out to them, "What are you boys conspiring about?"

Isaac flashed him a loving smile. "We are talking about religion."

In fact, Dan had been telling them about his boyhood desire to become a Catholic priest.

"Why didn't you do it?" Joseph asked.

"Well, I wanted to, but the church is, like, *sooo* repressive about homosexuality, about women's roles. And I really don't approve of what it's doing in Latin America and the Third World. That kind of rigidity is just not creative. And this pope really bugs me. He's, like, soooo conservative."

At Willa's end of the table, they were also discussing homosexuality and religion, this time in relation to the current controversy over federal funding of the arts. Last summer, the government, under pressure from conservative Republicans, had withdrawn its support for an exhibition of Robert Mapplethorpe photographs showing sadomasochistic sex between men, and from another that included a photograph by Andres Serrano of a crucifix dunked in a jar of the artist's own urine. It was tricky timing. The National Endowment for the Arts, the government's art-funding agency, was up for next year's allowance, and a lot of politicians were wondering why—if the endowment was just a clearinghouse for pornography and blasphemy—it should exist. Jesse Helms, a Republican senator from North Carolina, had pushed through the Senate an amendment prohibiting public monies from going to art that was obscene or religiously offensive, and the exhibition of Mapplethorpe's work had been cancelled. Now a special House and Senate committee was meeting in Washington that week to decide whether Helms's proposal should stand. The art world was up in arms.

Everywhere you heard the same inveighings against government repression, the chilling effect on the arts, and Gebler was getting sick of people repeating endlessly lines they had read in magazines or heard from other people who had also read them in magazines. Sometimes he felt as if all his friends had had their political opinions designed for them, with appropriate slogans, by an advertising agency. And Jesse Helms and his supporters had simply gone to a more cut-rate agency, except them—the people who were against obscene art—you never got to meet. At least not in New York. Just for once Gebler would have liked to meet somebody who favored censorship.

He repeated now a witticism of Emanuele Conti's about Helms, whose biggest constituent was North Carolina's tobacco industry. "Who is Jesse Helms? He is a man who thinks cigarettes are good for you and nudity is bad." Nobody laughed. Especially not Willa.

"You shouldn't even kid about it," said Willa. "The man's a Nazi—he should be wiped out."

"Pardon me, Willa—am I hearing right? Wiped out? Who's calling who Nazi?"

Willa ignored this. Just like Nixon said, in politics it was always the women who were red-hot. "The point is this," she continued. "We always knew Jesse Helms was the enemy. What gets me steamed are the collaborators. First of all, the National Endowment for the Arts is a bunch of gutless quislings—they're not curators, they're not . . . art historians, they're political appointees of the most repressive regime in American history, a regime that's whittling away at women's rights to abortion, that's . . . that's criminalizing AIDS, that's—"

"And what's more, not only have they sold their souls, they're not even, like, where the power is!" Dan, laughing, joined in. "I mean, to be in the Bush administration and stuck in the *art* department, that's like, Sorry, you can't be ambassador to Germany but we'll give you Nepal.

"Every time I go to Europe I feel, like, ashamed to be an American. I'm like, wait a minute, I've read about this, this is McCarthy all over again. Like, in Paris, they're building these *really* expensive new opera houses, museums, you name it—and here, we're, like, *demonizing* our artists."

Isaac spoke up. "How can you say you're ashamed to be an American?"

"Who?"

"You." He pointed to Dan accusingly.

Dan drew himself up, unexpectedly affronted. "*I'm* not ashamed to be an American. I'm from Massapequa. I was, like, the little boy marching in those Fourth of July parades on Main Street. Right outa Eastman Kodak. I was, like, *sooo* naive it kills me. We watched our boys—get that, 'our boys'—coming home from Vietnam, and my friends and me, we were, like, *wow*, these are heroes. I'm not having anybody cast aspersions on my—"

Gebler was feeling contrary. "What I don't see is why *not* getting a government grant equals persecution. I've never got a government grant. Am I being persecuted?"

Dolly, who was making a face, half in sympathy, half in dissent, interrupted. "It's true. Compared to Europe, we have no sense of patriotic pride in our artists, no sense of . . . of a national culture. We don't—"

"Yes, but sweetheart, who's filling up those European museums and those opera houses?" Gebler protested. "American artists. American composers, American painters, American choreographers. France isn't producing diddlyshit in the way of important music or painting."

"So what?" said Willa.

"So what? So America where artists are ignored is still the most creative country in the world, while France is a desert. Doesn't that strike you as a pretty good indicator that maybe all this government love and coddling isn't necessarily very healthy for the arts?"

"So what do you want to do?" demanded Willa, unnecessarily belligerent. "Stick us all in the Gulag and watch us put out?"

Dolly, who was shaking her head, interrupted. "I'm not saying it's good for the artists; I'm saying it's good for the government. Why do other countries look up to America? Because of its culture. I'm tired of artists from Illinois and Texas having to move to Europe to get appreciated."

"It's worse than the fifties, it's so fucking small-time," Willa complained. "This country is one big glob of happy Christian families who don't like blacks or queers or artists. Middle America is just Hitler with a two-car garage."

"Actually," put in Celia, "it's ironic, but the Europeans have to come here too. Even in Germany or Italy, they were, like, Who's Anselm Kiefer? Clemente who? until the New York dealers started listening."

"Nobody's listening to *me*," Gebler complained. "I'm trying to play the devil's advocate, and nobody's even listening. Especially not my high-minded wife." He seized Dolly's hand and kissed it.

"What do you think, Isaac?" Dolly asked, suddenly. She had been watching the young man glower in silence at the other end of the table.

Isaac polished his glasses, refusing to meet her eye. Angry-looking, as if this game weren't so funny. "What do I think about what?"

"About government funding of the arts."

He rode on the back legs of his chair. Hummed. Then spoke, deliberately. "I don't see why the U.S. government should bankroll artists who think it's fascist. Of course, I'm not too qualified to talk—I *come* from that Middle America Willa thinks is worse than Hitler. I've never been to Europe—I'd never even been to the theater till Alfred took me to *Ajax*. I thought it was pretty dry bones, too. I wouldn't have forked out a dime for that opera, if I was the U.S. government. I'd rather buy a Patriot missile any day. But don't ask me what I think—ask Joseph. He spent eight years trying to escape from the Soviet Union to get to repressive, fascist America."

There was a moment's awkward silence.

"Isaac's a New Hampshire Republican," Alfred ventured, by way of explanation.

It was a long evening. The last guests—Dan and Willa—sat around till two, smoking pot and talking about their first sexual encounters. Afterwards, Alfred and Dolly cleaned up, and stacked the dirty dishes in the washer. Alfred, unloading clam shells, teethed artichoke leaves, coffee grounds into a garbage can full of empty wine bottles, felt retrospectively oppressed by the rambling contentiousness of the conversation about government and the arts. Such arguments seemed to him pointless in society. Although the question of whether public patronage was good or bad for the arts was an interesting one, you didn't learn anything new. Everybody repeated clichés, and nobody listened. Although he felt dissatisfied with the evening, what he didn't want to admit was that the cause of his unease was the expression on his wife's face when Isaac had blown up.

When they got to bed, Alfred rolled over and went straight to sleep. Dolly kept her bedside light on and read for twenty minutes. Then she turned it out and lay awake, seething.

She chewed over the way Isaac had scrunched at the far end of the table all evening with that idiot Russian and Celia's pompous son. Refusing to look at her, pretending he hadn't heard her speak to him. And then, pressed, he had lashed out at Willa, whom he knew Dolly revered. Played right-wing redneck, just to insult Dolly's friend! Never had she encountered such churlishness. She had thought he was a giant, she had glamorized his mountain-man honesty, thrived on his stories of white-trash hardship, and imagined him some kind of Rousseauian prince of the spirit. No, he was just an ungracious little shit. And what was worse, he was pulling away from her, screwing up nerve for a break-up, and there wasn't a damn thing she could do about it.

After leaving the Geblers' apartment, Joseph and Isaac went on to the Cuban-Chinese coffee shop down the street, where they piled into a booth and ordered café con leche.

They were continuing their dinner conversation about religion and everyday morality, Isaac still speeding from his explosion at the Geblers'. "I think the central, the most ghastly fact in the world is this," he said, "that each one of us is locked up in the funhouse of his own ego. It's true. And we can't see out. Everyone else is all distorted—midgets, gnats, microscopic, subatomic particles compared to our own monstrous vastness. I mean, who created the human ego? What devil? Why are we so ungenerous? Why can't we ever take other people as seriously as we take ourselves? It's this barrier between people—the barrier of self—which any religion worth its salt's got to try to break down: the loving-thy-neighbor-as-thyself. Eliminating our largeness and the other's littleness.

"That's why I think communism was a kind of religion, after all—a social gospel. It wanted to make people equal in each other's eyes. Its mistake was thinking the sin lay in class, not in the ego, and that you could get equality by coercion."

"Communism wasn't trying to make people equal," Joseph objected.

"Maybe not Soviet, but, well, theoretical communism. If I were going to design a spiritual exercise, like . . . um . . . Ignatius Loyola, it would be to spend an hour every day trying to feel what another person is feeling, and to act upon the intuition."

Joseph, chewing on a plastic coffee stirrer, made a disparaging face. "Why do you want to help people? Most people doesn't know what they want, and people who know, they doesn't need your help. I know from personal experience: when I came in United States, I try to get my mother exit visa from Moscow. Years and years of bureaucrats saying no. Then when they give her visa, she decide she is wanting to stay! If you try to help other people, both of you get mad."

"Nonsense. People know exactly what they want. Everyone wants the same thing–love and plenty of it, piping hot, no questions asked. Did you ever read anything by Ramón Llull? He was a thirteenth-century theologian. Well, when he was seventy-five years old, he wrote a poem that goes, 'I want to die on the high seas of love.' Seventy-five and still longing. Only trouble is most of us are so starved we try to scratch out the eyes of anybody who comes close enough to give it. Why? Starved people don't like to eat."

Joseph shrugged, unconvinced. It honestly seemed to him that he did not seek love, only respect, that all he wanted was to get on with his work, and that if people had any respect, they would leave him alone.

"By the way," he said. "I have good news."

"Let's hear it."

"One of my paintings is going in group show."

Isaac, beaming, leaned over and clasped his friend's shoulder. "My gosh, Joseph, how wonderful! What great, great news. And why have you been keeping it from me all night, you sly little Russkie?"

"Oh well, it is not so great. It is only in public school in Staten Island. But there will be reception, with alcohol."

"I'm getting on the ferry right now."

"Well, it's not till May. Also, bring your girlfriend."

"I don't have a girlfriend."

"No, no, tell her she is invited."

"Which girlfriend?"

"Dolly."

Isaac looked at Joseph sharply. "She's not my girlfriend. She's Alfred's wife. She's my . . . patroness, my . . . friend."

"Anyway, whatever she is—she is in love, and woman in love brings luck."

Forty-three

BOBBY AND GEBLER were having lunch at Christ Cella, which was next door to Bobby's office. Bobby ordered Dover sole, even though it was a steak joint. Gebler, who had a steak and creamed spinach, felt his blood fortified. Good old protein, good old fat.

Once or twice a month he and Bobby met for lunch. Today Bobby was worried about Stephanie, his daughter from his first marriage, who was seventeen and desperate to be a fashion model. The kid was stunning, there was no doubt about it, and she had plenty of drive, but she was only five-seven. Then Bobby told him something that knocked Alfred for a loop. His wife, Sarah, was converting to Judaism.

"Get out of here! What the hell for?"

"Believe me, it wasn't my idea. You know she's been going to services for a couple of years and she's really into it. Now she's found this rabbi on the Upper West Side she's taking night classes from. It's wild. She even wants to kosher the kitchen."

"She wants to what?"

"The rabbi told her the most important part of Judaism is keeping kosher, and she swallowed it. Remember all that weirdo bullshit? No dairy for five hours after meat? All summer long we're taking the kids to the Lobster Pot and I'm, like, You guys having boiled or broiled? and she's, like, I don't think I feel like lobster. How about some scampi? No, honey, I'll think I'll have . . . chicken. Chicken? At the Lobster Pot? Now she won't go out Friday nights. I'm like . . ." Here he imitated a dropped jaw. "I haven't seen Sarah home from work before nine since we met. Now I get back Fridays and she's all dolled up with the Shabbas candles lit since sundown wanting me to say prayers."

"Do you remember them?" Bobby's house had been more religious than Alfred's.

Bobby shrugged. "I can hum a few bars. She's so smart I always thought she had a touch of the Jew in her. She already knows more than I ever did. I come home, she's, like, quoting Maimonides at me."

"Well, Maimonides is one thing—but kosher?"

"Don't I know it. No more shrimp roll. And it's complicated—like, what do we do about the kids? Do they get dunked too, or do we wait till they're old enough to decide for themselves?"

"They got kosher Chinese restaurants now," said Gebler, half-teasing, trying to keep the envy out of his voice.

"Yeah? They got diabetic ice cream, too. Ever tried it?"

"Well, life isn't all food, man. Think of your soul." Even though he could see from Bobby's proud wondering face Bobby didn't need bucking up, he was thrilled to bits.

"I gotta say, the kids are really into it."

"How come? We weren't."

"Well, they spruced it up some since we were kids. You know, these Manhattan synagogues, they look just like Episcopalian churches. And that's just the problem. Sarah's already chafing at the bit. I know she's gonna end up with a shaven head and wig in some basement *shtibl* in Crown Heights. . . ."

"Nah, she's too smart for that."

"Smart doesn't come into it." Bobby shook his head. "It's the curse. There's no fucking escaping it. You marry a girl from Beacon Hill looks like she stepped outa a Merchant-Ivory movie. 'Waspy' doesn't *begin* to describe Sarah when I met her. Ten years later she's turned into, like, not even your mother, your grandma from Zhitomir." He gestured to the maître d' to bring the check.

"How about you, Al? How's life treating you?"

Alfred shrugged. "I can't complain."

Then they went on to talk about the recession, and which of the Democrats were likely to stand against Bush in '92.

Riding back to work down Park Avenue South Gebler brooded over Bobby's news. He'd heard about the revival of Judaism, he'd seen it in his own neighborhood. Here it was. And it gave him an ugly lump in his stomach that was nothing but pig envy. Nothing but his thinking, How come Dolly never even asked me if I wanted her to convert? Or if I wanted the children to be Jewish, instead of goddamn pagans? I would have said no, but she could have asked. She could have showed a little interest. But she was just like her family—Jews were low-class. Uninteresting. All that history, all that passion, all that God and brain and poetry, well, they—the Christians—either stole it or they ignored it. They ignored it because they'd stolen it.

The image came into his mind of Bobby and Sarah and their two children standing around the Sabbath table over the braided bread, singing songs—an image half creepy, half touching. Especially in comparison to his own family life, which had become hospitable as Mars. Did Bobby wear a hat? He bet Sarah made him. For good or for bad, a woman can do what she wants with a man. All a man can do about it is hope he gets chosen by a woman who's for him.

And Sarah, aside from her own intellectual curiosity, her spiritual thirst, had understood this: that a young man escapes, because it stinks to him of parental failure, of poverty and sadness, but as he gets older he needs to find a way back, to be led home kicking and screaming, to have the intelligent outsider's eye show him all that's precious and rare in what he's tried to run from. Because Bobby couldn't have got back there on his own, any more than Gebler could. Not with a wife like a dead weight against it. Now that it was much too late, Gebler wished he could have done a little something for his kids that way. Given them an education at least, some pride in their inheritance of martyrs and kings and delectable neurotics.

Thinking of Bobby and Sarah, Gebler felt that his own life by comparison was bitter, carping, a grit of sand in the eye. And he was surprised, because he didn't think of himself as an envious person, but there it was. Envy.

Friday evening. Spring light, and the sun still high in the sky. The air was pregnant with the news of changing seasons, that the days of darkness at five had been folded away, and soon it would be light till suppertime. Isaac and Dolly were walking up Eighth Avenue in the rush-hour traffic.

They reached midtown. Isaac hadn't noticed before how many new buildings had gone up in the last few years. The Fifties were raw with unfinished construction. Some of the high-rises were cheap developments evidently jerry-built for maximum profit at minimum bother, but others were handsome solid towers of granite or glass worthy of an imperial city. He was counting the slices of pavement underfoot, trying not to step in any cracks. When they reached a red light, he stood and counted how many car horns honked before the light changed green.

Marconi had a theory that sound never died, and that someday you could develop an instrument capable of picking up every noise uttered in a particular space. Like those spiritualists who went to modern-day Antietam or Culloden and could see the ghostly armies plowing each other under in the mud. This was even truer of color, whose vibrations were eternal. Besides which, each color contained within itself the possibility, the ghost emanation of all the others.

They turned east along Fifty-seventh Street, passing Carnegie Hall, where already a few concertgoers were congregating. What a menagerie, if Marconi turned his instrument loose in Carnegie Hall!

"Would you like to stop somewhere for a drink?"

"No," Dolly said. "Let's keep walking." She walked fast, like him. It was one of his favorite things about her.

High wind, the clouds nimble and frisky. As they approached Central Park, the streets were full of bicyclists and RollerBladers returning home from the afternoon's outing. A child's hat blew away, and the little boy clapped his hand to his head, dumbfounded, while his mother raced in pursuit.

They turned into the park and, passing through the zoo and beyond the band shell and Bethesda Fountain, broke for the wide, level ground and big skies of the Sheep Meadow. Crocuses had sprung up in little clusters underneath the trees, and overhead the sky was now frowning gray. Two baseball teams playing in the dirt. Spring training. A Slavic-looking gang of young men playing soccer. Yugoslavs, Albanians, maybe.

By the weatherman's tower, Dolly and Isaac sat down in the damp grass. Ducks in the pond, half-hidden by bulrushes. Dolly picked up a stick, and now she peeled the bark off one end and poked it into the water.

Finally Isaac spoke. "I think it's time for me to leave New York." He threw clumps of grass into the pond and watched them float. "We can't go on like this."

Dolly froze. Stared into the water, biting her nails, as Isaac's sentences tumbled. How he felt false. How he had hated coming to her house for dinner, watching Alfred touch her, looking at the things she and Alfred had bought together, the children they'd made. How he couldn't ask her to live with him, and couldn't stomach any more sneaking around. How they had to stop before they lost what love they had.

Dolly looked down at the raw stumps of her fingernails. "I thought you liked what I've offered you—Goose Neck, friends you've met through me. . . . You've seemed very happy."

"I like it too much. I admire what you've shown me—you're the most generous woman in the world—but I am getting too far away from the things that make me want to express. My sources. What I know. I lost it the other night," he said slowly. "I was a jerk. I am a jerk. We shouldn't be parting angry. . . ."

She shrugged. "Please, don't let's talk about the protocol of breakups. That seems a little narcissistic."

"You know, I adore you, but it's got to end. You have your husband, your children. . . ."

"Look. I've never talked to you about my marriage—" Dolly began, but Isaac interrupted.

"Don't say it. I don't want you to leave your husband. It's us who don't belong together."

And now Dolly gazed down at the green muck on the pond's surface, no longer listening to his cardboard phrases, which spelled abandonment, emptiness. Mortality.

Eight months of ecstatic love. Eight months. Eight months was nothing, after so many decades of unhappiness. How many times had they slept a whole night through in each other's arms? Two? Three? How many times had she held him inside her? A hundred and fifty? Nothing. A hundred and fifty clutchings, five hundred hugs, a thousand kisses—nothing. Nothing against the cold failing remnant of life ahead. In another few years, she would be past fertility. Isaac was her last lover, and her best. There would never be another.

And why? Why was it impossible? Why should *he* feel false, when it was she who had had to confront every evening Alfred's barely suppressed hysteria, Johnny's disaffection, Carlotta's obvious contempt,

Leopold's flunking two courses in protest at his mother's neglect? What had she been asking of him, but to accept her passion gracefully?

"But we'd only just started," she said finally, looking up at him in flat despair.

And this is what Dolly kept repeating to herself, through that night and over the days that followed—that they had hardly started, she and Isaac, as if it were the abortiveness of this love that was the saddest part of all.

Forty-four

"'THE PRIMAL ENCOUNTER in Hooker's Old Testament narratives, with their smeared and saturated iconography of transgression and redemption, is that of the post-exilic urbanite grappling toward a Hegelian metatextuality, objectifying the dialogic tension between exile and the possibility of eternal recall, while the seductiveness of his notched, crotchety surfaces never altogether eliminates the underlying reminder that the radical manufacture of our "humanness" demands a certain decorative distancing—decor as decorum.' Man, I think this Spicer wants to get his hot little paws on your seductively notched crotch, guy, and maybe even—how does he put it?—do a little fancy transgression. Hey, this is a rave review, Hooker."

Isaac shrugged. "They sure write garbage, don't they?"

"It's a rave," Casey repeated, waving the magazine in the air.

Casey and Gina had stopped by Isaac's apartment for a drink. Isaac, who had never before had a place in which to offer people drinks, appeared indifferent to his own change of fortune. For the past few weeks he had barely been out of doors, and the loft was looking as dishevelled as its tenant.

Most of its furniture he had found on the street. The iron bed was salvaged from Manny's scrapyard on Twelfth Avenue. Two big battered leather armchairs he'd bought from the flea market, along with some old photographs he had framed himself. The cabinet where he kept art supplies Isaac had rescued from the sidewalk outside a parochial school. And Joseph's paintings.

Gina, who had not seen Isaac's place before, was amazed. "Why don't we get a place this big, Case?"

"I'm not rich and famous enough," joked Casey. "Isaac's living here rent-free. Isn't that what Edwardian guys used to do for their ballet girls?"

Isaac was not amused, although Casey, who considered himself solely responsible for his friend's success, was in such a buoyant mood that Isaac didn't have the heart to be cross. It was the first hot day of the year, when the mind and limbs start stirring into hope. And Gina, after two months in Europe, had just returned to her native shores. To celebrate, Casey had taken her for a dim-sum brunch at a two-story restaurant with escalators in Chinatown and then they'd sat in the new park at Battery Park City, basking in the tentative sun, watching the boats go by.

Isaac opened a bottle of champagne, and the three drank out of gas-station football mugs.

"What a day," said Casey.

"Strawberry ice cream," Isaac agreed.

"You should see spring in Paris," said Gina. "They got all these chestnut trees in bloom and these parks with pony rides for the little kids."

"I can see it," said Casey. "Springtime in Paris—strolling along the boulevards, loose change in my pocket, all the time in the world. Checking out the French babes in their miniskirts—ooh-la-la—ow!" (Gina had just cuffed him upside the head.)

"Sounds scrumptious," said Isaac, dryly.

"So what's stopping you, guy? Now you've got some cash in your jeans, why doncha make the grand tour? There's nothing happening in the art market, that's for sure—might as well take the money and run. Gina and I are planning to go back to Europe this summer—her friend she was living with says we can use her apartment for August. Why don't you come over'n' see us? It's only four hundred, five hundred bucks round-trip, and once you get there you can stay with us."

Isaac thought of the pictures he would like to see in the flesh— Mantegna's Saint Sebastian and Géricaults and Delacroixs and a roomful of Poussins. Why not? If he wasn't going to be with Dolly—and it was almost two weeks now that they hadn't even spoken—why stay?

"Anyway, this summer Paris is where it's happening." Casey, on his feet, was looking arch, meaningful. Now he came and perched on the arm of Gina's chair. Gina looked as if she were on the verge of bursting out laughing. Then he came out with it. "Isaac, we're . . . uh . . . me and Gina . . . we're . . . thinking of . . ."

Gina was laughing outright.

"Gina and I are getting married!"

Isaac was stunned. At first his mind went blank, and only then did he have the presence to give them each a hug. "You smart cookies! How'd you ever think up such a smart thing to do?"

"You think it's a good idea?" Casey, uncustomarily diffident. "I always thought I was too young, but suddenly, it just seemed kind of obvious."

"We both want lots of kids," explained Gina.

Casey by now had curled himself up in Gina's armchair, legs over hers. They kissed. A wet slurping sound.

"Hey," protested Isaac, "you start on the kids after the wedding, and not in my best armchair."

"Look." Casey seized Gina's long slim hand and held it out to Isaac. "Quite a diamond, huh? We bought it in the Mah-Fat shopping center in Chinatown."

"Superb," said Isaac, laughing.

"This cheapskate here." Gina gave her fiancé a loving swat.

"Where you going to do it? And when?"

"Well, that's the million-dollar question. My mom is such a flake, and Gina's—well, we'd rather not get families involved. So Gina thinks we should tie the knot in France. . . . Anyway, I want you to be best man. Not least because you're the only one of my real old-time friends who Gina doesn't think is preppy scum."

"And what are you going to do in the fall?"

"It's kind of a secret still, so keep it to yourself. Khazin is opening an uptown gallery. He's already got the space picked out—Madison Avenue. Look, it takes nerve, but the bottom of the recession is the time to start. . . . There's some major talent in the old Soviet bloc, and some megarich Russians anxious to launder their money. . . ."

The two of them looked so puppy-excited, so confident in the rightness of their future together that Isaac forgot his own misery and was cheered by this proof of the possibility of ordinary happiness.

"We have to have a party to celebrate," said Isaac. "We'll have a party right here, with a live band!" He laughed loud. "We'll hire a Russian band, and make 'em play 'A Million Scarlet Roses'!"

Johnny and Carlotta had a game they were fond of. It was called House, and the rules were simple. One of them walked into the playroom and collapsed into a chair, with a sigh. The other then sighed even louder. The sighing match rose from a gentle wistful exhalation to a sigh expressing deep reproach to an outright groan. They were playing their parents: aggrieved, sanctimonious, martyred, or just plain *tired*. Then, as the sighs escalated to the bray of a mating elephant, both collapsed into giggles.

Leopold, who persisted in some solemn Teutonic ideal of the sanctity of the home, even as embodied in their parents, disapproved. And when the girls cracked jokes about who would go with whom when Mom and Dad finally split, he fled to his room in tears.

Things were worse and worse in the Geblers' marriage. The sound of her husband's brushing his teeth or chewing his food provoked in Dolly an unconquerable physical revulsion.

And the worst of it was—now that she truly couldn't abide him—Alfred had turned clingy. In the evenings he no longer went out, but insisted on riding home with her from the office, sitting with her and the children after dinner, getting into bed when she did. She tried to freeze him, but he would not depart.

One night he reached over to draw her to him. Dolly flicked him off with such reflexive savagery that he lost his temper.

"This can't go on!"

"You're right, it can't," Dolly agreed, much relieved.

"We can't live like this—I don't feel like a human being."

"No," she agreed, "it's completely dehumanizing, for both of us."

They talked. Alfred, as usual when they discussed divorcing, grew so tearful that Dolly dropped the subject.

The next night, she was more businesslike. "So how should we go about it?"

"About what?"

"About splitting up."

A look of fury came over Alfred's face. "You've got to be out of your mind, sister. You really want to do that to our children? Over my dead body. We are in this thing together, and we are sticking."

She tried to broach the matter a couple more times, but Alfred wasn't having any of it. To Alfred's mind, his wife had had every right to be sore about Gina. He'd ended that one cold-turkey, and was now a model husband. He had even given up booze—half a bottle of white wine, max, over dinner. As for her, Alfred had no idea what she was or wasn't up to with Isaac, and didn't want to know. He could afford to be forbearing, because he understood something that Dolly perhaps had not yet grasped: Isaac was a young man just getting started in life, and no matter how dazzled he was by Dolly, how quixotically romantic, the last thing he needed was to bust up so long-established a marriage as the Geblers' in order to take on a neurotic, demanding forty-seven-year-old with a big household and three teenaged children.

But Dolly now resorted to hunter methods. If she couldn't evict her husband honestly, she would smoke him out. She stopped talking to Alfred, either at home or in the office. To herself, she maintained the unkind fiction that the only reason he refused a divorce was that he wanted her money. It now occurred to her, two decades later, that it had probably been William Orton who'd cooked up their incongruous liaison, told his aide-de-camp to glad-eye the lonely heiress. And Alfred, bored, greedy, expensive, had complied. Their life together, from its earliest Bellville days, had been a farce.

She deliberated over lawyers, started drawing up terms. Who would move out? The apartment was in her name, so was the farm. Would he fight her for the children? And what would they do about Aurora?

She had heard from bitter ex-wives that friends always sided with the husband. All the woman was left with was a ghetto of fellow divorcées. Would that be her fate—dining tête-à-tête at Shun Lee with Joan Buccam? Or bribing gay decorators to escort her to parties? New York could be ruthless to middle-aged single women. Whereas all the Inez Kleins and Joan Chavezes would be falling over Alfred. Would her children too abandon her? Well, she had lost Isaac already. Having lost Isaac, who for eight drenched golden months had been her proud lover, her life's blood, her very breath, what more was left to lose?

. . .

The young lady was asking Isaac about recurrent images in his work, but all he could think about was the serial number on the side of a bus he had seen that afternoon: 8633. The young lady had a peroxide crew cut and wore black. He kept thinking about the serial number of the bus and of other buses he had seen recently. Then he traced in his mind the different subway lines of the New York transit system, rolling off one by one each stop of the A train once it crossed the East River—High Street and Jay Street and Schermerhorn Street and Lafayette Avenue and Nostrand. The A train that went all the way out to Brownsville, where Alfred came from.

Isaac told her, "The rooster means time—workaday time. The rooster is a watchman, a symbolic conscience calling you to account, like Saint Peter's rooster. The window signifies the passage from one realm to another—from profane to sacred. The burning bush is sacred space. The tree combines both realms—it has its roots in the earth's infancy, its branches in heaven. The sea in the bathtub is the world."

The girl didn't know what he was talking about, but she took notes anyway. Then she sighed. "I guess I'd better not take up any more of your time." Isaac could tell she had not got what she had come for—that he had failed to utter those juicy, provocative, pungent sentences that instantly declared themselves quotable. And the D, once you got past the Brooklyn Museum—Parkside and Church Avenue and Beverley Road and Cortelyou and Newkirk. Out past Kings Highway and Sheepshead Bay to Brighton Beach. The B, D, and F culminated in Coney Island Avenue, which in turn culminated in the Atlantic Ocean, which culminated in Portugal. How many years before you could take the F train from East Broadway to Lisbon? He knew what those sentences she was waiting to hear might sound like, but he refused to shape them. It was enough of a battle not to break a chair over her head.

In the last couple of weeks, three reporters had shown up at Isaac's studio. One of them was writing a piece for *The New York Times Magazine* about Hanlon and the younger artists he had championed. Another was profiling Aurora. The third, reading a review of Isaac's show in *Time* by a critic who favored regional expressionism, had included Isaac in a movement she called "New American Gothic."

The writer for *Raw Vision*, a pretty young woman, asked him about his childhood and his experiences with the homeless. Isaac, prepared to sound off about Goya and Tintoretto, hesitated. Then, encouraged by her receptiveness, he told her—rather too much, he realized afterwards.

The next interviewer, a black-haired young man, asked the same questions about his working-class upbringing and life in the homeless shelters. When he wanted to know if Isaac's family too was fundamentalist, Isaac lost his patience.

That night he realized that it was at least six months since he'd done a lick of work or even had an inkling as to what he might do next, and this idleness he blamed largely on the corruptions of self-promotion. It was impossible to make art while thinking so opportunistically about what kind of art people might like to buy or trying to suck up to the critics who purveyed it. Every time he told some supercilious stranger that the man flying through the bathroom window was his father, Isaac was cutting off the possibility of another picture about his father. Art's wells must remain covered.

He mentioned his predicament to Joseph, feeling mightily ungrateful, as if complaining to a hungry man you've got heartburn. Joseph, however, was not unsympathetic, there being no shade of misanthropy that was alien to him. He considered it from a business angle. "Make up things," he suggested.

"It won't wash," said Isaac. They knew too much about him already, because it was his biography, not his work, that drew them—the picturesque tale.

"What does Dolly say?"

"She doesn't."

This reminder of what he was most anxious to forget put Isaac in an even fouler temper. There hadn't been an hour since their last encounter in which Isaac hadn't recollected with a shudder of loss the silvery sheen of Dolly's belly, the tumble of her breasts, the liquorous hive of her inner lips.

His ludicrous pettishness. His scruples that were no more than male cowardice, male vanity.

Where did they go, those missed chances—that skipped turning by which Dolly and Isaac might have spent years sunk deep in each other's arms and entrails, inventing preposterous love names, mating in hotel rooms, ferry terminals, and after-hours offices, looking at Vermeers in

Holland, Goyas at the Prado, promising that neither would ever again be alone, cold, hungry, misunderstood?

Abjectly jealous of Alfred, certain that Dolly now despised him. I am a selfish prig, I don't come as high as her knees.

Other times it seemed lunatic presumption to be imagining that this imperious, accomplished, and virtuous woman had genuinely loved him, had wanted to live with him—him! He reminded himself that dozens and dozens of artists had passed through Aurora over the years, and dozens more would come. One day she would be talking with some future squirt, her newest cultivation, and she'd say, I've just received a postcard from Isaac Hooker. Have you heard of him? He was a painter who was overnight fashionable and then vanished. A cautionary tale to young artists: Don't come out of nowhere and burn too bright. Learn to last.

Forty-five

I|T WAS SUNDAY AFTERNOON and Dolly and Alfred were in their bedroom. The children were spending the weekend with their aunt Sophie and her current boyfriend. Sophie's boyfriend had a farm in Bucks County—three hundred acres, horses, a stream running through it—and teenage children of his own. Too good to be true.

Carmen had been out since Thursday—both her kids had measles—and the Geblers' room had the slovenliness—sheets and blankets twisted into ropes about the foot of the bed, knotted clothes on the floor, a spoor of half-empty glasses—imparted by tenants who can no longer be bothered to go through the motions.

They were talking as they had been talking off and on for weeks now. The most trivial word triggered it, or else Alfred out of nowhere would collapse into tears, and the whole rigmarole would start again.

When the intercom rang, it was Dolly's inclination to let it go, but Alfred, congenitally optimistic, trotted off to answer it.

He returned. "Isaac."

Dolly visibly started. "Is he coming up?" she asked, frowning.

"You weren't expecting him, I gather."

She, still in her dressing gown, didn't bother to answer. The door-bell rang.

"Go entertain him, will you, Alfred? I'll be out in a moment."

Alfred went to open the door, greeting their guest with a languid handshake. Isaac, fortunately, did not look in a mood for conversation, either. He barrelled into the living room. Strode from wall to wall, counting under his breath. "Oh, you have a new picture."

"Yes, a Tom Allen," said Gebler. "I got it out in California. What will you have to drink?"

Isaac pushed out his lips in a silent whistle. "I'm trying not to drink."

Then conversation dried up again.

"Please, Alfred," said Isaac suddenly. "Do you think your wife might go for a walk with me?"

"Ask the lady herself." Alfred gesturing towards the door through which Dolly appeared.

Dolly did not seem overwhelmed by the invitation. She looked at Alfred, not quite head-on. "Are we done? Was there anything more we needed to talk about?"

"Nothing. What are we doing this evening?"

"Oh, Una left some dinner—will you be home?"

Alfred nodded. "We could go to a movie." The hollow novelty of its being just the two of them.

"Yes, why don't you take a look and see what's playing."

Alfred and Dolly spoke formally, but with less warmth than you might employ with a stranger.

Then she and Isaac left. They headed up Broadway, jostled by Sunday-afternoon families pouring out of Zabar's, Shakespeare and Company, Harry's Florsheim. A collective springtime gluttony for new books, new shoes. Amusement.

"I'm sorry to have dragged you out in the middle of your Sunday," Isaac ventured.

"That's quite all right," said Dolly, coldly. "We were just rehashing old ground. A great deal of marriage, you'll find someday, consists of repetition."

"Have you eaten lunch yet?" Isaac asked her. "I haven't been out of the house in days—I'm getting sick of stale doughnuts."

They stopped at Ollie's Chinese Noodle Shop, which even at four o'clock was jammed. Isaac ordered chow fun, Dolly steamed dumplings. They ate in silence, looking over the other customers.

Finally, Isaac spoke. "I have an idea for a project. But it's more ambitious than anything I've cooked up before."

Instantly Dolly's whole body changed. She craned forward eagerly, eyes boring into his.

"You know, I've gotten very fond of Enric Urgell. His parents came to visit several weeks ago," Isaac continued. "You know—of course you know—that his father and his grandfather and his great-grandfather were all mosaicists. Mr. Urgell showed me photographs of this Romanesque church in Barcelona they restored. Very austere—the floor coiled ropes and chains, in different shades of gray. Then he showed me pictures of a private chapel he built for a family in Majorca.

"Well, it was their first trip to America, but all Enric's father wanted to do was look at mosaics. Busman's holiday, right? We took him to the Metropolitan to look at the Roman floors, and we took him to several office buildings—nothing spectacular. And then we went to visit his friend, who has a mosaic workshop out in Queens—does bathrooms and swimming pools, mostly, for Mafia types—lovely swimming pools, with crabs and starfish and octopus, and he showed me how it's done."

Drawing from his pocket a tiny cube of blue-green glass, Isaac explained to Dolly how the little bits of marble and glass were planed into cubes on a lathe, how they then were placed along the cartoon of one's drawing and transferred to a bed of mortar.

"This is what gave me the idea. I'd like to make a whole room of mosaics. Floor, walls, ceiling. Enric's father and his friend tried to tell me the tricks, how you design it with the changing light in mind."

Looking sideways to check her reaction.

"I want to make a chapel filled with lives of the saints," he said, stammering. "The modern saints. I want it to be all the things I've painted up to now—the rooster, the burning bush, the black angel, my parents' house in Gilboa. Noah's rainbow. Plus scenes of New York—Luther and the subway train. The bonfire. You skating—who knows? Everything. New things. Modern scenes of hell. Of our contemporary saints and devils. The Russian Revolution, men on the moon. The fall of communism, with statues of Lenin, like the golden calf, being dismantled. Everything. A resurrection day, with husbands and wives climbing out of the grave. You know, I've always loved those Byzantine chapels from Ravenna and Sicily and Constantinople—not that I've ever seen 'em live—with their patriarchs and devils in gold and purple, like twelfth-century comic books. What do you think? I've been . . . stuck. . . . And now this came to me. What do you think?"

Her face had changed. Eyes shining now, mouth curled in a proud smile, the high color back in her cheeks. "My God, you are a wonder, after all."

Isaac watched her almost with trepidation. "So you think it's all right?"

"All right? I think it's the noblest, most soaring idea since . . . We must commission it. Aurora must. The question is, who should build it and where. You need the right space to house it in—I mean, we have to—Aurora has to—build you a space. You want something rather plain on the outside, rather Greek—whitewashed even, maybe, so you are the more startled by the color inside. You know, you really must go to Italy to see what those churches look like. . . . We will make you a permanent installation, a museum of—"

"No, not a museum," interrupted Isaac eagerly, leaning forward and tapping her on the knee. She took his hand, laughing. "A real church, a working church, a neighborhood church that everyone can come to. Why should beautiful things be mummified? Let it be a living church, with a priest and Eucharist and sermons and a soup kitchen."

"What an idea!" cried Dolly, alarmed. "Can we? But—listen, Isaac—I know just the place for it, too—the perfect site to raise your church on. My God, can we really do such a thing? No, I'm not going to tell you. You've surprised me, this afternoon. Now it will be my turn to surprise you."

They discussed Isaac's church until the waiter ejected them from their table to make way for more customers, and then Isaac walked Dolly home. As they reached the gates of her apartment building, he held her tight and kissed her, before the doorman's curious eyes. "You've got no idea how much I've missed you," he said, very low.

"Let's not talk about that." She looked away, angry suddenly. "That's water under the bridge." Then she disappeared into the courtyard.

The sun was setting when Isaac left Dolly at her doorstep, and the clouds had cleared. Isaac walked over to Riverside Park, by the Hudson River. He was walking fast, to dispel the dread that had come over him as soon as he'd left Dolly. You shouldn't have gone to see her. You ox, why did you go see her? And now it was too late.

For the last three days, he'd been possessed by his brainstorm, too agitated to sleep. Poised on the perpetual brink of revelation, as if–after these months' sterility–everything were about to be illuminated and he were to be shown the hidden connections in things. As if the disparate strands of his experience and consciousness were about to be melded in one tremendous unifying insight.

And he had to tell her, just to show that he was still whole and game, still green vital wood, not a crippled blasted thing she'd mistaken for talent, and because only she would understand.

But right in the middle of the telling, the idea had gone dead on him. The mosaic church had been disembowelled of its jewelled saints, and he was filled with self-loathing. It was a mortal mistake to confide your unhatched dreams to another soul. If your auditor criticized, you were crushed; if she was too enthusiastic, then that was even worse. In any event, it was no longer yours. You cretin, said Isaac–first glimmer you've had in months and now it's gone. This new Byzantium had vanished, and Isaac now acknowledged with shame that his prime motive in concocting it had been to see Dolly again. He had dreamed up a church solely in order to sleep with her!

The world suddenly seemed to him very ugly. The cars steaming along the West Side Highway on their way to the Bronx and New Jersey, the river dull as a dead fish. He tried to imagine this snake-thin territory cleared of people and their excrescences. How must it have looked before the first Indians arrived: virgin forest, bears and wild boar roaming what was now Broadway or Times Square? Alternatively, Manhattan in five hundred, a thousand years, once again a sliver of grassland, heaped in rubble: here the odd traffic light, there a ruined high-rise. There was a desolating comfort to this last image, the promise that this, too, shall pass.

Then the remembrance of his own immediate jam drove out Isaac's consoling dreams of nihilism. If my church idea is embarrassing garbage, I'll have to give back the loft to Aurora and find somewhere else to live. And if I cannot produce works for Celia to sell, how many months of savings do I have? And then what? It was back to menial jobs, or back on the streets.

When he got home—how huge and beautiful the space looked—Isaac seized a notebook and pencil, determined to set down some remnants of the church, but try as he might, he could not. His old visions he had already used up and could not cannibalize, and fresh ones did not come. He sat for several hours at the table, raking his mind for images, getting up from time to time, as if opening the window or turning on a light or devouring a Mars bar would undam his unconscious.

What made his current predicament hopeless was the recognition that so much of his earlier life had been immersed in just such blackness, such waste, and that this black emptiness, inevitably, was where his foolish feeling in love with the whole world and its fine women—loathsome folly! vain insincere destruction—led.

It was the blackness that was the truth. He thought of his own foul presumptions as a painter and of Joseph and how although the two of them spent hours discussing every brushstroke in Joseph's pictures, Joseph never mentioned Isaac's work—an inequity which previously he had attributed to Joseph's having so few people to talk to, whereas he was luckier, a neophyte who'd marginally caught the public eye. But now he saw Joseph's reticence in a truer light.

In *Anna Karenina* there is a scene in which Vronsky, a rich man who has taken up painting as a hobby, shows off his handiwork to a real painter. Tolstoy describes how the true artist feels as insulted by these vapid daubings and by Vronsky's complaints about the agonies of the artistic vocation as might a lover confronted with a man fondling on his lap a big doll, who imagines he is suffering the same despairs, enjoying the same raptures as the lover with his mistress. Was this not how Joseph felt about Isaac's mawkish talentlessness? Was his painting not a big—a not so big—wax doll? And now the doll had melted.

Back to zero, and the realization that although Dolly had invested so much hope and energy in him, he was about to disappoint her once again.

Towards eleven the telephone rang, but he didn't have the heart to answer it. After five rings, the machine picked up and a husky voice resounded. It was Dolly. "Isaac, I was sure you would be out, as usual, but I wanted you to know how extraordinarily excited and moved I am by your church. Let's talk in the morning—I have all sorts of thoughts about how to go about it. Anyway—good night."

Isaac climbed onto the roof with a bottle of Jim Beam. Overhead a couple of murky stars glinting in the pinkish-gray. That had been a surprise, on arriving in the city: how the night sky never went black, but remained a moist pink, like white mice's eyes. He wondered if he should leave New York, go back to Gilboa, but he figured that if he couldn't work in the country either, then he would truly drink himself to death or put a bullet through his brain. It was all the fault of Adam and Eve, who landed their descendants with the curse that not only must we work or else starve but we must work or else despise ourselves as useless slugs.

Over the next few days, Dolly left several more messages on Isaac's answering machine saying that she had discussed his plan for the chapel with Emanuele, who had a good suggestion about an architect, and that she had mentioned it—casually—to a few members of Aurora's board of directors, who were scandalized—maybe something absolutely ecumenical, like the Rothko chapel in Houston, might be worth considering—but she knew she could talk them around, and that she wanted as soon as possible to show him its future location. The first message was eager, chatty, the words tripping over themselves. "Call me as soon as you get this—I'll be at home this evening, I'll be up until midnight." Then a more anxious tone intruded. Had he gone away?

The last message was in a low monotone. "Please call me." And then no more.

When Celia said that she needed some new work from him and that what people really liked best were his early Gilboa pictures, Isaac had become so cringing that he plagiarized himself. Working from transparencies of his first paintings, he reproduced their gaudy colors and childish proportions.

He handed over a canvas and three watercolors and held his breath, waiting to be caught. But Celia said, "They're wonderful." As for clues to where he might go next, he had none.

Forty-six

THE TAXI DRIVER TAKING Gebler back uptown from work was called Nedim Elmankhly, and he was eager for a chat.

Gebler made the mistake of commenting on his name.

"We are a big clan in Egypt. Very many."

"How do you pronounce it?"

"Like 'Gene Kelly.' Remember, in *Singin' in the Rain*?"

"I sure do."

"Now you tell me—what is your name?"

Gebler told him.

The driver was amused. "That's not a name."

"What is it, then?"

"That's a profession. You're a gebbler—that's what you do for a living, maybe."

"What kind of profession?" Gebler wondered.

"Someone who talks a lot, maybe." Ha-ha-ha.

"Nice work if you can get it."

"Any work is good as long as you are onnis man." Then, "Let me ask you a personal question. What you think about the Second World War?"

"What do you mean what do I think about the Second World War?" Unfortunately he knew exactly what the Egyptian meant. Fucking Arabs—they were all alike, even the most civilized-seeming. "I think— Western Europe shouldn't have let Hitler invade Czechoslovakia; I think America shouldn't have let Russia annex Eastern Europe in 1945. . . ."

"You don't have to answer me if you don't want to."

Mr. Gebler gave up. "You mean what do I think about the Holocaust."

"Of course," said the driver, like a teacher whose student has finally caught on.

"What about it? I think Roosevelt should have bombed the train lines. I think we should have accepted refugees from Germany and Poland. . . ."

"That's not what I'm asking."

"Well, why ask me when all you want to do is tell me?"

"You're right. I will tell you. This is not my opinion—this is historical fact. In 1800s the British and the Jewiss people made a secret deal—"

"But in the 1800s there was no 'Jewish people' to make a deal with—"

"This is historical fact. To divide up the trade in Africa and India and Middle East."

"Bullshit."

"This is history. Now you want my opinion. My opinion is, in the Second War, the wrong Jewiss people died. The Jewiss people in the camps, they were onnis men who prayed. The quick ones who got away—the ones who paid the Germans gold to get away—they were the lobbyists. All the good Jewiss people died, the lobbyists got away."

Mr. Gebler himself got away, feeling sullied. Even in America. Even an urbane-looking taxi driver full of pleasant banter had it in for the Jews. That's why he felt uncomfortable with the cult of the Holocaust. Was this really what the Jews wanted to be idealized as—a bunch of skeletons in pajamas? Maybe the Zionists were right—better to trade in that image of victimhood for that of the beefy Israeli soldier with his skullcap and his Uzi. Just so some taxi driver didn't have the right to look at you in the rearview mirror and think Hitler let the wrong ones get away.

What a drain perpetually to have one's face shoved up against this uncomfortable fact of anti-Semitism, to be reminded that the world was full of strangers who wished one ill—yes, even him, who went so far out of his way to avoid a fight. And every time Alfred came up against this blood enmity, he remembered, I am a Jew and my children aren't. Was I wise to spare them the un-American burden of being hated, of carrying around this trace memory of huntedness? Or should I, on the contrary, have instilled them with a little ethnic patriotism—packed them off to kibbutzes for the summer, lit candles on Hanukkah? Again, he felt estranged from his wife, who could not possibly understand the dread his conversation with Mr. Elmankhly had roused in him, who would think him touchy, paranoid, embattled.

Several days ago Dolly had spoken to him about the neighboring lot on which they were planning to build their annex. She had a different idea, she said. She wanted to put there instead some kind of chapel to be decorated by Isaac. It was the first real conversation they had had in days, and Gebler was astounded. So astounded, in fact, that he found it difficult to come out straight with what it was he found so offensive about the idea. Instead, chewing his beard as he did when particularly upset, he had said, "I don't get it. For years you've been nagging the board to get the annex built. That's what we bought the land for. And now that we've finally got architects' plans and the board's go-ahead, you suddenly want to—"

"I think this project will be more important."

"A church? I'm baffled. All our lives we've been pushing modernism. This kid Isaac is making—voodoo art. You can't go from Schoenberg to . . . to 'On Top of Old Smokey' overnight. Are we going to be showing Grandma Moses next? Or . . . uh . . . holding big-tent revival meetings for all our friends?"

"He's not Grandma Moses—he's an artist with a sense of history, of tradition. He's a humanist."

"No, he's not. Joseph Beuys is a humanist. Isaac Hooker is a freak. In fact, it's worse than Grandma Moses—it's morbid, and the idea of building a whole church to him is just plain sick. And not very polite to me—it's tactless enough making me sit every night at dinner with that fucking black Jesus overhead, but to make me endorse some kind of Christian—"

"It doesn't have to be Christian, necessarily. It's—"

"Bullshit. Maybe you know what you're doing. Maybe you've figured out that our culture is so decadent that next flavor of the month in modern art is going to be Praise the Lord. But if it's true, I'm going into the linoleum business."

"It's just one project," his wife had said, uncharacteristically wheedling.

"Why should there be even one project that offends me?"

She had agreed to drop it for the time being, but Gebler was still livid.

Forty-seven

Dolly was sitting in the office, long after the last of her colleagues had left. She had cancelled her drink with Jerry Mehl and told Una to go ahead and give Alfred and the children dinner, as she didn't know when she was coming home. It had been a day stacked with meetings, appointments, phone calls, a hundred questions from Andy and Marlene and Costa, and by nightfall she wanted badly to be alone, in this cool glassy spaceship she had built.

She had just hung up from talking first to her mother and then to Beatrice about the latest nursing crisis—Mittie was threatening to quit, after her troublemaking co-nurse Lusandra had accused her of stealing Mrs. Diehl's sleeping pills. In another week, school would let out for the summer, and she would take the children to Norwood for a good long visit. Then she would be able to straighten out the nurses. Relieved to have an excuse to stay away from Goose Neck Farm, which had become unbearable to her. Reeking of loss.

When she heard the footsteps downstairs, she wasn't alarmed. Costa, who had keys to the building, sometimes came by after work to use their projector. She descended to investigate.

It was Isaac. He jumped, startled to be caught. And she too—annoyingly—found herself clutching the banister, faint at the sight of him. After so many weeks' silence. When she had given up.

"Oh. I didn't know you still had keys."

"Do you want me to give them back?"

"Well, not if they're of any use."

"I wanted to take a look at that bathtub painting you've got in the hall."

She gazed at him, questioning.

"It's not very good," he remarked. He followed her upstairs to her office and sat down. Looked at the pictures on the wall, at her books.

It was two months since they'd broken up, Dolly realized, and each hour had been customized hell. Hovering by the phone like a fifteen-year-old on a Friday night. Heart jumping hopeful at every ring of the doorbell, buzz of the intercom. Then plummeting. Waking up with a heart of lead, not knowing what was wrong, and then remembering–Isaac. Out of that dumb misery, that madness, he'd shown up on her doorstep to tell her about the mosaicked chapel. Then, silence. Her phone calls unreturned. Once or twice she had been on the point of picking up the telephone a last time, just to tell him how furious, how betrayed she felt, but she'd resisted. Even tonight she might have been willing to forgive him, if he had come to her with love. But what she saw was no shimmer of remorse or tenderness, only a sullen self-absorption.

He was sitting across the desk from her, like a student called in to see the principal. As if he didn't want to be there. "How's work?" he asked, finally.

Dolly told him, but he wasn't listening.

"Have you picked next year's artists? Who's getting castles and waterfalls this time?"

"Well, the foundation's not quite as loaded as it was in the eighties." Then she added, carefully, "I was sorry not to be able to include your mosaic chapel in our upcoming projects. I thought–I still think–it would have been one of the finest things we'd ever sponsored."

"Well, I've given up. You might as well put a pig on skates. I've said all that was in me to say, so I'm quitting."

"What can I tell you?" Dolly shrugged, sounding for a moment like her husband. "Maybe you'll come back to it later, maybe you won't."

There was a contempt in her tone that Isaac had encountered before in women of strong character and ability–the scornful impatience that if only I had your advantage, if only I were a man in this man's world, what heroic things I would do, compared to your bungling. It was the ruthlessness of the expert condemned to the sidelines. They say that women are the nurturing sex, but it is also true that a man can never be so unforgiving as a woman, because he feels too well within himself what it might be to fail and to fail publicly.

"Well, I'd better get uptown." Rising, Dolly paced the office fast, chewing on a ragged fingernail. Without noticing what she was doing, she packed up her attaché case, gathering the papers she needed to look at that night, rifling through drawers. Hands trembling. Damn.

"You want to know what we're doing next year?" She tossed him a mock-up, back from the graphic designer, of Aurora's latest prospectus.

Isaac flipped through, until he found the list of grants, of the future Isaacs she would be buttering up, buying Smithfield hams and Russian icons and silk long underwear, installing in prime properties. Then, unexpectedly, he exploded. "What makes you think it's good for artists, giving 'em real estate and drowning 'em in money? If you have a tender conscience about being so filthy rich, why don't you just write a check to the Salvation Army, not mess around with people's heads?"

An angry smile appeared on her face. "I'd forgotten what a preachy young man you are. What gives you the right to tell me what to do with my money?"

"Because you think your money gives you the right to tell artists what to do with their work!"

"Am I so very bossy? I suppose I must have thought I had enough critical judgment to make suggestions, and it seemed to me your work prospered from them."

"When the critic's the one with the wallet, those are pretty powerful suggestions."

She resumed pacing. "I never imagined we'd be descending to petty bickering and name-calling. I had such great plans for you, such noble things I imagined us accomplishing. I wish we'd never . . ."

"What?"

"I really thought you were the noblest person I'd ever met. Now I see I was a fool."

"But it's ridiculous!" he expostulated. "You can't pick up somebody out of the garbage can and make him an overnight wonder. Not unless you want to make a mockery of real talent."

She kept sorting through her papers, throwing things into the wastepaper basket. "I'm leaving," she said finally. "Let me give you a lift uptown."

They walked to the garage in silence.

Running a red across Houston, Dolly tried not to think about the first time they'd been in a car together. Then Isaac, tactlessly, said it. "Shall we go out to the North Fork?" he joked, smiling at her timidly.

"Get lost."

"Sorry," said Isaac.

She honked at a van that dawdled at the crosswalk until the lights had changed. "You know, lots of painters go through dry spells. Barnett Newman stopped painting for five years and studied science. Agnes Martin quit for decades. Of course, it helps having had academic training, just to get you through the motions. I don't doubt you'll get back to your work, as long as you don't worry at it too much."

"Yes, but I'm not a born painter," he persisted. "I just had a little luck at the beginning, because there were some things I wanted to work out, that I couldn't express any other way."

"What are you going to do?"

"I've still got almost eight thousand dollars left. On eight thousand you can do anything. Casey's telling me to go to Europe."

"How I would have loved to have taken you to Europe—seen everything through your eyes," she said, very low. "There were so many things that we never did. We hadn't even started. . . ."

"I know. I can't stay here. . . . It eats me up, being in the same city as you. I just wander around, hoping to bump into you on streets I know you've never set foot on. I might go up to New Hampshire for a while. . . ."

"Go back to your old girlfriend?"

"No. When do you want me out of the loft?"

"Oh, it's yours. Don't think twice about it. I don't know why you're making such a fuss about a couple months' rut. We've got plenty of artists on the payroll haven't turned out anything in decades."

"That's just what I'm telling you. And then you think you're doing people good!"

Past the window hurtled warehouses. The meat market, a rent-by-the-hour hotel. For anonymous fucks. For a moment she wished she could haul some stranger into one of those sordid cubicles, bang away for an hour, forget about intimacy, sympathy, trust. No more "love," no more preaching, just sweat and come. Then bars. Automobile showrooms. All the way up Tenth Avenue, a battalion of traffic lights, all green, all swaying madly in the wind. The city . . .

Isaac was looking at her hard, at her black brows joined in concentration as she drove, and his old longing for her came flooding back in a rush. When she pulled over at the curb outside his building, he took her hand, but her fingers were balled tight around the steering wheel. "Listen, I want us to be friends forever."

"You don't know the first thing about friendship. I'd rather be friends with a . . . rat or a wolf."

"I want you to teach me. I want us to talk on the telephone every day for the rest of our lives. I want you to come visit my grave or me yours, whichever one croaks first."

"I'll spit on your grave," said Dolly, laughing.

"Good."

"Because you're just a hypocritical sanctimonious boorish little . . ."

"I know."

". . . who doesn't have the balls—"

"I know. I know you did your hardest to give me a career and to make me famous. I know we could have been very happy—or very unhappy, but something better, anyway, than this nullity. And I'm grateful to you forever for wanting to risk it. But you can't do so much for other people—it just makes 'em feel helpless and hate themselves, and you—"

She jerked her head impatiently. "Please, cut the lecture."

"So are we friends for life?"

"No!"

"How come?"

She reached past him and opened his door. He clambered out, hesitated on the curb, in front of her half-open window.

"Because that's the kind of lie tenth-grade girls used to tell boys they never want to see again but don't have the decency to admit it."

"So can we at least be—"

"No!"

"—enemies?"

"No!"

When she got back to the apartment, much later that evening, they were sitting in the dining room, Alfred and the children. She heard the sound of their animated voices as she entered. Not sure she could face them. But wasn't that, finally, the grace of family life? Nine-tenths of the time, it drained you and drove you up the wall, having to devote your finest energies to its implacable pettiness, its refusal to rise above dishwashing detergent and homework and new shoelaces and doctor's appointments. And then, just occasionally, *it* buoyed *you*—became a raft of ordinariness and saving routine, on which the half-drowned soul might float, preserved for a moment from the destroying flood.

Conversation broke; her children looked up. They were talking about horses. She hovered in the doorway. Then, to Alfred's surprise, she gave him a wan smile.

"Have you eaten?" he asked. "Let me get Una to warm up some dinner."

"Yes . . . I'm ravenous."

"It's yucky," warned Leopold. "It's all . . . bare *bones*."

"It's osso buco," said Alfred.

Then the children pitched right back into the argument that had been raging when their mother walked in. Carlotta, it turned out, was trying to talk Alfred into buying her a horse. Last year Sophie's boyfriend, Bob, had got his daughter a hunter named Ned, only to discover that Jennifer was allergic to horses. Every weekend Carlotta had been going down to the farm in Bucks County to ride Ned. Now Bob had called up Alfred and asked him if he wanted to buy the horse. Alfred, petrified of animals, said no way. But unfortunately Bob had also mentioned the idea to Carlotta, who maintained that if they didn't get Ned, she was moving down to Pennsylvania. An ultimatum. An elopement. Johnny and Leopold, of course, were on Carlotta's side. As was Sophie.

"What do you say, Dolly?"

Into Dolly's mind came marching images of damage—of Carlotta's getting thrown, breaking her back at a jump. Horses were so damn skittish—one stray leaf and you could end up a paraplegic. The imagination of disaster.

"Anyway, who's going to be left walking it when you go off to college?" said Alfred, laughing.

Carlotta didn't think that was funny. "What do you think, Mom?"

"I don't know, sweetheart. How much does Bob want for it? And where would we board it? We're having a pretty lean year—horses are expensive."

Carlotta looked huffy, as if she'd been accused of insensitivity. "Well, how was I to know? When it's not a lean year, you don't exactly go around saying, Hey, we're really rolling in dough, anything you kids want?"

Dolly laid a hand on her shoulder, rubbed the child's straight back.

"We could board it out at Sunny Acres," suggested Johnny. Sunny

Acres was the stable on the North Fork where Carlotta had first learned to ride. "That wouldn't cost so much, would it?"

"Let's think about it," said Dolly. "Let me talk to Bob, and make a couple of calls. . . ." Sneakily she liked the idea of something that would keep Carlotta out at Goose Neck more often and happily, and Carlotta, sensing in her mother an unexpected ally, allowed herself to be massaged.

"How was your day?" asked Alfred.

"Dull." Dolly, scooping the marrow jelly from the bone, made a face. "I think I'm getting tired of contemporary art."

"Well, you picked a fine time to get tired of it," said Alfred jocularly. "Just when the market's collapsed because everyone else is sick of it, too. So what shall we do instead?"

Then Leopold started telling them about his friend Kent's birthday party: Kent's parents had taken the whole class to a Japanese puppet show, in which the puppets were life-sized. Afterwards, they had eaten green-tea ice cream, except for Warren Zimroth, who had gotten sick and had to be taken home early.

As Isaac reached the fourth story, he saw a dark figure seated outside his apartment. He raced up the remaining flight of stairs, wondering whether it was Luther or Scout wanting help. When he got to the top, he recognized Joseph, who lately had taken to dropping around at night. "Hail, Isaac," said Joseph, rising to his feet and reaching out a hand.

They went around the corner to the Blue Sky, where Mary had just come on duty. Isaac ordered a bacon cheeseburger and a black-and-white milkshake, Joseph coffee and a Greek salad without the feta.

"Is this salad with black olives or green olives?" he asked.

"Black," said Mary, winking at Isaac.

"No olives."

"Let me get this right," said Mary. "You want a Greek salad without the feta and without the olives. You want to make that a garden salad, by any chance?"

"Whatever," said Joseph.

"You're just like my kid brother," said Isaac, affectionately. "He wouldn't eat anything but frozen french fries and black-raspberry sherbet without the pips. When he got sick of black-raspberry sherbet too we nearly murdered him."

"It's been weird week," said Joseph, emptying three packets of sugar into his coffee. "I'm working on picture—abstract, of course—and I keep seeing faces in picture. Eyes, nose. Every time I scratch out one face, new face appears another place. Now there is shape that looks like dog. I think God is playing tricks with me—Here I made this wonderful world. How arrogant you are to ignore it."

"Sounds more like the devil."

"Poor guy—did you read in newspaper?—has spent twenty-five years to discover computer program that proves existence of God." Joseph screwed an index finger into the side of his skull, indicating idiocy.

"Misses the point, doesn't it? I remember my old girlfriend saying, The question isn't do you believe in God but does God believe in you. She said, Why should He? You're just a snot-nosed little twerp—and besides, there's two billion more where you came from. What's the proof of *your* existence?"

"So am I right that mankind is very stupid accident?"

By now, they'd left the Blue Sky and crossed the highway to the river. The Hudson River gleaming slick as an oil spill, the lights of New Jersey refracted in its glib flood, and one long barge slipping by.

"Well, no God doesn't really get us off the hook, does it? I mean, what's the percentage in atheism? Precisely because there's no God—maybe—because this world is a charming mistake—maybe—we have no choice but to do our best to help one another."

"So why paint angels, if there isn't no God? Then you're like street painters in Paris who makes clowns and kittens for tourist trade."

"No," said Isaac. "I am trying to believe, and that's a start. Once in a long while I do believe, and then I betray my own belief so far that I have to start again from below zero. But if I keep on slow and steady, maybe by the time I'm eighty I'll have worked my way round to a first principle—a modest one, one of those fortune-cookie mottoes like Love thy neighbor as thyself. Hard to live by—ambiguous, given the ubiquity of human self-hatred, but . . . challenging."

Joseph looked unimpressed. "I like better Hippocratic oath. 'Do no harm' is more realistic."

A NOTE ON THE TYPE

This book was set in Garamond, a type named for the famous Parisian type cutter Claude Garamond (ca. 1480–1561). Garamond, a pupil of Geoffroy Tory, based his letter on the types of the Aldine Press in Venice, but he introduced a number of important differences, and it is to him that we owe the letter now known as "old style."

Composed by Dix, Syracuse, New York
Printed and bound by Berryville Graphics, Berryville, Virginia
Designed by Robert C. Olsson